Always Been You

ALEX TAYLOR

Always Been You

Destined Love Book 1

Alex Taylor

Character art by Paige Moreland

Cover Design by Kimberly at KBG Designs

Editing by Sophie at Wonder and Wander Editing Co.

Print ISBN 978-1-0688632-0-2

Ebook ISBN 978-1-0688632-1-9

To all the girls who think you're not enough.
You're wrong.
You are enough and you always will be.

Author's Note

Please note that some of the subject matter in this book may be
triggering for some people.
If any of the following subjects cross a line for you, please do not
continue.
Your mental health matters.

Talks of body shaming
Cheating (not between the MC's)
Ex with stalker tendencies
Pregnancy
Sexual degradation
Explicit sex scenes

Looking for a Dicktionary? Check out the back of the book

Playlist

Zombie
The Cranberries

Can I Be Him
James Arthur

Flowers
Lauren Spencer Smith

I Hope
Gabby Barrett

Before He Cheats
Carrie Underwood

Look What God Gave Her
Thomas Rhett

Figure You Out
Voila

Cruel Summer
Taylor Swift

Best Shot
Jimmy Allen

Paper Rings
Taylor Swift

Die First
Nessa Barrett

Dancing With Our Hands Tied
Taylor Swift

That Part
Lauren Spencer Smith

Lover
Taylor Swift

They Don't Know About Us
One Direction

Beside Me, Besides You
Jake Austin Walker

Taylor Swift
Matt Cooper

Heaven
Kane Brown

Those Eyes
New West

Do It All Again
Lauren Spencer Smith

Dandelions
Ruth B.

Til Forever Falls Apart
Ashe, Finneas

Look After You
The Fray

Little Bit More
Suriel Hess

I Forgot That You Existed
Taylor Swift

CHAPTER 1

Olivia

Today's the day. Today I turn twenty-five. I've always adored my birthday. Growing up, my family always made it special. My mom would prepare a special breakfast, and we would do some sort of family activity, followed by dinner at my favourite restaurant, then movies and popcorn on the couch at home. Even after I started university, my family always made time on the Saturday right after my birthday to do something. Going to school in the same city I grew up in made it easier to maintain the tradition.

This year, my parents are out of town for work and my younger sister, Gianna, is away at school, so my older brother Matt and I are meeting for lunch and then my best friends have an evening planned for us.

Standing in the washroom, my excited eyes stare back at me. My freshly washed and dried hair feels soft as I pull it into a ponytail before getting dressed for the day. As I lock the front door, I send Matt a text.

LIV

Hey! Just leaving my place now. Heading to the SkyTrain, be there in about 20 mins.

MATTY

Sounds good

Popping in my headphones, I pull up my favourite playlist and head to the restaurant. The station and trains are full of people as usual. I find a spot near the door, grabbing hold of the yellow pole as the train makes its way to the various stations. Getting off the train, I make my way to street level and towards the restaurant, feeling the sun on my face as the sound of traffic and people fills my ears. My smile widens I've always enjoyed the hustle and bustle of the city. As I round the last corner to the restaurant, I walk straight into a wall—or rather a hard, muscular chest.

"Oh my god, I'm so sorry," I say quickly, as firm hands reach out gripping my waist, steadying me.

My gaze slowly takes in the sight in front of me, starting with a muscular stomach and broad chest wrapped in a perfectly fitting dress shirt, then all the way up a square jaw, a crooked nose, and into piercing green eyes. Green eyes I recognize.

My breath catches in my lungs as I realize I'm staring at Josh Lincoln, my brother's best friend.

Inhaling deeply, I inadvertently get a lung full of his scent. God, he's sexy. I take in his raised eyebrow and the smirk playing on his face, he clearly caught me checking him out. I can't help myself though. Growing up, I had the biggest crush on him, and he has only gotten better with age. I immediately take a step back ensuring I'm out of arm's reach and run my hands down my clothes to straighten them as he drops his hands to his sides.

"Hey Josh," I say, my voice coming out breathier than I intended.

"Hey Olivia, happy birthday."

A blush warms my cheeks; I'm surprised he remembers. Maybe Matt said something to him? Josh has always been close to my family; he and Matt met in second grade and ever since, they have been inseparable, playing the same sports and going to concerts together. They even took it as far as going to the same university. Josh and I were friends growing up, but I always thought he saw me as Matt's annoying younger sister who liked to tag along with them. Although at the time, he never did complain about it. When Matt and Josh became best friends, Josh's sister Emily joined us too. She's our sister Gi's age, so they grew closer than the rest of us.

I pull one arm across my chest and grip the opposite arm, giving him a smile. "Thanks, Josh. What are you up to?"

"Oh, not much, just looking for something for lunch. What about you? Any special plans for your birthday?"

"I'm actually on my way to meet Matt for a birthday lunch at the Blue Spoon..." I admit, looking up at him through my lashes. "You maybe wanna join us?"

He seems to hesitate for a few seconds before responding. "Are you sure? I wouldn't want to invade your birthday lunch."

I can't remember the last time Josh and I spent time together. At the prospect, a nervous energy spreads through me. "Yeah, it will be great. You and I can catch up and I know you and Matt have that spectacular bromance; he will be happy to see you too," I say with a wide smile. Sometimes I find Matt and Josh's relationship a little odd, but I'm used to it now.

He chuckles. "Well, Matt truly is my soulmate. Never had one like him and never want another to replace him." We both laugh.

"That settles it, you're joining us." I smile up at him.

He nods, stepping aside and gesturing for me to go first before falling into step beside me. I can feel the heat radiating off his body, and that, in conjunction with the warmth of the spring sun has me beginning to sweat. I pull the neck of my shirt away from my skin a bit, hoping a little airflow will help cool me down.

"It's just down the block," I say.

Shoving his hands into his pockets, he nods. I try to take him in more as we walk. He looks like he did the last time I saw him, but there's something different about him that I can't put my finger on.

"Sounds good. So, what's new with you, Olivia?"

"Oh, you know, not much. I still spend my days trying to tame a bunch of sixth graders and deal with their sometimes even worse parents. We have parent-teacher conferences coming up soon, so I've been busy prepping for those."

"Sounds like a lot."

I smile fondly, thinking about my students. "It is, but I love it," I say.

When we get to the restaurant, Josh opens the door for me and we enter together. The place is bustling with people as servers run around checking on their tables. Music plays softly in the background, so softly that if you weren't paying attention, you likely wouldn't notice. The hum of active conversation wraps around us as

I step up to the host stand. I see Matt at a table in the back corner. Looking at the hostess, I point to my brother with a smile, she nods her understanding and we make our way to his table.

His large six-foot-two frame is hunched over the table and his brown wavy tendrils rest on his forehead.

He looks up from his phone, noticing me and Josh and something flashes in his brown eyes before he smiles. He stands up and pulls me into a hug. I smile into his chest. The same sense of safety I've always gotten from him envelopes me. Matt is the best big brother a girl could ask for. Standing beside him, I feel so small, but it's also easy for me to see all our similarities, our matching eyes from our dad, the colour of our hair, and the shape of our noses.

Pulling away, I say, "Look who I ran into around the corner, your favourite person in the world," I jest with a smile.

He chuckles, planting a kiss on my cheek. "My favourite non-blood related person, today you're my number one. Happy birthday, Livvy."

"Thanks, Matt."

He pulls Josh into a bro hug, patting him on the back. "Hey, man. Good to see you. Planning to join us for lunch?"

"If that's alright with you. Olivia insisted."

"Of course, man, take a seat."

Josh grabs the chair across from Matt and pulls it out, nodding, indicating for me to sit. He helps me push the seat in before taking the seat next to me. Being this close to Josh has my skin feeling like it's on fire. I don't even have to look at him to feel the energy radiating off of him. Unease fills me at the fact that I never feel like this with my boyfriend Drew.

We each grab a menu and begin to peruse the options. I know what I am getting. I get the same thing almost every time. Lasagna with bolognese. My family teases me for it, but I am a strong believer that if I am going to spend a decent amount of money on something, I want to know that I will like it. Teaching doesn't pay well so I'm always cautious about how I spend my money.

Like he can read my thoughts, Josh leans closer and whispers in my ear, his warm breath skating over my ear. "Order something new; today's on me." I blush and shake my head.

I don't recall ever telling Josh that I always order the same thing.

I don't remember going out to eat with him enough that he would have noticed.

"Olivia, please don't fight me on this." His voice is insistent, "It's your birthday. Lunch is on me."

I look up and to my left, making eye contact with him. "Thanks, Josh."

When I glance at Matt, he is watching us with a small smile, like he knows some secret the two of us don't. Growing up, I never told anyone about my crush on Josh. He was the attractive older guy—star of the hockey team, smart, and funny. Plus, with him being Matt's best friend, I always knew he was off-limits. Not only that, but I never thought Josh would go for someone like me. I am average height, with unruly hair that I sometimes have issues taming and I'm plus-size.

Don't get me wrong, I've learned to embrace my body and to stop comparing myself to all the other girls at school, but it's not something that's been easy. There are times I have had major difficulties with my body image. I have dated; I've been with Drew for almost two years. Unfortunately, not all guys will date the plus-size girl, and it's taken a lot of support and encouragement from my friends and self reflection for me to be able to accept that.

Our server comes up and takes our orders. I decide on something new this time, switching to a baked tortellini with alfredo sauce. When I order, Matt's head visibly jerks back in surprise, and Josh chuckles beside me.

"So, Liv, how's work?" Matt asks.

"You know, same old, same old. We have parent-teacher conferences next week, so I am preparing for those. I just redid my seating chart—I put Sarah and Jake together, so I am looking forward to seeing how that turns out," I chuckle.

Matt shakes his head while trying not to laugh. He looks at Josh. "Sarah and Jake are two students that Liv swears up and down have a crush on each other. She is attempting to play matchmaker."

Josh turns to me, his eyes a little wider than normal, a small smile tugging at the corner of his mouth. Looking between these two men, I smile. "What? I am a hopeless romantic. I feel like I have to do my part."

Josh regards me like he can't quite figure something out, and

Matt stares at me for a second longer before nodding. Matt clears his throat and changes the subject. "So, how's Drew?"

I typically avoid talking about Drew with Matt. I know he's not Drew's biggest fan. Matt has made remarks about how Drew should act his age or how he should treat me better. I know he says these things because he loves me, but he doesn't get to see the Drew I do when it's just us.

"He's good. He has some family stuff he's been dealing with," I say, playing with the edge of my napkin.

"Does he have anything planned for your birthday?"

"No, well… The girls have something planned for me, actually. Drew is with his family this weekend; he is helping them with something. He said he will try to meet up with us wherever we end up going. But we are supposed to go apartment hunting tomorrow. We are talking about moving in together. My lease is up on June 30, so I have to let my landlord know in a couple of weeks or go month to month."

As I speak, both Josh and Matt visibly tense. I am not surprised my brother isn't completely thrilled at the idea of me moving in with Drew, but I wonder why Josh cares?

Matt straightens himself and takes a deep breath. "So, you're really serious about him then? Moving in together." I can tell he's not saying everything that he wants to.

I nod and move the napkin I'm playing with onto my lap. "Yeah, I am. I love him and I am excited about building a future with him."

Matt nods just as our server drops off our food. As we dig in, we move on to lighter conversation, Matt and Josh discuss upcoming games for the recreational hockey team they play on with some friends. We sit enjoying conversation and laughing with each other, and just as I finish eating, my phone buzzes with a calendar reminder. I look down and see it's already two p.m.

"Hey, I'm sorry, but I have to run. I have an appointment before the girls all show up at my place," I say, standing up and giving Matt a peck on the cheek and a hug. "Thanks for meeting me for lunch. I'll call you later this week to set up something else soon."

"Yeah, of course. I love you, Liv. Happy Birthday."

"Thanks"

I move over to Josh and he stands, so I offer him a quick hug. "Thanks for lunch, Josh."

"Anytime. Happy birthday, Olivia."

I grab my bag and head to the restaurant exit, making my way to the nail salon for my mani-pedi.

CHAPTER 2

Josh

The last person I would have thought I'd run into this afternoon was Olivia Carter. Seeing her for the first time in around a year was surprising, to say the least, but it was definitely a pleasant surprise. I know I was the one who decided to distance myself after learning about her relationship; but seeing her again, her smile, hearing her laugh, watching her and Matt interact, I'm beginning to regret that decision. How much have I missed out on these last months? Can I push past how I feel about her and just be friends? I always have a sense of calm when I'm around her, and I miss that.

"Can I get a scotch on the rocks, please?" Matt asks our server as she passes by.

"Make that two, please," I add.

Matt runs his hands over his face before he leans over the table, clasping his hands together, and looks at me.

"I can't believe she is moving in with that guy." He shakes his head before continuing, "I can't say anything to her about it, it's her life and I have to let her do her own thing, but I just don't like the guy. I've seen how he treats her, always asking her to do everything for him, but never offering to do things for her. I don't think he makes enough time for her, either. I mean, it's her birthday, man. Who doesn't spend the day with their girlfriend on their birthday, especially if you are talking about moving in together?" He lets out a heavy sigh.

Taking a deep breath, I shake my head slightly. "I don't know, man. She's an adult. There's not much you can do but hope she's happy."

I'm not sure if I'm talking more to Matt or myself. I knew Olivia was in a relationship. I've met the guy and heard Matt complain about him enough, but hearing that she is planning on moving in with him has me feeling like I'm going to be sick.

When we were younger, Olivia was just Matt's younger sister. She would tag along with us, whether to the mall or the park, and she came to all our hockey practices and games.

Then I hit university; I came back to visit over Christmas with Matt, and my sister and I went to the Carter's Christmas party. We went every year, so it wasn't anything new, but when I got there and saw Olivia walking down the stairs, I stood stunned in the entryway. All I could think was, *God, she's gorgeous.* She had always been beautiful. I don't know if it was just her, my time away, or me growing up more, but she was the most stunning woman I had ever seen.

Her hair hung loosely around her face, and her red dress hugged her curves perfectly. My mouth went dry at the sight of her and the smile she had as she said hello to me. I was done for.

It wasn't just her looks that had pulled me in that winter break, though. While I was home, I hung out with Matt at his parents' house—watching hockey games—and Olivia would join us on the couch. She got into the games just as much as we did, sometimes more so, and she knew what she was talking about too. We talked more that trip home and I got to know the grown-up Olivia. She was the same as when we were kids, just with a little more sophistication and knowledge. Being around her was so much fun; she made me laugh, smile, and remember what I love about being home.

But she was Matt's younger sister, so I knew I could never make a move on her. My relationship with Matt was and still is too important to wreck.

I'm pulled out of my thoughts when our server drops off our drinks. "Can I get the bill too, please?" I ask, and she nods and smiles at me before walking off again.

"I know you're right, but I worry about her. I do want her to be happy, but I fear she's settling. With her being a romantic the way she is, it surprises me too. I see my parents' or your parents' relationships and I know there's no need to settle. You can find something good out there." He shakes his head while spinning his drink on the table. "Don't get me wrong, I enjoy the easy casual thing too, but I know when I am ready, I won't settle."

"I hear you. If you're really worried about it, you have a couple of weeks before she gives her landlord notice. Maybe help her out." I finish my drink in one go as the server drops off the bill.

I pull out my credit card and she holds up a finger as she runs off to get the credit card machine.

"You're right, man, but enough of this talk. Are you coming to my place later for Liv's surprise party? Grayson and Caleb are coming too."

"Yeah, I'll be there. You need me to bring anything?"

"Nope." He takes another sip of his drink. "Zoey has it all covered. She has the girls decorating at my place right now. I'm going straight home to help them with anything that still needs to be done."

I look at him in shock. "You let three women loose in your apartment and you're not freaking out? Are you okay, Matt? You always make sure women leave your apartment before you."

He scratches his jaw and shrugs. "I trust Zoey, and it's for Liv. I'd do anything for her and Gi, including letting three women loose in my apartment." He chuckles.

"You're a good brother, man. If you need anything for tonight, let me know."

"Thanks, man. You don't have to get lunch, let me get it. We invited you and it's my sister's birthday."

I shake my head and grab the card machine from the server as she arrives. She stares at me unabashedly. "No man, you're already throwing a surprise party at your place. I'm getting lunch."

I finish with the machine and pass it back to the server. Her eyes flick to the billfold on the table that I never looked at and I reach out to pass it back to her. She smiles at me, pink tinging her cheeks and the tips of her ears as she says, "Oh, no you keep that. Have a good day," and hurries off to the back of the restaurant.

Matt shakes his head with a laugh. "What do you wanna bet that she left her number in there? She is probably sad that you didn't even look inside and is hoping you will before we leave."

Laughing, I open the billfold and sure enough, at the top of our receipt written in pen, it says, "Call me ☺" with a phone number written beneath it. Our server is cute. She's about five-foot-eight, her blonde hair is pulled back into a ponytail, and she has a friendly smile; She just isn't doing anything for me. I spin the billfold toward him, and he laughs.

"Keep it," I say.

"You sure man? I'm sure that wasn't meant for me."

"Yeah, I won't use it."

He leans forward on the table so he's closer to me, and drops his voice. "You good, man? When was the last time you got laid? I haven't heard any of your stories or seen you with someone in a while."

Honestly, the thought of sleeping with anyone right now has my stomach tightening and bile rising in my throat. I've had a few one-night stands over the last few years, but that's it. Even though I know Olivia is in a relationship now and I want her to be happy, I can't even think about anyone else right now. Seeing her again has reignited something in me. I don't know what to say to Matt, so I go with a partial truth.

"Yeah, I'm good. Just been busy lately. Haven't been interested."

"Okay, well, when you are, let me know and I'll wingman for you, just like old times."

He stands and pats me on the shoulder before he folds the bill and puts it into his pocket. Just past him, I see the server watching, and she raises a brow. She doesn't look upset, just intrigued.

I stand too and pull him into a hug. "I'll see you later."

"Yeah, see ya."

We walk to the front of the restaurant and head in separate directions. Needing to pick up Olivia's gift I ordered, I decide to walk, using the time to clear my head. Olivia is moving in with her long-term boyfriend. Matt is still playing the field like he wants to. And I'm... What? I don't have an interest in a string of one-night stands. Maybe I should have taken the server's number. She was pretty and maybe she's looking for more than someone to warm her bed for a night.

Grabbing Olivia's gift and a card, I head home to shower and get ready.

CHAPTER 3

Olivia

I sip my coffee and admire my new nails as I walk home. I love spring so wanting to enjoy it, I take the long way home—walking through the park and stopping to take pictures of the water and trees. A light breeze whips my ponytail, I slow and take in the feeling of it on my skin, the smell of the flowers, and the sound of people and dogs around me. Contentment washes over me, causing me to smile. My smile remains all the way to my apartment.

When I arrive at my building, Max, one of our daytime concierges, greets me. I've been in this building for a few years and have grown friendly with him. He's in his late fifties, with salt and pepper hair that nowadays leans a little more towards salt than pepper. He and his wife have lived in the city for a while, and they have two daughters around my age. I always enjoy hearing his stories about them; he speaks about his family with such fondness.

"Good afternoon, Olivia'" He smiles. "I have a delivery here for you."

Smiling back, I join him at his desk. "Thank you, Max. How are you?"

"Oh, no complaints today. How about you?"

"It's been good. Celebrated my birthday with my brother and a friend earlier. By the way, the girls will be stopping by later this evening. I know they're on my list, but thought I'd give you the heads-up."

"Not a problem." He taps the counter before walking around the corner and returning with a glass vase full of red and white roses. My smile widens as he places them on the counter in front of me. "Here you go. Are these from the boyfriend?"

I shake my head. "I honestly don't know who they're from. I have been getting bouquets on my birthday for years from an anonymous sender."

"How sweet. Well, happy birthday, Olivia."

"Thanks," I say, grabbing the bouquet. I head toward the elevators and scan my fob, hitting the twenty-second floor and heading to my apartment.

Matt helped me find this place after I graduated from my program. It's in a wonderful location, safe, close to the school I work at, and close to Matt, which was a plus for him but not a necessity for me. He is still protective of both Gi and me, even though we are grown now. I know he worries about Gi being so far away for school, so if it helps him to have me close, I'll give it to him. Plus, this is a nice apartment.

Pushing through the front door, I drop my purse on the entryway table and walk into my living room. I place the vase of roses on the end table beside where I love to sit and look for a card. I find a white card tucked in between a few of the rosebuds.

Happy Birthday Sunshine,
I hope you have a day as amazing as you are.
Xoxo

Leaning down, I place my face right into the bouquet and inhale deeply; the smell makes my smile grow. I take the card, my fingers playing with it as I walk to my bedroom and into my closet. My hands push aside some things on the top shelf, and when I get to the back, I find the shoe box I keep of sentimental items I've collected over the years. I pull it down and take it to my bed. Opening the box, I pull out the bundle of similar white cards, all from the bouquets I've received over the years.

It all started on my sixteenth birthday. I was at school and a small bouquet was delivered to me in my first class. It garnered some attention too, as someone walked right into the classroom, called my name, and dropped them off at my desk. Then, it happened again the next two years. When I got to university, they were delivered to my dorm room, and the bouquet was nicer, with more expensive flowers. When I started at my current school, they were delivered to my classroom. Someone would walk them from the front office and deliver them to me. It gained some oohs and awws from my students. Now they are large bouquets made up of red and white roses, my favourite flowers.

The messages on the cards were all different, but along the same lines. The only thing that's always the same is the term of endearment—Sunshine—on all of them, but no one I know calls me that.

I haven't figured out who is sending them, but I have kept every card. Part of me knows I should be wary about someone anonymously sending me flowers, but seeing as they haven't tried anything, I choose to happily enjoy them. Every year, seeing the flowers sends warmth throughout my body and soul knowing someone cares enough to send my favourite flowers to me on my birthday.

I place the card with the others, bundling them together again, before going through the remaining contents. I look at pictures of me with my parents at my high school and university graduations, various pictures with Matt and Gi, and pictures with Hannah, Zoey, and Eliza. At the bottom, I have pictures of Matt, Josh, and me after one of their hockey practices. There are some of Matt and Josh playing hockey, some of us in a park on the swings, tickets from a concert I went to with them, and pictures with both of them before my prom. I also have pictures from all the various graduations of Gianna, Matt, Josh, and the girls. Pictures that memorialize the important events in our lives.

It's weird to think I used to be so close to both Josh and Em when I was younger, and now we all live in the same city again and it's not the same. We aren't distant or unfriendly, I just don't see them as much as I used to.

Placing the lid back on the box, I put it back in the same spot in my closet. My nostalgic thoughts continue to linger. I check the time on my phone—it's 5 p.m. The girls will be here at 6 p.m. to help me get ready, so I have time to shower.

Ideas of what to wear tonight fill my head. When I started

discussing plans for my birthday, they stopped me right away and told me they had it completely handled. So, I left tonight in their capable hands.

I don't realize how long I've been scrolling on my phone since my shower when I hear my front door open and the voices of my friends carry through the apartment. I grab my robe, secure it around my waist, and meet them in the hallway where I'm automatically pulled into a group hug.

"Happy birthday, babe," Zoey says as she pulls back.

"Happy birthday, Liv," Eliza says, giving me a kiss on the cheek.

"Happy birthday," Hannah says, squeezing me before releasing me.

The four of us head into my kitchen where I mix myself a rum and Coke Zero and the girls open a bottle of white wine. I won't drink the stuff, but I always keep a small supply for when it's my turn to host.

Zoey claps her hands together. "Okay, so I am going to take care of your makeup, Han is going to do your hair, and Liz has got your outfit. All you have to do is sit back, let us work, and of course, drink!"

Grabbing my hand, Zoey pulls me into my bedroom, pushing me into the chair in front of the vanity. Music starts blaring from the Bluetooth speaker now connected to Hannah's phone. This takes me back to our college days, getting ready for a party together, helping each other as we listen to music and pre-game.

One night years ago, we were all chilling at one of our places listening to music. We all have different tastes, so we created a shared playlist to give us a mix of music every time we hang out. A song I added, "Zombie" by The Cranberries, plays through the speaker.

As Zo rummages through my makeup she asks, "So Mr. Anonymous sent flowers again this year? I saw them when we walked in. I think they might be bigger than last year. They are gorgeous."

I blush, "Yeah, I still have no idea who has been sending them. Every year they make me smile."

"I'm glad, you deserve nice things, babe." She smiles at me over her shoulder. "So, what have you done so far today?"

"Went to lunch with Matt at Blue Spoon, got my nails done, and walked through the park," I say. I hem and haw whether or not to tell them about meeting up with Josh, and decide they're my best friends, I might as well. "Guess who I ran into before lunch, though?"

"Who?" Hannah asks.

"Joshua Lincoln."

Eliza stops rifling through my closet and pops her head out. "You mean the super-hot, billionaire, CEO, your brother has a bromance with—Joshua Lincoln?"

I look over at her and nod. "Yeah, and he ended up joining us for lunch. It was nice being able to catch up. He remembered it was my birthday too, paid for lunch and encouraged me to try something new. I did, and I actually liked it."

All three of them swing their heads to me. "You're saying that Josh got you to try something new at your favourite restaurant, even though your family has been trying to get you to for years?" Zoey asks. Zoey probably knows me the best because we went to grade school together, while we met Hannah and Eliza at university.

"Yeah, he insisted. It's not a big deal." I feel the blush spread across my cheeks as they give me an *as-if* look before resuming their tasks.

Hannah uses the straightener on my hair to loosely curl it and tells us stories about the recent cases she's had to deal with as a nurse at Vancouver Memorial. She talks about a guy who came into the ER after running his arm up a Sawzall, a kid who shoved marbles up *both* nostrils, and an artist who attempted to cut off his ear to be 'more in touch with Van Gogh'. I know it's wrong to laugh at what these people have gone through, but some of these things just lack common sense.

"You know, even with all those crazy cases, this week wouldn't have been that bad if it wasn't for Dr. Maxwell." I can hear the disdain in her voice as she scrunches her nose, causing her eyes to close slightly, making the same face she always does when she talks about him.

Grayson Maxwell is a friend of Matt and Josh's who works in the ER at Vancouver Memorial with Hannah. I have never had a problem with Grayson. From every interaction I've had with him, he seems nice enough. I know he's close enough with Matt and Josh, that should I ever need anything, I could call him, and he'd be there. But ever since last year, Hannah cannot stand the man. She won't talk about what happened, so we have all let it be, knowing she will tell us when she's ready. I guess Liz decides to give it another go, because she asks, "What did he do?" from my closet as she bends over to go through my shoes.

"The usual Grayson stuff, being a stuck-up jerk and leaving his shit lying around the nurses' station while flirting with every nurse. I end up having to be the one to pick up after him too. God, you'd think the nurses would ignore him, seeing as how much he gets around. But nope, he flashes them that smile and it's like all their panties melt simultaneously," she says with a huff.

I hold back a chuckle and say, "You know, Han, if you're interested in him, you could always just ask him out. You know he's not that bad of a guy."

"Han, you should go for it. I think you need a good lay. If you don't want to take it any further, you don't have to," Zoey adds.

Hannah rolls her eyes at Zoey and me through the mirror. "Nope, not going there. I don't need any STIs, thank you very much."

"Maybe you need to find another doctor at the hospital then, Han. Maybe a good lay will make Grayson a little less annoying to you, and maybe make him a little jealous in the process," Eliza adds as she walks out of my closet with an arm full of clothes and a pair of heels in her hand.

"I don't think a good lay, or even a great lay, could make Dr. Grayson Maxwell any less stuck up or annoying. I also have no desire to make him jealous," Hannah says as she turns the straightener off, placing it on the vanity and grabbing the hairspray. She gives me a good spray, takes a step back, and says, "Perfect Liv, you're gorgeous!" Wrapping her arms around me, she gives me a quick squeeze from behind before getting comfortable on the end of my bed.

"Next weekend, we're going out and getting you laid, and we'll put this theory to the test," Zoey says as she points the makeup brush in her hand at Hannah.

"Sure, sure, Zo. Whatever you say," Hannah replies, knowing

there's no point in arguing with her. Once Zoey gets an idea in her head, there is no talking her out of it, especially if she thinks it's best for her friends.

"I can do Saturday evening if Drew and I find a place tomorrow," I say.

"Have you picked out any places yet? Any areas you want to live?" Liz asks.

"We're still deciding. I would like to stay close to here; it's close to work, I love this park, and it's a great neighbourhood. Plus, I'm sure Matt wants me to stay close. Drew wants something a little more downtown, but I don't want to move again anytime soon, so I want something bigger that we can expand in. Maybe start our family in one day, you know?"

Through the mirror, the girls exchange quick looks before Zoey says, "You'll figure it out," while squeezing my arm.

Zoey finishes with my makeup, telling us about her law school classes at UBC, and then takes me back to my bed, where Liz has my outfit laid out.

Being plus-size, I've always been one to cover up more than my friends, but Liz has picked out a nice black lace bra with matching panties, high-waisted black skinny jeans, a sheer red shirt, and black pumps. It's sexy and stylish, showing off a little more than I usually do. As I get dressed, the girls grab their bags and get changed too.

I walk over to the full-length mirror on the wall and take in what the girls have done to me. My auburn hair is in loose curls, ending around my shoulders. My makeup is done nicely, a little more glamorous than my natural look, with a deep red lip, and the outfit is amazing. The jeans accentuate the waist I do have, and, paired with the black pumps, my legs look longer. The red top looks good with my pale skin and the black lace bra makes my boobs look fantastic.

Once I am done looking in the mirror, they drag me into the kitchen where Hannah pours us four shots of Jager. We all lift our shot glasses as they cheer, "To Liv," and down our shots. While Hannah pours the next round, Eliza orders our Uber. Two more shots and we gather for a couple of selfies in my living room before grabbing our jackets and heading downstairs to meet the Uber.

In the elevator, I open my Instagram and post our pictures with the caption, *Celebrating my birthday with my ride-or-dies* .

When we get downstairs to the Uber, Hannah pulls a scarf from her purse and stands behind me, tying it around my eyes.

Making sure it's secure, she leans in and whispers in my ear, "It's a surprise after all." She helps me into the back of the car, and we head to our destination.

CHAPTER 4

Josh

I make sure I arrive at Matt's apartment early enough to assist with any last-minute details. I use my key to his place and head straight up. Walking in the front door, I hang my coat up in his entry closet and make sure Olivia's gift is securely in the pocket.

I take in the changes made to Matt's usual bachelor pad. As soon as I walk into his living room, I'm assaulted by purple streamers hanging from the top of the archway. Fondness fills my chest as I take in the dark purple, blue, and silver decorations. Olivia's favourite colour combination.

My heart skips a beat as I take in the rest of the decorations. Enlarged photos from Olivia's life are scattered throughout the place.

I stop in front of a photo of me pushing her on a swing. Matt stands on the one beside it with a huge grin on his face while Liv has her head tipped backwards as she swings. Just looking at this photo, I can hear her laugh. The next photo is of the three of us after one of our hockey practices. She's squished between Matt and I, in all our gear, grinning from ear to ear.

Moving to the next room, pictures of her with friends and family fill the space. I recognize a photo from her high school graduation. It's her entire family, Emily, and I. I've seen this picture before. As I get closer, I see I'm smiling, but I'm not looking at the camera—my eyes are fixed on Olivia.

All this time, I thought I kept my feelings for Olivia hidden, but this picture right here captured everything. My love for her is written all over my face. I just hope no one else has caught it.

Shaking my head, I move to the kitchen where Matt is setting out food on the dining table and setting up a bar on the kitchen counter.

"Hey, man." I pat him on the shoulder. "Need a hand with anything?"

"Hey," he says. "If you wanna finish setting up the plates and napkins, that would be great. Everyone should be arriving soon."

"Sure, no problem. I saw the decorations and pictures when I came in—you guys are going all out for this party."

"Yeah, it's her twenty-fifth, so we wanted to make it special. Although Zoey took charge of the decorations and delegated the food. All I am doing is offering my place and adding some finishing touches before everyone gets here." The love Matt has for his sister is obvious in his voice.

"Still, she will love this."

"I hope so," he says with a smile.

Together, we put the final touches in place. Around 7:30 p.m., people start arriving. Everyone was told to be here before 8 p.m., so they're here before the girls are supposed to leave Olivia's place.

The smell of beer and alcohol fills my nose while the sounds of people mingling and low music floats through the air. Grayson and Caleb arrive at 8 p.m., joining Matt and me in the kitchen, where we are making a couple of drinks. Matt looks up, spotting them, and sets down the stuff in his hand to walk over and pull them each into a hug, slapping their backs.

"Thanks for coming guys. Liv and the girls should be here soon."

"Of course. We saw those pictures out there. You three looked close growing up," Grayson says.

Matt and I met Caleb and Grayson at a bar one of our first weeks back from Harvard. We all started talking and our friendship grew from there. They know Matt and I have known each other for years and our families are everything to us. I guess we never went into a lot of detail about it.

"Yeah, Liv liked to follow us wherever we went. She was at every one of our hockey practices and games. She knows just as much about hockey as we do. Never get between that girl and watching the Cyclone play. She can be feral," Matt says, chuckling.

"Man, do you remember our first year at Harvard? When we were home for Christmas, and we were at your parents' place watching the game? I swore she was going to throw her bowl of popcorn at the TV when the ref made that tripping call against Vancouver. She was pissed, yelling at the TV, cussing out the refs," I say to Matt, holding back a laugh.

"Yeah, she's definitely entertaining to watch hockey with," Matt agrees.

"Why don't you invite her to our games, then? Might be nice to have someone watching who actually knows the sport." Grayson asks Matt with a grin.

"I haven't thought about it, but I'll ask her."

Matt's phone goes off and he pulls it out, checking it. He smiles, turns the music off, and motions toward the living room. Standing on his couch, he announces, "Everybody, they are on their way up now."

He jumps off the couch, and we all move closer to the entryway to greet the birthday girl. Silence fills the air until the door opens, and Olivia walks in with her friends.

Olivia is blindfolded with a scarf. Her auburn hair cascades in loose curls to her shoulders and her lips are painted a dark red. My eyes take in the sight of black skinny jeans hugging her every curve, paired with black heels that make her legs look amazing. Her red sheer top teases me, allowing me to see the black lace bra underneath.

The sight of her has my heart racing and my jeans tightening. God, my mouth is dry; has someone suddenly cranked up the heat, sucking all the moisture out of the air?

Olivia is gorgeous.

I take a quick sip of my drink to fight the sudden dryness in my mouth. Grayson gives me a knowing look like he can sense my internal turmoil.

Zoey unties the scarf from around Olivia's eyes and the entire group yells, "Surprise!" Her eyes widen, and her jaw drops as she takes in the room around her. She scans the room, looking at the pictures, decorations, her friends from work, some others I recognize from her high school days, her brother, and then her eyes land on me and they widen in shock for a second as a smile crosses her face.

Turning around, she looks at Zoey, Hannah, and Eliza and pulls them into a group hug. She must whisper something to them because they all erupt in laughter.

Everyone in the room goes back to their conversations, allowing Olivia to make the rounds. Turning back to us, she walks up to Matt and pulls him into an enormous hug.

"Thank you so much, Matt. This looks amazing," she says.

"Of course, anything for you Liv, but to be honest, Zo handled most of it. She and the girls were here while we were at lunch, decorating and everything."

Her eyes go comically wide. "Wait, you're telling me you let my friends into your apartment by themselves, and you sat and had a calm lunch with Josh and me, without having a coronary?" she asks, dumbfounded. Caleb and Grayson chuckle beside us.

"Yeah, it wasn't a big deal." He shrugs. "Now let's celebrate my little sister turning twenty-five!" He reaches into his pocket and turns the music back on—it's the stuff Olivia usually listens to.

She gives Grayson and Caleb quick side hugs before turning to me. Matt and the guys walk over to Olivia's friends, leaving the two of us to talk.

"Twice in one day, huh, Josh? I don't think I've seen you this much since you were at Harvard and visited for the holidays."

I laugh. "Yeah, we should probably fix that. But right now, let's get you a drink. Rum and Coke Zero, right?"

Surprise fills her face. "Ummm... Yeah! You remember?" she asks.

"Of course I remember, Olivia."

Extending my arm to indicate I'll follow her, she walks ahead of me and I put my hand on the small of her back. I can feel heat radiating through her shirt and into my hand as we walk. In the kitchen, I fix her a drink, handing it to her and lifting my glass to hers. "Happy birthday, Olivia." She clinks her plastic cup with mine and takes a sip.

"Perfect." She smiles at me before one of her friends comes and steals her away.

I wander around and eventually find Grayson, Caleb, and Matt in a corner talking. I catch the end of their conversation about last night's playoff game between Boston and Florida.

"What's going on with you and Hannah?" I ask Grayson.

He grimaces slightly before he lifts his beer to his lips. "What do you mean?" he asks, taking a long draw from his beer.

"You're going to play dumb? You two work together and she has been shooting death glares your way and avoiding this side of the room all night. So... What the fuck did you do to deserve that reaction from her?"

"Man, I don't know." He looks around the room, finding Hannah, before looking back at me. "She's just being Hannah. She's standoffish at work too. She does her job, but she gives me the cold shoulder."

"You must have done something to fuck up because that's not Hannah. I have known her for years and she is nice unless you give her a reason not to be," Matt says.

"Have you asked her what happened?" Caleb asks.

"Nope, I figure she'll say something eventually if she wants to, but we work together fine. So, until it impacts that, I'm going to let sleeping dogs lie."

"You sure? I can ask Liv for you if you want," Matt pushes.

"Yeah, it's fine. Don't ask Liv," Grayson says.

Zoey comes up to us then, placing a hand on Matt's arm. He looks down at her with a small smile and she smiles back. "I think we should cut the cake. Do you want to come help?"

"Yeah, of course, let's go." He nods at us before he follows Zoey into the kitchen, guiding her with a hand on her lower back.

"I'm gonna grab a beer. You guys want another?" I ask Grayson and Caleb. They both shake their heads, and I turn and follow Matt into the kitchen. Grabbing a beer from the bucket of ice, I scan the room and notice Olivia across the room talking with a group of her friends, her head tipped back as a huge laugh fills the room. She looks so happy and carefree.

Her smile and laughter make me feel light, but jealous at the same time. I want her smiles. I want to be the person who makes her laugh so hard she throws her head back.

Matt walks past me carrying a black forest cake with candles on it and makes his way over to the corner where Olivia is. I follow behind and when he stops in front of her and starts singing "Happy Birthday," everyone joins in as she turns and faces us, a blush creeping up her neck and cheeks.

I still, wondering if I were to peel her top off if I would see it extending down her chest too. Would her skin be warm to the touch? If I trailed my fingers over the skin there, would she erupt in goosebumps? She has never been someone who enjoys being the centre of attention, but she is just a person who sucks in those around her. She's infectious in all the best possible ways. She sucked me into her orbit years ago, and even though I have tried to create space between us in recent years, I've found myself pulled right back in within less than twenty-four hours.

When we all finish singing, she closes her eyes for a few seconds before leaning forward and blowing out the candles. I close my eyes to avoid catching a glimpse down her top. Matt takes the cake over to the table and Zoey cuts it. She hands a piece to Olivia, and she passes it to Matt. "Thanks for all of this, Matt."

"Don't worry about it, Liv."

She then hands the next piece to me. "Thanks for being here, Josh"

Reaching forward, I place my hand on the top of her arm and smile down at her. "I wouldn't miss your birthday, Olivia. I'm glad I'm here. I promise I won't miss any future birthdays, either."

She smiles up at me with a gleam in her eyes. "I'm glad you're here too."

Just after 1 a.m., I am talking with Grayson and Caleb, and I notice everyone has left. Making my way to the kitchen with them behind me, I find Matt doing shots with Olivia, Zoey, Hannah, and Eliza, and they're all wasted.

Matt looks up and grins at me. "Jooooosssssshhhhhh, hey, man! I'm so glad you're here." He walks over to me and pulls me into a hug. "I love you man, you're the brother I never had," he says as he pats me on the back. "Sometimes I wish you really were my brother."

I chuckle and pat him on the back, too. "Love you too, man. Maybe it's time to call it a night?"

He pulls back, resting his hands on my shoulders. "More shots!" he exclaims, and the girls join him.

"More shots!" Zoey proceeds to pour another round of tequila shots for them. They toss them back at the same time and she gets to work on pouring another round.

"I think this might be your final round, guys," Caleb suggests, joining us at the kitchen counter. He grabs the bottle of tequila as they all toss back a round. Grayson is just leaning against the fridge, enjoying the sight before him.

"Come on, we'll give you guys a ride home. Where are you all going?" Caleb asks them.

"Hannah's coming to my place, Zoey's going home, and Liv's going home," Eliza explains, sounding like she might be the most sober of the bunch even though she's still three sheets to the wind.

"Okay, we can work with that. You guys grab your stuff. We'll make sure Matt gets to bed and then take you home."

Grayson leads Matt down the hallway to his bedroom and gets him settled, while Caleb and I make sure the girls have everything. Standing in the entryway, Caleb and I get the addresses of the girls.

"Caleb, can you take Liz and Hannah? Grayson, can you take Zoey, and I'll take Olivia?" The guys nod and we make our way into the hallway.

I lock the door and lead Olivia to the elevator. She leans into me and wraps herself around my arm as we walk.

"Thanks for being such a good man and getting us home, Josh," she murmurs, patting my chest.

"Olivia, I will always make sure you're safe."

I feel my body temperature rising as she continues to hold onto me. We step into the elevator, and she looks up at me through her long lashes. "You're a good man." Everyone is looking at us now. Olivia leans towards her friends and fails in her attempt at whispering, "He is like all muscle; I don't think I can feel an ounce of fat on him at all."

The girls start laughing, and Grayson and Caleb look at me with grins spread across their faces. Drunk Olivia apparently speaks her mind. I shake my head as they continue to look at me. Grayson, the shit disturber that he is, looks at Olivia and asks, "Liv, how much of Josh have you felt to come to that assessment?"

She completely shocks me, because she looks him in the eyes and says, "Not as much as I wish." One of the girls makes a sound and Olivia turns to them. "I can window shop, I just can't buy. I'm in a relationship, not blind."

Right then, the elevator doors open, and everyone laughs at Olivia's statement. "Okay, well, I think it's time to get these drunk girls home," I say as I usher Olivia towards my car.

"Don't do anything I wouldn't," Grayson calls after me with the biggest grin. I won't be doing anything besides making sure Olivia makes it home safely. Firstly, she's drunk, and secondly, even if she was completely sober, she's in a relationship.

I open the passenger door and help Olivia inside. She works on her seatbelt but is having difficulties, so I reach across her and fasten it for her. I turn my face and look her in the eyes. "All good?"

She nods and places her hands on either side of my face. "Anyone ever told you that you have the most gorgeous eyes?" she whispers. I continue to stare into hers, shaking my head.

"No Olivia, no one has ever said that. Thank you."

She takes her hands and runs them up my cheeks until her fingers are gripping the hair on the back of my head. I hold back a groan. "Well, they are gorgeous. I could get lost staring at them." Her words have my body heating. Olivia has never spoken to me like this. It's sending my mind reeling. Her delicate touch and her fingers in my hair are giving my dick the wrong idea. I need to get my mind and body under control.

Reaching up, I grab her hands, remove them from my hair, and place them in her lap. "Thank you, Olivia. Are you good? I should get you home."

She nods and something flashes through her eyes for a second before disappearing. I close the door before rounding the front of my car and getting in. Throwing the car into drive, I speed out of the parking garage.

Olivia leans against the window, looking out as we drive down the streets to her apartment. After about five minutes, she turns and looks at me.

"Why did we grow apart, Josh? I miss you. I don't know what happened." She looks sad like she did when she lost her favourite toy growing up.

"I don't know, Olivia. I miss you too. You haven't lost me, though; we can spend more time together if you want," I tell her. I never thought she genuinely noticed that I wasn't around her as much. I knew we were close growing up, but I always thought she hung out with me because of Matt.

"Yeah, I do. I'd like that," she says before leaning against the window again. "Drew didn't come tonight," she whispers so softly I almost don't hear it. I don't know what to say to make it better, so I just keep driving.

When we get to her place, I pull into the parking garage and round the car, opening the door for her. She's still groggy, so I loop my arm around her waist, and she leans in as if it's the most natural thing in the world. I wish that was the case. I wish she wasn't with Drew, that she wasn't my best friend's little sister, that we were in any other situation where I could just tell her how I feel.

Fobbing us into the elevator, I help Liv to her apartment, remembering where it is from when I helped Matt move her in. I help her inside and down the hallway to her bedroom.

Her bedroom is completely her, there are pictures on her night-stand and vanity, and there's a stack of books and a candle beside her bed. Her bed is covered in pillows and the room is still a mess from her getting ready earlier.

I help her onto her bed, and she nestles into her pillow with a contented sigh. Grabbing an extra blanket from the end of her bed, I cover her with it. She is going to wake up with a killer headache, so I head into her washroom and grab some Advil and a bottle of water from her kitchen. I write a brief note and leave it with the water and pills before placing a gentle kiss on her forehead and quietly exiting her room.

Needing to be close to her for a little longer, I take in her living room. She has a shelf full of books, pictures, and knickknacks. There are decorative throw pillows all over her couch, and a blanket on each end. I notice on one end table she has her TV remote, a book, and a bouquet of red and white roses, and I smile to myself. They're her favourite flowers, and she has placed them where she usually sits.

Reaching into the pocket of my coat, I grab Olivia's present and leave it on the table before stepping outside her apartment, closing the door softly.

CHAPTER 5

Olivia

B*uzz, buzz, buzz.*
Buzz, buzz, buzz.
Buzz, buzz, buzz.

"Ugh," I groan as I roll over and search for my phone. My mouth is so fucking dry, and my head feels like there's a tiny construction crew inside using a jackhammer on my skull. Finally locating my phone, I slowly lift it into my line of sight. Cracking one eye, I check to see why it's buzzing and notice it's already eleven in the morning. I have texts from both Matt and the girls' group chat. Closing my eyes again, I take a deep breath and tell myself, *I can do this; I can survive the feeling of death today.*

I push myself onto my elbows and slowly open my eyes. My blackout curtains are still closed, so the light isn't too harsh. Looking at my nightstand, I notice two Advil and a bottle of water with a note beside it sitting on top.

Drink the water and take these. Feel better.
-Josh

I force myself all the way up and rub my eyes with the heel of my hands. God, what happened last night? Looking back at my phone, I open the texts from Matt.

MATTY

Hey Liv, you alive?

How are you feeling?

Call me when you can.

Next, I switch over to the group chat with the girls.

HAN

Ugh, tequila shots, remind me never again.

ZO

I have the worst case of cottonmouth, shots are
not my thing.

LIZ

Who's up for a greasy brunch?

HAN

I'm down.

ZO

Same. I need something to absorb all the alcohol
Liv convinced me to drink last night.

LIV

I'm down for greasy food. Sammy's in 45?

What do you mean I did the convincing? I can
barely remember last night. The last thing I
remember is doing the shots which MATT
convinced us to do. I say we blame my brother
😅.

LIZ

Sammy's sounds good.

ZO

Yup to Sammy's.

HAN

Sammy's it is.

Matt can take the blame for the first two, but girl,
after that you were throwing them back. Good
thing Josh took you home.

ZO

Yeah, in the words of drunk Liv last night 'Josh is such a good guy,' oh and 'he's got muscles I don't think he has an ounce of fat on him,' and 'I can window shop, I just can't buy,' lol, drunk Liv is a blast. 😊😊 🔥

LIV

I did not say that, did I??? God help me!

LIZ

You did, in fact, say that as well as, you haven't felt as much of him as you'd like, all while clinging to his arm as he walked you to his car.

LIV

God! So embarrassing! This is why I don't drink. Drunk Liv does stupid things. Why did you guys let me do that? How did you guys get home last night?

LIZ

Grayson drove Zo home and Caleb drove us to my place. Now that is one hunk of a man.

HAN

Oh yeah, Liz kept giving Caleb fuck me eyes on the car ride home.

LIZ

I was not, take that back. 😠

HAN

Babe, you were. If you two had been alone, I wouldn't have been surprised if you had crawled onto his lap and started kissing him.

LIZ

Okay, so Sammy's in 45, let's get ready bitches.

LIV

See you soon

I go back to my conversation with Matt and respond.

LIV

I feel like hell. Shots, really? And tequila… The girls and I are fucked this morning 🤢

MATTY

You were the one who kept everyone going, Liv.
When will I learn to never drink with you?

LIV

Not sure 😅

Going for brunch with the girls will call you later.

I have thirty minutes to shower and get changed before I need to be out the door. Mustering what little energy I have, I get out of bed, and make my way to the washroom, turning the shower on. God, looking at myself in the mirror, I see I have raccoon eyes and my lips are so dry they are visibly beginning to crack. I step into the shower, allowing the hot water to run through my tangled hair and down my body as I close my eyes and try to piece last night together.

I remember getting to the party. The memories of dancing and socializing come back to me, and I remember seeing the cake which turned into shots with Matt and the girls. Matt gave me my birthday present: a gift certificate for a massage at a nice place downtown, and a gift certificate to the bookstore. The girls all pitched in and got me a new Apple watch with a band for me to dress it up.

I remember texting Drew to see if he was going to make it to the party, but he couldn't. Grabbing the shampoo, I work it into my hair before rinsing and moving to the conditioner. As I massage my scalp, an image of Josh kissing my forehead comes into my mind, but I can't tell if it's a memory or a dream. I finish my shower before grabbing my phone and scrolling to Josh's number.

LIV

Hey, thanks for taking care of me last night. It means a lot to me. I always feel safe with you. Sorry if I did or said anything stupid; drunk Liv doesn't always think.

JOSH

No need to thank me. I am just glad we got you home safe. And no need to apologize for anything; drunk Liv is funny.

I smile broadly, reading his text before putting my phone down, and finish getting ready. As I walk out the front door, my phone begins to blare Gianna's ringtone.

"Hey, Gi! How are you?" I answer with a smile. I miss my sister, but I know she's at a top tier school getting a degree she wants, so I'm happy for her. As her big sister though, I wish she was closer.

"Hey, I'm good. Sorry, I couldn't make it to your birthday bash yesterday; Matt told me all the plans. That's why I waited until today to call you; I knew I wouldn't be able to keep the secret." I can hear the smile in her voice. "How was it?"

"It was amazing. I loved it. They went all out on decorations and food, and they got my favourite black forest cake, too. But then I let Matt talk us into tequila shots, so I'm heading to meet the girls at Sammy's for some greasy hangover food. How is school? We miss you. When will you be home?"

"School is good. My finals are coming up soon. I'll be on the first flight home after finals. I miss you guys too. We need to do a siblings' lunch when I get home."

"Of course, Matt will be down for that. Let me know when you book your flight and I'll pick you up at the airport."

"Will do. I have to go. I'm meeting with a study group. Love you Liv! Happy birthday."

"Love you too, Gi! Talk to you soon."

I put my phone away and turn the corner towards Sammy's. We stumbled upon Sammy's one of the first weeks after I moved into my apartment; we had been drinking and found this little twenty-four-hour diner down the street and decided to try it out. We've been coming here ever since.

I slide into the booth and greet the girls as Sam walks up to our booth. Sam is the owner and regularly works the floor serving. She is tall, with long blonde hair she usually keeps up in either a ponytail or bun. She's in her late 40s or early 50s and is one of the friendliest people I know.

"Hello, girls. So nice to see you all. How are you?"

"Hey Sam, we're good," Zoey says. "Nursing some nasty hangovers after Liv's birthday party last night. We need some good, greasy food!"

Sam smiles at me. "Happy Birthday, Liv. Well, I can do that for y'all. Pancakes with hash browns, eggs, and bacon for the table?"

We all look at her with a smile and a universal, "Sounds great!"

Sam walks behind the counter and puts our order in and returns with four coffees. "Anything else I can get you, ladies?"

We shake our heads and say thank you before she returns to help the rest of the customers in the diner.

I look over to Eliza and ask, "So, what's going on with you and Caleb, Liz?"

She groans and rolls her eyes. Using the spoon she just stirred her coffee with, she points at each of us. "I'm gonna say this once, got it? Nothing is going on between me and Caleb. Is that man fine as fuck? Yes. You'd have to be blind to miss that, but that's the extent of it."

"So..." Zoey starts and I know she's going to dig. "You're saying that if Caleb asked to sleep with you, you'd turn him down?" Zoey asks, quirking her brow at our friend, who is the most serious of the group.

"If Caleb asked, no, I would probably be down, but right now I am perfectly content with enjoying the view. Plus, I have no desire to get involved with a cop. Liv, what happened with Josh after he took you home last night? You were all over him," Eliza says, trying to move the conversation away from her, and it works.

Shaking my head, I look at my friends' curious faces. "Nothing happened. Josh is an old friend. He took me home, put me to bed and left me a bottle of water and a couple of Advil on my nightstand. That's it. Plus, Josh knows I'm with Drew; he wouldn't try anything, and I won't cheat. I'd end it before that."

Hannah sighs into her coffee before putting it down. Reaching across the table, she takes my hand and squeezes it. "Liv, why are you still with Drew? The guy doesn't treat you right. You deserve to have someone who will worship you. You are a fierce girl, but you're also smart, kind, funny, and loyal as hell. The guy couldn't even make it to your birthday party last night, and he barely texted you at all yesterday. He didn't call you once, did he? Has he even checked in today?" I hear the emotion in her voice.

My friends haven't said much about my relationship with Drew, so this is new. It does hurt that Drew didn't make it yesterday or reach out today, but I know he's been dealing with family issues. I have to allow him the space and time to be there to support his family.

I squeeze her hand back. "I love him. We've been together for two years and are planning on moving in together. I know he's a good guy, he just has a lot going on right now. Once he figures everything out with his family, it will all go back to normal. But thank you for looking out for me. I love you, Han."

Eliza adds her hand on top of Hannah's and looks at me. "We're here for you if you need us, babe. You just have to text or call, you know that, right?"

Zoey places hers on top of Eliza's. She adds, "Liv, we want you to be happy. You are such an amazing person. You deserve the world, babe."

I look at them with tears in my eyes and place my free hand on top of Zoey's so the three of their hands are between mine. "You guys are the best friends a girl could ask for. I love you all. How did I get so lucky to deserve you?"

"We are just as lucky," Hannah says. We each give one more hand squeeze before taking our hands back. As we separate, Sam comes back with our food, and we dig in. We talk about our upcoming week.

We pay our bill and head out. Outside of Sammy's, we all hug and agree that they will all meet at my place on Saturday for a night out. As I walk to the SkyTrain, I call Matt.

"Hey Liv, how's the hangover?"

"Better, thanks. I just left Sammy's, the girls and I had breakfast. How are you after last night?"

"Oh, my head isn't killing me anymore." He chuckles. "Josh took you home last night, right? I'm assuming you made it home safe and sound?"

"Yeah, Josh took me home, Caleb took Han and Liz to Liz's place, and Grayson took Zo home. Your friends made sure your little sister and her friends made it home safe and sound." I smile and laugh.

"Well, I am glad. Did you talk to Drew after last night? I noticed he didn't make it." My stomach clenches. Both my brother and my friends noticed my boyfriend didn't make it to celebrate my twenty-fifth birthday.

I sigh. "No, he texted me last night to let me know he wouldn't make it. We're supposed to go look at a couple of places today. I'm on my way to his place now." There's a pause on the other end of the line, and I can tell that Matt is thinking about what he wants to say. After a few seconds, he lets out a breath.

"Let me know if you want any help looking." I know how hard that was for my brother to not stick his nose into the issue and just offer help without his opinion.

"I will, but I think we are fine for now. Thank you. What are your plans for the rest of the day?" I ask, wanting to move the subject along, knowing Matt isn't one hundred percent supportive of this move.

"Nothing much today, might hit the batting cages with the guys."

"Sounds fun. Oh, I talked to Gi today. She said she'll be on the first flight home after her finals. She wants to have lunch with us when she gets back. I offered to get her at the airport when she lands."

"I'm down for lunch, for sure. Let me know about her flight home. I'll try to go with you to pick her up."

"Will do. I'll talk to you later. Love you."

"Love you too, bye."

Putting my phone away, I grab my transit pass from my purse and tap it to get onto the SkyTrain. It's only a couple of stops to Drew's place, so I scroll on my phone before hopping off and making the walk to his place. I use my fob for his building to enter the lobby and make my way up to his apartment.

Getting to his door, I twist the door handle and it's unlocked, so I walk in.

"Hey babe, I'm here. You ready to go?" I call out.

"Liv?" Drew calls, and he sounds surprised I'm here. "Yeah, just give me a minute." I hear some noise coming from his bedroom and assume he's just finishing getting dressed. I go into the kitchen and grab a bottle of water, downing half of it in two sips.

He slips out of his bedroom and closes the door behind him. Drew's short blonde hair is slightly dishevelled and his glacier-blue eyes take me in as he makes his way to me, stopping to kiss me on the cheek before leaning against the kitchen counter. He shoves his hands in the pockets of his jeans that hang off his narrow hips. He looks a little uncomfortable. I take him in. He's dressed in a pair of dark wash jeans and a plain green t-shirt that looks wrinkled, like he just picked it up off the floor. His hair is a mess, and he won't hold eye contact with me.

"Hey Liv, I forgot you were coming over today. What's up?" he asks.

"Umm... We have two appointments to look at apartments today. Are you still good to do that?" I'm worried he might bail, seeing as he missed last night.

"Oh, yeah, totally." He reaches into the fridge and grabs a bottle of water. He turns to me and says, "Let's head out."

Grabbing his keys, he ushers me out of the apartment. When we get into the hallway, he locks the door and then reaches for my hand. His hand is clammy and warm, which is not normal for him.

I look up at him. "You, okay? Your hand is all warm and clammy. If you're sick, we can reschedule, and I can make you soup or something."

"Nope, all good," he rushes out. "Let's go to these appointments."

"You sure? You're acting weird." His behaviour has something niggling inside my mind, but I push it to the side, figuring his mind is probably focused on the issues with his family.

"Yeah, sorry. I just have a lot going on. Trying to wrap my head around it all."

Climbing into the elevator, Drew selects the parking level where he keeps his car. "So, how is everything with your family?" I finally ask after a long silence.

"We're still figuring some stuff out, but it should all be good soon." Sensing he doesn't want to talk about it, I change the subject to our upcoming appointments.

"That's good, so the first place we have an appointment at is the one over on Pacific, close to my place, and then we have another over on Homer."

"Sounds good," he says, sounding disinterested. I'm not sure we should do this today, but he was the one that had brought up moving in together and he was so excited.

Getting off the elevator, we make our way to his car. He gets in and turns on his playlist before pulling out of the parking garage and heading in the direction of our first appointment.

Drew is silent as we make our way through the streets of downtown. The silence is ripe with tension and I'm not sure why. I feel like no matter what I say, he's going to be disinterested, and it hurts. After a few minutes of silence, I look at him and say, "I missed you last night."

He looks over at me for a second, then returns his eyes to the road and readjusts his hands on the steering wheel. He seems extremely fidgety. A few seconds pass without a word before he answers, "Yeah, I'm sorry I couldn't make it. This stuff with my family has taken a lot of my time. Once we get that all figured out, why don't we take a weekend away? Just the two of us." He smiles at me.

"That sounds great." We haven't done a trip away before, so it will be nice to have some time for just us. "Is there anything I can do to help with this family situation? Can you tell me what's going on? I would like to help you."

"Sorry, Liv, the family wants to keep it quiet for now. As soon as I can tell you, I will."

"Okay, well I'm here for you if you need it." I reach over and place my hand on his thigh, giving it a small squeeze.

"Thanks."

We arrive at the first place, and he pulls up to the curb outside the building. Getting out, we make our way to the front door. I send a text to the agent we are meeting. A minute later, a tall blonde woman dressed in a form-fitting navy dress with a square neckline opens the door.

"Olivia?" she asks.

"That's me." I smile and gesture to Drew. "This is my boyfriend, Drew. We will be renting the place together."

She smiles and lets us in, reaching a hand out to Drew and me, both of us shaking it. "Thanks for meeting us," I say.

"I'm glad to." She adds, "So this place is on the thirty-fourth floor. It's a two-bed, two-bath with hardwood floors, new appliances in the kitchen, and it has a magnificent view of the water."

"I am excited to see it."

We make our way to the elevator and make small talk on the way up to the apartment. When we get up there, she unlocks the door and leads us inside.

It's an open floor plan. The kitchen is the main focal point when you walk in with stainless-steel appliances and an island. Making our way further into the apartment, we walk into the living room, which has floor-to-ceiling windows that look over the water and park below. Hardwood floors are in every room of the apartment. Moving from the living room, we head towards the master bedroom.

The master bedroom is large enough to fit a king-size bed comfortably with two nightstands. It has a his-and-her walk-in closet and features the same floor-to-ceiling windows and view as the living room. The ensuite bathroom has a luxurious tub I can't wait to use. I can imagine the lit candles and the bubbles as I lay there with a good book and soft music playing after a long day.

The second bedroom is perfect for a guest room. Excitement fills me as we finish the tour. This is somewhere I can see myself living.

Making our way back into the kitchen, I find the realtor looking over some paperwork. Looking at Drew, I say, "I love it. It's a great location and I love the space in the closet and kitchen."

"I think it's perfect for us," Drew says, smiling.

"Okay, well, this sounds great. Let's go over a couple of things. The rent will be twenty-five hundred a month and the deposit is half a month's rent. You don't have any pets, do you?" the realtor asks us.

"No, no pets," I say.

"Okay, that's good. The owner has looked at the application you filled out online, and your references and credit checks came back positive. So, if you guys want the place, it's yours. All we need for you to proceed is a cheque for the deposit."

"Can you give us just a minute?" I ask her. She nods and I grab Drew's hand and lead him onto the balcony outside the living room.

"So, what do you think?" I ask Drew once we are outside and the door is closed.

"I think it's great if this is the place you want. I don't have my chequebook with me, but I can drop a cheque off tomorrow after work and then we can sign the contract next weekend."

"That works. Oh my god, I can't believe we're doing this." I squeal a little with excitement. "This place is perfect. I love the location, the park is right downstairs, it's close to work, and this view is amazing. Just think, in a month this place will be ours." I squeeze his hand and smile.

Drew pulls me into a hug. "Yup, this will be all ours, and I will get to see you every day, and fall asleep and wake up beside you every day, too."

Looking up at him, I go onto my tiptoes and kiss the corner of his mouth. "I can't wait. I love you."

"Me too."

Grabbing my hand, we head back inside and set up a time next Saturday afternoon to sign the contract and for Drew to drop off the cheque tomorrow. We down to the car and Drew pulls out his phone.

"Hey Liv, I have something I need to take care of. Can I drop you off at your place? We can pick up some boxes on the way so you can start packing."

My stomach drops. I was hoping to spend the day with him because I didn't see him yesterday.

"Yeah, that's okay." Even I can hear the blatant disappointment in my voice. "Is everything all good?"

"Yeah, nothing to worry about."

The drive to get boxes and to my apartment is done in silence.

CHAPTER 6

Olivia

Drew drops me off and helps me carry the boxes we grabbed upstairs. Walking into my apartment, I take it all in. Pretty soon, this will no longer be my home. I'll be living in a nice two-bedroom apartment with Drew. It's a bittersweet revelation. This was the first place I could truly call my own and I'm going to miss it, but I'm also looking forward to my future with Drew.

Drew kisses me and makes his way to the front door after letting me know he'll text me later today. Once he leaves, I settle in my usual spot on the couch and open my group chat with the girls.

LIV

We found a place!!!! It's perfect, it's a 2-bed 2-bath, great kitchen, amazing view, lots of closet space… we sign the lease next weekend and move in on June 30th!!!!

ZO

Yay! I'm so happy for you! Do you need help packing? You buy pizza and I'll be there, lol

HAN

Where is this place??? I can't wait to see it!!!

And same as what Zo said, just let me know when!

LIZ

So happy for you guys!!! Let me know when you
need help! 💜

LIV

It's on Pacific, not far from my place now. It's right
by the park, I should have taken pictures, but I was
too excited!!!

I will buy the pizza and the wine 😌

ZO

Just let me know when!

LIZ

Same!

I then text Matt.

LIV

Found a place, sign the lease next Saturday. It's
close to my current place, safe, 24-hour concierge,
and close to work.

MATTY

Happy for you Liv, when do you move in? Do you
need help moving?

LIV

We move in on June 30th. If you could help, that
would be great.

MATTY

I'll be there, I'll see if the guys can help too. I
remember all the shit you have 😅

LIV

It's not shit. 🙄

MATTY

Sure sis, let me know what time to meet at your
place.

LIV

Will do.

Settling into my spot, the exhaustion of the day hits me, so I
decide to read for a bit before I make dinner. When I turn to the side

table where my most recent book sits I notice a gift covered in purple wrapping paper and a card on top. I recognize the handwriting on the outside of the envelope. It's Josh's

Open the gift first, then open the card.

I slowly peel the paper open. A smile overtakes my face when I see he got me a Kindle. It's one of the new ones with 32 GB of storage and wireless charging. I then open the card.

Olivia,

I know how much you love your books and thought you might enjoy this. I hope the romance lover in you gets everything you need from this. There is a year subscription to Kindle Unlimited in here too so you can read as much as your heart desires. I hope you have an amazing 25th birthday and this year brings you joy and love. You deserve it all, Olivia.

Josh

Josh is one of the few people who uses my full name. Most people, including my friends and family, only really call me Liv. I kind of love it when he uses my full name. As a kid, I hated it. I wanted a nickname because it was super cool to have one. As I've grown up, I've come to love my name more and more.

I can't believe he got me this. He must have left it when he dropped me off yesterday. This is so unbelievably thoughtful of him; I have debated for some time about getting myself one. I grab my phone immediately and pull up Josh's number so I can thank him right away.

LIV

I just found the gift you left for me. It is so thoughtful. I love it. Thank you so much, Josh. I wish I could say thank you in person. Can we do lunch this week?

JOSH

You're welcome, Olivia. Yeah, we can do that. What day works for you? I'll check my schedule.

LIV

Saturday noon?

JOSH

Sounds good. I'll make a reservation. I'll text you the details.

LIV

Perfect. Again, thank you, Josh.

JOSH

No thanks needed. I hope you enjoy it.

I browse books until my stomach growls and I make dinner before settling in bed for the night.

During the week I give my landlord notice, make it through my conferences, and start to pack some of the less used things in my apartment.

When I get up Saturday morning, I shower and get ready for my lunch with Josh. I'm meeting with Drew after to sign the new lease so before I leave, I make sure I have my ID and a direct deposit form for rent withdrawals. I am so excited we got this place and I'll be living with Drew. I can't help doing my little excited dance and letting out a squeal before leaving my apartment.

Josh made reservations at a restaurant between our two places. While he lives closer to the business centre of downtown—since that's where his company is located—I live closer to parks, in a more family-oriented part of downtown. I walk toward the train, running to catch the one pulling up to the platform.

It's a quick ride and I make my way through the crowd and up the stairs to the station's exit, checking my watch to make sure I'm still on time. As I make it to the top, I see Josh waiting. He's looking at his phone and I take the time to slowly take him in. With dark wash jeans and a Harvard t-shirt, he looks effortlessly casual and relaxed, leaning against the wall. His hair is messy, like he's been running his fingers through it. I can never get over how good he looks and how much he's filled out since we were younger.

He looks away from his phone as the crowd bustles past him, and when he finds me, he smiles and pushes off the wall. Electricity travels through me as he gets closer and my heart rate increases.

I feel nervous.

Josh and I have been friends for years, but mostly when we hung out, Matt was there too, and it's been a while since we last spent alone time together. I'm not sure how either of us has changed over the years. When we reach each other, he pulls me into a hug.

"I'm so happy to see you," he says into my hair.

"Me too. You didn't have to meet me here though." I smile up at him as we pull away.

"It's all good. I figured you'd take the train. Parking is horrible here anyway, and we can walk to the restaurant together."

Chuckling, I walk beside him. "Yeah, there are days I question why the streets are so busy when you can take a train or bus anywhere downtown."

"I know, but I guess I am guilty of that, too. I prefer to drive to work every day. I'm not a huge fan of the crowds on the train during the normal work commute."

"Do you really work normal work hours?" I look up at him. "I feel like you're a control freak at work, and you work ridiculous hours to make sure everything is done right."

He places a hand over his heart and feigns pain. "Ouch Olivia, you really do have me pegged." He laughs. "But I do have a decent work-life balance. I have hockey with the guys, poker every Saturday night. I see Em as often as possible and go to my parents once a month."

"Okay," I chuckle. "I believe you, but tell me you aren't at work every morning by 6 a.m. and don't leave until 7 p.m. unless you have a game."

"7 a.m. and I leave between 5 p.m. and 6 p.m." He elbows me

lightly in the side. "And don't act like you don't work ridiculous hours too. I know you. You may only be at school at 7:30 a.m. and leave at 3:30 p.m., but I know you take work home with you." It's crazy that years later Josh still can peg me like that.

I put my hands up, surrendering. "Okay, you got me there."

We get to the restaurant and Josh places his hand on my lower back, guiding me inside. Heat radiates up my back from where his hand is resting. I can feel it through my clothes. I don't have this visceral reaction when I'm with Drew. A single touch doesn't warm my body, causing me to want to melt into it. Giving my head a slight shake to rid myself of these thoughts, I remind myself that I love Drew. We have built a solid foundation and are taking the next steps in our relationship. Steps I am looking forward to.

We wait at the host stand as Josh gives his name, and she leads us to the back corner. It's an upscale restaurant, nicer than I probably would have chosen. I almost feel underdressed in my leggings and chiffon tank top. Looking around, it seems like every person in here has money, even those who are dressed casually are dressed in name-brand clothes I could never afford on my teacher's salary.

I take in the decor of the restaurant; the walls are painted a dark red with black wall sconces spaced evenly around the entire restaurant. Each table is decorated with a black tablecloth and a candle in the centre. The lights are low enough that the room has an intimate feeling, even for lunch.

When we get to our table, Josh pulls out my chair and I take a seat. The hostess hands us menus, her eyes lingering on Josh for a few seconds longer than necessary and tells us our server will be right over.

As I open the menu, Josh says, "The eggs Benedict are amazing here. I'm sure you'll love them."

Without looking at the other options, I set the menu down. "Okay decision made, eggs Benedict," I say cheerfully.

Smiling, he closes his too and sets it down. The server comes over and gives all her attention to Josh. Even as I place my order, she continues to completely ignore me. I roll my eyes. I'm not Josh's girlfriend, but I am here with him. It would be nice if the server didn't completely ignore me.

"So, how were your parent-teacher conferences?" Josh asks.

"Good, no drama this year, which was nice. I was able to make it home at a decent hour every day so I could start packing."

Josh stiffens. Our server drops off our drinks, and Josh nods as he downs half of his water in a single sip.

"Uhh... So you found a place with Drew then?"

"Yeah, it's this great place, close to my current one, and it's got a great kitchen, closet space and a view of the water. We move in on June 30th."

Josh swirls his glass on the table and avoids eye contact with me. Clearing his throat, he says, "That's great, Olivia. I'm happy for you." His tone doesn't exactly match his words, but I'm not sure why that would be the case.

Deciding not to read into it too much, I say, "Thanks, we are signing the lease this afternoon. I can't wait. It's going to be great. How are you? What's new with you?"

"Not much. Life is the same. Our summer league is picking up now. So that keeps me busy, along with work."

"God, I remember how much time I used to spend at the rink with you guys. But watching you play was amazing. Are you both still as fast as you were then?"

Josh chuckles. "Yeah, the three of us basically lived at the rink." He smiles fondly like he's gone back to those days in his mind. "I wouldn't be surprised if they put your name on the stands you were there so often. You'll have to come to a game and tell me if we're as fast. I know Matt said he was going to invite you to one soon."

"That would be nice. I miss watching you guys play." I run my fingers through the condensation on my glass as we continue talking about his hockey games and our memories of the rinks growing up.

Our food arrives, and we eat and reminisce about the old days. While we eat, I notice a few different women checking Josh out, lingering glances here and there, some with blatantly jealous looks at me for being the one eating with him, but he pays no one any attention but me. When we finish, Josh asks for the bill.

"Josh, you don't have to pay for my breakfast. I invited you. I've got the bill."

"Don't be silly, Olivia. Just let me get this."

I go to reach for the bill, but he grabs it faster. At Josh's signal the server brings over the machine, and Josh hands her his card before I can.

"Got to be faster than that, Olivia." His teasing tone reminds me of growing up with him and the way we would pick on each other. I smile at the thought.

"Okay, but the next one is on me."

"Whatever you say," Josh says with a chuckle, and I don't believe he will ever let me get the bill.

The server processes the payment, writing something on the receipt before handing it to Josh. He looks at it and slips it into the billfold before standing and making his way to the washroom. While he's gone, I peek inside and written on the bill is a phone number. It has my stomach twisting. This woman gave him her number with me sitting right there. The audacity that she did it right in front of me, too. Josh and I are just friends, but if I saw two people out to eat, I would assume it's a date.

When Josh returns, we gather our stuff and head towards the front of the restaurant. When we get outside, I turn to face him. "Thanks for lunch today. It was nice to spend some time together again." Going onto my tiptoes, I pull him in for a hug, and he wraps his arms around my waist, holding me for a few seconds.

"Yes, it was, Olivia. I enjoyed it. Are you taking the train home?"

I nod. "I'm taking it to meet Drew."

His jaw tightens, and he nods slightly. "I'll walk you to the train?"

"You don't have to, but that would be nice."

We start walking to the SkyTrain station and spend the few minutes in silence. When we get to the station at the top of the stairs, Josh turns to me and leans down, placing a chaste kiss on my cheek. It's friendly and nothing more, but it sends tingles through my body. I have to control this. I'm with Drew and I don't cheat. I know this is entirely friendly, and Josh and I grew up together. This is nothing more than a friendly goodbye.

"Take care of yourself, Olivia," Josh says.

"You too," I say before turning and walking down the stairs towards the train.

Getting off near Drew's, I walk the couple of blocks to his place, using my fob and key to get inside. I don't see Drew when I walk in, but I hear noises coming from somewhere in the apartment—from what appears to be his bedroom.

The door is cracked, and I slowly make my way towards it, thinking he might be taking a nap. After a couple of steps, I can distinguish the sounds. It's grunting and moaning, not snoring and it's coming from two people. One sounds like a woman. I feel a lead ball drop into my stomach. I clench my fists, squeezing as my nails bite into my palms.

"Yes, Drew, harder," the woman moans. I stop dead in my tracks, the blood rushes from my face. Drew is sleeping with someone else. Bile creeps up my throat as I summon the energy to continue to move forward. I need to confirm this. I need to see it for myself. I take a few slow steps forward, making sure to remain quiet, I hear more.

"Take my cock, just like that."

I hear Drew and the slapping of flesh the closer I get. Stopping outside the bedroom door, I see Drew on the bed, kneeling behind a skinny blonde on her knees with her face shoved into the mattress and facing away from me. I think I might puke.

"Just like that Drew, fuck me harder," she moans. Her moans seem so over the top, almost like a porn star. He grabs her hips harder and starts pounding into her. Neither seem to have noticed me standing here. Wet heat pools behind my eyes, and I feel like I'm going to throw up. I am standing in my boyfriend's apartment on the day we are supposed to sign a lease to move in together, and he is here, fucking some other girl. My insides twist and I can't take a full breath. I place one hand around my throat and the other over my stomach, as if that will help the pain and nausea radiating through me.

The woman continues to moan, and Drew continues to talk as he fucks her. My hand moves up from my throat. I can feel how cold my skin is as it moves to my mouth, holding back the scream threatening to rip from my throat.

I've seen enough. I need to get the hell out of this apartment and as far away from this as soon as possible. I don't want either of them to see or hear me.

Slowly, I back away from the bedroom door, making sure to be quiet.

The last thing I need right now is to confront Drew. I'm not sure I could take it. I don't know if I'd scream and punch him or collapse into a ball on the ground. I'm not strong enough for this right now.

Needing fresh air, I get through the front door as quietly as I can before running down the hallway. I jab the elevator button fast several times in succession. I know this won't make the elevator come any faster, but I need to get out of here as quickly as possible. All rational thought has left me at this point. It feels like the walls of the hallway are closing in on me as I stand here waiting. My breathing becomes quick and shallow. I bend over and put my hands on my knees, hoping to catch my breath again. When the elevator dings, signalling its arrival, I get in, pushing the lobby floor button and then the close door button the same way I did the call button. The walls stop closing in on me, but my breathing hasn't returned to normal.

My mind begins to fill with questions as I descend. Has he even had issues with his family, or has it all been some elaborate ruse to cheat behind my back? How long has this been going on? Do I know the blonde girl? Has he introduced us before? Does she know he's in a relationship? My brain is on overdrive trying to process the fucked-up shit I walked in on. I trusted him. I loved him, and I was changing my life so we could live together because he asked me to. I've given notice to my landlord. How the hell am I supposed to move on from this? Not only did the man I love cheat on me, but he has ripped my world out from under me. I have no place to live now. What in the hell am I supposed to do at the end of June?

Getting to the lobby, I rush out the front door and make it onto the sidewalk, moving out of the way before I stop and clutch at my chest and look up to the sky. The tears I've been fighting find their way past my control. I feel the first one make its way down my cheek as I stand here. I quickly swipe at it, working to keep the rest at bay. I can't start crying in the middle of the sidewalk. Taking a deep breath, I do my best to gather myself. I don't want to take the train right now. There is a store around the corner I decide to walk to, knowing I can hide in the washroom out of sight.

As I make my way there, I call Zoey to ask if she can pick me up. She agrees and I make my way to hide until she tells me she's here.

CHAPTER 7

Josh

After lunch with Olivia, I head home to get a workout in before I need to set up for poker tonight with the guys. It's my turn to host and they should be arriving around 5 p.m.

My workout is longer than usual. I push myself to try to get thoughts of Olivia out of my head. On top of being my friend and my best friend's little sister, she has a boyfriend. I know I want her in my life and if that means that our relationship is strictly platonic, then that's the way it has to be, but that doesn't stop me from wishing it could be so much more.

Spending time with Olivia has been so easy since reconnecting with her, but it's been a reminder of why I've kept my distance since coming home. Seeing her smile, hearing her laugh, or watching how her cheeks turn pink when she blushes reminds me of all the feelings I had for her before. The time apart has only allowed her to grow and blossom, making all those little things about her so much better.

I run on the treadmill, pushing myself harder than usual, not stopping until I'm panting for breath. When I finish, I grab a towel, patting my face dry, and wrap it around my shoulders before grabbing a bottle of water from the mini-fridge. Opening the bottle, I chug it, finishing it in one go, crumpling the empty bottle when I'm done.

The front door opens as I enter the kitchen and Matt strolls in, carrying a couple of six-packs of beer.

"Hey man," he says as he puts the beer in the fridge.

"Hey," I say, looking at my watch.

Matt catches me and says, "Yeah, I'm early, thought I'd come by, and we could throw the four o'clock game on before the guys get here."

Nodding, I reply, "Sure, put it on. I'm just gonna jump in the shower real quick."

Matt nods before opening a beer and moving into the living room, dropping on my couch, and propping his feet on the coffee table. Matt and I have always been close, we have keys to each other's places, so it isn't weird he showed up unannounced, but what is weird is I was just pushing myself harder than normal in the gym to rid myself of dirty thoughts I've been having about his younger sister.

I shower quickly before joining Matt. The game is still zero-zero. I walk into the kitchen and call out, "Need another beer?"

"Sure," he calls back. I grab two beers, pop the tops off them and join Matt on the couch, handing him one.

"What did you do today?" he asks as I settle beside him. My beer hovers in front of my lips as I look at him. He knows Olivia and I are friends, and I have no intention of hiding that we went to brunch today, but I'm not sure how he'll react to it.

"I went to brunch with Olivia, then came home and worked out. You?" I ask and take a sip of my beer, keeping my eyes on Matt, gauging his response. He turns his head towards me, raising an eyebrow.

"Brunch with Liv? How was that?" he questions before continuing. "I know she missed you when we first got back from Harvard. She asked about you a few times."

I never knew that. I never knew she missed me until she said something to me this week. I'm more surprised that Matt is saying his sister missed me. I missed her, too. Conversation with her is always so easy and silence has never been awkward. It's always been nice to just be with her.

"She did?" Matt nods. "Brunch was good. We caught up and talked about the old days. I missed the easy conversation with her." As I pick at my beer label, I add, "She went to sign her lease for the new place with Drew afterwards." Matt's jaw tenses and he takes a long drink from his beer.

"She's an adult and can make her own choices, but I don't like that guy." Matt sighs before continuing, "Something about him bothers the crap out of me. But she can make her own choices." I know it's hard for Matt to say that; he's always been protective, but respectful of his sisters, allowing them to live their own lives.

We watch the game for a while. Caleb and Grayson show up around 5 p.m. and join us on the couch and we finish watching the game before we move to the table for poker.

We're sitting around the table, a couple of hands in, and Caleb is telling us a story from this week at work.

"It took three officers chasing him five blocks to catch him. I was just thankful their car was closer. I did not want that naked fucker in my car," Caleb says, shaking his head.

Laughing, I shake my head too. "I'm not sure how you deal with shit like that. I think I much prefer people in stuffy suits and boardrooms."

"Well, some days I question it too," Caleb says.

"You know, last week we had a guy come into the ER after putting his arm through a Sawzall. It's a wonder the human species has survived so long," Grayson says, laughing.

Laughing, Matt claps me on the shoulder. "I've gotta agree with Josh on this. I prefer my office."

I enjoy our poker nights. The stories told are often just as hilarious as today's and I definitely needed the distraction.

Matt places his beer on the table and starts shuffling and dealing. Just as he tosses the last card to Caleb, his phone buzzes next to him. He looks at it and his brow furrows and he looks at me. "It's Zoey. She would only call if it's important. I gotta take this." I nod and get up and move to the kitchen, looking for another beer.

"Hey Zoey, what's up?" He sits up straight in his chair. "What happened..." "Yeah, I'll be there, does she need anything else..." "Okay, everything will be okay."

He stands quickly and faces me. "Hey man, I've got to go. Liv needs her locks changed; Zoey didn't want to tell me what happened over the phone but said it should be done sooner rather than later."

"Yeah, of course. Let me grab my tools and I'll drive you."

"Thanks, man," he says before taking his bottle to the kitchen.

"We'll head out," Caleb says, getting up from the table. "Let us know how Liv is once you're done."

Matt pats his shoulder. "Will do."

We say goodbye to Grayson and Caleb and I grab my tool bag and my keys before we walk out the front door, only stopping at the hardware store before going to Olivia's place.

CHAPTER 8

Olivia

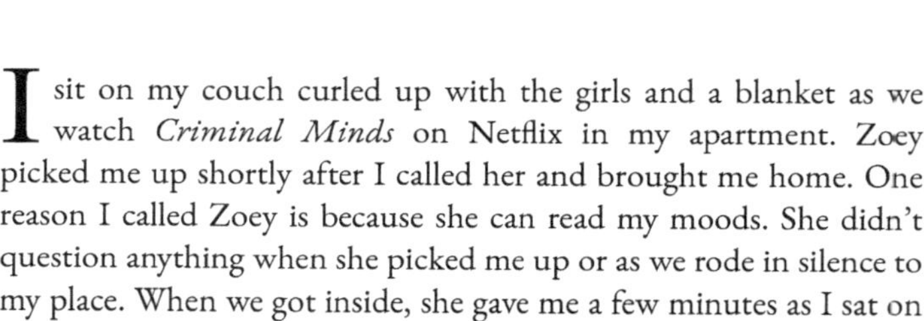

I sit on my couch curled up with the girls and a blanket as we watch *Criminal Minds* on Netflix in my apartment. Zoey picked me up shortly after I called her and brought me home. One reason I called Zoey is because she can read my moods. She didn't question anything when she picked me up or as we rode in silence to my place. When we got inside, she gave me a few minutes as I sat on my couch and cried while she held me, and then she asked, "Do you want me to call the girls?" I nodded and within forty-five minutes, Hannah and Liz showed up at my apartment with food and booze.

The girls made me a drink, we started eating pizza, and I told them what I walked in on at Drew's place. He's texted me a few times and tried calling after I missed our appointment. They must have contacted him because I doubt he remembered, as he had been fucking some skank when we were supposed to be meeting. I hate to think nasty things about her. She might not have known that he was in a relationship, but bile rises in my throat every time I flash back to standing outside his bedroom.

I haven't responded to any of the texts or returned his calls. I have no idea what I am going to do. I gave notice on my apartment, and now I have nowhere to go at the end of my lease. It's going to be hard to find another place on such short notice, and I need to make sure I get my name off the lease at the new place. I don't want to be tied to that place in any way.

After I tell them everything, they hold me as I cry, and then Eliza asks, "Liv, doesn't Drew have a key to your place?" My breath catches in my throat, my arms immediately wrap around my stomach, protecting myself, and I nod. I didn't think about that; Drew could choose to show up here whenever he wants.

"I'll call Matt and we'll get your locks changed," Zoey says before she gets up and calls my brother.

Oh, god. I'm not ready for Matt to know about this. He didn't like Drew to begin with, but he didn't push the matter. I knew it, and now Matt is going to be proven right. I know he won't rub it in, and he'll just be pissed about the whole situation, but no one wants their older brother to be right about something. I begin to cry again as my world continues to crumble around me. How did I let this happen? How did I miss the signs? Was I that desperate to have someone other than my family and the girls love me that I just ignored everything? I feel like such an idiot.

We sit and watch the show while we wait for Matt to show up. When the lock clicks, the girls sit up and look, and I notice Hannah and Zoey move to block my view in case it's Drew. I hear Matt's voice before I see him. He is talking to someone when he comes in. God, I hope it's not Drew.

Matt rounds the corner with Josh and they both stand there, taking in the situation, concern written over both their faces. There are empty pizza boxes on the living room table and alcohol spread out, too. I probably have mascara streaked down my cheeks, and I know my nose is red and my eyes are puffy. The worry on their faces causes me to break into tears again and wrap my arms around myself. Matt is across the room in seconds, pulling me to his chest and running his hand over my hair the way he used to when I was a kid.

"Shhhh, shhhh, you're alright, Livvy. What's wrong? What can I do?" he whispers.

I can't make myself form words. I wrap my arms around my brother and absorb his strength as he attempts to comfort me. Hurt and shame course through me at the same time. Hurt from Drew cheating and catching him in the act, and shame because Matt warned me against the guy and now, here I am crying in front of him and Josh. I take all the strength I can from my brother.

I still can't manage to get words out. Matt turns to Zoey. "Zo, what happened to her?" he asks, worry coating each word.

She makes eye contact with me, and I see the unasked question in her eyes. 'Can I tell him?' I nod. Matt's my big brother and I know all he wants to do is protect me. Josh is Matt's best friend and my friend as well. He'd find out, eventually. I just wish I didn't have to witness it.

Zoey takes a deep breath and Hannah rubs my back. "Liv went to Drew's after brunch with Josh, so they could sign the new lease." She reaches out and squeezes my arm, lending some of her strength as she continues, "She walked into his place and saw him fucking some girl in his bed. She didn't confront him about it, and she doesn't think he saw her, but he's called and texted her about missing the meeting. He has keys to her place; we're worried he might show up here. She has also already given her landlord notice and now doesn't have a place to go when her lease is up," Zoey says.

I feel Matt tense. "Motherfucker," I hear him curse in a whisper. I release my hold on him and sit back on the couch, wrapping my arms around myself again.

"I should have listened to you," I whisper to Matt as I look at my crossed legs.

"Don't. Don't blame yourself for any of this." There's a harshness to his words, but not one that scares me. It makes me feel safe, knowing Matt will always protect me. He places his fingers under my chin, forcing me to look him in the eyes as he says, "This is all on that stupid motherfucker. You did nothing wrong, Liv. Everything will be fine. You'll get through this. You are strong."

Looking into his eyes, I see the truth in his words and the anger he's holding back. I nod, allowing some of the shame to fade away. I look past Matt at Josh. His face is full of anger and his hands are in fists at his side. I can't force myself to make eye contact with him. Having him know this happened is too much. I drop my gaze back to my lap.

Matt grips my knee. "Josh and I will change your locks for you. It's going to be okay."

I nod as he gets up, and they move to the front door. I hear a drill as they work. When they finish, I pull together the energy to stand and hug my brother, Josh comes over next and pulls me into a hug as well, he leans down and whispers in my ear, "It's his loss, Olivia. That man is an idiot. Don't let him make you feel less than or bad about yourself. You are amazing and you deserve someone who will treat you like a goddess. Keep your chin up." I nod into his chest, taking a deep breath and inhaling his scent before taking a step back.

Everyone turns towards the front door as we hear the sounds of keys trying and failing to open the front door. I stiffen. Drew must be here. Matt moves to the door; I place my hand on his arm and shake my head. I need to put on my big girl panties and deal with this. It has to happen sometime, so what better time than now when I have people here to back me up?

"Liv, it's me. Open up." Drew's voice comes from the other side of the door.

I slowly move into the entryway; I can feel everyone move with me, with Matt and Josh in front of the girls. They stop a few feet behind me as I open the door. Drew looks at me with furrowed brows and I brace one arm on the door frame, not allowing him the space to enter my apartment.

When he sees me, a smile spreads across his face, along with a look of relief. "Liv, I've tried texting and calling you. You missed our appointment with the rental agency." He looks over my shoulder and sees the gathering of my friends and brother. "What happened?" Drew asks.

Standing straighter and pulling my shoulders back, I take a deep breath, gathering my strength. "What were you doing before our appointment today, Drew?"

His eyes dart between me and the people behind me. "Grading," he answers.

I take a deep breath. He's not going to own up to the truth. I guess I'll have to say it. "So, you weren't fucking some skinny blonde chick from behind in your bed, then?" I spit at him.

He staggers back slightly and the colour drains from his face. He puts his hands up defensively. "Look Liv, can we talk about this? Please, let's talk." He looks over my shoulder again. "Alone, please."

Are you fucking kidding me? I pretty much just told him I caught him cheating on me and he wants me to talk to him about it. To be in a room with him alone. He has obviously lost his ever-loving mind. I think it's the casualness of the way he asks that pisses me off the most, though, as if cheating is a normal occurrence in a relationship. I feel the anger rising in my body from my toes to my ears. I go rigid as I try to not completely explode.

This man has the fucking gall.

"You want to fucking talk, Drew. Are you kidding me? The time for talking was when you realized you were interested in other women. The time for talking was before you slept with some skinny, blonde bitch. Before we agreed to get a place together. You will not be getting anything more from me. Leave. Me. The. Fuck. Alone. Don't come here again, and lose my number, don't contact me again." My chest is heaving with anger.

He looks me up and down. "We got a place together, Liv. You can't do this. You made a commitment to me and our new place. We can work on this. You can start going to the gym with me, and we can cook together. We can work on you and our relationship when we live together."

I have always been self-conscious about my body, but Drew is flat-out saying this to me now. My body wants to curl up on itself. I'm beyond angry. I pull my right hand back and slap him across the face and he staggers.

"I owe you nothing, and I haven't signed a lease, so I'm not on the hook for that. But thank you for showing me what a piece of shit you are."

Drew's face is bright red where I slapped him. Anger fills his eyes, and he takes a step toward me. "You bitch," he spits, but before he can get any more out, Josh stomps past me and has Drew pinned against the wall across from my apartment.

"Careful what you say next," Josh grits out.

Matt walks forward and steps in front of me, blocking any access Drew might have to me. I lean around Matt to get a look at what's happening in the hallway. Josh leans in and says something into Drew's ear. I can't hear it, but Drew loses all colour in his face. Josh lets him go and Drew makes his way down the hallway, staring at Josh, Matt, and me.

The guys usher me inside and all the energy leave my body as I crumble onto the couch. Josh hands me my drink once I'm settled and I give him a slight smile before I finish every last drop.

"We're going to stay with her tonight," Zoey says to Matt, and he nods.

"Can you text me the contact information of the rental agency? I'll email them to ensure your name is off the lease," he says, and I only have the energy to nod at him. "Your new keys are on the entryway table. I have your spare key," he says, kissing me on the cheek and leaving with Josh, locking the door behind them.

I look at the girls as they curl up on the couch with me. "Thank you, guys," I whisper.

"Liv, there's nothing to thank us for. We love you; we are here for you," Hannah says.

Liz squeezes my knee as she nods. We turn *Criminal Minds* back on, finish the pizza, and have some more drinks before we pull out my air mattress and set up the living room for us to sleep. Today may have been one of the worst days I have ever experienced, but I was reminded that I have amazing friends and a brother who will always be there for me. Tomorrow is another day, and I have so much to figure out now, but I have a support system that will help me through it.

I wake up in the morning, and the events of yesterday come flooding back. Drew's cheating, the girls coming over, Matt and Josh showing up, and the confrontation with Drew. I take a deep breath, trying to release the tension from my body, but it doesn't work. I sit up on the air mattress and see that Han and Liz are already awake and sitting in the kitchen with coffee. Zo is still asleep beside me.

I rub my eyes, get up, and shuffle into the kitchen and head to the coffeepot. I look at them and see the worry that floats in their eyes. I take a deep breath and turn to them with a full cup. "I'm okay... or I'll be okay." I let out a sigh. "At least I found out before we moved in together." They both have solemn looks on their face, and they nod. "I do need to start the apartment hunt, though. Can you guys help? Send me anything you find."

"Of course," Han says. "If you need, you can crash on my couch. It's not super comfortable, but it'll work."

"Thanks, Han, I might need that."

She looks down at her watch. "I'm sorry babe, I have a shift at the hospital. I need to get home and change." Getting up, she puts her coffee mug in the sink and hugs me. "Call me if you need anything. I love you, Liv. You're strong, you'll be okay," she tells me before pulling back.

"I love you too, thanks for being here last night," I say. She smiles before grabbing her purse and heading out the front door.

I putter around the kitchen and make a simple breakfast for Liz, Zo, and me. We eat at my kitchen table and have an easy conversation about nothing. The girls stay for a few hours before they head home for the night. I grab my phone, checking it for the first time today when they leave.

I have several texts and missed calls from Drew—I ignore them all—a couple of texts from Matt and one from Josh. I go into my phone and block Drew's number, so I don't have to deal with him anymore and delete all his texts. I open the texts from Matt next.

MATTY

Liv, you're strong, you're going to be okay.

Let me know if you need anything. I'm here for you.

We are supposed to go to dinner at Mom and Dad's tomorrow. I'll pick you up at 5:30.

LIV

Thanks Matt, love you too. See you then.

MATTY

You're good then?

LIV

Will be.

I completely forgot about dinner with my parents, but it's been a while and being with my family will help me. I then open Josh's text.

JOSH

Don't forget that you are amazing. Don't let that douchebag make you feel bad about yourself, Olivia. Please let me know if you need anything.

LIV

Thanks Josh, you're a good friend.

I decide to spend the rest of the night taking a bath with candles and Netflix queued up on my laptop. Relaxing in the water, I close my eyes and my mind goes over my entire relationship with Drew, trying to figure out where I went wrong. What could I have done differently?

I shake my head before pinching my nose and plunging myself under the water. I am not going to go down that road. It's not my fault Drew cheated on me. That's his shortcoming, not mine. Drew was distant in our relationship; he didn't prioritize us. I am not going to put any energy into that man anymore.

I am going to put all my time and energy into me, now. I'm going to spend tomorrow with my family. I am going to power through the remainder of the school year and then I am going to take my summer and enjoy nature. I'm going to read my books, find myself a nice place, and I'm going to have fun.

After my bath, I settle into my bed with this new motivation and wrap myself in my blankets and fall asleep.

CHAPTER 9

Josh

I stare at my computer, trying to focus on the report my assistant Kate forwarded me from our financial department. I run my hand through my hair in frustration. I've had a hard time concentrating on anything since Saturday night. After Matt and I left Olivia's place, we went back to mine, and we drank, ordered Chinese food, and watched an old fight on TV.

Both Matt and I were pissed. Liv was hurt, and we couldn't do anything about it. When Drew showed up at her place, I wanted to punch him in the face. It took everything in me not to. I got the pleasure of seeing his face drain of all colour when I had him up against the hallway wall. I told him how I would do more than shove him against a wall if he contacted or visited Liv again, and if he enjoyed his ability to walk, he needed to leave right then. Hopefully, he knows how serious I was about that.

My office door opens, and I look up to see Matt stroll in and take a seat across from me.

"Hey man, what's up?" I ask him once he's settled. He runs both his hands down his face as he takes a deep breath.

"I'm trying to not beat the shit out of my sister's dick of an ex and I haven't found a place for her to move. It's so close to the end of her lease, I don't think we can find anything before she has to leave. The girls and I have all offered her our couches, but that's temporary. I want to get her out of her place as soon as possible to prevent any run-ins with Drew. I don't know what to do." He leans forward and places his elbows on his knees. "We had dinner at Mom and Dad's this weekend, and she seemed to be in a much better place, like something clicked in her, but I am worried about her. I feel like I failed to protect her." Torment fills his eyes.

"Man, you know Olivia doesn't blame you for anything. She's an adult, and you were there for her on Saturday when she needed you." I lean back in my chair and run a hand down my face as I take a deep breath.

I have spare rooms. I've got plenty of space and could offer one to Olivia until she gets on her feet. Could I really live with her, though? Could I spend months seeing her every day and not want to take our relationship to another level? She's just getting out of a terrible relationship. She just found out her boyfriend was cheating on her. She's in a vulnerable place right now.

Am I really going to do this? Am I going to put myself in a position that may make this worse? Yup, I'm going to do this because I would do anything for Olivia. I take a deep breath before I say, "If she needs a place to stay, I have a spare room, and we can rent a storage unit for her furniture. The spare room is completely furnished, and she would have her privacy."

He whips his head up. "You'd do that? You'd let her stay with you?" he asks, a mix of relief and something else playing across his face.

I lean forward, placing my arms on the edge of my desk. "Matt, I would do anything for you and Olivia. Yeah, if she needs a place, she can take one of my spare rooms. It's not like I am using it."

Genuine relief washes over Matt's face. He runs his hands down his face again as he leans back in his chair and his chest deflates as he lets out a huge breath.

"Man, you have no idea how much that means to me. I know she'll be safe there. Let me take you to lunch."

"Of course, man. You want to hit the pub down the block again?"

He pats his hands on his knees and rises from his chair. "Yeah, sounds good." I stand and grab my jacket from the back of my chair. It's not like I am making any progress on these reports, might as well take a break and get some food and fresh air.

Walking out of my office, I tell Kate to hold my calls until I'm back later.

Matt and I head down the block to the pub we frequent when he visits me at the office. We grab a seat at the bar and order a burger with fries and a beer each. Matt and I have been friends for years, we don't need to say much when we spend time together, we can just watch a game or grab a bite, but I'm still worried about Olivia and I'm hoping he might have some more information.

The bartender drops off our beers and I take a sip of mine. "So, have you heard more about how Olivia is doing?" I ask him.

He runs his fingers through the condensation on his beer. "I called Zoey yesterday to get an update. I don't want to bug Liv. Zo said she thinks Liv is handling this better than she would. Said that Liv isn't letting it get her down. She has come up with this list of things she wants to do this summer once school is done. No more crying, I guess, but I don't know. I'm not sure if this is her ignoring it and not processing it, or if she really is fine. You'll let me know if you notice anything, right?" he asks as he turns and faces me on his bar stool.

"Yeah, of course, I'll make sure she's all good." He nods, and our food is delivered. We eat in silence as we watch the sports highlights. When I finish my food and beer, I pull out my wallet and put some bills on the bar before grasping Matt's shoulder. "I've got to get back to the office. I'll see you later."

"See you later, man." He nods and hands the money back to me. "This is on me, man, please." I pocket the money before heading back to the office. I manage to make it through a few more hours of work before I grab my coat and head out of the office at 5 p.m. Kate is still sitting at her desk when I walk out of my office. "Head home and enjoy the rest of your night," I say as I leave.

I grab Chinese food from one of my favourite places near my office, and head to Olivia's.

I press the buzzer and it rings before Olivia answers, "Hello?"

"Olivia, it's me. I brought dinner. Wanna buzz me up?"

"Ummm..." I can hear the confusion in her voice. "Sure, Josh."

The system buzzes, and the gate opens, allowing me into the parkade. Grabbing the food and heading to the lobby entrance, I buzz her again and the door unlocks. Taking the elevator up to her floor, I knock on her apartment door.

Seconds later, she opens the door; she's dressed in a pair of pyjama pants, and a UBC t-shirt. Her hair is in a messy bun, with little tendrils of her auburn hair out, shaping her face. She smiles questioningly and opens the door more for me to slip into her apartment. I place a quick kiss on her cheek before I make my way to the kitchen, and she follows behind me, silently grabbing plates and cutlery.

"Soooo, not that it's not nice to see you Josh, but what's up? What's with the dinner and random visit?" she asks as she opens the fridge to grab a beer and points it at me as a question. I nod, and she passes it to me and grabs a cooler for herself. She settles in a chair across from me.

"Matt came to see me at work today. He mentioned you're having a problem finding a place to move when your lease is up. He also mentioned that he's worried about potential drop-ins from Drew." Her shoulders slump as she dishes some food onto her plate.

She lets out a long breath before speaking. "Yeah, it's been difficult. It's so close to the end of my lease. I thought I'd have issues, just not this bad. I think I'm going to have to crash on Zoey's couch for a bit while I try to find a place." I can hear how defeated she is and it crushes me. I never want her to feel this way.

"So that's why I'm here. I have a spare room. Why don't you take it for the summer? It will give you plenty of time to find a place you like."

Her head shoots up as she looks at me. She swallows as she takes in what I just said. I can see all the questions running through her mind.

"Are you sure? I really don't want to impose, Josh; I don't want to be in your way." She nibbles on her lip nervously.

I take a bite of my food. Olivia could never be a bother, and it would be nice to see her more often. I don't tell her that. Instead, I say, "Olivia, I wouldn't offer if I didn't mean it. Couch surfing is not something you should have to do. Get a storage unit for your bigger furniture. The bedroom is furnished. Come over whenever you want, and I'll show it to you."

"Josh..." She pauses before continuing. "That would be amazing. Of course, I'll pay rent—"

I cut her off before she can continue. "Nope, not necessary. The room isn't being used right now. It's all yours."

Her entire body visibly relaxes, and I hope that means she's going to take me up on my offer. "Thanks, Josh, I'll at least cook and clean. I appreciate this. I've been stressing and you've taken a huge weight off my shoulders."

I nod. "Anything for you, Olivia." I don't think she realizes how true that statement is. I would do anything to make her happy.

We finish our dinner while she tells me about some of her students and we talk about this weekend's hockey game. When we finish, I help her clear the table and put the leftovers in her fridge. While she walks me out, I make sure she has my address and the buzzer code. We make arrangements for her to move in this weekend. It's a full month before her lease is up, but we don't want any chances of Drew showing up.

I throw myself into my work over the next few days; I have my housekeeper make sure there's fresh sheets on the bed in the spare room Olivia will be using, and I get a new set of keys and a fob made.

It's noon on Saturday when my phone rings with a call from the buzzer. I answer, "Olivia?"

"Yup," she answers. I buzz her up and head to the front door.

I'm waiting in the open door when the elevator opens at the end of the hallway. She's pulling a suitcase and dressed casually in a pair of dark blue skinny jeans and a silky tank top that does nothing to hide her curves or ample chest. I hurriedly drag my eyes up to her face, hoping I didn't get caught checking her out.

"So, this is it," I say.

She leaves her bag as she makes her way to the floor-to-ceiling windows in the living room that look over the city. I join her and take it all in, trying to see it from her point of view. I've lived here for a few years, so the view is nothing new to me, but I remember seeing it the first time I moved in, and it is amazing.

"It's beautiful," she finally says, looking over at me with a tentative smile. She seems unsure about being here. I want her to know that she is completely welcome here.

I grab her suitcase and say, "Let me show you your room," and she follows behind me.

There is a hallway on either side of the front door. When you walk, the one on the left has my bedroom, a washroom, storage closets, and my office, and the one on the right has three spare rooms, a washroom, and my gym. Walking down the one on the right, I stop at the end and open the door and Olivia follows me in.

My sister helped me furnish my place when I moved in. This room has a queen bed in the centre of the room with black sheets, a navy-blue comforter, and nightstands on either side. There's a walk-in closet to the left of the bedroom door and beside it is an ensuite washroom. I pull her bag into the closet and join her in the room.

"So, this is your room. There are fresh sheets on the bed and towels in the washroom. My housekeeper will change the sheets once a week on Mondays. There should be enough towels in the washroom, but if you need more, let me know. There is an in-home gym two doors down on the right and my room and office are on the other side of the apartment, so you'll have plenty of privacy. Help yourself to anything in the kitchen. My housekeeper stocks it when she comes on Mondays as well."

She nods and twists her hands in front of her like she's deciding what to say. "Thanks, Josh... If you want, I can do the grocery shopping and cleaning. I don't mind. School is out soon, so I have the time." She is chewing on her lip now, something she's done for years when she is nervous.

I shake my head. "All good, there's no need, but I won't stop you if you want to. This is your home now too, so please do what you like. Let me know if you need anything, Olivia. Do you have anything else in your car?"

"Yeah, a few boxes, and I think I'll bring my vanity tomorrow and move my stuff into storage this week."

"Let's go get your boxes and then we can take my car and go get your vanity today. I can help you move stuff to storage tomorrow."

I head to work before Olivia wakes up and drudge through my day before I finally pack everything up and head home at 6 p.m. Arriving home, I open the front door and smell a mix of seasonings wafting from the kitchen, along with the sound of music playing from a Bluetooth speaker.

Walking into the living room, I take off my suit jacket, laying it over the back of a chair before I loosen my tie, and roll the sleeves of my dress shirt up to my elbows. I watch as Liv stirs something on the stove, moving to the music, completely oblivious to the fact that I've walked in. I cross my arms over my chest and, leaning against the back of the couch, I take her in.

In a pair of black leggings, a loose-fitting tank top, and her hair pulled back in a ponytail, she moves like she has no care in the world, bobbing her head to the music. It's nice to see her happy and enjoying something. Spinning around to move to the sink, she lets out a scream and clutches her chest. I try my hardest not to laugh.

"Jesus Christ, you scared the shit out of me," she exhales, dropping the spatula in the sink.

"I didn't mean to," I say, smiling.

She stares at me for a second before saying, "Well, I made dinner. I just need to drain the noodles and it's done. Why don't you wash up and I'll finish this, and we can eat."

"Yes ma'am," I joke, pushing off the couch and heading to the washroom. Returning to the kitchen, Olivia has set the dining room table with plates, cutlery, and food. I only eat at my dining room table when my family comes over and that's not often as we usually go to my parents' place.

"Do you want a beer?" Olivia calls from the kitchen.

"Yeah, that would be great, thanks."

I sit down at the table as she returns with a beer for me and a cooler for herself. She settles down beside me at the table, takes a sip of her drink, and fiddles with the label. Things seem awkward with this being the first time we've sat down and shared a meal since she moved in. I don't like it. Things have never been awkward between us before.

"Thank you for cooking, Olivia. It looks amazing," I say, breaking the silence.

She reaches for the salad bowl and passes it to me. "Don't worry about it. It's the least I could do since you're letting me stay here with you."

"You don't have to cook for me, Olivia," I say. "I appreciate it, though. I can't remember the last time I had a home-cooked meal, probably when I was at my parents' for family dinner."

I can cook, and my mom made sure I could take care of myself, but I often find myself ordering takeout or going to a bar after work to watch whatever game is on instead of cooking for myself. I never really enjoyed cooking for only one person. I put some salad on my plate before handing the bowl back to her and grab the pasta.

"It's nice to cook for someone else besides myself," she says as she follows suit with the salad and pasta.

I take a bite of the pasta; the flavours erupt on my tongue, and I let out an appreciative moan. I don't remember her being such an amazing cook. Her cheeks pinken at the sound of my moan. "This is amazing," I say to make sure she understands how much I'm enjoying this.

"It's not bad," she mumbles while using her fork to push her pasta around her plate like she's embarrassed.

"It's more than okay," I tell her. She remains quiet. "So, how was your day?" I ask.

"It was good. I went to my place and cleaned, handed my keys back to the landlord, got my security deposit back, and spent some time with Gi. Came back here and I read a book on the balcony. That view you have is amazing," she says, looking at me with a soft smile.

"That sounds great. How is Gi? She just got back to town, right?"

"Yeah, she got in on Wednesday. Matt and I picked her up at the airport and had lunch with her. She's doing well and adjusting to being back. The weather is different and everything."

"I can understand that. I'm glad you enjoy the balcony; I enjoy that view. I sit out there when I have issues sleeping, the sound of the traffic below, people going about their lives, it's nice." She nods as she listens.

"I did enjoy it. I think I'll be spending a good amount of time out there. How was work?"

"Had a few meetings, nothing special."

We finish eating with some easy, casual conversation. When we finish, I stand and collect the dishes and make my way to the kitchen with them. She follows behind me and tries to help, but I stop her.

"You cooked; I'll clean. That's the rule." She stares at me for a second, her lips parted, like I just told her something scandalous.

"Thanks," she says before grabbing the remaining items.

"What are you going to do now?" she asks as I put the last of the leftovers in the fridge.

"I was going to watch something on Netflix. Wanna join me?"

"Sounds good," she says. We wander over to the living room and settle on opposite ends of the couch. She grabs the blanket off the back of the couch, and we pick a new show neither of us has watched. This feels easy and comfortable, sitting and watching TV with Olivia after a day at work and sharing dinner. I could get used to this, and that scares the shit out of me, because what will I do when she moves into her own place?

CHAPTER 10

Olivia

T he next few weeks pass quickly as Josh and I get used to living together. Josh has hockey games on Tuesday and Thursday this week, but the rest of the week, I cook dinner, he cleans up and then we settle on the couch together and watch our show. It's weird, calling it our show, but neither of us will watch it without the other, so it is our show.

On Saturday, Josh leaves in the afternoon to run errands and then heads straight to poker with the guys. The girls show up at 4 p.m. with grocery bags of snacks and booze. I answer the door and guide them in, and we head into the kitchen. Their eyes go wide as they take in the apartment. We've all lived in decent one-bedroom apartments in the city, but nothing as nice as Josh's place.

"So how about a tour?" Hannah asks after I finish putting the drinks in the fridge.

I chuckle at her obvious excitement. "Sure."

I take them to my new room. My bedroom here is about the size of my living room at my old place. I open the door and the girls shuffle in behind me.

"This is nice," Zoey says as she wanders into my closet.

"That looks like a great tub," Liz calls from the ensuite washroom.

On our way to the balcony, I point out the in-home gym Josh

told me about. Despite it being late June, there's a cool breeze coming through. I wrap my arms around myself as we take in the view before grabbing drinks and settling onto the huge sectional couch.

"So..." Zoey takes a sip of her drink, looking around the room before her gaze settles back on me. "How is living with Josh?"

It has felt so natural and normal. It's been nice having someone to share a meal and conversation with at the end of the day, but I don't tell them that.

"It's been good," I say as nonchalantly as possible.

I feel all three of their intense gazes on me. I take a big sip of my drink as they stare at me. "Just good? That's all you're going to give us?" Hannah asks.

"Yeah, it's been a few weeks. I make dinner on the nights he's home. He cleans and does the dishes after, then we watch Netflix together. He's had plans the last few weekends, so he hasn't been around."

"How domestic," Zoey says, her voice laced with humour.

"He's letting me live here rent-free. The least I can do is cook him dinner when he's home."

"You know, if I were you, I would be trying to climb him like a tree by now. He is single, isn't he?" Hannah asks.

I shoot her a glare across the couch. "He's just a friend, *and* he's my brother's best friend. Not happening. Besides, I just got out of a long-term relationship and Josh doesn't see me that way," I say.

"You keep telling yourself that, girl," Zoey says, shaking her head.

"Have you not seen the way that man watches you?" Liz asks.

I pause my drink on its way to my mouth for a second. Liz is probably the most observant of the group. I take a sip before asking, "What do you mean, 'watches me'?"

"Girl, at your birthday party, it was like he couldn't take his eyes off you. Then there was that weekend at your place. I swore he was going to beat the shit out of Drew when he started calling you names, and before that, his hands were in tight fists when he heard the story," Eliza says.

I don't remember him watching me at my party. Since I moved in, I have caught his small smiles when he doesn't think I'm looking, when I finish cooking us dinner or when we curl up on opposite ends of the couch and watch TV.

"He's just a good friend," I say.

"You sure, babe? He moved you into his apartment and is giving you completely free rein in it, letting you have us over and everything."

"He did it as a favour to Matt," I say. He told me Matt came and visited him at his office the day Josh came to my place and made the offer.

Zoey looks at Hannah and Eliza before looking back at me. She puts her hand on my knee. "Liv, Matt didn't ask Josh. He offered it, unprompted. Matt had been calling me for updates on you because he was worried and didn't want to constantly call you. He called me that day and told me that when he stopped by Josh's office, he had offered the spare room."

I stare at her, trying to figure out what this all means. Matt must have mentioned he was worried about me and I needed a place to stay. That's all this was.

"Josh is just being a good friend," I say. "So, what are we ordering for dinner?" I ask to change the topic. The girls get that I am done with this conversation, so we leave it there. I place an order for two large pizzas and garlic sticks before queuing one of our favourite nostalgic movies, *The Princess Diaries*.

I slowly open my eyes to light coming in through the opening in my bedroom curtains. Rolling over, I notice the bed is empty—Zoey isn't there with me. I check the air mattress and it's empty, too. My phone says it's only 9 a.m. and the girls' bags are still in my bedroom.

Throwing my legs over the edge of the bed, I grab my robe before venturing out into the living room. I stop dead in my tracks as soon as I get into view of the kitchen. Josh is in front of the stove wearing a thin black t-shirt that clings to every inch of him and a pair of gym shorts, while my friends are gathered at the dining table. They each have empty plates in front of them and a glass of orange juice or a mug of coffee.

"Good morning, sleepyhead," Hannah chimes when she notices me. I close my mouth, which seems to have dropped to the ground.

Looking over at her, I rub my eyes. "Morning," I croak out. "What's going on?" I ask, looking around the room.

"Josh is making us breakfast," Zoey says with a wicked grin.

I swivel my head to Josh, watching as he walks a cup of coffee to me. He slowly does a head-to-toe scan of me before his eyes meet mine. His pupils are huge. He hands me the coffee and our fingers graze. A shiver runs through my entire body.

"Good morning, Olivia," he says with a smile. "Breakfast will be done in just a moment. I was just going to send one of the girls for you."

"Thanks." My throat is so dry, I barely manage to get the word out as I stare at him. He nods before turning around and going back to the stove.

I take an empty chair near the head of the table and look down at my coffee. I notice it's already had milk, and I suspect sugar, added to it. Taking a quick sip, my eyebrows shoot up. It's exactly how I take it. I look up and I notice the girls are staring at me.

"What?" I ask.

"Josh," Eliza whispers to me. I check over my shoulder to make sure he can't hear us.

"What about him?" I whisper.

"We came out this morning, ready to get coffee and leave, and when he saw us, he said he was making breakfast for the two of you and that we should stay and join. He added more plates to the table and got us drinks. When Hannah said good morning to you, he immediately looked at you with a smile and made you a coffee. Like it was something he does every day..."

Josh was going to make us breakfast and then invited my friends to stay? I continue to stare at her until I finally shake my head. Before I can say anything, Josh comes striding into the dining area with plates full of food. He puts down a plate stacked with French toast and another with bacon, going back into the kitchen he comes back with more: one with eggs, a bowl with cut strawberries and blueberries, and tucked under his arm a can of whipped cream.

My heart begins to race as realization hits me. Josh got up this morning and decided to make my favourite breakfast. The last person to do that for me was my mom. I rub my hand over my chest to tamper down the ache growing there.

He sits down beside me and claps his hands and rubs them together. "Let's dig in," he says.

"Thank you, Josh," Eliza says.

"Thanks, Josh," Hannah says next.

"Looks amazing, thanks Josh," Zoey chimes in, and he nods.

I stare at the layout before me. My favourite breakfast is in front of me, and he knows how to make my coffee. I turn and face Josh, placing my hand on his wrist. "Thank you, Josh. This means a lot."

"No problem," he says and hands me the plate of French toast. We load our plates with food. The girls talk about their week and upcoming plans, and Josh asks questions of everyone and listens intently.

I feel like I have stepped into some weird alternate reality. I don't remember a time when I ever did anything like this with Drew. I don't remember easy conversation between him and my friends. This isn't my normal life, is it?

I listen to the surrounding conversation contributing very little when Eliza asks me a question that pulls me out of my fog. Everyone is looking at me, waiting for an answer.

"Sorry Liz, what did you ask?"

"How is completing your list coming along?"

Heat fills my cheeks: I made a list of things I want to do this summer since breaking up with Drew. Some items on the list are sexual experiences I want now that I'm single. My eyes dart to Josh, who's looking at me. I tuck a piece of hair behind my ear.

"Um, I finished writing it, but haven't started it yet," I tell her.

"What's this list?" Josh asks as he takes another bite of French toast.

"Olivia here has created a list of *aaallll* the things she wants to do since breaking up with Drew," Zoey says with a mischievous grin.

"Okay, what's on this list?" he asks.

"Um, nothing really," I say, avoiding his gaze.

"Not true. Last we talked about it, you said a trip to Banff was on it, as well as a trip to the island." Hannah's eyes dash to Josh.

"And a few more things," she says with the same grin as Zoey, probably remembering some of the more explicit items on the list.

"That sounds fun. I'm sure we can tackle this list this summer, Olivia," Josh says with a smile.

My neck and face feel so warm. I'm sure Josh would be very capable of helping with *every* item on it. Thoughts of him helping has me breathing faster. I give him a small smile and a slight nod. My throat is so dry, and I think I'm sweating. I'm not sure I can form words right now.

"Oh, that's so nice of you to offer to help her, Josh. Liv, you should show Josh the list later," Zoey says. She's sitting across from me, so I kick her under the table and glare at her, earning me a grimace. The last thing I want to do is show the list to Josh. He doesn't need to know my sexual fantasies. That is a step way too far past the friend line we have drawn in the sand.

"There's no need for that," I say through clenched teeth.

"I'd love to see it; I'll help you get everything checked off before summer ends," Josh says.

"Won't that just be great Liv, checking off the list with Josh?" This time, it's Hannah chiming in.

She's too far away for me to kick her under the table so I smile and tilt my head before saying, "Well Hannah, why don't you create your own summer to-do list and ask Dr. Maxwell to help you with it."

Her jaw drops, and she glares at me. "I'd rather get poison ivy over my entire body and sprayed by a skunk," she says.

Josh chokes a little. I turn and look at him, and his eyes are wide. "Sorry Josh," she mumbles.

He uses a napkin and wipes his mouth. "All good... Out of curiosity, what did he do to garnish that reaction?" he asks.

She avoids eye contact, stabbing at the eggs on her plate. "Plenty," is all she says. I lean closer to Josh and whisper, "She won't tell us what happened, but it's been like this for a while."

He nods and whispers back, "I'm not sure if Grayson is oblivious or was playing stupid, but when I asked him at your party, he didn't seem to know what happened."

We finish our breakfast with more casual conversation, thankfully the topic of my summer to-do list is dropped. When we're all done, I get up and start clearing the table. Josh moves to stand and help, but I put a hand on his shoulder and push him back down. Leaning over, I whisper, "You cooked, I clean. That's the rule, remember?"

He turns his head and pulls back so he's looking me in the eyes. I could get lost in his gorgeous green ones. They have an inner ring of hazel surrounding his pupil. He takes a deep breath, and his pupils dilate. He closes his eyes for a second, like he's gathering himself before he opens them again and looks at me.

"Can I at least make myself another cup of coffee?" he asks in a whisper.

I nod. "That is acceptable."

The girls help me, and we make quick work of the cleanup.

"We should get going," Hannah says once we finish. Josh is still sitting at the dining table scrolling through his phone. "Thanks for breakfast Josh, it was great."

Zoey and Eliza say their thank you's too and we head to my bedroom. Once we're all inside, Zoey closes the door and leans against it.

"Okay babe, if you don't try to jump that fine piece of man, I think I will. He made you breakfast, and when he saw us still here with you, he invited us to stay. He engaged in conversation with all of us and offered to help you with your summer checklist, without knowing what's on it. Which you should totally take him up on. That man probably has some mad skill in the bedroom."

"I have to agree with Zoey on this, Liv. You should go after him," Hannah chimes in.

"Put some feelers out, at least see where he stands on this," Eliza says.

"I just got out of a relationship. I'm damaged goods," I say, but I know the girls aren't going to let this go, so I add, "I'll think about it."

We strip the air mattress and get changed before the girls grab their bags, and we head back into the living room. I walk them to the door and hug them goodbye.

"Thanks, Josh," they each yell out as they walk out the door.

"See you later," he shouts back.

Jump him, Zoey mouths before she turns and walks down the

hallway with the girls. Closing the door, I turn and join Josh, who has relocated to the couch. Instead of sitting on the opposite side of the couch though, I sit next to him with one leg lifted and bent so I can face him and the other hanging off the edge and an arm bent on the back of the couch. My index finger runs across the material on the back of the couch as I gather myself. After a few seconds, Josh locks his phone, sets it down beside him, and turns to face me, mirroring my position.

"Thanks for that Josh, for making breakfast and inviting my friends to stay. You didn't have to," I say. His fingers start to run up and down my arm that's on the back of the couch.

"I know, but I wanted to. It was nice to see you with them. You're always so carefree when you're with your friends. I like to see you that way."

He continues to run his fingers slowly over my arm. It's sending sparks of electricity across my skin and making it hard to focus. I close my eyes and take a deep breath, releasing it slowly in an attempt to gather myself.

"Any plans for today?" I ask.

"Meeting up with Caleb to help him with a few things, you?"

"Nope, thought I'd just relax and read today."

"Well, have fun. I should get ready and head out."

He stands up and I immediately want him to sit back down, missing his touch.

The week passes by quickly. Matt, Gi, and I head to my parents' on the 1st for their Canada Day neighbourhood barbecue and gathering. Josh and Em are there too and we watch the fireworks and spend time catching up with people we haven't seen in a while. The next week, I spend a few days with Gi, catching up, and doing some shopping. I spend a couple of days looking up some new things I might want to incorporate into my classroom next year.

Josh comes home from running some errands on Sunday and meets me in the kitchen as I'm grabbing a water bottle from the fridge.

"Hey, how are you?" I smile.

"Hey, good. You?"

"Good. Any plans today?"

"I have dinner at my parents' tonight. Em actually asked me to bring you with me. You want to go?"

Growing up, I ate at the Lincoln's house often. Between Matt and Josh being friends and then Em and Gi, our families grew close, and we often had dinner together once a month. I always loved his parents. Eleanor and Logan were so welcoming towards us, and from what I remember, Eleanor was a skilled cook. It's been some time since I've spent time with his family. It would be nice to see them again.

"Sure, sounds fun. What time do we need to leave?"

"Em will be here at 4:30 p.m. We'll give her a ride there and drop her off back at her place on campus after."

I check the time on my phone, it's 12:30 p.m. "We still have a few hours. Wanna watch *Manifest*? I've been dying to watch the next episode, but didn't want to watch without you."

He smiles brightly. "Yeah, put it on."

I turn turn it on and settle into the couch, and Josh sits right beside me. I sit with my legs crossed in front of me and lean back into the cushions. Josh plays with the little hairs on my neck as we watch like it's the most normal thing in the world. I've always loved having my hair played with. It relaxes me. I lean into his touch and his light touches turn into a deeper rubbing of my scalp.

After three episodes, I pause the TV and turn to face him. His hand is still in my hair. "I think I'm going to get a snack and then get ready. Do you want anything?" I ask.

He shakes his head, and I get up and grab a small bowl of fruit. I eat it quickly in the kitchen before going to get ready.

I take a fast shower and blow dry my hair, deciding to leave it in a straighter look for the night, pulling the top of my hair back and securing it with bobby pins. Leaving my makeup more natural, I change into a pair of dark blue jean shorts, a black tank top, with a black sheer button-up top over it, and my favourite pair of black flats.

Standing in the living room, I slip the flats on. As I finish, Josh walks out of his room. His hair is wet from his recent shower, and he's dressed in a light grey button-down, hugging his every muscle and navy-blue chinos that stretch across his muscular thighs. God, this man is sex on a stick. I take in every part of him as he adjusts his sleeves, not noticing me. Looking up, his eyes meet mine and he takes in my outfit and his lips part slightly.

A knock on the door pulls me out of my staring. Em must be here. Josh continues to stare at me for a few seconds before he moves towards the front door, clearing his throat. I stand up as he opens it and hugs Em.

I'm always surprised by how beautiful Emily is. Tonight, her gorgeous long, blonde hair is in loose waves down her back and her makeup highlights her green eyes and the soft features of her face. She and Josh are the complete opposite in looks. She steps into the apartment, her eyes land on me, and her smile widens. She walks over to me and pulls me into a hug.

"Oh my god, Olivia, it's been way too long." Pulling back, she holds onto my arms. Her eyes take me in, and she lets out a low whistle. "Girl, you look hot," she says and looks over her shoulder at her brother. "Josh, doesn't Olivia look hot?"

He stares at us. I can feel his eyes burning into me. "Josh?" Emily prompts.

He coughs lightly. "Yeah," he says before turning and grabbing his keys.

"Um, we should get going," he says and opens the door, waiting for us to exit before he locks it. Emily hooks her arm through mine as we walk down the hallway.

"We have so much to catch up on. You'll need to tell me what it's like living with this weirdo," she says, tilting her head toward her brother.

Josh, ever the gentleman, opens the car door for Emily and I. Traffic isn't too bad this time of day, so we manage to make it out of the city easily, using the time to catch up.

Josh pulls into the driveway of his parents' house before getting out and opening the doors for us again. His parents live in the same house they did when we were growing up. It's a nice three-bedroom, two-bathroom with a big backyard. Eleanor has flowers planted on both sides of the driveway and the path leading up to the front porch. In front of the porch, she has various rose bushes. Stepping off the pathway, I walk over to the blooming white roses and stick my nose in them.

I hear Josh and Emily climb the steps up the front porch and knock. The door creaks a little as it swings open and Eleanor's voice sweeps over me.

"Oh, my babies are home. Where is Olivia?" she asks.

"Over here, Mrs. Lincoln. I was just admiring your beautiful rose bushes."

At the sound of my voice, she steps out onto the front porch. Eleanor Lincoln looks good for being in her early fifties. Tonight, she has her dark black hair pulled back into a tight bun at the nape of her neck. She's wearing minimal makeup and her grey eyes are bright. A smile spreads across her face as she looks at me, stepping away from her roses.

"Well, I'm glad someone other than myself appreciates them, and it's Eleanor, Olivia." I join her and she pulls me into a giant hug. "Oh, it's so nice to see you Olivia," she says and releases me.

"It's so nice to see you, Eleanor. Thank you for extending the invitation for dinner."

"You will always be welcome here. Why don't we go inside and get some drinks? I'd love to hear all about what you've been up to over the last few years."

She takes my arm and walks me inside. Walking in the front door is nostalgic. I haven't been here since Gianna went off to university. A little den sits to the right of the entryway that the Lincolns use as an office and library, and on the left is their open, spacious living room. Mr. Lincoln is sitting in his recliner with a beer in his hand. He looks up at us and sets his beer down, giving each of his children a hug. He looks at me and a big smile stretches across his face.

"Is this Olivia Carter? We haven't seen you in this house in some time, dear. Where have you been hiding?" he says, pulling me into a hug. Logan Lincoln is in his late fifties. Since I've seen him, grey has started to mix in with his chestnut brown hair. Looking at him and Josh, it's easy to see the family resemblance. They have the same eyes, high cheekbones, and strong jaws.

"Hi Mr. Lincoln, it's nice to see you. I've been around." I smile brightly at him.

"It's Logan, dear. I'm glad you're here."

We move into the living room and Emily and I get settled with Logan while Eleanor and Josh go into the kitchen. A few minutes later, they return and Josh hands me a glass with dark liquid in it and sits next to me. I take a sip and the rich taste of rum mixed with Coke Zero hits my tongue. My go-to drink. I turn and smile at Josh as I process the fact that Josh didn't even ask what I wanted to drink. He just knew.

Josh

Conversation is easy as we all sit in the living room of my childhood home. When Mom says dinner's ready, we move into the dining room. Mom and Dad each take seats at the head of the table. Em takes her usual seat on Mom's left, and I pull the chair across from Emily out and nod at Olivia. She looks at me for a second before taking a seat and quietly saying, "Thank you."

I grab the seat between her and my dad. We pass the food around the table and make our plates. As soon as everyone has food, Emily starts the conversation.

"So, Liv, what is it like living with Josh?"

That peaks Mom and Dad's interest. I mentioned reconnecting with her a few weeks ago, but hadn't gotten the chance to tell them about her moving in.

"It's been nice. It was so nice of him to offer me his spare room," Olivia says as she pushes some food around on her plate.

"I'm sorry dear, I didn't realize you had moved in with Josh," Mom says. "What caused that?"

"She needed a place to stay, Mom," I say, hoping she won't probe too much into it. I don't want Olivia to feel obligated to talk about what happened with Drew.

"What about your boyfriend?" Emily asks. "Josh mentioned a while ago you were serious with someone."

I shoot Emily a powerful stare, silently telling her to drop it.

Olivia swallows harshly and lifts her gaze to Emily. I reach under the table, rest my hand on her leg, squeezing it and lean back in my chair. She looks at me and I give her a nod, letting her know I'm here for her. She gives me a slight smile and looks back at Emily.

"I did. We broke up a few weeks ago. We were going to move in together, but I caught him cheating right after I had given my landlord notice. I couldn't find a place on such short notice, and Josh was nice enough to offer his spare room."

I give her leg another hard squeeze to show my support. I hate that this happened to her, but she seems to be doing okay. She resumes eating her dinner. Emily looks at me and then back to Olivia. "I'm so sorry. You are better off without him. You deserve someone who will worship you," Em says before reaching across the table and grabbing Liv's hand.

"Thanks," she says back with a smile.

I let go of Olivia's leg, lean in and whisper in her ear, "She's right, you deserve to be a man's world." I watch goosebumps rise on her skin as I pull away.

"So, do you have any plans this summer, Olivia?" Mom asks, trying to move the conversation along.

"Not much right now, but I'll make plans," she says smiling.

I bump my shoulder into hers. "What about that list the girls were talking about?"

I watch the blush rise up her neck and into her cheeks and her eyes dart down to her plate. She's embarrassed by this list, but I'm not sure why.

"Oohhhh, this must be good and juicy. You're blushing, Liv. Share this list with me," Emily says.

"It's nothing. I got drunk with the girls one night and wrote it, it's mostly travel and there are some..." She hesitates before finishing, "other things on it."

Emily raises a brow. "Other things? Okay, now I have to see it."

"I've yet to see this list and I've agreed to help you with it," I say with a grin.

Her head shoots up and she shakes it. "No, you don't need to do that. I don't need you to help, but thank you," she rushes out quickly. Mom and Dad are deep in conversation, and I join in. Out of the corner of my eye, I see Olivia hand her phone across the table to Emily. Her eyes move as she scrolls through the list, and then her eyes go big and her jaw drops.

I look over at her and she leans closer to Liv. "Josh is going to help you with this?"

"Noooo, when he offered, he hadn't seen it. He is not helping with it. Nope, someone else," she whispers, thinking I'm not paying attention. Emily goes to hand Olivia her phone back, but before Olivia can grab it, I take it from my sister.

"If I'm going to help you with this list, I think it's better if I know what's on it so I can plan."

Olivia's face pales as she reaches to get the phone back from me and Emily tries to cover her laughter. Olivia continues to try and reach across me to grab her phone, but my arms are too long.

I turn to read the list.

Olivia's Summer List
- Camp in Banff
- Travel the Ice Fields
- Weekend in Whistler
- Camp on Hornby Island
- Trip to Victoria
- Trip to Seattle
- Go to a concert

These aren't that bad. I continue reading.

- Have a guy kneel for me and make me come
- Be tied up in bed
- Tie a guy up in bed
- Experience multiple orgasms in a night
- Try spanking
- Try sexual degradation

I look back at Olivia, and her face is pale white, and she's staring at her plate and Emily is watching us as she plays with her wine glass and tries to hide her laughter. Mom notices Emily, then looks across at Olivia and me, and her brows furrow.

"What's going on?"

I hand Olivia her phone under the table. "Nothing Mom, just Emily being Emily."

Olivia grabs her phone and shoves it into her back pocket. As the conversation moves to Emily's studies and how Gianna and Matt are doing, my mind keeps wandering back to that list.

When we finish eating, I help clear the table and help Mom with dishes while Dad goes back into the living room to watch sports highlights and Emily and Olivia move to the back deck.

When we finish the dishes, Mom joins Dad in the living room, and I grab a beer and sit at the kitchen table. My mind wanders back to Olivia's list. The beginning is innocent stuff, camping and travelling, but the end and all the sexual experiences she wants to have this summer has me hard just thinking about it.

I think about being the guy to kneel before her with my face between her legs, eating her until she comes so hard her legs give out. Taking her to my bed and tying her to it where I perform a repeat before climbing between her legs and fucking her until she screams my name.

I am painfully hard; I reach down and adjust myself to try and quell the aching feeling. I down the rest of my beer before dropping the bottle in the recycling bin and heading towards the back door. I stand in the doorway as Emily and Olivia talk.

"If he offered, would you let him?" Em asks Olivia.

"I'm not sure. I don't think I could do casual with him. There's too much history there and I wouldn't want to ruin the relationship that we already have. He means way too much to me to lose him trying to complete this list."

"Have you thought about a relationship with him?" Em asks, not noticing my presence.

I know I shouldn't be listening, but it's like my feet are glued to the ground and won't move. I want to know who they're talking about. Who could she not do casual with? Who is so important to her that she couldn't stand to lose them?

"You have to promise not to say anything. I haven't said these words out loud to a single person, not even the girls," Olivia says her voice serious.

"Pinky promise, not a word."

"Growing up, I had the biggest crush on him, but I never

thought he would see me that way. You know we were friends, but I've always been Matt's little sister. A relationship with him could be amazing. I value his friendship. I've always been able to be myself around him, and I feel safe with him. I think I need to find somewhere else to live soon, because the way we're going it feels way too natural and I could get used to it, so when he starts to bring other women over, I think it could break my heart. I am going to focus on completing my list and finding a place to live."

My breath can't seem to escape my lungs. Olivia is talking about me. She had a crush on me growing up? She couldn't do casual with me and wants a relationship? Should I make a move and let her know I want one with her? I need to do something before she finds a new place. I like having her at my place too much to just let her leave now.

"You should talk to him, Liv," Emily encourages.

"I haven't heard of a single long-term relationship he's had. Is he someone who does relationships?" Liv asks incredulously.

"I think he just needs the right person," Em says. They sit in silence before they move their conversation on to other summer plans.

I clear my throat a minute later, and the girls turn and look at me. I smile. "You ladies ready to go?" They both nod and push up from the bench. I hold the door open and follow them into the living room.

"Mom, we're going to head home. I have to drop Em off at her place. Thank you for dinner. I'll call you this week." I hug her and place a peck on her cheek before moving to give my dad a quick hug.

"Thank you so much for having me tonight, Eleanor," Olivia says as my mom pulls her into a hug.

"Anytime Olivia, I hope we will see you more often," Mom says as she looks at me like she knows something the rest of us don't. I've been getting that look from people more often lately.

I help Emily and Olivia into their jackets before we head out to the car.

"I'm being dropped off first. You take the front seat, Liv," Em calls as we round the front of the car toward the passenger side. I open both doors for them and they climb in. I let Emily hook her phone up to the speakers and the girls talk the entire way to SFU about different artists and other random topics. It's nice seeing how easily Emily and Olivia get along.

I pull into the parking lot in front of Emily's dorm and turn to Olivia. "I'm going to walk Em up, stay here and keep the doors locked." She agrees and I get out, walking around and helping Em out of the car.

"I think you'd be good for her," Emily says once she opens the front door of her building.

"What do you mean?" I ask.

"You don't need to play dumb with me, Josh. I know you well, and I've known this for years. You like Olivia, and more than as a friend."

I furrow my brows. I didn't think anyone else had known, let alone my little sister.

"I'm not sure what you're talking about," I say.

"Cut the crap, Josh. You might be my big brother, but I still know a thing or two. You like that girl and based on the way she blushed when talking about you and that list, she likes you too. My advice, make a move before she finds another man to move on with."

I figure there's no point in hiding it from her anymore. "Okay, what do you recommend I do?"

"Do something that lets her know you want more, but be careful with her, okay? Only make a move if you're ready to build something with her."

Emily unlocks the door, before stepping inside and looking at me. "I am, thank you." I give her a hug and a kiss on top of her head. "Goodnight, Em. I love you."

"Love you too Josh, go back to Liv."

I step back into the hall and Emily closes her door. When I hear the click of the lock, I make my way back to the car. Getting in, I see Olivia's head is leaning against the window. It appears she's fallen asleep.

I keep the music quiet and use the drive to think over my conversation with Emily; I need to let Olivia know I want more with her. When I get to the parkade, she stirs and rubs her eyes before looking at me with a small smile. I smile back and park before helping Olivia out.

Unlocking the front door, I let her walk in first. She looks at me with a small smile before saying, "Goodnight, Josh." She starts to walk towards her bedroom, and I call out her name. She stops and turns to face me.

"Yeah, Josh?"

I close the space between us, putting my hand in her hair at the base of her head. I lower my head down to hers. I'm done being worried about the things outside of Olivia and me. I've spent too much time not acting on how I feel for her. No more, I'm taking what I want. I wait for a second, giving her time to say no. Her breath fans against my lips as mine hover over hers. Her chest begins to rise and fall rapidly. When she doesn't stop me, I lower my lips to hers.

I've spent years thinking about this moment. What it would feel like to finally kiss the girl I've pined over for years. Her lips are soft and sweet from tonight's dessert. She seems hesitant. I move my lips over hers slowly, and she kisses me back. Her arms wrap around my neck, pulling me closer. I walk us to the wall pressing her back against it, and I deepen the kiss, using my tongue to trace the seam of her lips, urging her to open to me.

Her lips part and our tongues meet. A groan leaves my chest, and she kisses me back more urgently. I break the kiss as I trail kisses across her jaw and down her neck. "Josh," she whispers as I reach a spot behind her ear that seems to drive her crazy.

I run my tongue over it again before trailing my mouth back across her jaw. I kiss her again and push my hips against her stomach, allowing her to feel how hard I am for her. Releasing my hand from her hair, I trail it down her body, skimming over her breast and down her side before gripping her ass and pulling her body further into mine.

"Do you feel what you do to me, Olivia? How hard you make me?" I whisper against her lips. She nods slightly before I kiss her again.

"If you want me to stop, tell me now, Olivia."

"Keep going, Josh," she says as she moves her hips closer to me. I move my leg between hers, pressing my thigh into her centre. She grinds against it, seeking the friction she so desperately needs. As I continue to devour her, I use my hands on her ass to help her grind harder on my thigh. Breaking the kiss, I work my way down her throat and a mewl leaves her. She's enjoying this as much as I am. Her grip tightens in my hair as she works herself fast against me.

"Come for me, Olivia," I whisper in her ear.

My hot breath causes goosebumps to break out across her skin. Seconds later, she's calling out my name as her legs give out. I move my hands up, wrapping my arm around her waist to keep her upright. When she comes down from her high, I place a chaste peck on her lips and keep my forehead planted on hers.

"I want to help you with your list, Olivia, but I want more. I want a relationship with you. I don't just want to cross items off your list. I want dates, talks about your hopes and dreams. I want talks about the future. Don't answer me right now. Take the night to think about it."

With another quick kiss, I whisper, "Goodnight, Olivia," before walking down the hall towards my bedroom to deal with my throbbing cock, which is begging for release.

CHAPTER 12

Olivia

My eyes are fixed on Josh's retreating back as he walks towards his room. I can barely wrap my head around what the hell just happened. I reach up and run my hands up my face to my hair and rake my fingers through the strands. Taking a deep breath, I head to my bedroom, shutting the door behind me and leaning against it. Closing my eyes, my mind immediately replays the moments in the hallway.

The feel of Josh's grip in my hair as he pulled my head back, the feel of his warm breath against my lips, the feeling of his soft lips as he kissed me, him running his tongue over my lips, coaxing me to open for him, our tongues dancing as we kissed. I was so turned on as he pushed me against the wall and pressed his hard cock into my stomach. When he kissed across my jaw and down my neck, finding the sensitive spot behind my ear, it drove me crazy.

The needy way I ground myself against his thigh, seeking my release is all I can think about. My breathing picks up again as the sensations come back, flooding my system. I need a cold shower, asap.

I quickly strip out of my clothes and turn the shower on, hopping into it right away. I close my eyes, my mind reeling. Did that really just happen? Did Joshua Lincoln just give me an orgasm in the hallway of his apartment and tell me he wants a relationship?

Wrapped in a towel, I move out into my bedroom and text the girls.

LIV

911, help are you guys awake???

ZO

What's up?

HAN

Girl, what happened?

LIZ

You okay?

LIV

I don't know, I may need to be committed, because I still can't wrap my head around what just happened…

I went to dinner with Josh and Emily at their parents' house. Josh mentioned my list, and I showed it to Em. Josh stole my phone and read it… But that's not what's getting to me. When we got home, he KISSED me, and not just a little peck, like a life-altering, dominating kiss, and then he helped me dry hump his thigh in the hallway until I came. When I was done, he told me he wants to help me with my list, but he wants a relationship with me. I'm freaking out.

Like, did this really happen?

Am I dreaming? Am I asleep?

This is Joshua FUCKING Lincoln we're talking about.

ZO

Life-altering kiss, an orgasm, and he wants a relationship. Plus, he's hot as fuck. Kinda sounds like a dream boat, Liv, I say go for it.

HAN

You are awake; you don't need to be committed. Babe, take the jump, try a relationship with him. It's been almost 2 months since the shit show with Drew. You deserve this.

LIZ

Liv, you're fine. What do you want?

LIV

I never thought this was a possibility, not gonna lie. I had a crush on him growing up, but I never thought I'd kiss him, let alone get an orgasm or a relationship.

ZO

Sweetheart, we all knew you had a crush on him.

LIZ

^^^ true

HAN

I think the only person who doesn't/didn't know is Josh.

LIV

You guys suck. Why didn't you say anything??? What the fuck am I supposed to do now? When I finished, he told me to sleep on it and then went to his room.

ZO

Do you think you're ready for another relationship?

LIV

Maybe. With Josh, there's so much history and we're friends. I'm worried I'll lose his friendship.

LIZ

Talk to him, let him know that. I'm sure it will all work out. Don't not do it just because you're scared. You'll regret it.

LIV

He's usually gone for work before I get up in the morning and he has a game tomorrow. I guess I'll have to wait until he gets home from his game, or I'll wait it out until Tuesday. Ughhhh...

HAN

This will all be good. Don't stress, get some sleep, babe.

LIV

Thanks. I'll talk to you guys tomorrow. Love you.

Plugging my phone in, I settle into bed and try to fall asleep. I toss and turn for what seems like hours before sleep overcomes me.

I groan as I roll over the next morning; reaching for my phone, I see the time. It's 11 a.m. I throw the blankets off me as I pad to the washroom. My eyes catch my reflection in the mirror and memories of last night flood my mind. Liz is right. I'll regret this if I don't at least have a conversation with Josh and give this a shot.

Josh won't be home for hours; I decide that I'll make myself some breakfast and then get some cleaning done in the kitchen before settling in with a book. I throw on some clothes before heading to the kitchen to make breakfast.

I pull up my favourite upbeat playlist and connect to the speakers set up in the apartment. The dance music plays through the living room, dining room, and kitchen, and I begin cooking. When I finish eating, I turn up the music to a blasting volume and dance as I clean the kitchen.

JOSH

I wrap up my last meeting at 1:30 p.m. and head from the conference room to my office. Sitting at my desk, I run my hands through my hair and down my face.

This morning I left for work before Olivia was even up, which is normal, but today my entire body's on edge, not knowing what she's going to do after last night. After I left her in the hallway, I made my way to my washroom and jerked off in the shower to the memory of the feel of her skin, how she responded to my touch, and the sound of her moans as she ground herself against my thigh.

I check my calendar to confirm I have nothing pressing I need to attend to today. I have a game tonight, and I don't want to wait that long to get an answer from Olivia. Closing my laptop, I put it in my bag along with a couple of files before I head out of my office.

"Kate, I'm heading home for the day. Take messages for any calls that come in, and text me if anything urgent comes up. You can leave at 3 p.m. for the day. I'll see you tomorrow."

"Of course, see you tomorrow, Mr. Lincoln," she says with a nod before returning to her computer and I head to my car.

Unlocking the front door, I hear loud music as I step inside. I set my bag down and toe off my shoes before heading into the living room. Taking my suit jacket off, I lay it over the back of a chair in the living room and roll up the sleeves of my dress shirt.

As I walk into the kitchen, I watch Olivia dancing in a T-shirt with her hair in a messy bun. She's behind the island, so I can't see any more. I watch as she bounces from foot to foot. She has her hands in the air as she sings "Look What God Gave Her" into a serving spoon. This song fits her perfectly. I can't take my eyes off her.

I lean against the wall, cross my legs at the ankles, and my arms over my chest as I watch her in her carefree spirit, dancing around the kitchen. I could stand here for hours watching her. I can see how happy she is as she dances and sings to her music. I wish that every moment of her life could be like this, where she has no care in the world. She moves out from behind the island and I notice she isn't wearing any pants. She raises her arms above her head again and her t-shirt rises enough that the sexy pair of black lace panties peeks out from under the hem.

I tilt my head back and do my best to stifle my groan. Taking a deep breath, I lower my head just as she screams while clutching her chest. She stares at me for a second before she remembers she's only wearing panties on her lower half and shuffles behind the island.

"Josh, you scared the shit out of me. I thought you wouldn't be home until after your game tonight."

"That was the plan, but I wanted to see you. See if you thought about what I said last night. I couldn't wait until after my game. Can't say I'm mad, I got a great little show for coming home early." I grin.

She visibly swallows. I push off the wall and walk towards her. She moves until her back is pressed into the counter. I stop when I'm only a couple of inches in front of her.

"So, Olivia, do you have an answer for me?" I ask.

She stares into my eyes for what feels like a whole minute before she gives me a small nod and a whispered, "Yes," escapes her.

The word is barely out of her mouth before I lean down and claim her mouth. I use my right hand to grip her hair, tilting her head back to allow me to consume more of her mouth. She slides her hands up my arms and into my hair, scraping at my scalp.

I lick along her lips slowly to get her to open to me. She opens with a gasp as my free hand grabs her ass and pulls her body into mine. Our tongues meet, exploring each other. I can taste strawberries on her as we kiss. I slow down, removing my tongue, changing the kiss to a few pecks at the corners of her mouth.

Resting my forehead on hers, I close my eyes. We stay like that for a few moments as we work to catch our breath. When I open my eyes, she's looking up at me with eyes full of questions.

"Olivia, if we do this, you're mine. I don't share. It will be just you and me. Got that?" She nods once. "I need to hear the words, Olivia."

"Yes, Josh, just you and me," she whispers.

I lean in and give her a quick kiss. "Good, now I want to take you to lunch. Why don't you go get dressed and we can head out?"

She nods and I step back, giving her space to retreat into her bedroom.

CHAPTER 13

Olivia

I close my bedroom door and lean my back against it, tilting my head back, replaying the moment we just shared in the kitchen. *If we do this, you're mine. I don't share. It will be just you and me.* It was a major turn-on.

A smile spreads across my face because all of this is so surreal.

Pushing off the door, I quickly get dressed and put my hair in a tasteful ponytail. Giving myself a brief look in the mirror, I smile as I join Josh in the living room.

Josh looks up at me and smiles, lifting himself off the couch. My body warms as he draws closer and stops in front of me. "You look beautiful, Olivia." He places a kiss on my cheek before his hand finds my lower back and he leads me out of the apartment.

We make our way down the hallway and into the elevator. He presses the first floor for the lobby.

"I thought I'd show you one of my favourite places just down the block," he says, smiling down at me. I nod in acknowledgement and clasp my hands in front of me.

I'm not sure how to approach any of this. Josh and I have been friends for years, so realistically, this shouldn't change anything. We can just touch each other more freely and kiss. I smile at that thought, being able to reach out to him whenever I want.

"What's got you smiling like that?" Josh asks, watching me intently.

"Nothing, just thinking about life." I'm not sure what to say. Do I say, *Oh, I'm smiling because I can touch you whenever I want now?* I don't want to come across as clingy when we literally just decided to try this out.

He leans down and whispers in my ear, "I like your smile. I want you to keep doing that." The elevator dings, and he pulls back, his hand returning to my lower back, leading me out of the lobby and turning right down the block.

Arriving at the restaurant, Josh opens the door for me. A hostess greets and seats us. Josh pulls my chair out and takes a seat across from me. I smile at him and look around the restaurant. It's a casual place. The walls are painted white with large scenery pictures all over them. One wall has a large image of the Golden Gate Bridge and another of the CN Tower in Toronto. I also see the Statue of Liberty and Niagara Falls.

The place has a very open and welcoming feeling. I look back to Josh and he's watching me take in everything with a slight smile. I grab my menu and look at it to avoid his stare. Feeling myself warming under it, I try not to squirm. I don't want our relationship to become awkward now. We've been friends for too long and no matter what, I don't want to lose that. I also have to acknowledge that he's my brother's best friend.

Quickly skimming the menu I make a decision before our server comes by, and we place our order all at once and she leaves.

"So, you left work early for an answer?" I ask Josh.

He leans forward and places his clasped hands on the table. Josh has rolled up the sleeves of his dress shirt and I watch the muscles of his forearms strain as he puts weight on them. I've read a lot of romance novels—they're my go-to books—and I've read about female main characters being into watching their partner's forearms. I've never understood it until watching Josh.

Drew was always kind of scrawny, and kind of unsure of himself. He didn't have this energy that just pulls you in the way Josh does.

"Yes, I spent my morning distracted by it being unanswered. So, as soon as I finished my last meeting, I decided to come home. I have to say I'm very happy I did." He grins.

"Me too." I grin back; I have a few worries though, and I want to address them now before we get too far into this. "Josh," I start, and his grin slips a little. I reach out and grab one of his hands. "I want this, I want us, but can we keep this quiet from Matt for a little bit? You guys are best friends and the last thing I want is to get between you guys. I want to enjoy this and see where we go and then tell him when we're ready."

Josh studies me from across the table. He gives my hand a small squeeze and nods. "If that's what you want to do, then of course; but Olivia, I want to give this a real shot. I want to see how great we can be together. We'll tell him when you're ready."

I smile and squeeze his hand before sitting back in my chair.

"So, tell me how your season is going so far. This is your summer league, right?" I ask.

"Yeah, it's a lot of the same guys, but it's a different league. I like playing year-round. It's a great workout and when I've had a shit day at work, it's nice to push my body. I also like seeing the guys, too."

I nod. "I remember you slamming a few guys into the boards when we were in high school." I send him a huge smile with a small chuckle.

"Yeah, I think there may have been a year when I spent a good amount of time in the box for roughing," he chuckles.

"You seem oh-so-proud of that." I nudge his leg under the table.

"I protect my guys," he says matter-of-factly.

Our food is delivered, and we continue to talk about hockey from when we were kids, and he tells me about his new leagues.

"Olivia, I was serious about wanting to help you with your list. I don't have any games this weekend. Why don't we go up to Whistler? We can hike, do some shopping in the village, and there are a few museums we can hit, too."

I nearly choke on my drink at the mention of my list. I have no idea what he thinks about some items on it, but a trip to Whistler does sound nice. It will also give us some time to explore what we could be without the pressure of my brother being around.

"That sounds great, Josh. I'd love to go with you." I smile.

When our server drops off our bill, Josh pays before we head home. When we get home, he unlocks the front door, holding it open, and gesturing for me to go in first.

"Thank you for lunch, Olivia," he says, giving me a peck on the cheek. "I have a few things to deal with before I head out for my game. I'll see you later. I had fun."

"I did too. Say bye before you leave?" I ask.

"Of course." With a quick kiss, he walks down the hallway to his office.

I make my way into my bedroom, throw myself on my bed, and let out an excited squeal while kicking my legs. I just went on a first date with Joshua fucking Lincoln, and it was great. It was easy and fun. He wants to go away this weekend to help me with my list. Wow, a weekend away with Josh in Whistler, away from the city and our friends, just the two of us.

I sit up and lean against my headboard, grabbing my phone to text the girls.

LIV

I just went on a first date with Joshua Lincoln, OMG!!!

ZO

Seriously, how are we just hearing about this?
Details girl. Don't leave anything out you owe us.

HAN

What have we missed since last night??? Girl, details!!!

LIZ

…. Liv, don't leave us hanging.

LIV

Group call???

We agree to call in thirty minutes, so I call Matt in the meantime.

"Hey Liv, is everything all good?" he answers.

"Yup, I just realized it's been a while since we talked, wanted to chat. What are you up to tonight?" I ask knowing full well he has hockey with Josh.

"I have a game tonight. What about you?"

"Not sure. Might hang out with the girls tonight. What rink are you playing at?"

"Kits at 7 p.m." I make a noise of acknowledgement.

"You played at that one in high school sometimes, didn't you?"
I ask.

"Yeah, it's a decent rink. How's living with Josh going?"

"It's fine. Between work, hockey, and other things, he's not home a lot. When he is, we eat dinner together, maybe watch an episode of a show together." I keep it brief so he doesn't get any indication of Josh and me.

"I'm glad it's working out, sis. Hey, I've got a meeting I have to go to. I'll talk to you later."

Matt hangs up, and I lay my head back against the headboard when my phone rings again. I look down and Zoey's face fills the screen. I answer and the screen splits, showing Zoey, Hannah, and Eliza.

"Okay girl, spill," Zoey says, skipping any greeting. A huge smile spreads across my face.

I recap them on my morning, including Josh offering to go to Whistler this weekend. They're silent for a while before I hear squeals. "You're going away for the weekend together?" Zoey asks.

"Yeah." I nod. "He said he wanted to help me complete my list."

"Babe, a guy doesn't offer to go away for the weekend to just help with a list. He wants to go away with you," Liz says matter-of-factly. Did Josh offer because he wants to go away with me? I know he said he wants to give this a shot, but a weekend away? Just going away together is a big deal.

I give my head a slight shake to get those thoughts out of my head. I can't be dwelling on these kinds of things right now. We're too new. We haven't even labelled what we are. I know we're seeing what we can be, and we're exclusive, but an entire weekend away for anything other than checking an item off my list seems far-fetched at this point.

"So, they have a hockey game tonight... Do you guys wanna go with me? It would be under the premise of going to support Matt though."

All three of them nod and say, "Yes," and we make plans to meet there before hanging up.

I check the time and see I have two hours before I have to leave to meet the girls at the rink. Deciding to see about getting a ride from

Josh, I head down the hall to his office. I knock softly and hear a "Come-in" called from the other side.

Opening the door, I lean against the door frame while Josh looks at his laptop. His brows are furrowed as he stares intently like he's trying to solve a complex problem. He looks hot with his confused look; his eyes eventually move and meet mine and a smile comes onto his face.

"What's up?" he asks.

"I was wondering what time you're leaving for your game?"

"5:15 p.m., why?"

"Can I bum a ride with you?" I ask with a smile.

"Sure. You want to come?" he asks incredulously.

"Yeah, it's been a while since I've watched you guys play. The girls are going to meet me there."

"Okay, sounds good. What are you up to right now?" he asks with a mischievous grin, getting out of his chair and walking over to me.

"Nothing. Did you have something in mind?" I ask, looking up at him through my lashes. He wraps his arms around my waist and pulls me into him. He leans down so I can feel his warm breath on my lips as he whispers, "I was thinking we could do a little of this."

He closes the last centimetres that separate our lips, kissing me slowly at first, savouring the feeling and taste of our kiss. His right hand moves from my waist up my back and into my hair, gripping it tightly. A deep moan leaves my throat and I grip the front of his shirt. He uses my moan to slip his tongue into my mouth, finding mine. Our tongues play with each other as they explore. I squeeze my legs together, trying to ease the ache growing between my thighs.

He moves me so my back is pressed against the wall and uses his leg to spread mine, pushing his thigh into my centre. I break the kiss, moaning in pleasure at the pressure he's applying. God, this feels so good. Josh trails kisses down my neck and I lean my head to the side, granting him better access. He licks and kisses his way down to my collarbone until he is just above my breasts.

His left hand trails down my body as he kisses across my chest. My breathing is quick and shallow now. My skin is burning up, and my panties are ruined, I'm so wet.

He kisses his way back up to my lips before leaning his forehead against mine. "Babe, if we keep going like this, I am definitely going to be late." He leaves a quick kiss on my lips before he turns around and heads back to his desk. When he settles in his chair, he reaches down and adjusts himself. I stop and work to catch my breath before I leave his office and head back to my room to change my panties before we head to his game.

CHAPTER 14

Josh

After finishing with a few items for work, I make my way into my bedroom. I quickly hop in the shower, giving myself a passing once over, knowing I'll take a better shower after the game.

Getting dressed, I head to the living room and find Olivia sitting in an armchair reading on her Kindle. I smile, knowing she's using her birthday gift. Her hair is still damp from the shower, and she's wearing a pair of leggings with knee-high boots and a plain maroon t-shirt, with a hoodie lying over the back of the chair.

I walk up to her and place a kiss on the top of her head. "I'm just going to grab my bag from the gym and then we can head out." She looks up at me with a smile and nods. I do a slight jog down the hallway to the gym and grab my hockey bag, tossing it over my shoulder and grabbing two sticks that are leaning against the wall.

Heading back into the living room, Olivia gets up when she spots me. She grabs her purse and sweatshirt before walking over to me. I open the door for her, and she grabs my sticks as she walks into the hallway. It's like it's the most natural thing in the world for her to grab my sticks before heading out for a game. I smile at the thought that doing this regularly could be considered our normal.

I lock the front door and reach for her hand as we head down to the car. I throw my bag, along with my sticks, into the back of my SUV and move to open the passenger door for Olivia. She gets in and I steal a fleeting kiss before closing the door. I need to keep it quick, otherwise, I'm not sure we'll make it out of the garage, let alone the game.

I round the car and hop into the driver's side, starting the car up. Reaching across, I place my hand on her thigh as I drive us toward the rink.

"When was the last time you went to a game?" I ask.

"Ummm, I went to a Cyclones' game last year with Matt, but I haven't been to one of his games since he was in high school."

"Well, I'm glad you'll be there tonight," I say, smiling and giving her leg a slight squeeze.

"Me too." She smiles, her hand coming to mine.

We pull into the parking lot of the rink, and I open the door for her before we head to the back of the car. I grab my bag and she grabs my sticks again.

"You don't have to carry those, Olivia," I say, reaching for them.

"I know, I want to," she says, pulling them out of my reach.

I shake my head with a smile then close and lock the car. There are plenty of cars in the lot, and I quickly look around to see if there's anyone around us. When I find no one, I grab Olivia's wrist and pull her into me. "One pre-game kiss before we have to act like it's not killing me to not have my hands on you."

A blush creeps up her skin and I lean down, letting her close the distance between us. I kiss her, slowly, enjoying the kiss before I pull away.

"I want another one of those after the game," I tease her.

She looks at me with a mischievous look in her eye. "If you score tonight, I might just drop to my knees and reward you for a job well done," she says before turning and walking toward the front door, leaving me with my mouth hanging open. I have to reach down and adjust myself. The image of Olivia on her knees for me has me getting hard. I never thought she would say something like that, let alone be on the receiving end of the comment.

She looks over her shoulder at me, winking before saying, "You coming or not?"

I close my mouth and hurriedly catch up to her. When I'm right beside her, I say low enough so no one else can hear me. "I'm not sure what I'm going to do with that dirty mouth of yours."

She grins, her face lighting up. "Well hopefully, later, you'll be fucking it."

I never knew Olivia Carter had such a dirty mouth, but I'm loving it. I'm walking beside her with a semi, hoping no one around us can see what her words have done to me.

Inside the lobby, there are screens that show what teams are playing at each rink. Seeing we're on rink two, I lead Olivia through the doors to our right. As soon as we step inside, we are hit with a blast of cold air from the ice. We walk toward the centre of the building, which leads to the dressing rooms and connects all the rinks.

We pass a few guys and I notice the full head-to-toe looks she gets from some of them. It takes everything in me not to reach over and pull Olivia into my side so they all know she's with me, but she's worried about her brother, and I respect that. So, I ball my hands into fists at my side. I may not be able to touch her and show that she's mine, but that doesn't stop me from glaring at each guy who is clearly checking her out.

Turning the corner, I stop right outside the dressing room; I look at Olivia and she's holding her hoodie over one of her arms and is standing there in just her t-shirt and leggings.

"Are you going to be warm enough?" I ask.

"Josh, I've been to plenty of games in my lifetime. I'll survive."

I hear a throat clear beside us and I look over and a couple of our teammates, Nick, Sam, and Luke, are staring at us.

"Hey guys," I say, nodding at them. I look back at Olivia and hear one of them clear their throats again.

I look back at them, and Luke says, "Aren't you going to introduce us?"

I roll my eyes and say, "This is Olivia. Olivia, this is Nick, Sam, and Luke," I point at each of them. They give me questioning looks as their eyes move between Olivia and me. They take their time doing a head-to-toe look over her. The questioning looks don't surprise me. I've never brought anyone to a game with me. My fists clench at my side and Luke notices.

"Hey guys, nice to meet you," she says in her upbeat voice.

They each say a version of 'You too' or 'Same'.

"Olivia is Matt's younger sister," I say, and their eyes widen.

She passes me my sticks and takes a step back. "I'm gonna text the girls. I'll meet you back here after the game. You still take an hour after the game to finish?" she asks as she continues to walk backwards.

"Yeah, I'll text you when I finish."

"Sounds good, score for me!" she says before turning around and rounding the corner towards where we came in.

The guys walk past me, and Luke bumps my shoulder. "Score a goal for her," he says and chuckles as we head into the dressing room. I find my usual spot, dropping my bag and sitting down. Checking my sticks, I decide to re-tape one of them. I remove the tape and begin wrapping it when Matt walks in, dropping his bag beside mine.

"Hey man," he says, sitting down.

"Hey, what's up?"

"Nothing much, you?"

"Same," I say, finishing with my stick and getting changed into my gear.

"So, Matt, I met your sister earlier," Luke calls from the other side of the room.

Matt's head shoots up from what he's doing and looks at me. "Liv's here?"

"Yeah, I thought she would have said something to you," I say.

"Nope, I talked to her earlier, and told her about the game," he says, which surprises me because, based on her earlier comments, she knew we had a game.

"She said the girls are coming."

He looks at me incredulously. "Zoey is coming to a game, really?" he asks, his tone sounding like I just told him the world's biggest joke.

"She said the three of them were meeting her here."

He throws his head back and laughs. "Zoey at a hockey game. Zoey at a hockey game without professional players. Yeah, I'll believe that when I see it," he says through his laugh.

"Your sister is bringing friends?" Luke calls out again.

"According to Josh, here."

"They as hot as your sister?" Luke asks.

I glare his way, and a resounding "Watch it," is called from Matt and me. Luke's eyes get large and look like they might pop out of his head as he puts his hands up in surrender.

"Okay, sister is a touchy subject. What about her friends?"

Nick and Sam look up at that. "How many friends is she bringing?" Nick asks.

"Three," I say, and the three of them look at each other with Cheshire grins.

"Those girls will chew you three up and spit you out," Grayson says, walking in. "Especially Hannah, although that might be fun to watch." He chuckles.

"Just cause she's got your panties in a twist over there, Gray," I say through a laugh.

His head snaps to me. "One, I don't wear panties, *Joshua*, and two, she did nothing of the sort. I work with the girl, and I've seen and heard my fair share of her carnage. Third, I'm not the one living with my buddy's sister."

Everyone's eyes snap to me. "I had the space, and she needed somewhere to stay, plus Hannah has had some interesting things to say." I lean down and tie my skates. "The girls were over for breakfast on Sunday morning, and Hannah does not have anything nice to say about you." He just shakes his head and continues to get ready.

"Really, but you're going to score a goal for her?" Nick adds, and I glare at him.

Matt just laughs beside me. He's used to mine and Olivia's antics when it comes to hockey. "Are you two going to revive your old pre-game ritual?"

Luke laughs. "Josh and your sister have a pre-game ritual?"

Matt shakes his head and chuckles. "Yeah, when we played in high school, Liv was at all our practices and games. They had the same ritual our freshman year through to the last game of our senior year."

"Do you have a pre-game ritual with your sister?" Nick asks. I know he's trying to stir the pot and start shit.

Matt stops tying his laces, thinks for a second, and looks at me. "No, come to think of it, I don't. Seems you stole my sister, dude," he says, humour filling his voice.

I shake my head and stand up. Grabbing my sticks, I head out to the ice to warm up. Olivia and her friends have grabbed some seats on the bleachers right beside our bench. She looks at me as I place one of my sticks behind the bench. I smile at her before heading onto the ice.

I skate a few laps around our half of the ice before getting down on the ice for some stretches. When I finish those, I test the flex of my stick on the ice and then do some practice shots on the net. When the game horn sounds for us to clear the ice, I head to the bench.

"So, what do you say, Livvy, we bringing back our pre-game ritual?" I ask, throwing in the nickname I used when we were in school.

She grins and claps her hands before getting up and meeting me. I grab a pull-top water bottle and place it on the edge of the boards beside her. She makes a fist with her right hand, and I make one with mine. Hers starts above mine and then comes down as mine goes up, and we repeat it three times, then we fist pump three times, we turn and hip bump once and then she grabs the water bottle and sprays my hair. I smile, and she smiles back, and we just stare at each other for a few seconds.

A chuckle from behind me has me breaking eye contact. Her friends are staring with their mouths hanging wide open. I turn and see every member of our team staring; some guys from the other team, and the refs, are watching us. Olivia notices and her entire face turns a beautiful shade of pink; it spreads down her neck to the tops of her breasts.

Matt walks up and claps me on the shoulder with a wide-ass grin.

"Hey Liv." He kisses her on the cheek. "Nice to see you here. I wish you had said something. Although with you two doing your pre-game ritual again, hopefully, that means we'll win this season." He chuckles.

"It was a last-minute decision," she says. "Good luck," she calls as she turns around and joins her friends.

CHAPTER 15

Olivia

Oh my god, I can still feel myself blushing as I return to sit with the girls. I feel their eyes on me. Hannah is the first to say something.

"What in the hell was that?" she whisper-hisses at me. I turn and face them.

"When we were younger, I was at all of Josh and Matt's practices and games. The summer before their freshman year, he was trying to come up with a pre-game ritual. I offered to help, and we came up with that. They won their first game. They did really well in their season, so we decided to keep it up through their senior year." I shrug like it's no big deal, but I remember coming up with that with Josh over that summer, it was hard at times doing it while we were in school and I had feelings for him, but I was able to work through it. Now we're seeing what we can be, and he wanted to do it again in front of his team. I feel the blush that was fading come back in full force.

"You had a pre-game ritual with Josh for four years?" Liz asks.

"Yeah, it's not a big deal," I say and turn back to face the ice.

I feel Zoey's stare on me. She was there in high school. I'm sure she remembers I was at all the practices and games, and I'm sure she also remembers how much I loved our little pre-game routine then, too.

The guys are now skating toward centre ice, getting ready for the opening face-off. Josh is at the centre getting into his stance gripping his stick as he lowers his upper body. Matt's a defenceman and is getting into position too.

Hannah, who is sitting right behind me, leans forward, placing her chin on my shoulder. "It is a big deal, and you are so going to be fucked." She sounds like she's super happy about that.

I turn and face my friends in a quick movement, sending Hannah rearing back. "First, it's not a big deal, and two, I love you guys. I'm glad to have you here, but I actually want to watch this game."

I turn and face the ice again, throwing my hoodie on.

"Babe, you know we don't understand hockey," Zoey says.

"I'll explain the calls, but we will watch this game," I say seriously.

The puck is dropped at centre ice. Josh wins the face-off, sending the puck back and to his right and the guys are skating toward the other team's goal. The puck is passed to Josh, who skates to his left and then passes it to Sam as he skates behind the other team's goal. He gets slammed into the boards, fighting for the puck.

They battle against the boards for the puck, and the other team gets it. It's passed, and they start skating back to centre ice. They cross centre and Matt skates past, stealing the puck and passing it to Josh. Josh connects and skates back to the other team's goal. He shoots and scores in the top right corner. I jump out of my seat, cheering. His team surrounds him on the ice, and he skates up to his team on the bench as he bumps all their fists. He skates down the boards before coming in front of us and he points at me and mouths 'for you'. Once again, I feel the blush across my cheeks and down my neck, remembering the promise I made him in the parking lot.

He returns to the bench and a new line heads out to the ice for the face-off. Zoey is sitting beside me, and shoulder bumps me.

"What was that?" she whispers.

"Nothing," I say, avoiding looking at her.

The puck drops at centre ice again the other team wins it. The play moves along with a hooking call made against our team. The puck drop is now to the right of our goal, our team wins it and sends it flying behind the net, the puck connects with Luke's stick, and he skates to the other side of the ice, he passes to Nick, the puck connects, he shoots, and the goalie catches it in his glove.

The game keeps moving. I explain any calls to the girls and at the end of the first period it is 1-0. The guys all skate off the ice, get water and do a shift change. I look over and Josh is already looking at me with a smile. I smile back, tucking a stray piece of hair behind my ear. One of his teammates calls for him and he looks away.

I turn and face the girls. "So, what do you think so far?" I ask, knowing they aren't really into hockey.

"I think you are in dangerous territory with Josh. I think you could easily fall head over heels for him," Liz says with a serious expression.

"We are seeing where this goes, but we are not telling Matt yet. The last thing I need is to ruin their friendship if this doesn't work out," I say.

"I don't think you have anything to fear," Zoey says. "I think Matt would be happy for the two of you."

The game starts again, and I watch, but my mind is split between the game and what Zoey said about her thinking that Matt would be happy for Josh and me.

At the end of the second period, I stand and look at my friends. "I want some hot chocolate. Do you guys want some?"

"Sure, I'll join you," Hannah says as she stands. "Zo, Liz ,you want some?"

They both nod, and Hannah and I make our way towards the front of the building and upstairs to the bar. I order four hot choco-lates and we wait for the bartender to get them.

"Hey, so about all this stuff going on with Josh. I know we have razzed you about it, but we just want you to be happy and don't want you to get hurt," Hannah says with such a sincere look. I reach and grab her hand that's sitting on the bar and give it a quick squeeze.

"I know. This is all so new—like twenty-four hours new. I don't want to rush anything and make it into more than it is. I want to enjoy what we have and see where it takes us. You know I love you girls for always being there for me. I don't know what I would have done after the whole Drew fiasco if it wasn't for you three. I love you." I pull her into a hug. I know my friends only want the best for me.

"I love you too," she says into my hair before pulling back, keeping her hands on my shoulders, and squeezing. "We will always be here for you."

"I know, I'll always be here for you guys, too."

The bartender delivers our drinks. I pay, and we head back to the game. I pass a drink to Zoey and take my seat. Looking over to the bench I see Josh sitting on the end, looking at me. *You okay?* he mouths. I smile and nod, holding up my hot chocolate. He smiles back.

I turn back to the game. It's still early in the third period and Josh jumps onto the ice. He skates to the other side of the ice, his stick connecting with a pass. He takes the puck to the end of the ice, passing it to Nick, who skates around the net and passes it back to Josh; he has it for three seconds before he fakes a shot to the right and sends a slap shot into the bottom left corner of the net. The girls and I jump up and cheer.

There's five minutes left, the puck drops again, and we watch as the game ends, 2-0 as all the players meet in the centre fist-bumping each other before they all skate off the ice to head to the dressing rooms. The girls and I head over to the dressing room door to talk to Matt and Josh before they head in.

"You guys have dinner?" I ask the three of them.

"Nope, have something in mind?" Liz asks.

"I have to wait for Josh, so I was thinking I'd head up to the bar while they shower and change."

"Sounds good to me. Zo? Han?" They both nod.

"Well, if it isn't our lucky charm!" I hear Matt's voice as he approaches with the team. "I don't think I've seen Josh go that hard in years."

Josh shoulder bumps him. I think I see a slight blush on his cheeks, but that could be from the cold or the adrenaline. "I play just fine, thanks, asshat," he says with a chuckle.

"I think it might have been your pre-game ritual," Matt says, bumping him back.

Josh shakes his head at my brother and stops right in front of me.

"I'll be quick, Olivia."

"Don't worry about it. The girls and I are going to head up to the bar. We haven't had dinner yet. You want me to order you a burger and fries to be delivered in an hour?" I ask.

"That sounds great, thanks."

"Get me one too, Liv. I'll join you guys," Matt says to me, but he's looking at Zoey like he is trying to solve some kind of puzzle.

"Sounds good. I'll see you both in an hour." I look over at Josh. "You played great. I missed this." I hip-bump him before walking away with the girls.

We head up to the bar and grab a spot at a huge high top. We each order a drink and look at the menu. I decide to get the same burger that I'm going to order for Josh and pick one for Matt.

I put my menu down and look at Zoey, who's sitting across from me. Eliza is to her right and Hannah is to my left.

"Zoey, what is going on with you and my brother?" I ask her. Her jaw drops on the other side of her menu and Liz and Hannah look over at her.

"Nothing. Nothing is going on with Matt," she rushes out.

"You know I wouldn't care if you guys wanted to actually date? I just don't want anything to be awkward. You know how important Matt and Gi are to me, and you girls are important to me too. I like that we can all hang out together."

"It's all good, Liv. Nothing is going on with Matt." She picks up her drink and takes a big sip of it.

"Okay, but just know that I'm okay if you guys decide to start something."

Zoey changes the topic, and we move on to a couple of the books that we've read recently, sharing recommendations and talking about our favourites. We eventually order our food. Twenty minutes later, I hear Matt's and Josh's voices as they enter the bar. Looking over, I see them, along with Grayson, Caleb, Nick, Sam, and Luke. I get up and meet the guys at the end of the table. I hug Matt and he kisses my cheek. Caleb and Grayson do the same thing, followed by Josh, who wraps both arms around me and whispers in my ear, "I wish I could kiss you right now."

"Me too," I whisper back.

Josh pulls back, and I wave behind him to Nick, Sam, and Luke.

"I've ordered you two burgers," I say, pointing at Matt and Josh, "but you guys still need to order." I wave at our server, and she notices me right away, nodding. We take our seats with Josh beside me and Matt across from him.

"Girls, this is Nick, Sam, and Luke. Guys, these are my friends, Hannah, Eliza, and Zoey."

They all smile and wave to the opposite sides of the table.

Our server arrives and the guys place their orders, getting a couple of pitchers of beer to share and food.

"So, Olivia, I saw your pre-game ritual with Josh here. I hear you guys did that in high school too," Luke says, leaning over the table and trying to make eye contact with me.

I nod. "Yeah, we came up with it the summer before Matt and Josh's freshman year. It started as something dumb, but when they started winning games, he insisted we keep it up. I was already at all the games, so I didn't see the harm," I say with a shrug.

"What was your pre-game ritual with Matt?" Zoey asks, a little mischievous glint in her eyes.

"We didn't have one. Let's see Matt's freshman year, I think he was too obsessed with trying to impress—what was her name—the blonde," I snap my fingers. "Oh, it was Kimberly De Marco, right? Then your sophomore year, it was the redhead who threw around daddy's money. Samantha, right? Junior year it was the girl from down the street, Rebecca Wilder, and then when she got a boyfriend, it was Cassidy Smith, and your senior year it was Taylor Price, Kennedy Notion, and Kate Kelly," I say.

Josh puts his arm around the back of my chair and leans back, hiding a smirk behind his beer as he takes a sip.

I look at him. "Oh, don't you act so smug there, mister." I elbow him in the side, and he pulls away. "Don't act like you were so perfect. I still remember your nickname from your junior and senior year." He winces and takes another sip of his beer.

"That was years ago, Olivia," he says weakly.

"I have got to hear this. What was his nickname, Liv?" Hannah asks, grabbing my hand, squeezing it excitedly.

"Oh, we don't have to do this," Josh says pleadingly.

I look him in the eyes. "But you were so proud of it in high school." I grin widely, and look at the girls. "For his last two years of high school, the girls called him 'Monster Josh' after he supposedly hooked up with a girl during a party at the beginning of the year."

Their jaws drop, and the guys start laughing. I look over at Josh, whose face is now beet-red, and I know it has nothing to do with the cold or the game. He takes another sip of his beer.

"So, let me get this straight. You were always chasing girls," Hannah says, pointing at Matt, "and you were known for the size of your dick." She points at Josh, and then the girls start laughing, full-on belly laughs. I join them and we all clutch our stomachs as we continue. As our laughing subsides, our server, along with another server, arrives with the first round of food.

"Burger with mushrooms," she asks me. I point at Matt. "Bacon cheeseburgers, medium rare with fries," she says next, and I point to Josh and myself.

"Thanks," I say as she places the food in front of us. "Can I get another Long Island when you get a second?"

"Of course, hun, I'll be right back."

"Thanks."

I turn back to my food. The girls are already digging in. "Did you really order yourself and Josh the same thing?" Matt asks, causing everyone to look at me.

"Yeah, it looked good, plus I know Josh will eat whatever I feed him," I say with a shrug.

"Will he," Zoey says, chuckling and I kick her under the table.

"Yes, not everyone is as picky as I am. It makes it easy." I glare at her, knowing she's thinking of dirty things.

"Olivia is probably the pickiest eater I have ever met," Josh chuckles and I elbow him again.

"Hey, don't pick on me when I have been cooking your dinners lately."

He puts his burger down and hands up in surrender. "Okay, don't poison my food, please," he says with a grin.

Grayson nearly spits his beer out. "Liv, you've been cooking him dinner every night?" Everyone seems interested in this line of conversation. Little grins are on each of the girls' faces and even on Matt's, and confusion on everyone else's.

"Yeah, I'm kind of living with the man. For free might I add. The least I can do is make sure he has a hot meal on the table when he comes home from work. Anyway, I enjoy cooking and I'm not a huge fan of cooking for just myself, so I make enough for four, our dinner and lunch for each of us the next day. I enjoy it. It's not a big deal, really."

"Dude, your sister is living with your best friend, and she cooks him dinner like every night. You're okay with this?" Nick asks from the other side of the table. "I'm not sure I would be okay with that if it was my sister." He shakes his head as the rest of the food is put on the table.

"They've been friends for as long as Josh and I have been. I have no problem with any of it," Matt says as he digs in and finishes off his burger.

"So, you'd have no problem if I asked Olivia for her number, then?" Luke asks Matt.

I stiffen and Josh's left hand finds my leg under the table and squeezes it.

"Liv is an adult and can make her own decisions, but just know that anyone who hurts either of my sisters is a dead man," Matt says with a look of total seriousness.

"I think Josh might beat you to that," Hannah says with a laugh. "I swore I would have to call 911 after the incident with Drew at her apartment. He could have passed out with how tightly Josh held him against the wall."

I look over at Hannah and glare at her. "Let's not talk about doucheface."

"Sorry, babe, but that look on Josh's face was one out of our books. Think Alex Volkov when Christian showed up at Alex and Ava's and Christian was about to threaten Ava so he could see Stella."

Zoey and Eliza point at her. "Exactly like that," Liz says and the three of them start laughing. I feel the heat rise in my cheeks. I remember that night. I remember how hot it had been to have Josh stand up and protect me. At the time, I thought it was just a big brother type of thing, but now I know it must have been more. Josh squeezes my leg again and smiles at me before leaning in and finishing his burger.

Matt points a finger at the girls. "That. That is why I'm not worried about Liv living with Josh. I know for a fact that he will protect her."

I shake my head quickly, before changing the conversation topic, "Matt, Gi and I are getting lunch on Wednesday if you want to join us?"

He nods and throws a fry in his mouth. "Sounds good. Just let me know the details."

"How is Gi?" Caleb asks while picking at his fries.

"Who is Gi?" Nick asks.

"Gi's our younger sister. She's studying public relations at Stanford, she's home for the summer. Gi's good from the last time I talked with her. She just dumped the guy she was seeing. She called him an idiotic, limp dicked, shithead, I believe. Something about being unsatisfied in the relationship," I say.

Matt's face goes red, and I hear choking sounds and chuckles around the table. "One, I didn't even know she was dating someone, and two I don't need to hear about her sex life, or yours, thank you very much. We may be close, but I don't need to know that my sisters are unsatisfied in the bedroom."

"Hey, I didn't say I was unsatisfied," I say with a grin, knowing it will bug him even more. I feel Josh tense a little beside me and look at me with an apprehensive smile.

Matt groans. "Please don't tell me you're back with Drew."

I throw a fry at his head. "God, you idiot, no! I'm not back with that piece of shit."

He throws his hands up in front of him. "Okay, I just wanted to make sure. I don't need to know anything more about your hookups."

Josh runs his napkin down his face. His body is still tense as he says, "I have an early morning tomorrow. You ready, Olivia?"

"Yup."

He flags down the server and gets the bill for Hannah, Liz, Zoey, me, and him.

"You don't have to do that Josh," I hear Eliza whisper to him, he shrugs and whispers back so only the girls and I can hear him. "You guys took care of Olivia after that day with Drew and kept her company tonight. Dinner's on me." He smiles at them.

The girls get up and meet me at the end of the table and hug me goodbye, and they each, surprisingly, hug Josh as well. He hugs them back before meeting Matt and giving him a bro hug. Matt says something to Josh, and he nods. Matt hugs me and we wave our goodbyes to everyone before I follow Josh out to his car.

CHAPTER 16

Josh

I flex and relax my fingers as Liv and I walk out towards my car; I want nothing more than to reach for her hand and lace our fingers together or put my arm around her shoulders and pull her into me, but I can't.

Before we left, Matt thanked me for taking care of his sister. I felt a little guilty for not telling him about us, but I want to respect her wishes. Hearing Matt say Olivia is an adult and can make her own decisions gave me hope he won't kill me when he finds out about us.

We get to the car and I open the passenger door for her, and she hops in. I take a quick look around and when I don't see anyone, I lean in and place a kiss on her lips.

"Hi," I say with a smile before pulling back. "I really needed to do that."

"Me too," she says with a huge grin.

"So what was that comment about being sexually satisfied?" I ask. Her cheeks turn pink again and she tucks a piece of hair behind her ear.

"I just wanted to get under his skin. There hasn't been anyone since Drew, just you."

I lean down and whisper over her lips, "Good. I'm glad." Closing the distance, I give her another quick kiss.

I get in and we make our way back home. As I drive, I keep my hand on Olivia's leg. It feels so natural, driving and being able to touch her so freely. I never want to lose this.

"It was nice to be at a game again. I didn't realize how much I missed it," she says with a relaxed smile.

I give her leg a squeeze. "You're welcome to come whenever you want. It was nice having you there again." I forgot how much I enjoyed having Olivia at our games growing up, to know we always had someone there cheering for us.

When we get home, Olivia helps me get my gear upstairs and into the gym where I hang it up to air out and grab my towels to throw them in the wash.

"I forgot how stinky your gear gets," Olivia says with a laugh.

"Yeah, it can get pretty bad." I grab the fabric Febreze and spray my gear before turning on the fan. She leans the sticks against the wall before heading into the living room.

I meet her in the entryway where she's stopped. When I stop in front of her, she goes onto her tiptoes and wraps her arms around my neck. "I believe I promised you something for that goal you scored," she whispers against my ear. I wrap my arms around her and grab her ass.

Her words and the feeling of her breath instantly have me hard. "I believe you did," I say as I kiss along her neck. I grab her hand and pull away before placing a soft kiss on her lips and leading her into my bedroom. Turning, I face her and place my hands on either side of her face, looking her in the eyes.

"You know you don't have to do anything you don't want to, right?" I ask, needing her to know just how serious I am. I don't want her to do anything out of a sense of obligation.

She looks me straight in the eyes. "Josh, I feel unbelievably safe with you. I know you will never force me to do something I don't want to do. I want to be with you. I want a relationship. I want sexual and emotional intimacy with you. I want it all." She drops to her knees and a salacious grin spreads across her face. "And right now I want to get on my knees and have you fuck my mouth until your cum is dripping down my throat."

God, having Olivia Carter on her knees right now is doing things to me. I don't have the time or mental capacity to analyze it before she reaches up and hooks her fingers into the waistband of my joggers and boxer briefs and drags them down my legs slowly. Once they're around my ankles, I step out of them and kick them to the side. She is staring at me with wide eyes as she takes me in. "I guess there was merit to that nickname," she whispers as she reaches up and wraps a hand around my length. Her fingers don't meet, and she leans forward and licks me from base to tip, flicking her tongue over the tip.

She repeats this and then leans forward and sucks one of my balls into her mouth.

"Fuck," I groan out, throwing my head back and gripping her hair. She releases it and looks up at me with a smile before wrapping her lips around the tip. She takes me in while her hand assists her at my base. I want to be careful with her. I restrain my hips from bucking.

She reaches up with her free hand and grips my hand that's in her hair and she pushes my hand further into her hair, giving me permission. I remember what she said as she dropped to her knees. She wants me to fuck her mouth.

I look down at her and run my thumb along her cheek before my hand returns to her hair and my grip tightens. She nods as much as she can with me in her mouth.

"Relax for me, babe," I say, and she does.

Tightening my grip, my hips buck into her face, and I do just that. I fuck her mouth. I feel the tip of my cock hit her throat as I continue my movements. Tears start at the corners of her eyes, and I wipe them away and begin to pull away, but Olivia's free hand grabs my ass, her nails digging in, and holding me in place.

Her hand continues to work in tandem with her mouth as I move in and out of it. I feel the tingle at the base of my spine. I work myself into her mouth faster, as Olivia twists her hand at my base and the hand that was on my ass leaves and plays with my balls. I'm seconds away from coming. The heat in my body is building and I feel my balls heavy and drawing closer to my body.

"I'm going to come, Olivia," I say, and she moans around me. I feel the vibration all the way through me. That does it. It sends me over the edge and I'm releasing myself in her mouth. She continues to work me, drawing out my orgasm as much as she can.

When I'm done, she sits back on her heels, smiling up at me. She drags her thumb across her bottom lip as she wipes a stray drop of cum and licks it off. I'm currently standing in my bedroom with a t-shirt on and nothing below the waist while she kneels completely clothed in front of me after giving me a mind-blowing orgasm, and probably the best blow job I've ever received. I'm in complete and utter awe as I look at her. I never thought I'd be in this situation, yet here I am. I plan to enjoy every moment of it.

I smile down at her as I hook my hands under her arms and help her stand. I kiss her intensely, licking the seam of her mouth and coaxing her to open for me. Her tongue meets mine when she opens, and I taste myself on her as we deepen the kiss.

I moan into her mouth and tightly grip her hair, angling her mouth so I can completely devour her. She moans as my grip tightens.

She reaches forward and grabs my shirt, pushing it up. I reach behind me and grip the neck of it, breaking the kiss just long enough to remove my shirt, tossing it to the side.

"I can't be the only one naked," I say against her lips. I reach forward and grab the hem of her shirt, pulling it over her head before kissing her again.

I walk her towards my bed and when her legs hit the edge; I help her on to the mattress gently, following her down.

I kiss down her neck and across the top of her breasts. Latching on to one of her nipples through the lace of her black bra, I flick my tongue over the sensitive bud, and she arches her back. I reach behind her and unhook her bra. Leaning back on my heels, I pull the straps of her bra down her arms and throw it onto the floor.

I stare at her, taking in her taut pink nipples and the rise and fall of her chest as she continues to breathe heavily. I lean back down, and my mouth covers her nipple again and I flick my tongue over the tightened bud. She moans my name, and her hand reaches into my hair, gripping it firmly.

I kiss across to the other, doing the same things to that one, releasing it with a pop. I kiss down her body and shuffle off the bed until I'm standing between her legs that are still dangling off the bed.

I take in the sight of Olivia half-naked on my bed with her auburn hair splayed across my comforter, her naked chest rising and falling with her harsh breath, her full breasts and nipples glistening from having my mouth wrapped around them, her soft stomach, and her beautiful brown eyes staring back at me.

She is breathtaking.

I reach forward and put my fingers into the waistband of her leggings and panties. She lifts her hips and I pull them down her legs, dropping them with the rest of our clothing. I continue to stand there as she shuffles onto the bed, placing her head on the pillows. I climb between her legs as she leaves them bent at the knees open, allowing me to look straight at her glistening, pink pussy.

I make eye contact with her as I crawl up between her legs. "You look absolutely stunning, Olivia," I say before placing a reverent kiss on her lips. "I'm now going to worship your pussy the way it deserves to be worshipped."

She moans as she squirms. I kiss my way back down her body until I reach that sweet spot between her legs, allowing my hot breath to cover it before I crawl down and kiss my way up one leg, stopping before I get to the place she's aching for me to touch. I do this again with her other leg. This time I don't stop. When I get to the top of her leg, I lick my way from her entrance to her clit. Her hips buck at the sudden sensation of pressure on her most sensitive place.

I wrap my arm under her leg and put my hand on her stomach, holding her flat to the mattress.

"Josh," she moans as I circle her clit before pulling it into my mouth.

Hearing her moan my name like that has me hard as a rock again, but this isn't about me, it's entirely about her.

"Oh God, yes!" she moans, louder this time.

I release her clit from my mouth and enter her with a finger. "My name is Josh, Olivia. That is the name you will be calling out." I crook my finger, finding that sensitive spot inside of her.

Her hips buck off the bed again. I pull my finger out and enter her again, this time with two fingers. I lean my mouth forward and flick and circle her clit again. She reaches down and grips my hair, pulling my face deeper into her soaked pussy.

My tongue moves faster and faster; she moans louder, her grip tightening in my hair, and her hips buck faster into my face. I don't let up. I need to feel Olivia completely lose control on my tongue, to feel her pussy grip my fingers as her clit pulses under my tongue.

I pull her clit into my mouth again, gently scraping my teeth against it and that does it. Her pussy clenches my fingers as her hips lift off the bed and she is calling out my name like it's a chant that will save her.

I continue to crook my fingers, massaging the sensitive spot inside her as I use my tongue on her clit, drawing out every ounce of her orgasm. I pull back as her moaning subsides and I reach down and give myself a quick squeeze to try to calm my aching cock before climbing back up her body and kissing her.

"That was... That was..." She can't finish her sentence. She continues to work to catch her breath, her chest heaving while she recovers from her orgasm.

"Amazing to watch," I say before kissing her again.

I roll over onto my back before pulling her into me. I kiss the top of her head. After a few minutes, I get up and go into my en suite washroom, clean myself up and brush my teeth. When I return to the room, Olivia is in the same spot on my bed as when I left her. I walk up beside her, her eyes are closed, and I kiss her forehead. "Babe, you should go to the washroom and brush your teeth."

"In a minute," she mumbles. I reach up and brush my hand over the top of her head a few times. "Babe, you're falling asleep. Come on, you can come right back here in a minute," I say, gripping her hand and helping her sit up.

She opens her eyes and looks at me. "I was almost asleep. Why do you have to be so considerate after you blew my mind with that orgasm?"

I lean down and kiss her. "You can come back to bed in sec babe, let's get you cleaned up first."

She lets out a huff and then gets up and makes her way into the washroom. While she's in there, I gather our clothes and place them on the chair outside my closet and return to the bed, pulling the blankets back. I climb into bed and plug my phone in before setting my alarms for work.

When I place my phone down on my nightstand, I look up. Olivia is standing in the doorway of the washroom with her arms wrapped around her centre with an unsure look.

"Babe, come to bed," I say. She looks at me and then over at her clothes on the chair. With her arms still wrapped around herself, she walks over to the chair and starts to grab her clothes. I quickly climb out of bed and walk over to her, putting my finger under her chin, and forcing her to look at me.

I'm not sure what's going on in that gorgeous head of hers, but I can't have her being unsure of us. Not after what just happened in my bed. I don't think I can give that up. I won't force her into anything, but I will fight for this.

"Babe, are you regretting what we just did?" I ask when her eyes meet mine.

Her eyes widen. "No. No, I don't regret it. Do you?"

She seems hesitant when she asks the question. I lean down and place a kiss on her lips.

"I don't regret a single second of it. What's going on in your pretty little head? You seem hesitant."

She tries to look away from me, but my thumb goes onto her chin, holding her head in place. "Babe, what's wrong?" I ask, worried.

"I just want to cover up," she whispers. I'm not sure why she's so worried about this now after I just had her spread naked on my bed, but I want to get to the bottom of this and make sure that she's comfortable.

I release her chin and let her grab her shirt and pull it over her head. It comes down just past her butt, and then I grab her hand and pull her to the bed with me. I sit on the edge and position her between my legs, and grab both of her hands. Looking up at her, she looks everywhere but my eyes.

"Babe, I need you to look me in the eye," I say softly, and she finally does. "Talk to me. What has you freaking out and wanting to cover yourself?"

She closes her eyes and takes a deep breath. Tears form in the corner of her eyes. I use my thumbs to brush them away as they begin to fall. She opens her eyes and when they meet mine, they're full of vulnerability and fear.

"Josh, I'm not skinny. I have a tummy and thick thighs and I don't look like most girls. I like to cover up." She whispers her confession and closes her eyes as more tears fall. "Drew was always pushing me to go to the gym more. To lose weight, to eat healthier. I know that's probably the reason he cheated on me."

A weight drops in my stomach. That she has been made to feel anything other than beautiful kills me.

I continue to stroke her cheeks as tears run down them. "Olivia, you are gorgeous. If you want to cover up right now, that's your choice. If you want me to cover up, I will. But I do not want you to feel like you have to. I want us to be able to have these conversations with each other, to be open and honest with each other. I think you are beautiful, inside and out, and I want you to think the same about yourself."

I pull her mouth down to mine and kiss her softly, slowly, showing her how beautiful I think she is with this kiss. Her fingers go into my hair, and she holds my face to hers as she kisses me back.

"Thank you," she whispers against my lips as she breaks the kiss.

"Babe, you don't have to thank me. My job is to ensure you know how beautiful I find you." I kiss her softly again. "Let's get into bed and get some sleep."

She nods and climbs onto the bed and crawls to the spot beside where I was when she walked out of the washroom. I settle into the mattress and pull her into me until she has her head on my chest, her arm thrown over my stomach, and her leg over mine. I run my fingers through her hair as I listen to her breathing slow until soft snores are coming out of her.

I lay there thinking I would be so lucky to spend the rest of my life like this.

CHAPTER 17

Olivia

I feel the weight of an arm wrapped around me as I stir. The sound of an alarm fills the room. I nuzzle deeper into my pillow as I try to ignore the annoying sound. The weight is removed, and I groan at the loss of heat at my back, and the sound stops. The bed dips and I feel lips kiss my hair and hear a whispered, "Go back to sleep, babe," before falling back asleep.

When I wake up later, I notice I'm not in my bed and pull the blanket up to my neck as I smile at the memories of last night. His smell hits me as I inhale deeply. I get up and grab my leggings before heading back down the hallway to my bedroom to shower.

Once I'm out, I quickly get dressed and grab my phone. Seeing it has a low battery, I grab my charger on my way to the kitchen to get some breakfast. Prepping yogurt and some fresh fruit, I settle at the kitchen island before starting chores for the day. I decide to bring Josh lunch. I quickly whip something up before packing it up.

The SkyTrain ride to his office is quick. The sound of high heels echoes across the white marble in the expansive lobby. I make my way to the elevator bank and take one up to the top floor of the building.

Stepping off the elevator, I walk to the receptionist's desk. "Hi, I'm looking for Josh Lincoln's office," I say when she looks up at me with a polite smile.

Her eyes take me in before she says, "Is he expecting you?" I swallow, wondering if it was a bad idea to stop by.

"No, my name is Olivia. I brought him lunch."

I hold up the bag I'm carrying and hope she'll let me back to see him. Maybe I should have called or texted him to make sure it was okay that I dropped by. He could be in a meeting or out of the office. I fidget, playing with the hem of my shirt. This was a bad idea, but I've come this far. No sense in turning back now.

She looks at me again like she can't believe I'm here for him, but she picks up her phone and makes a call.

"Kate, I have an Olivia here for Mr. Lincoln..." Her face contorts at whatever she hears on the other end of the call. "Okay, sure... Alright Kate."

She looks at me again with a look of confusion. "You can go in. Just walk straight to the end of the hallway."

She points down the left side of her desk.

"Thank you," I say with a smile before heading down the hallway.

A thin blonde woman about my age is sitting outside Josh's office when I arrive. She smiles widely and rises from her desk when she sees me.

"You must be Olivia," she says.

"Yes, and you're Kate?" I ask cheerily.

"Yes. It's lovely to meet you. He just finished his call so you can head in." She points to his door.

"Thank you, Kate."

I knock lightly before opening the door. When I step inside, he shifts his head from what he was looking at on his computer. When he notices it's me, he smiles.

"Hey, what a lovely surprise. What brings you here?" he asks as he rounds his desk, pulling me in for a kiss.

I hold up the cloth bag. "I thought since I didn't make dinner last night and you don't have any leftovers, I'd bring you lunch today."

He leans down and kisses me again. "You didn't have to do that, babe, but I am happy to see you."

He pops his head out and speaks to Kate. "Kate, go ahead and take lunch." He comes back in, closing the door, and we move to the couch he has set up with a coffee table in front of it.

He's in a large corner office with floor-to-ceiling windows that look over the city. A large wooden desk sits on one side with his computer and stacks of folders. His degrees are in frames on the bookshelves behind his desk, along with photos of him with friends and family, and tons of books. Across from his desk are two expensive-looking wingback chairs. A tall plant sits in the corner beside the couch and there is a door that leads to what looks like a private bathroom.

"So, I made a chicken Caesar salad, dressing on the side, and homemade chocolate chip cookies for after," I say as I unpack the food.

"Sounds amazing." We each grab a salad and add dressing to it before getting comfortable on the couch.

"How'd you sleep last night? You kind of woke up when I left this morning, but you seemed to pass out again quickly," he chuckles.

"I slept great, you?"

"Best sleep I've had in a long time." A huge grin lights his face and I blush. This is nice, having lunch with Josh in his office, and being able to show up unannounced to surprise him.

"What have you done this morning?" he asks as he continues to eat his salad.

"I showered, had breakfast, stripped your bed and put it in the washer, started a new book, made lunch, and researched some things I want to do in Whistler," I say.

"You didn't have to strip the bed, babe," he says, holding his fork in his salad.

"It's all good, I don't mind."

"Okay, but really, you don't have to do that." He studies me before continuing, "What did you find that you want to do in Whistler?"

I pull my phone out and hand it to him. He places his salad on the table and takes it from me. "You're really into your lists," he teases.

I shove his shoulder lightly. "I believe seeing my last list is what contributed to me getting on my knees for you, so don't tease."

He holds his hands up in surrender. "You're right, I do love your lists. Send both of them to me. I'm going to book our room for Whistler. Are you okay with one room?" he asks.

"Yes, should I not be?" I ask, unsure. Does he not want to share a room with me after last night? Did he not enjoy it the same way I did? Questions swirl in my head and Josh obviously sees that my mind is taking me all over the place because he places a hand on my leg, bringing me out of my thoughts and back to the conversation.

"Babe, no. I just wanted to check with you. I don't want to push you into anything," he assures me. "I want to know that you're comfortable with everything we do. Trust me, I want to share a room with you."

I reach out and grab his hand. "Josh, you're not pushing me into anything I don't want. How about this? I promise you I'll tell you if I want to slow down or take a step back and you do the same. We promise to communicate with each other."

He leans forward, grabbing my lunch and placing it on the table before placing his hands on either side of my face. "Promise," he says before kissing me. He kisses me deeply, his tongue seeking entrance to my mouth. I open for him, moaning. My hands grip his shirt and I shift closer to him, kissing him back just as severely as he kisses me.

There's a knock at the door, and we break apart. He straightens his shirt, fixing where my hands gripped the fabric, and adjusts himself in his pants.

"Come in," he calls.

The door swings open and a middle-aged man with a receding hairline in a black suit and navy tie stands in the doorway. He has a folder in one hand. When he sees Josh and I sitting on the couch, he looks a little taken aback.

"Oh, I'm sorry Mr. Lincoln, I didn't realize you were busy," he rushes out, an uncomfortable look on his face.

Josh stands up. "It's all good Liam. This is my girlfriend, Olivia. She stopped by for lunch. Olivia, this is Liam. He works in our financial department."

Holy shit, did Josh just refer to me as his girlfriend in front of one of his staff? I am Joshua Lincoln's girlfriend, and he is my boyfriend. Butterflies fill my stomach. This is my biggest teenage dream come true.

Standing up, I run my hands over my dark-coloured skinny jeans and reach out and shake Liam's hand. "Nice to meet you," I manage to get out as my mind continues to run a mile a minute, processing this.

"You too, ma'am," he says with a polite smile. "I have the quotes for you regarding the Samson file you requested," Liam says to Josh and hands him the file.

"Thanks, Liam."

Liam turns and leaves Josh's office, closing the door behind him.

I turn to Josh and smile. As he places the folder down on his desk, looking up at me, his brows draw together. "What?" he asks.

"Girlfriend, huh?" I say with the biggest grin still plastered on my face. He walks forward and wraps his arms around my waist, his hands sitting just above my ass.

"What else would I call the girl that I am exclusively seeing, and is sleeping in my bed?"

"I like it," I say as I go up on my tiptoes and kiss him.

"I'm glad. I like it too."

He leans down and kisses me again. Wrapping my arms around his neck, my fingers play with the hair at the nape of his neck, and his hands grip my ass firmly. He pulls me into him and kisses me deeper. Our tongues meet, and we explore each other's mouths. No matter how many times we kiss, it still feels like the first time, like we still have so much to learn and explore. I feel myself getting wet as his hands continue to grab my ass and our bodies mould together. I break the kiss, attempting to catch my breath, and he leans his forehead against mine.

"Josh, as much I want to continue this, I should let you get back to work. I'll see you when you get home tonight."

I give him a soft kiss before extracting myself from his arms. I pack the containers from our lunch and grab a cookie before handing him the rest of them.

"For you," I say.

Stepping out of his office, I call, "Bye," closing the door behind me. It takes everything in me to hold myself together as I make my way down the hallway to the elevator. As soon as I am on the elevator and by myself, I do a little happy dance.

Before settling on the couch with my Kindle, I text the girls gushing about Josh calling me his girlfriend at lunch and my phone buzzes with a text from an unknown number.

UNKNOWN NUMBER

Liv, baby, can we please talk? I want to figure this out and make us work. I've given you space to cool down. Let's talk and figure this out. I love you, baby.

I stare at my phone open-mouthed. It's Drew. I blocked his number after we broke up, so he must have gotten a new number. The last thing I want is to talk to him, let alone try to work this out. How can he claim to love me while he was fucking another girl? I take a screenshot and send it to the group chat.

LIV

Look what the fucker just sent me.

ZO

Are you fucking kidding me? I could kill him with my bare hands.

LIZ

Calm down, Zo, I don't think any of us want to be bailing you out of jail, but I agree, he is a fucker. Ignore him, Liv. You are happy with Josh. You deserve so much more than Drew. We are here for you.

HAN

If he hobbled his way into my ER, I'm not sure I would save him. Cheating scum are the worst. We're here for you. Liv. Girls night again Saturday?

LIV

Can't, Josh and I are heading to Whistler this weekend.

LIZ

You will have to keep us updated about your weekend.

Olivia

On Friday Josh only heads into work in the morning and is back by 1 p.m. so we can get on the road before traffic gets bad on the Sea-to-Sky highway. As I pack, I get another text from Drew. They've been coming all week.

You lose service partway up the Sea-to-Sky, so I downloaded a couple of playlists to make sure we have music. We take our bags down to the car and head out onto the road. You can't have a true road trip without a stop at Tim Hortons, so we stop at Timmies and grab an Ice Capp and a bagel for me, and a double-double for Josh.

We listen to music, and I sing along to some of my favourite songs while Josh drives one-handed, resting his other hand on my thigh.

I look out the window and take in the view as we make the two-hour drive. I watch the ferries on the water and the ripples of waves that trail them and the birds flying overhead. I can see how the highway winds its way up through the mountainside away from the ocean. It slowly takes you out of the bustling city and into the calmness that is the small towns between Vancouver and Whistler. It's been a long time since I've been up this way and I'm reminded of the beauty of the drive.

Pulling into Whistler, we drive through the village and Josh takes us straight to our hotel to get checked in. Walking into the expansive lobby, the black and grey marble floors shine. In the centre, the hotel logo is engraved on the floor in gold.

We make our way over to the reception desk, hand in hand, where a pretty, blonde girl with bright, blue eyes greets us.

"Good afternoon. Do you have a reservation?" she asks as she bats her eyelashes at Josh.

"Yes, I have a suite booked under Lincoln," Josh says. He squeezes my hand and pulls me into his side, his hand resting on my hip. His thumb makes slow movements against my skin.

"Yes, of course. Here we go." She looks between Josh and me, almost as if wondering if it's just the one room. "We have you in suite 1505. This suite only has one bed," she says, giving Josh a questioning look.

"Yeah, my girlfriend and I only need one." He smiles and looks back at me, flashing me a wink.

I take a step back from Josh and wrap an arm around myself. Is this how it will always be? People questioning Josh being with me? Will I have to watch other women check him out everywhere we go and have them think they would be better with him? Drew always said I was so lucky to be with him because it would be hard to find someone who could look past my plus-size body and love me. It took a lot of work to be able to push those thoughts out of my mind and ignore him, but was he right? Would Josh prefer to be with someone like the pretty, thin, blonde receptionist? Will he also try to change me?

"Okay, well, here are your keys. The elevators are just to your right here around the desk. Please let us know if you need anything. Enjoy your stay with us." She smiles tightly as she hands Josh the keys. Stepping inside the elevators, Josh presses the button for the top floor, and we follow the signs to our room. Waving the key over the lock, he holds the door open for me. I only make it a few steps in before I stop, taking in the room before me.

I am standing in what looks like a living room, with a couch and two chairs in front of a large flat-screen TV. A dark brown table sits in front of a window with a view of the village. Along the wall behind the couch, there is a counter with a coffee maker, microwave, and a mini fridge hidden below. The door leading to the bedroom is to the right of the TV. To the right of where I am standing is a huge washroom. Sitting in the centre of the wall is an opulent clawfoot tub and to the left is a walk-in shower.

Josh leans in behind me and places his mouth beside my ear. "You like it?" he whispers, and I nod slowly.

This room seems like way too much. I can't believe he got us a room like this. I would have been fine with a regular hotel room. A room with a basic bathroom, a bed, dresser, and TV. He's gone above and beyond for this trip so far.

"Good. Let's put our stuff down and get ready. I made dinner reservations."

I turn and look at him. "You did?"

"Yeah. Now let's get ready." He kisses me before moving around me and making his way into the bedroom. I follow behind him and place my bag on a chair in the corner of the room. A king-size bed sits in the centre of the room with a dresser and flat-screen TV across from the foot of the bed. A door connecting to the washroom is to my right..

"Where are we going?" I ask.

I did pack something nice, just in case. I always make sure I have everything I might need when I go on a trip, but I want to make sure I dress appropriately.

"It's a surprise," he says, trying to hide his smile.

"Well, what should I wear?"

"Whatever you would like, Olivia."

I shake my head. "What are you wearing, Josh?"

"Dress slacks and a button-up."

"Okay. What time do we need to leave?"

"Our reservation is for 6:30 p.m., so we should leave here at 6:15 p.m."

I nod, still a little stunned by all the effort he's put into this weekend. It seems like too much to just check items off my list.

"Sounds good," I say as I walk over to where he is sitting on the edge of the bed. I step between his legs, and wrap my arms around his neck. He tilts his head back to look at me.

"Thank you for bringing me this weekend, Josh," I say, leaning down and kissing him softly. He wraps his arms around my waist, pulling me further into him.

My fingers grip the hair at the back of his head, and I lean into him more. His tongue licks at the seam of my lips. I open for him. I moan into the kiss as his right hand tightly grips my ass.

I break the kiss, working to catch my breath and rest my forehead against his.

"I should probably get ready." I smile at him.

"Yeah," he says, but neither of us makes a move to separate from one another. I stand there staring into his beautiful green eyes. There are flecks of brown that float around the deep emerald rings. I lean down and give him a quick peck before slowly removing myself from between his legs. Josh looks at me with a playful frown on his face.

"I'm going to get ready, and then we'll go to dinner," I say as I head to my bag. I grab my make-up bag and hair straightener and head into the washroom.

"I have a quick errand to run Babe, I'll be back before we have to leave. I have my phone if you need me." He meets me in the washroom and gives me a swift kiss before heading out of the hotel room.

Once I hear the click of the hotel door, I grab my phone, open the group chat with the girls, and hit the video call button. While it rings, I plug in my hair straightener and turn it on.

Hannah answers first, "Hey girl!" Then Zoey and Eliza answer.

"Hey guys!" I say when all their faces appear on the screen.

"Aren't you supposed to be in Whistler with your boyfriend?" Zoey asks, her brows pinched together in confusion.

"I am. He had to go out for an errand quickly and I am getting ready for the dinner reservation he made us."

Grabbing my phone, I make my way toward the window in our bedroom and flip the camera. "Look at this view he got us. We're in an actual suite with a living room and a separate bedroom."

I pan over the view from our bedroom window and head back into the washroom before propping my phone against the mirror. I separate my hair and use the straightener to curl it.

"He went all out," Liz says, her voice soft.

"Yeah, this room is really nice, and he made a reservation for dinner somewhere nice enough that he's wearing suit pants and a button down. I'm not sure what our plans are for the rest of the weekend."

"Josh will probably have it all planned out. Don't worry about it. Enjoy it," Hannah says.

"Yeah, I'm glad I packed something I could wear to dinner tonight, though. He didn't say anything before we left." Josh left the plans for this weekend a secret.

"Well, what did he say when you asked him what to wear tonight?" Liz asks.

"He said I could wear whatever I want to."

The girls are silent on the other end of the call. I can hear the wheels turning in their heads, but no one says anything. "What?" I ask.

"Nothing, babe." Zoey pauses and a soft smile crosses her face. "Just, that's nice."

"We should let you go. Have fun this weekend, we will catch up this week. Take lots of pictures for us," Liz says.

"Will do, bye."

"Have fun. Bye," Hannah and Zoey say before they all hang up.

I put some music on and finish my hair and makeup. Moving back into the bedroom, I grab a change of clothes and bring them into the washroom with me closing the door. I know Josh saw me naked on Monday, and I've slept beside him this week, but I still don't feel completely comfortable with him seeing me naked, especially in the harsh light of the hotel room. When I was with Drew, I was only naked in front of him in complete darkness. I was never comfortable exposing myself in the harshness of light. He was always making comments about how I needed to take better care of myself, go to the gym, and eat healthier. I'm realizing more and more just how much he slowly chipped away at my self-confidence over the years.

I change into a black pencil skirt and a teal blouse, tucking it into my skirt and pulling it up just a bit so that it folds over the top of my pencil skirt, which sits at my waist. I touch up my perfume and head into the bedroom to change into black flats.

When I open the door, all thoughts leave my brain. I didn't hear him come in, but Josh is standing at the end of the bed in a pair of black dress slacks and a light blue button-down. He's left the top few buttons undone and I can see his perfectly sculpted chest. I watch as he rolls up the sleeve of his right arm to his elbow to match his left. As he rolls up the sleeve, I see the veins and muscles move with the movements. His hair is unruly, like it usually is when he's been running his hands through it. He looks sexy like this, watching how confident he is in himself. I see it every day in the way he walks and does everyday tasks. I squeeze my legs together, hoping to quench the desire growing between them. I feel my skin getting warm and a flush move up my neck and across my cheeks.

Josh looks up at me with a smile and does a head-to-toe look over me as well, and his smile broadens. He looks over me again and clears his throat. He adjusts himself in his slacks and I smile to myself.

"You look amazing, babe. Are you ready to go?" he asks.

I close the distance between us and grip the open parts of his button-down. "You don't look so bad yourself. Just let me put my shoes on and I'm ready."

I go onto my tiptoes to kiss him, and he wraps his arms around my waist, resting his combined hands on the top of my ass. He kisses me intensely, but slowly, savouring it. "Let's get out of here," he whispers across my lips.

He steps away, allowing me to move around him and grab my shoes. I quickly slip them on and grab my purse, throwing my phone inside. It's warm enough outside that I shouldn't need a jacket.

We leave the room and Josh grabs my hand. Arriving in the lobby, I look at the girl who checked us in and smile and wave as she watches us leave hand-in-hand.

We walk a few blocks until we reach the centre of the village. There are people all around, going between shops and heading into restaurants. Josh leads us toward an elegant restaurant, the outside walls made completely of windows. He opens the front door, gesturing for me to enter. The hostess takes us straight to our table. The atmosphere is expensive and romantic. Soft music plays, the lights are low, and candles flicker on the tables with enough space between them to offer privacy.

Josh pulls my seat out and kisses my cheek once I'm seated. I sink into the comfortable black leather chair and run my hands over the black tablecloth. The fabric is soft under my fingers and feels expensive.

We browse the menu, selecting drinks, an appetizer to share, and our entrees. As our server leaves after delivering our drinks, Josh asks, "So, why Whistler?"

I take a sip of my drink. "It's been a while since I've been here.

When I came last time, it was only for a single day. I wanted to come again and enjoy it more. We live so close to all these amazing places, and we rarely take advantage of them. I want to change that this summer. I want to find myself again, to be really, truly happy again."

"You're right. We do live so close to all these amazing places. I'm glad I get to enjoy them with you this summer." He leans forward, placing his forearms on the table. "Were you not happy before, Olivia?"

I roll the question around in my mind. I don't know how to articulate how I've been feeling the last few years. I know I haven't felt like myself. I don't think I was super happy. While I was with Drew, I stopped doing some of the things I used to love because they didn't align with his interests. I lost myself in the relationship. I don't think I truly realized it until I was out of the relationship.

"I haven't felt like myself the last few years. I dropped some of the things and connections I had, and because of that, I wasn't truly happy. I just was." I lift my right shoulder.

Josh seems to ponder over what I've just told him. It's a lot to tell someone that you've spent the last few years unhappy and were just going through the motions of life. I'm not sure how I would process that if one of my friends or Josh told me the same.

"Are you finding that happiness again?"

"Yeah, I think I am."

I take another sip of my drink. That's the truth. These last few weeks I've felt a change in myself. I've spent more time with my friends and my family. I've been taking time to read and go for walks. Being with Josh makes me happy, the way he always checks in with me, making sure that I'm comfortable with what's going on. The simplicity of eating dinner together and sitting on the couch with him after he gets home from work. How he lets me be entirely myself when we're together. No talks of me attempting to change some-thing about myself to better suit him. All these changes in my life have me feeling incredibly happy.

As we eat, he tells me about the small travelling he did to surrounding cities while he was at Harvard, and I tell him about some of the stupid stuff Hannah, Zoey, Eliza, and I got into while at UBC. When we finish our entrees, my phone starts to buzz in my purse. I silence the call without checking it and we continue our conversation. My phone rings again and I check it in case it's important. It's an unknown number, which means it's likely Drew, and I silence it immediately.

"Is everything okay?" Josh asks, concern filling his voice, but it also feels like his voice is so much further away than it is.

I don't want to talk to Drew ever again. There is no reason for us to. I've been ignoring his texts. I thought that might be enough of a hint. The phone rings again. I silence it and turn my phone off, this time putting it back in my purse. The messages Drew has been sending have been a mix of *I miss you, we can work this out, you won't find anyone better than me*, and *do you really think someone is willing to help you get better?* Every time I read his texts, I feel like the world around me is closing in. I feel like everyone is staring at me and judging. I can't make out what is going on around me. My body feels tense and I just want to fall in on myself.

"Babe?" Josh asks.

He grabs my hand, giving it a quick squeeze, pulling me from this horrible feeling and back into the present as my body slowly relaxes.

I look up and meet his eyes, concern filling them. What would he say if I told him that Drew was trying to contact me again, that he's been texting me and now he's calling? I don't want to ruin our trip, so I decide I'll tell him later.

"Yup, all good. It's nothing important." My voice is soft and unsure. He gives me a skeptical look, but doesn't press the issue and nods.

We decide against dessert. Josh pays our bill, and we head out into the warm summer night. Josh slips his hand into mine as we walk back to the hotel. We find a bench across the street from the hotel entrance and sit. I stare up at the sky, taking in the view of the mixing colours as the sun begins to set. The actual sunset won't happen for a bit, but I enjoy watching the sky change slowly from day to night, the transition period when the world often moves from the hustle and bustle to a more relaxed state as people head home and spend time with family and friends, to curl up with a book, or watch movies.

"It's peaceful here," Josh says softly beside me.

I lean against his side, and he wraps an arm around me. I feel safe in this spot. I've noticed that just having Josh near me makes me feel safe.

"Yeah, it is. I enjoy living in the city, but I enjoy the silence and nature of being further away too. It makes sense that this place is so popular for tourists."

"Do you always want to live in the city?"

"I don't know. I know I want a proper backyard when I have kids. I don't want them only surrounded by concrete. If I could find that and afford it in the city, I might consider it."

I turn my head and look at Josh, who is already watching me with a small smile as he sits and stares at me.

"What?" I ask as he continues to watch me in silence.

He shakes his head. "Nothing, you ready to head inside?"

"Yeah." He gets up and offers me his hand as we walk to our room in comfortable silence.

CHAPTER 19

Josh

Dinner with Olivia tonight was more than expected. It was hard to hear she's been unhappy these last few years, but hearing her say she's finding happiness again and hoping I'm a part of that made my heart race. Conversation with Olivia flows so easily, but we can also enjoy silence comfortably, like we did, sitting on the bench across from the hotel.

Listening to her talk about wanting kids made me realize even more that I want that with her someday. I want us to be a family, to see little girls who look just like her running around our home, little boys skating on the ice like I did as a kid. Realizing that, I just sat there and stared at her. I know how crazy it all sounds, too. To be thinking about wanting to marry her and have kids when we have only started dating. The thing is, we have this foundation of friendship we are building our romantic relationship on. We were friends as kids; we grew apart afterwards, and when we reconnected, it was seamless. I've never questioned where I stand with her, or how genuine she is with our interactions. She has always been uniquely her.

We are silent as we make our way, hand in hand, to our hotel room. Olivia and I have been intimate, but haven't had sex yet. I want it to happen naturally, but I can feel myself getting nervous as we get closer to our room. With Olivia, this is different. Not only have we known each other for years, but she is someone I can see a future with. Someone I want a future with. I want marriage, a big house with a yard for the kids and dog to run around in. The last thing I want to do is screw this up.

It doesn't feel like we just started dating. All the years of our friendship have led us to the place we are now and having her live in my place for weeks before we started dating adds to this feeling. I felt comfortable having her in my space. I looked forward to going home and spending time with her. This has all been building gradually and I know that means this is going to make it all so much better.

Opening the door, I allow Olivia to walk into the room first. She kicks her shoes off beside the entertainment unit in the living room before positioning herself on the couch. I follow her into the room and toe off my shoes beside hers. I lean over Olivia, placing a swift kiss on her lips, pulling back, and letting my lips hover just a few centimetres from hers.

"I am going to take a shower, I'll be right back." I place another quick kiss on her lips after she nods.

Turning on the shower, I move quickly, dressing in a pair of gym shorts when finished. Liv grabs a few items I assume are her pajamas, and heads into the washroom.

When I hear the water turn on, I head over to my bag and start grabbing some things I packed for the weekend. I grab out a few unscented candles, placing them on the dresser across from the bed and a few on the windowsill, and place two lavender-scented ones on the nightstands beside the bed. Inside the nightstand, I place the new box of condoms I bought. I bring up a playlist and connect my phone to my portable speaker. I make my way around the room, lighting the candles, turning off the lights, setting the scene for a romantic evening.

I close the bedroom door as I hear Olivia open the washroom door and her intake of breath. She looks around the room slowly before her eyes land on me.

She is standing there in a maroon negligee, with lace around the triangles of fabric covering her breasts. Her hair is dry and loose down her back and her face has been washed of any makeup she had on earlier.

She is absolutely gorgeous.

We walk towards each other, meeting halfway. I look down at her as I wrap my arms around her back and she wraps hers around my neck.

"You look beautiful," I say before kissing her softly. "I want you to know I don't expect anything from you, but I do want to spend a romantic night in bed with you. Maybe watch a movie or we can just talk and listen to music. Whatever you want as long as we can do it together."

Olivia plays with the hair at the nape of my neck before she rises on her tiptoes and kisses me. It's a slow and intimate kiss, one that says so much more than words could possibly express.

Her lips leave mine, but she stays on her tiptoes as she whispers, "I know, Josh. I know you won't push me. I feel so unbelievably safe with you. I trust you."

Those words cause my insides to warm; it's all I could ever ask for.

She drops back down, grabs my hand, and leads me to the bed. She pulls the blankets back and climbs on, kneeling as she faces me and wraps her arms around my neck again. Pressing her lips to mine, this time she kisses me more hungrily. Her tongue licks at my lips and I open to her, groaning into the kiss as she grips the hair at the base of my neck. Her nails scrape my scalp.

My arms wrap around her, and I step closer to the bed, pulling her into me. Her ample breasts press against my chest, and she shuffles closer to the edge of the bed, trying to get closer. My lips move from hers and trail along her skin. I kiss softly across her jaw and down her neck.

I pull back and look her in the eyes. "Olivia, you are entirely in control. If you want me to stop at any time, I just need you to tell me, and I will stop immediately. Tell me you understand."

She nods. "I need words, babe. I need to know one-hundred-percent that you understand."

"I understand, Josh."

"Good, now why don't you climb into the middle of the bed for me?"

She complies immediately, shuffling to the centre of the bed, laying on her back. I take a few seconds to take her in as she lies there, spread out for me. The light from the candles flickers over her, creating an ethereal look. She is breathtaking. I climb on the bed, settling beside her, running a hand through her hair, admiring how soft it feels between my fingers.

"You are stunning, Olivia; I don't ever want you to question that."

She looks at me like she's trying to find some sort of sign I am not telling her the truth. It only solidifies in my head that people in her past have made her feel like shit about herself and I will do everything I can to fix that.

I kiss her again, but more urgently this time. Using my tongue to part her lips, I explore every part of her mouth, tasting every inch. Her tongue joins mine. My hand moves into her hair, gripping it at the base of her skull, causing her to moan. I tighten my grip a little and she moans again, her hands gliding over my naked chest and around to my back, her nails scraping at my skin looking for purchase.

I kiss across her jaw and down her neck, finding the sensitive spot behind her ear that drives her crazy. She writhes under me. Moving down, I nip at her collarbone and then lick across the same place. I kiss my way down her chest to the tops of her breasts, softly kissing the tops before flicking my tongue over her hardened nipples through the fabric of the negligee. She moans as she pushes on my chest, breaking the contact of my tongue against her nipple.

I lift, looking her in the eyes to see if she wants me to stop. My chest is rising and falling harshly, and my cock is hard and straining against my boxer briefs. She doesn't say anything, just pushes me so I'm forced to lie back. She takes off her negligee so she's completely naked for me and moves to her knees before she kisses across my chest. Her tongue darts out and flicks my nipple, pulling a low groan out of me. I never knew that was something I enjoyed before, or maybe I didn't, and it's just Olivia that does it for me. She smiles against my skin as she continues to kiss my exposed skin. Feeling her soft lips on my skin is driving me wild, but I hold back from taking control again. Olivia needs this.

When she reaches just above the top of my shorts, her hands grip the waistband of my shorts and boxer briefs. I lift my hips to help her pull them down. Sitting back on her heels, her gaze drags over my body. Starting at my face, she slowly works her way down over my chest, down my abs, before settling her eyes on my erection. Her eyes flick to mine before she leans forward and flicks her tongue across the slit at the pre-cum gathered there. I throw my head back and groan, fisting the sheets.

Olivia sucks the tip into her mouth, swirling her tongue around it, before taking in more of me. One hand grips the base of my cock while the other reaches up and rolls my balls. Her hand squeezes tight when she has me reaching the back of her throat. She repeats this several times and I find myself trying to repeat hockey stats to prevent myself from finishing prematurely. It's not working. I reach out and grab her head, forcing her to release me from her mouth.

She smiles and I move to be able to kiss her.

I whisper over her lips, "I don't want to come yet babe, lay down for me. I want you to come on my tongue."

She quickly moves to lie on her back and spreads her legs for me. When she's in position, I move between her legs, using my hands on each thigh, holding her legs open for me. While keeping eye contact with her, I slowly lick from her entrance up to her clit, circling it once. I repeat the motion two more times.

She bucks her hip under me. "Josh, I need more, please... More."

Hearing her beg for me is everything. I remove one hand from her thigh and enter her with one finger, bending it until I find that one spot that will drive her crazy. I apply pressure before slowly moving my finger in and out of her as my tongue flicks over her swollen clit.

Her hips buck faster, and I remove my finger, adding another as I push back in. My fingers and tongue move faster, and she tightens around my fingers and her moans sound more breathless.

"That's it, sweetheart. Come for me. Come on my tongue like a good girl."

That does it. She bucks furiously as she calls my name in a chant, reaching her arms out, looking to grab anything that will ground her. I work every second of her orgasm out of her before I remove my fingers and climb up her body. Making eye contact, I place my fingers in my mouth, licking every last drop of her off them.

I reach over to the nightstand and open the drawer. Grabbing a condom out of the box. I look at Olivia before lifting it to my mouth to open the wrapper. I wait for a signal from her. A slight nod is all I need before I rip it open and roll it down my painfully hard cock. I pump myself a couple of times before Olivia reaches down and positions me at her opening.

"Please Josh, I need you. I need you inside me," she says as she lifts her hips to meet me.

I slowly press inside of her, watching her face as I sink inch by inch deeper into her, stretching her. Her face contorts as she adjusts.

When I'm fully inside her, I run my hand over her hair. "Are you okay?"

We make eye contact for a few seconds before a huge smile spreads across her face. "Yeah Josh, I'm perfect. I need you to move. I need you to fuck me."

I slowly pull out of her and push back in, burying my head in her neck as I pick up my pace. I relish in the feel of her wrapped around me as the room fills with the sound of our moans and skin slapping skin. I feel her building, almost tipping over the edge.

I grab her right leg and lift it high around me, allowing me to fill her deeper. My hand seeks hers as our fingers lace around each other's. I hold her hand beside her head as I kiss her. This is so much more than sex. She tightens even more around me, the nails of her free hand scratching at my back so harshly I know it's going to leave marks—but marks I'm proud of.

"Yes, Josh, there. Right there." She gasps.

I fuck her harder, hitting the same spot over and over. Within seconds, her back is lifting off the bed as she tightens around me, calling my name. Her orgasm sets off my own. I groan her name into her neck as I empty myself into the condom. We stay connected as we both work to catch our breath. When I am breathing normally, I roll over onto my back and link our hands together. We roll to face each other and her smile is blinding..

"Wow, that was... I have no words," she says.

"Yeah. I agree," I say, leaning in for a kiss.

Getting up, I make my way to the washroom, removing the condom, and cleaning myself up before returning to the room. While Olivia takes my place in the washroom, I blow out the candles and make my way to the bed. I climb under the covers, hoping Olivia will come to bed how she wants and won't feel the need to cover herself.

When she comes out of the washroom, it's pitch-black in the

room except for a small sliver of light coming through the curtains. She pads her way to the bed and climbs in, curling into my side. I run my hand slowly up and down her back, stopping to play with the ends of her hair at times.

"That was amazing, Olivia," I whisper into the dark. She throws her leg over mine and wraps an arm around my stomach, pulling her body closer to mine.

"Yeah it was," she says.

We continue to lie in silence, and I listen to her breathing even out as she falls asleep on my chest, and I follow not long behind her.

CHAPTER 20

Olivia

I moan as Josh flicks his tongue against my clit before moving down to lick from my entrance back up, circling my clit with his tongue. I feel myself get wetter and wetter with each move his tongue makes. This dream feels so realistic, but I keep my eyes closed, not wanting to lose this feeling. He sucks my clit into his mouth, causing my back to arch off the bed. He inserts a finger in me, bending it and hitting that sensitive spot.

My eyes fly open. This feels all too real to be a dream.

I look down at my body and see Josh's head between my thighs. When he notices me looking at him, he lifts his head with a mischievous grin as his finger continues to pump in and out of my wet pussy.

I feel myself building and building. I'm on the edge of the cliff. His head dips back down and his teeth scrape along my clit, sending me over into an all-consuming orgasm, calling out his name. He continues to work me as I slowly come down from the high.

Josh withdraws his finger and climbs up my body, placing kisses along my skin as he moves up. He flicks his tongue over each nipple as he reaches my breasts. He continues to kiss up my body until he reaches my lips. He kisses me deeply; I taste myself on him as his tongue seeks every part of my mouth. His erection presses into my thigh. He breaks the kiss and plants a few chaste kisses on my lips.

"Good morning, babe," he says when I open my eyes and connect with his deep green ones.

A smile spreads across my face. "Good morning, indeed."

I reach over to the nightstand as Josh did last night and grab a condom before ripping it open with my mouth. Reaching between our bodies, I roll it down his erection as Josh places soft, slow kisses down my neck and across my collarbone. Once it's on, he positions himself at my entrance and thrusts inside me. My hands move to his back, feeling his muscles move as he moves inside me. My eyes roll back in my head as he fills me.

He moves at a fast and unrelenting pace. "God, you feel so good, Olivia. So tight and warm," he moans into my ear. He lifts himself up, keeping us connected as he lifts my hips. His pace picks up. His thumb moves to my clit and circles it, applying just the right amount of pressure to it.

"Look at how well you take me, Olivia," he groans as I tighten around him. His thumb continues to work my clit, my pussy clenches around his cock, and my hands fist the sheets.

"That's it, be a good girl and come for me, Olivia." His words send me over the edge and stars burst in my vision.

Once I'm coherent again, Josh pulls out of me. "On your knees."

I comply as quickly as my satiated body will let me. Once I'm on my knees, he places his hands between my shoulder blades and pushes my face into the mattress. I feel so exposed, but so desired at the same time. I comply, twisting my head to the side as I arch with my chest pressed against the mattress and my ass in the air.

He repositions himself at my entrance and grips my hips so tightly I know there will be bruises, but I want them. I want that reminder of how much Josh wants me at this moment. He thrusts into me, reaching a spot deeper than he did last night. I moan his name as he works in and out of me.

"God, Olivia. You look so good taking my cock like this. Such a good girl."

I clench around him. His words make me wetter than I already was. I hear how wet I am as he continues to fuck me from behind. His hand comes down on my right ass cheek as the sound reverberates through the room. I moan at the feeling. His hand rubs at the sting, soothing it.

"Do you like that, Olivia? Do you like when I spank you while I fuck you from behind?"

I moan, surprised by the effect his words have on me.

He spanks me again. "Words, Olivia. Tell me how much you like it."

"I... I... I love it, Josh," I breathe out before his hand connects with my ass again, sending me right over the edge in the most powerful orgasm I've ever had.

My vision goes black and all I see are spots of white. I feel liquid gush down my thighs as my pussy tightens around Josh. He groans my name as he comes with me, leaning over my back, panting.

He places soft and reverent kisses along my back before pulling out slowly. I mewl at the loss. He lies beside me, staring at me. His chest rises and falls, and I lower my hips down to the mattress and feel a wet spot.

Josh reaches over and brushes my now unruly, just-fucked hair behind my ear before giving me a quick kiss.

"I'm going to shower before we head out for breakfast."

I smile and nod. My legs feel like jelly, but as soon as he's inside the washroom, I quickly shuffle off the bed and see a giant wet spot. I don't know what happened, but I remove the sheets and throw them into a pile on the floor at the foot of the bed and then pad into the washroom behind Josh.

He's standing in the shower with his head tipped back. I stand there for a few seconds, enjoying the view of the water running down his body, and how the droplets move through the creases of his muscles. Stepping into the shower, I reach for his soap, rubbing it between my hands, getting it sudsy. I wash his chest. Josh smiles and tucks a piece of hair behind my ear, kissing me. After the kiss, I move my way down his taught stomach and legs.

When I make my way back up his body, I kiss him before having him turn and give me his back and repeat the same process. I reach for the shampoo and start massaging it into his scalp. I've always enjoyed having my hair played with and my scalp massaged. Washing Josh and washing his hair feels more intimate than the sex we just had.

When I'm done, I move him under the water, running my fingers through his scalp, helping the shampoo rinse out. I pull him out of the water, reach for my conditioner and add it to his hair.

When I reach for my bar of soap, Josh silently takes it out of my hand and does the same thing for me, washing every inch of my body slowly and with care. When he finishes with my body, he moves on to my hair, massaging my scalp with shampoo, and then applies conditioner to the ends. Once I rinse my hair, Josh pulls me close to his body, resting his forehead against mine with his eyes closed. I close mine too and enjoy the feeling of being under the water with Josh.

"I'm glad we're here," he whispers.

I open my eyes and look at him. There is so much behind his beautiful eyes, but I can't fully decipher it.

"Me too," I whisper back.

He reaches around me and turns the water off before stepping out of the shower and wrapping a towel around his waist. He reaches for another towel, wraps it around me, and places a kiss on my forehead. We dry off and head into the bedroom, where Josh notices I stripped the sheets off the bed. He turns to me with a questioning look.

"How come you stripped the bed?"

Heat climbs my cheeks. "Um, I just wanted to make sure they gave us clean sheets," I say before making my way to my bag and digging in it for clothes. He walks up behind me and wraps his arms around me as he leans down and places his mouth right beside my ear so I can feel his hot breath on my skin.

"You mean because you squirted all over my cock as I fucked you from behind?" he whispers.

I tense in his arms, and stop looking for clothes. Josh turns me to face him. He looks me in the eye and brushes my hair behind my ear.

"Babe, it's nothing to be embarrassed about. If anything, it makes me proud I made you do that."

"I've never done that before." My voice is soft, and I try to look anywhere but his face.

He grips my chin and forces me to look him in the eyes. "Babe, that just means I did something right where other men haven't. Please don't be embarrassed because I plan to make you do that again and again."

He holds eye contact with me before I nod slightly. He kisses me as he reaches around me and slaps my ass.

"Good. Now let's get dressed so we can head to breakfast. I was thinking we would hit up a museum and then grab some lunch supplies before heading on a walk and having a picnic."

"Sounds good!"

Getting dressed, we head out and Josh takes me to do everything I could possibly want before we return and he proceeds to give me three more orgasms, and I fall asleep in his arms.

"This is what I loved to do in the park by my old place, lie in the grass listening to children play, people riding their bikes, the water lapping nearby, watching the clouds overhead," I say wistfully. Josh holds my hand as we lay here, taking in our surroundings. My free hand plays with the soft grass and I inhale deeply, enjoying the clean, fresh air. There's a certain stillness being here.

"I don't take enough time to enjoy this. Maybe we can do that together. Enjoy more time outdoors."

I turn my head toward him with a smile. "I'd like that."

We continue to lie there for a while before we return to the car and leave Whistler.

When we get home, Josh drops our bags in the laundry room before we make our way into the living room, and settle onto the couch.

"I have to get a few things done for work. I'm going to grab my laptop. I'll be right back."

I nod, grab my Kindle and the blanket off the back of the couch, and get settled in. I continue the book I was reading before we left. Josh comes back and settles on the middle cushion, throwing his feet up on the coffee table. We're silent, enjoying each other's company. I eventually nod off. I wake to Josh holding my Kindle, his eyes scanning over the screen and changing pages.

"Um, what's up?" I ask, watching him carefully, not sure which of my books he's chosen.

He looks at me with a smirk. "So, this is what you like to read?"

I blush. "What book are you reading?"

I need to know just how intense the book is. Is it one of my dark romances? Small town? Feel good?

"The one you were reading when you fell asleep."

My blush deepens. I was reading a dark, mafia, arranged marriage romance. Josh places my Kindle on the coffee table and leans over me.

"Is this where some of those ideas on your list came from? Does reading these books make you wet, Olivia?"

My mouth goes dry. I look over Josh's shoulder, not being able to look him in the eyes, and nod slightly. He grips my chin and forces me to look at him. "Olivia, look at me. I like to hear the words. Do these books make your pretty pussy wet?"

"Yes."

"Good to know. Let's go to bed."

He backs up, giving me space to get up off the couch. I kiss him, but before I can make it down the hall to my bedroom, Josh grabs my wrist, stopping me. I face him with a confused look. He steps closer, wrapping his arms around me.

"I want you in my bed, Olivia. I want to fall asleep and wake up next to you every day. We can move your stuff into my room tomorrow, but please spend the night with me."

I wrap my arms around his neck, reach up and kiss him softly. "Yes, let me grab a shower and something to sleep in, and I'll be right in."

"Okay." With a peck he walks down the hall to his room, and I return to mine, showering, throwing on a negligee and grabbing my phone charger before making my way to Josh's room. I settle on the bed, plug my charger in and check my phone for the first time all weekend. I have a couple of texts from Matt and Gi. The group chat with the girls has tons of texts, and I have missed calls and texts from Drew's new number.

I open the texts from Matt first.

MATTY

Hey how's your weekend?

Hey, I heard from Zoey you went out of town for the weekend. Is everything all good?

Just checking in. Can you text me back?

LIV

Yeah, headed up to Whistler for the weekend. It was on a list of things I want to do this summer. Home safe and sound.

MATTY

Sounds good. Glad you're home safe.

GI

Hey, Matt's been asking where you are. Are you good?

Apparently, he called Zo. She said you went away for the weekend. He's a little worried cause you didn't say anything.

LIV

All good, home safe and sound. Just texted Matt.

GI

ZO

Liv, Matt called looking for you. I just said you went out of town. Didn't say anything about Josh, but you owe us all the deets.

HAN

Yes, tell us everything!!!!!

LIZ

When will you be home?

ZO

Did you have sex?

How was it? It had to be good. It must have been. This is Joshua Lincoln we are talking about.

HAN

He is probably a god in bed.

LIZ

I would have to agree.

HAN

I bet no woman leaves his bed unsatisfied. 🔥 🔥
🔥

ZO

They probably leave wanting more 😊

Liv, we need to know now. I can't not know.

HAN

Liv???

Liv, are you getting it that much you can't respond??? 😏 🔥 💦

LIV

We are home now. Dinner tomorrow night? I'll give you the details then!

LIZ

In

HAN

ZO

UNKNOWN NUMBER

Baby, please let me explain.

Please talk to me. I went to your place, and you weren't there.

I went by your place again and they said you don't live there anymore. Can we please meet?

Liv, please meet me.

I can explain. Let's meet. I love you, baby.

LIV

Leave me alone. I'm not your 'baby' anymore.

Josh walks into the bedroom as I send the text to Drew. He's wearing a pair of gym shorts low on his hips and is using a towel to dry his hair.

"You okay?" he asks with a worried expression.

"Yup, just answering all the texts I missed this weekend. I guess I forgot to tell Matt and Gi that I was heading out of town for the weekend, so he sent me a few texts, and I guess he reached out to Zo, who told him. I just told him I went to Whistler, though I didn't say we went together." I avoid his eyes at the last part.

He throws his towel into his laundry hamper and climbs into bed beside me.

"You know I respect your decision not to tell Matt about us yet, but I want you to know that when you're ready, I'll be there with you to tell him."

"I know, and I want you to know I'm not ashamed or anything. In fact, it's the complete opposite of that. I just don't want to ruin your relationship with Matt. I want to see where this goes first."

He leans over and kisses me slowly, his hand moving into my hair, angling my head for him to kiss me more thoroughly.

"I know, babe. I'm proud to be yours and that you're mine." His words send a thrill through me. I never thought I'd hear those words from him. I settle into the bed and wrap my arms around him, placing my head on his chest.

"Good night, Josh."

"Good night, Olivia."

CHAPTER 21

Olivia

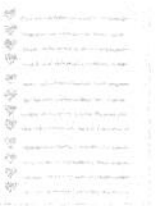

T he next morning, I wake to an empty bed. I settle in with some breakfast and work, texting Josh around lunch time.

LIV

Hey! I'm just getting ready to make myself lunch. I won't be home for dinner. I'm going out with the girls. Do you want me to leave you some food for dinner???

MY MAN

Hey, no need. I think I'll meet up with the guys for a beer. Have fun tonight. Let me know if you need me to pick you up.

LIV

Okay, have fun. I'll take an Uber if needed.

MY MAN

Okay, have fun, be safe.

LIV

You too

I do some reading and chores before getting ready to meet the girls. We chose a nice restaurant not far from Josh's place. I dress in a skirt, a nice blouse, and a pair of black flats.

As I walk to the restaurant, a gentle breeze sweeps through the streets, helping cool the warm summer air and bringing the smell of food out of the nearby restaurants. When I get there, Zoey is already there with a table. I join her, pulling her in for a hug before sitting across from her.

"Okay, so we will keep the juicy details for when the girls get here, but how are you?" Zoey asks.

"Good, really good. I'm glad we went. I think I would have enjoyed it solo, but it was better being there with him." My cheeks hurt from how big my smile is.

"I'm sure it was. I haven't been in a while, but I remember it being a nice place to escape."

"Yeah. It was gorgeous and relaxing. A pleasant change of pace from the city. How are you?"

"Good, nothing special on my front. I did get that unexpected call from your brother wondering where you were. I didn't say anything about Josh, but I'm surprised he didn't call him."

"I never thought to ask him if Matt called. Although I wouldn't be surprised if Matt used it as an excuse to call you. He seems to do that a lot."

I'm not sure what's going on with Matt and Zoey, although I wouldn't have any problems as long as I'm not left in a tough position if something happens. I want them both to be happy. I think they'd be good together, but I don't think my brother is ready for a committed relationship quite yet.

"Nothing is happening between Matt and me, but if that changes, I promise to tell you. You've already given us permission."

Liz and Hannah come in, hugging both of us before taking their seats. We order drinks and a few appetizers. As soon as our server leaves, Hannah claps her hands together. "Okay, tell us everything."

I settle into my chair and turn and face the three of them.

"So, after our Facetime, we went out for dinner and went on a short walk around before getting back to the hotel. When I was in the shower, he lit candles and put music on. He then proceeded to make me come several times. In the morning, he woke me up with his face between my thighs, and he then fucked me until I came twice." I feel the blush creeping up my neck and face and I lean in closer, dropping my voice to whisper, "He made me squirt. I've never done that before, and he was so proud of that."

The girls are looking at me with slack jaws. Hannah is the first to recover.

"He made you do something no other man ever has? Wow, he must be good."

I nod. "He's good, but it was not just the sex, it was the dirty talk too, and uhhh... He spanked me too."

"He really is helping with your list," Eliza says with a gleam in her eyes.

"Yup, that's three things off the list so far. There's something else though, not Josh-related." I play with my napkin, deciding how to go into this new topic. "Drew got a new number and has been texting and calling me. He wants to talk. I sent him one text to leave me alone, but otherwise, I've ignored him."

Concern fills their faces as they look at me. "Babe, let us know if you need us to do anything. We are here for you. Maybe you should tell Matt and Josh, though," Eliza says.

I shake my head and spin my drink on the table. "I don't want them to worry about it. It's my problem. I have to deal with it." I don't want to be that girl who is always running to her brother or boyfriend because they need help. I already did that right after the breakup when I needed somewhere to stay. I need to handle this myself.

"You know they won't view it that way. They will want to know and want to help you," Hannah says.

"If it gets worse, I promise to say something. Until then, I want to keep it just between us."

The girls exchange looks before conceding the point.

Our food is delivered, and they catch me up on their weekends. I tell them about the small birthday party my parents are throwing for Matt at their place this Saturday, and they all say they'll be there. We spend the rest of dinner talking, laughing, and drinking.

We hug goodbye outside the restaurant and the three of them head to the train while I walk back to Josh's. It's a warm summer night, warm enough for me to be fine without a jacket, and the sky is so clear you can see the sliver of moon. I make my way slowly back to the apartment. When I get upstairs Josh is sitting on the couch with a beer, watching sports highlights.

I walk over and kiss him hello. "Were you waiting up for me?" I ask.

"Of course. I needed to know you were home safe. How was dinner with the girls? How are they?"

I settle beside him on the couch, facing him. "They're good. Zoey is doing an internship at a firm downtown right now. Liz is busy at work, but enjoying it, and Hannah has been busy in the ER. They're going to be at Matt's birthday party on Saturday. How was dinner with the guys? How are they?"

"Oh, that's good. They're good. We have a game tomorrow, and they wanted to know if you'll be there. I told them I didn't know, to which they said they hope you are 'cause they think you're our new good luck charm."

I throw my head back and laugh. These big tough guys think I'm their good luck charm.

"Yeah, I'll be there. Just let me know what time we have to leave. I'm beat. I'm going to head to bed."

I kiss him before heading to his room. Josh follows shortly behind me, pulling me into his chest and cuddles behind me.

We slip into a routine the rest of the week, including my phone blowing up with texts from Drew, all of which I ignore in the hopes he'll get the message and leave me alone. Despite spending every night in Josh's room, I haven't moved my things in there yet. He hasn't pushed me and has given me the space I need with that decision.

On Friday, I call Matt, wishing him a happy birthday and he goes out with Josh, Caleb, and Grayson. On Saturday, Josh and I go shopping to get Matt's gift; I find an off-season sale on Cyclone jerseys and get him one, while Josh gets him an extravagant bottle of scotch.

Dressed in a casual summer dress and sandals and Josh in a pair of shorts and a short-sleeved button-down, we grab the gifts and head downstairs. Zoey is meeting us there later, but Hannah and Eliza are getting a ride with us to my parents' place.

The drive to my parents is easy. They live only a few streets away from Josh's parents in the same house that Matt, Gi, and I grew up in. Josh gives me control of the music, so I put on mine and the girls' collective playlist, and we jam out. The entire time he drives, Josh has his hand on my thigh. I can tell the girls notice, but don't say anything. When we get to my parents, Josh parks on the street outside their house and opens the car doors for each of us. We make our way up the steps to the front door and my mom opens it before we even have a chance to knock.

"Liv, how are you?" she asks, pulling me into a hug.

"I'm good, Mom." She releases me and hugs Eliza and Hannah before catching sight of Josh, who's standing at the back of our group.

"Joshua, look at you. How are you?"

She hugs him as well before dragging us all into the house. When I get inside, there are a few people here already. I find my dad and hug him before moving around and finding Gi and Emily sitting in the kitchen. I come up behind Gi and hug her tightly.

"How is my baby sis?" She holds onto my hands and squeezes them.

"Good, how are you? How was your trip to Whistler?" Emily looks at me when Gi says that.

"Um, it was good, spent a lot of time walking and enjoying the fresh air, and hit a museum too."

"You went to Whistler last weekend?" Emily asks with a smile.

"Yeah," I say, she's still smiling at me. She must know Josh went too, but thankfully, she doesn't say anything.

"How's school, Em? Josh mentioned you are taking a few summer classes to finish early."

"Yeah, it's going well. I'm hoping to finish at least a semester early, but we will see."

Matt and the rest of the guys file into the kitchen shortly after. The guys are carrying cases of beer, and they each make their way around, giving Em, Gi, and I a kiss on the cheek before heading outside to the deck. Matt comes to Gi and me and we jump out of our seats and pull him into our sibling group hug, making sure we squeeze him nice and tight.

"Happy birthday, Matty," I say before giving a cheek kiss and Gi does the same.

"Thanks guys, I'm glad you're both here."

"Nowhere else I'd be," I say and Gi says, "Same."

My dad comes up behind Matt, slapping him on the shoulder. "Food's ready. Let's head outside."

Everyone shuffles outside and finds a seat, and we all load our plates with food. As we eat, laughter fills the backyard. I sit back in my chair and enjoy the feeling of having a group of people I care about all together in the same place, enjoying good food and each other's company.

When Zoey shows up, she walks through the sliding glass door with a gift bag, stopping between Josh and Matt. She hands Matt the gift and whispers something to him, which Josh hears. Both men push their chairs back and make their way inside the house.

Everyone takes notice but leaves them be. Zoey does the rounds, saying hello to everyone before making her way towards us. Just before she gets to where we're seated, I hear raised voices coming from inside. I push my chair back and make my way towards the house. Zoey grabs my wrist and stops me.

"Liv, you might not want to." Her face is etched with worry.

"What's going on?"

"It's not a big deal."

When the voices get louder, I look at Zoey and then back at the house. She knows I'm going to go in, so she releases my wrist and follows. When I make it to the front door, all the blood drains from my face and I stop dead in my tracks. Drew is standing outside my parents' front door. Josh and Matt are both working to get him to leave, but he won't budge. He notices me standing there and calls my name. Both Matt and Josh look over their shoulders at me. Their faces are full of concern at what this encounter will do to me. I feel and hear everyone else making their way inside to see what's going on.

"Liv, baby, please let me talk to you."

"Drew, no. I'm not your baby anymore. Leave me alone."

"Liv, we can work this out. We love each other, we were moving in together. Can we at least talk? Let me explain."

Josh's hands fist at his side, and Matt is standing straight as an arrow. The muscles of his back are tense as he listens to our exchange. I walk closer to the door and place a hand on each of Matt and Josh's arms before stepping between them.

"No, Drew, we will not be talking, and how dare you show up at my parents' house during my brother's birthday celebration? You have no right. You need to leave now."

"Not until you talk to me. You won't answer my calls or my texts. We need to talk."

The air hums as both guys tense even more behind me. "You think, maybe, that's because I have nothing to say to you? That I don't want to talk to you, that I don't want you in my life?"

"Baby, please let me explain. I want to go back to what we were. I want to move in together. Where are you living now? I know you're not at your old place."

"Explain what, Drew? How I walked into your apartment when we were supposed to go sign the lease and found you fucking some blonde? How it had probably been going on for a while, and I wouldn't be surprised if you were fucking her or someone else on my birthday? We will never live together. You need to leave my family's house and leave me and them alone. I don't want to hear from you again."

He reaches out to grab my hand, but before he makes contact, Josh has his wrist and twists his arm behind his back. "She already told you to leave. Matt and I have told you to leave. You need to respect that and get the fuck off this property, and you better well remember what I told you the last time you showed up at her apartment."

My body is completely tense from head to toe, being this close to Drew again, and having everyone hear about what went down. Josh gets Drew out of the house and Matt follows to make sure he leaves. I feel the walls closing in on me. There is a vice-like grip on my stomach and throat. I work to get more air into my lungs as I stand in the entryway.

I turn around and see everyone looking at the entire exchange. Zoey and my mom help usher everyone outside back to the food and I collapse on the floor, crying as all the tension leaves my body. Josh sits next to me, pulling me into his chest allowing me to cry it out. His hand works through my hair the way he's learned I like, and he kisses the top of my head as he whispers that everything is going to be alright.

"I've got you, babe. It's going to be okay. I'm right here." His hand continues to work through my hair when I hear the front door open.

I see Matt standing there. I sit up and wipe the tears from my eyes.

"I'm sorry he ruined your party, Matt," I say in a small whisper.

He crouches in front of me and runs his hand over my head in the same way Josh was just doing. "Don't worry about it, Livvy, it's not your fault. He's gone. It's all going to be okay."

I nod and he helps me stand and the three of us make our way back to the party. Before we get outside, Josh stops me. "Just let me know when you want to go and we will leave, okay?"

I nod and grab his hand, giving it a quick squeeze before heading out to join everyone.

CHAPTER 22

Josh

I manage to keep myself calm on the car ride home because Hannah and Liz are in the car. When we get back to our building, we all say our goodbyes before they make their way to the train and Olivia and I head upstairs. When I finally close the front door, I pull Olivia into a hug, kissing the top of her head.

"Why didn't you tell me he was contacting you, babe?" I ask.

Her body tightens in my hold and I move my hand through her hair to help her relax. After a minute, I feel the tension slowly leave her.

"I didn't want to drag you into it. It's my problem. I should figure it out myself."

I loosen my arms around her and move back so I can look into her eyes. "Look at me, babe, I am here for all of it. I am here to support you with everything. Olivia, we no longer have your problems and my problems. We work together and lean on each other. Okay?"

She looks into my eyes for a minute before closing hers and nodding as her arms come around me again and we hold each other for a few minutes.

I lead her to our bedroom. Even though she hasn't moved her stuff, I still view it that way as she sleeps with me every night. When we step into the room, I close the door and stand in front of her.

"I would like to cross off an item from your list. Do you have a preference, or can I pick?" I ask.

Her cheeks pinken, and she plays with the side seam of her dress. "You can pick."

I lead her towards the bed, lean down and kiss her. I grip her hips, pulling her into me so her curves melt into the hardness of my body. She opens her mouth to me and wraps her arms around my neck. I hold her like I never want to let her go because I don't.

Every aspect of being with Olivia feels right. I kiss down her neck and she tilts her head, allowing me more access. When I reach that spot behind her ear, she moans, and it vibrates through her entire body. My hands find the hem of her dress and I drag it slowly up her body before dropping it on the floor. Reaching behind her, I unhook her bra and slowly bring it off her shoulders and down her arms before dropping it with her dress.

My hands reach out and cup her breasts, feeling their weight in my hands as I roll her nipples under my thumbs. Her skin is soft, and she reacts to my every little touch, sending thrills through me.

This woman is magnificent, and I get to call her mine right now, and if I have my way, I'll get to call her mine for the rest of my life. I'll give her my last name. She will be the mother of my children, and we'll grow old together. I will get to experience moments like this with her for the rest of our lives.

Leaning forward, I flick my tongue over a nipple. She thrusts her breast into my face. I move to the other, sucking it into my mouth and releasing it with a popping sound. "Your tits look so pretty wet from my mouth," I say against her skin before I drop to my knees in front of her.

I help Olivia spread her legs, allowing me access to the sweet spot between them. When they're far enough apart, I move my face right into her wet heat, my tongue finding her clit through the fabric of her panties. I taste her through them. She is absolutely soaked. My fingers grab the waistband of her panties and pull them down, helping her step out of them. I move back, flicking my tongue over her clit. She moves onto her tiptoes, grabbing fistfuls of my hair before arching her back and pushing her pussy further into my face.

I insert one finger into her slowly, knuckle by knuckle, until it's fully inside her. When it is, I slowly work it out, each time picking up the pace. She continues to moan my name and buck into my face, seeking more friction. Inserting another finger into her, I feel her stretch around my fingers as I find that sensitive spot inside her. Her breathing picks up, and she begins to clench around my fingers. Before she comes, I pull my fingers out and insert a third, slowly, allowing her to feel the stretch. I work her slowly and her grip on my hair tightens even further.

When I feel her close, I remove my mouth and look up at her. "That's it, baby, come for me. Be a good girl and come on my fingers and face."

I give her clit one more flick and her body begins to convulse. I reach up and hold her up as she rides out her orgasm.

When she's done, I help her onto the bed, positioning her near the top. When she's settled, I head into my closet and grab two ties. She opens her eyes and looks at me, seeing the ties. Her pupils dilate even further. Walking to the bed, I wrap a tie around each wrist, securing it, before attaching them to the headboard.

"Are you okay?" I ask her.

When she nods, I quickly remove my clothes before climbing onto the bed between her legs. I lean down and kiss her, making her taste herself. I go to reach for a condom in the drawer of my nightstand when she shakes her head.

"I'm clear and I'm on the pill," she whispers.

I look into her eyes and see a sense of vulnerability there. God, I would love to feel her bare. My body hums with anticipation and a feeling I can't quite name. I've never done this with someone else. I've never been one for a lot of one-night stands, but I have always used a condom.

"Are you sure?"

She nods vigorously. "Yes, I want to feel you completely. I need to fully feel you. I don't want anything between us."

I kiss her again, slowly trying to communicate my feelings for her through this kiss.

"I'm clear. I've never gone without," I whisper against her lips.

I position myself at her opening before slowly thrusting into her, feeling every inch of her pussy gripping my cock. When I'm fully inside, she wraps her wrists around the ties once and lifts her legs, wrapping them around my hips. I squeeze my eyes shut, feeling her hot, slick pussy bare like this has me on edge. I can't come yet, but she's clenched around me and I'm on edge.

I groan. "God, you feel amazing, Olivia. I want it like this every time," I whisper into her ear. She nods her head against mine.

I slowly pull out before thrusting back deep inside of her. I lean down and wrap my lips around her right nipple as I continue to move in and out of her dripping pussy.

"Yes, Josh, yes... Yes... Just like that."

I move to her left nipple and one hand reaches between us and my thumb finds her clit, circling it and applying the pressure I know she likes.

"Olivia, come for me. Be my good girl and come. Soak my cock," I tell her.

She clenches around me. A few more swipes of my thumb, and she falls over the edge. I don't relent. I quicken my pace as the sound of slapping skin fills the room with her moans. She tightens again, and she's over the edge again. This time I follow with her, groaning her name as I empty myself inside her.

When the air begins to re-enter my lungs, I reach up and untie her wrists from the headboard. I kiss her cheek, then her nose and eyelids, before I place a kiss on her forehead. I crawl off her and head into the washroom, cleaning myself before grabbing a washcloth and wetting it with warm water.

Standing in the doorway to the bedroom, I watch Olivia lay on the bed with a satiated smile, enjoying the sight.

I make my way back into the bedroom and use the cloth to clean Olivia up before climbing into bed with her.

"Is that something you want to do again?" I ask her.

She turns to face me with a smile and a blush. "Yes, Josh. You can tie me up again."

She kisses me slowly, her hands going into my hair. It feels like her kiss is saying so many things. That she is happy. This is exactly where she wants to be, that I am who she wants, and I hope I'm right.

"Josh, wake your ass up, man!" I wake to the sound of Matt walking through my apartment calling for me and Olivia stirs next to me. She turns and faces me when Matt's voice comes out again. "Do I need to drag your ass out of bed?"

She bolts upright and climbs out of bed. Grabbing her clothes, she runs into the bathroom, closing the door. I grab a pair of joggers, throwing them on and go into the bathroom. Olivia's face is full of worry.

"Josh, he can't see me like this. He knows what I wore yesterday. This isn't how I want him to find out.

I nod before saying, "I'll take him to the balcony, so he doesn't see you. Come find us after you've changed." She nods, and I kiss her before heading into the living room.

As much as I love Matt, he's my best friend and the brother I never had, he's fucking up my chance at morning sex. I'm not going to push Olivia into telling her brother about us, but I hope she decides to tell him soon because it's killing me that I have to find a way to sneak her out of my bedroom.

Matt is sitting in the kitchen with a cup of coffee. I make myself a cup before turning to him.

"Good morning. What do I owe for this early morning impromptu visit?" I ask.

"I need to talk to you about last night," he says. I nod and motion to the balcony and he follows me. Not exactly where I thought this was going to go, but I agree that Drew needs to be handled. I see Liv make her way down the hallway while Matt has his back turned.

"What about last night?"

"Drew—did you know he was contacting Liv? She hadn't said anything to me. I had no idea he was bothering her."

I shake my head. "No, I had no idea. Last night she told me she didn't want to bother us, that it was her problem and she had to deal with it herself. I think she feels like a burden with everything that's happened, and she wants to stand on her own two feet."

Matt looks at me for a few seconds before letting out a deep breath he seems to have been holding in.

"Man, I want to be there for her. She is my sister. She's not a burden. I want her to know that."

"I think it will just take some time. Over the last month, I've realized that some people have done some terrible things to her self-esteem, and Drew probably did the worst of it. She'll get better. She's been smiling and joking, so I hope that means she's happier."

The door to the balcony opens and Liv steps out in a new sundress, her hair brushed up in a ponytail. "Hey Matt, what's up?" She walks over and hugs him before smiling at me.

"Not much, just needed to talk to Josh. How are you?"

"Good. Better after last night," she smiles at him.

He wraps his arm around her shoulders and pulls her close to him, kissing the top of her head.

"I'm glad. You know I'm here for you, right? Always, no matter what, you can always tell me anything."

"Yeah, I know. I just don't want to burden you," she whispers.

"You are never a burden, Liv. Please know that."

She nods, and he places a kiss on her forehead before releasing her.

"You want to hit the batting cages?" Matt asks me.

"Sure, let me grab my gear and we can head out."

I head into the gym, grab my gear, and meet Matt by the front door. Olivia is in the kitchen making herself coffee, and it takes everything in me not to go over and kiss her before walking out the door. Instead, I settle for calling out goodbye before heading down to my car with Matt.

When we get to the batting cages, we pay our entrance fee and make our way inside. Matt sets himself up and starts hitting the balls as they are launched his way.

After a few hits, I ask, "You all good? You're quieter than normal and you're swinging that bat like it's done something to personally offend you."

He lets out a deep sigh and swings the bat at the ball that was just released.

"I feel like I've let Liv down. I should have said more to encourage her to leave Drew before it got to this point. I keep thinking that if I had said something earlier, she wouldn't be experiencing this pain. I worry Gi is going to go through the same kind of pain, and I won't be able to do anything about it. I feel like I'm failing as the older brother here."

I can't believe he's feeling this way, because I sure as shit know his sisters don't think that. As his best friend, I need to get Matt's head out of his ass and make him see this situation for what it is.

"Matt, you can't believe that. When your sisters need support or help, you're the one they turn to. They know that you're there for them. I'm sure that Olivia is thankful you didn't say anything to her about Drew, that you supported her and her decision and were there for her when she needed you. I know that if either Olivia or Gianna needed you, they would call you and they know you would drop whatever you were doing to help them. You can't beat yourself up over this, man. You're a great brother and they know that."

Matt drops his bat and looks at me, his shoulder sagging a little. "I'm not sure. Liv didn't even call me after she caught him. She called Zoey, and the girls were all there before I even got a call, and it was Zo who called me, not Liv."

"You know Olivia, though. She wouldn't have let Zoey call you if she didn't want you there. She let Zoey tell you the whole sordid story too, not just that they broke up, and the fact that Zoey knew to call you and not someone else says a lot. Her best friend knew the person to call when she needed support the most was you. I know how much she loves and relies on you. I think she's just worried she does it too much. Maybe you guys should spend a day together, talk to her about this."

"Yeah, I guess you're right."

I take my turn in the cage, hitting a few balls, and we talk about nothing of importance. When I get home, Olivia is in the kitchen making lunch while her music blasts through the speaker system. I stand and watch her dance around the kitchen for a minute before I walk up behind her and wrap my arms around her, placing my chin on her shoulder after kissing her on the cheek. She leans back into me as she continues to season the chicken she has on the stove.

"Hey babe, smells good."

"Thanks. How were the cages with Matt?"

"Good. He needed to work through some things. I'm hoping our talk helped him."

"Is he okay? He's always worrying about Gi and me. I'm not sure he takes proper care of himself. I worry about him at times," she says sadly.

"I think he's fine, just needed to talk some stuff out."

"Well, I'm glad you were there for him. I wish he would share more with me."

"It's nice knowing how much you guys love each other." I kiss the top of her head before turning to the fridge, grabbing a water bottle out and drinking half of it at once.

"What can I do to help?" I ask.

"If you want to set the table, I'll have the food done in a minute."

As I set the table, I think about Emily. Seeing what Matt and Liv are going through, I wonder if she knows how much I love her and that I'm always here for her. I decide to make plans to spend the day together soon.

"So, we have no games over the long weekend," I say. "I was thinking we could cross off a few places on your summer list. We can hit Banff and the ice fields, and I found a concert in Calgary we could hit. Cross three things off your list at once. We could leave on Thursday morning and come home Monday. Then we could take the next weekend to go camp on Hornby Island, maybe make it a group trip. You invite the girls, I'll invite the guys, and the following weekend we could do Victoria and Seattle, go over to Victoria, spend a day and then take the ferry to Seattle for a day and drive back up?"

Olivia pushes her food around her plate for a minute, not saying anything, and I worry I overstepped somehow. I look at her and she isn't looking at me.

"Olivia? Did I do something wrong?"

She shakes her head slightly before looking up at me. "No, it's just... You put a lot of thought into this."

I'm beginning to think maybe that's a bad thing. I thought we were going to do this list together, and she wanted to complete it together.

"Yeah, you wanted to complete it this summer. I thought we'd do just that. We have only a month and a half before you go back to work."

She gives her head a quick shake. "Yeah, sounds great. I'll text the girls about the trip to Hornby Island."

I reach across the table and grab her hand, giving it a quick squeeze. "Babe, something is bothering you. What's going on? If you don't like those plans, we can change them. I just want to help you with this."

She looks me in the eye, searching for something. "I don't know. I think it's my insecurities coming out. You've made these plans and my mind is saying you've done it to complete the list faster, and that's leaving me unsure, I guess."

I know the list is what started this, but I thought she knew I want a long-term relationship with her, and we aren't together just because of the list. I reach for her chair and pull her close to me. I position us so her legs are between mine.

"Olivia, I do want to complete this list as soon as possible, but simply because I want to make sure it's done before you go back to work. It has nothing to do with our relationship. I'm in this for the long haul. As long as you'll put up with me, I'm here."

She takes a visibly deep breath before slowly releasing it. "Okay. Thank you, Josh. I think I'm just dealing with some insecurities. I'm trying to work on them."

My heart squeezes at her words. I'm glad she is voicing this so I know where her head is, but it kills me that she feels this way or that any part of her questions my reasoning for being with her.

"Babe, that's okay, and I'm here to support you through that. I want you to be able to talk to me about anything." She nods and I pull her into me, wrapping my arms around her before placing a lingering kiss on her forehead. After a few minutes, I clean up the dishes from lunch.

She sits at the table, watching me as I load the dishwasher and make my way back to her. I brace myself with one hand on the back of her chair and the other on the table, caging her in.

"How about a few episodes before my game?" She nods, and I kiss her before grabbing her hand and helping her up. I lead her to the couch where we settle in. She cuddles into my side while we watch before we leave for my game.

On Saturday, after confirming details with Olivia for our trips, I text the group chat with the guys.

JOSH

You guys free the weekend of the 13th-15th?

MATT

Yeah, what's up?

CALEB

What are you thinking?

GRAYSON

Should be.

JOSH

Olivia wants to do a camping trip on Hornby. She thought about doing a group trip and I said I'd ask.

GRAYSON

She asked you and not Matt?

JOSH

She kind of lives here, so she asked.

CALEB

I'm in. How long is Liv living with you?

My chest tightens. I know this started as a temporary arrangement, and it would be moving our relationship quickly, but I don't want her to leave. Just the thought of it has panic and uneasiness run through me.

I love being able to climb into bed and pull her into me, falling asleep with the smell of her lavender shampoo, coming home to her dancing while she cooks, or watching her curled up on the couch with her Kindle reading a book. It all feels so right, and I don't think I can handle losing it.

JOSH

As long as she needs and wants.

MATT:

I'm in on camping. Let me know how much it is.
Guessing we should carpool for the three ferries.
Of course, my sister has to pick such a difficult place. 😫

GRAYSON

Not surprised.

JOSH

Grayson, can you keep your shit with Hannah together for this trip?

CALEB

Shit with Hannah?

MATT

What did you do to her?

GRAYSON

Seriously guys, why do you think I did something wrong?

CALEB

Your playboy ways.

MATT

The way you seem to have no relationship with women.

GRAYSON

Loving the support here, guys. Yes, Josh, everything will be fine with Hannah.

CHAPTER 23

Olivia

On Thursday morning, I pack the remaining items I need for our road trip. Josh comes behind me and wraps his arms around my waist, kissing my neck. "There is something I want you to do for me before we leave," he whispers against my skin and I lean back into him, melting at the feeling of his lips on me.

"What would that be?" I ask, slightly breathless.

"I want you to download a couple of your naughty books as audiobooks for us to listen to on the car ride. I want to see what has you so fascinated."

My skin heats as a blush creeps across my cheeks and down my neck, and I stiffen. Don't get me wrong, when it comes to the girls, we share book recommendations, and no one yucks anyone's yum, but to share that with Josh... Some of the books I read are dark romance and some deal with kinks I'm not sure I want him to know I enjoy reading about.

"Babe, I want you to pick the dirtiest book you can find. I want to get into it with you. Don't worry, nothing is going to scare me." He kisses down my neck and across my shoulder. My panties get wetter as his lips trail over my skin. His teeth scrape the skin on my shoulder before he releases me and heads out of the bedroom.

I grab my phone off the nightstand, open my audiobook app, and find a couple of books that are on my TBR. I find a small-town romance, a couple of mafia romances, a marriage of convenience, and a single dad/nanny romance. I download them so we can listen to them when we lose service.

When that's done, I make my way into the living room, where Josh is packing a few things into a cooler. I watch his muscles move under his tight blue Henley. He looks up at me and smiles. "All ready, babe?"

"Yup."

"Okay, I packed the camping gear in the car already. We're good to go."

In the car, I connect my phone and select the small-town romance, thinking we should ease into this. The book plays as I look out the window, watching the passing scenery. Josh rests his hand on my thigh, his thumb moving slowly over it. The book starts innocently enough. It's about a city girl who leaves to get away from her overbearing parents and winds up in a small town on the other side of the country. She takes a position in the office of a local construction company, taking care of their accounts and she butts heads with the owner of the company, but there is something about her that draws him in. After a late night in the office, he drives her home and walks her to her door and he finally decides, *screw it,* and kisses her and they tumble into her house and into her bedroom.

As the spicy scene starts, I pause the book. He looks at me. "What was that?" Confusion fills his voice.

"Um... We don't have to listen to that," I say, wringing my hands in my lap, filled with a mix of embarrassment and something else.

I've never shared my spicy books with anyone other than the girls, and now that I'm sitting in the confines of Josh's car and the book is about to explicitly describe the characters having sex, I'm having an internal freak-out. What will Josh think when he hears it? When he finds out exactly what I sit on his couch reading every day? I shift my body and face the door, looking out the window, trying to hide myself from him as much as I can in the car. We are still on the highway through the mountains separating the lower mainland from the interior of BC.

"Babe, can you please look at me?" Josh pleads.

I readjust myself, but keep my eyes down, not able to muster the courage to look at him yet. His fingers come under my chin as he forces my head up. He looks at me for a few seconds before his eyes return to the road.

"I don't want you to be embarrassed about this. I want you to feel comfortable sharing this with me. I'm not going to judge you or make fun of you for listening to and reading these books."

Drew always made it seem like reading romance wasn't true reading. I trust Josh, though. I know he's telling me the truth when he says he won't judge me. He looks at me for a second before reaching forward and playing the book again.

I adjust myself again, looking out the window and listening to the narrator describe the main male character going down on the female main character. Listening to the description and having the images the story conjures in my mind is getting me wet. I squeeze my thighs together, trying to quench the desire growing between my thighs.

I glance over at Josh and notice him getting visibly hard in his shorts. God, the fact that this man is currently on my desired road trip, listening to my smut book, and getting turned on by it has me feeling all sorts of things. It turns me on, but it also has my heart pounding in my chest. Josh never ceases to surprise me.

He reaches down and adjusts himself, and I squeeze my thighs together harder. Josh notices the movement and where my eyes are and smirks.

"Olivia, I want you to pull your dress up for me and spread your thighs."

I do as he says, leaving my black lace thong visible, and I feel the leather seats on my bare ass cheeks. "Good girl, now I want you to pull your panties aside and play with your clit."

I stop. I've never been able to get myself off with my fingers. Josh notices my hesitation.

"Josh, I've never been able to get myself off with my fingers. I've only been able to do it with a vibrator," I whisper.

He's silent for a minute before he says, "Okay, I want you to play with yourself, get yourself ready for me and I'll bring you over the finish line, but I want to watch you play with your pretty pussy for me."

I'm soaked, and Josh's words only add to it. The book is still playing, and I lean my head back and close my eyes, my right hand moving down my stomach and between my thighs. My pointer finger goes to my entrance, gathering moisture before I bring it to my clit, circling it. Moaning, my hips buck off the seat at the sensation. Josh hisses beside me. I listen to the book and my movements pick up. The pressure begins to build, but it takes me nowhere. I try adding pressure and moving faster and nothing.

I open my eyes and turn my head to face Josh.

"Babe, I need you. I need to come."

My body is wound so tight, I need release. Seconds later, I feel Josh's hand trail up my thigh until he reaches my dripping pussy.

"You're so wet for me, Olivia," he groans.

His fingers enter me, pumping in and out a few times before they move up to my clit, circling and applying pressure. My hips buck against his hand, and he moves faster. I can hear how wet I am as his fingers move.

The pressure low inside me continues to build. I feel the orgasm within reach, and Josh moves his finger down to my entrance and I groan at the change, losing the orgasm that was right there.

He brings his fingers back up to my clit, working faster and harder this time. My chest rising and falling rapidly. I reach out, griping anything I can get my hands on, and my body continues to wind tighter and tighter. "Come for me Olivia, come on my fingers," Josh says, and it sends me flying over the edge. My hips leave the seat, seeking more pressure on my clit to draw out my orgasm and at the same time looking to remove his fingers it's so sensitive.

After a minute, Josh removes his fingers, and I peel my eyes open just as he puts his fingers in his mouth and sucks me off them, all while watching the road. It's fucking hot.

This isn't the first time Josh has done that, sucked me off his fingers after getting me off, but each and every time I find it so erotic and it gets me rearing for more.

Josh gives me a knowing smile. He reaches down and adjusts himself again. Reaching over, I open the button and zipper of his shorts, deciding to return the favour. I grip his cock and pump him a few times. His thighs flex and his grip on the steering wheel tightens. I take my thumb and run it over his slit, gathering the pre-cum and using it to lube his cock. I tighten my grip and he groans. I can see the effort he is using to keep his concentration on the road.

"Olivia, I don't think we should do this," he barely manages to grit out, but his hips buck into my hand. I continue to pump him in my hand, twisting every once in a while. His breathing accelerates and his hips buck more often, meeting my hand as I work his hard length.

I love knowing what I do to Josh, knowing I am the reason he's in a frenzy right now. Because he's driving, I take pity on him and tighten my grip slightly and twist in my seat, allowing my right hand to reach over and take hold of his balls as I roll them while my left hand moves faster. Within seconds, he's groaning my name and coming in my hand.

I release him, open the glove box, finding a few napkins and clean my hand. I'm definitely going to need to wash them as soon as we make a stop. I tuck Josh back into his shorts, zip him up, and relax in my seat as we continue to listen to the book.

We stop in Kamloops for gas, and I head inside and wash my hands in the washroom before returning to the car where Josh is leaning against my door with his legs crossed at the ankles and his arms crossed over his chest, causing his shirt to stretch and strain. My steps slow as I take in the man in front of me, thinking about what we have become to each other. Josh is no longer just my friend, but rather he's someone I see spending the rest of my life with. Everything with him seems so natural, and that should scare the shit out of me, seeing as we've only been intimate for a couple of months now, but it feels almost inevitable now.

When I get a few steps away from the car, he uncrosses his arms and his hands come to my hips. I have to widen my stance, so I have a leg on either side of his outstretched ones. He pulls me close and kisses me. It starts slowly and moves into a hungry, all-consuming kiss.

"Do you have any idea how hot it was watching you play with your pussy while one of your spicy books played and I drove?"

I blush and look around to see if anyone heard him. Satisfied no one did, I wrap my arms around his neck and whisper in his ear, "I think that hard-on you were sporting was proof enough, but you can always show me when we get to the campground."

I take a step back and reach around him to grab the handle. Josh pushes off the door and whispers back, "Be careful what you wish for, babe." He places a kiss on my temple, opening my door before walking around the car as heat rises in my cheeks.

Our first stop is Revelstoke. We drive up the mountain, taking in the view as we wind our way to the top. We find a hiking trail to a viewpoint, stopping at the top. My breath catches as I take in the gorgeous view. You can see wilderness stretched out below for miles. I stand in silence as I take it all in and absorb the sounds of the birds and the wind whistling through the trees. The wind helps cut some of the stifling heat that's sticking to my skin. I feel Josh standing behind me. He wraps his arms around me, and I melt into his chest.

I pull my phone out and take pictures of the view before turning the camera and taking a few selfies of Josh and me. He smiles in them. I catch a few of him looking at me, some of him kissing my cheek, and a few of us kissing. Josh kisses my temple and asks, "Ready to go, babe?" I nod and he takes my hand, and we hike back to the car.

For lunch, we find a pub in town. There are TVs placed so that no matter where you sit, you can see one. People chatter at tables and the bar as we find a table in the corner. We both order a burger with fries, and sit in comfortable silence as we watch the Blue Jays' game, digging in when our food is delivered. It's nice to be able to spend time with Josh and be comfortable with the silence. There's no need for either of us to fill it with noise or random conversation.

While we finish our drive to Banff, we listen to a dark mafia romance. It's a book I've already read but found out the audiobook is narrated by one of my favourite narrators and wanted to listen to it. The soothing voice of the male narrator has me falling asleep against the door.

I'm woken up by the feeling of Josh's fingers brushing my hair behind my ear and him softly saying, "Babe, we're here. It's time to wake up."

I nuzzle my face into his hand and make a noise of contentment. I feel his lips on my forehead and my eyes flutter open and I make eye contact with him. A smile pulls at my lips when I look at him.

"Hi." He smiles softly at me as his fingers continue to move through my hair.

"Hi," I whisper back.

"We're here." I look out the windshield and see we are at the campground.

"Where do you want to set this up?" he asks me, as he grabs the tent.

I find a nice flat area near the trees, and he gets to work while I unload the camping barbecue and some food and get to work on making dinner. When he finishes getting everything in the tent, he joins me at the picnic table. He gets the dishes set and I plate up our food. While we eat, we make plans for our time here.

"So, I finished the book while you were asleep," Josh says, as I have a fork full of salad in my hand.

I look at him and ask, "What did you think?" And take a bite of salad.

He smirks. "It was informative. Tell me, Olivia, do you want the things that happen in your books to happen to you?"

I swallow and mull over my answer for a few seconds. I feel comfortable with Josh, and everything feels right and natural with us, but do I risk telling him just how much I want to try some of the things that happen in my books, the book he listened to had sexual degradation and light choking in it. I study Josh for a second and know he won't judge me for telling him the truth.

"I, um, I want to experiment with some of it," I tell him and take a sip of my drink.

Our plates are empty now and Josh stands and cleans up. That was not the response I was expecting. He hasn't said anything at all. I stiffen, as if preparing for a physical blow in the form of a verbal one.

"Um, Josh..." I say, dragging out his name.

"Yes, babe." Babe, he's still using his term of endearment, so he can't be responding that badly to my answer. My body doesn't relax, though. I'm worried my admission will have Josh changing his mind about our relationship.

"Are we okay? You haven't said anything." My voice is weak, weaker than I wish it was, but I'm so worried about what he might say. He stops what he's doing and walks over to me, placing his fingers under my chin, lifting it, and forcing me to make eye contact with him.

"Olivia, I want to experiment with you, too. So, I am going to clean up to ensure we don't get any bears and then we are going to climb into that tent together and we are going to try some of the things in your dirty little book and then I'm going to hold you in my arms as we fall asleep."

I'm both turned on and emotionally warmed by his words. He wants to experiment with me and then hold me. I want that too. I immediately get up from the table, causing Josh to chuckle, and I quickly start packing what I can into the car as Josh finishes cleaning. When everything is in the car, we climb into the tent where I see Josh has zipped two sleeping bags together so we can share them.

I remove my clothes as soon as the tent is closed. Josh grins as he does the same. When I'm naked, I climb into the sleeping bag and Josh is right behind me. He kisses me deeply before trailing kisses down my neck and across my collarbone. His hand slowly moves down my body. His fingers graze across my belly before they dip down, finding how wet I am for him.

He groans into my neck as he drags his wet fingers from my entrance to my clit. "Always so wet for me, Olivia." My hips lift, seeking more pressure from his finger. "My needy little slut, aren't you, Olivia?" His words send more heat down my body, and I close my eyes as my pussy clenches.

"You like that, Olivia; do you like me calling you my little slut?" I nod, trying not to analyze why that does something for me.

His fingers continue to work my clit as his teeth pull my earlobe. My body winds tighter and tighter as he continues to work me. I grip the sleeping bag as I turn my face into his chest and moan.

"You're going to come for me now, Olivia." He groans as he puts two fingers inside me and his thumb presses down on my clit. My back arches as I come around his fingers. He continues to work me until every last bit of my orgasm has been pulled from my body and my back is flat against the ground again. He removes his fingers from my wet pussy and puts them into his mouth, making eye contact with me.

"Your pussy is delicious," he murmurs as a blush spreads across my cheeks and down my neck.

Josh moves and positions his body between my legs, his cock nudging my entrance. I lift my hips encouraging him, and his right hand moves to come around my throat, tightening slightly, just enough that I can feel light pressure. My pussy clenches around nothing, wishing it was squeezing Josh's thick cock.

He leans down and whispers in my ear, "You may be my needy little slut, but you get my cock when I say you do."

I close my eyes, revelling in the feeling of his hot breath against my cheek and the way his words send a rush of wetness between my legs.

"Please," I beg in a breathy moan.

He grips his cock with his free hand and rubs the tip against my clit. I feel myself building as he continues to use his cock to play with it. When I feel close, he stops, and my eyes fly open. A wave of disappointment crashes over me. He looks down at me with a wicked grin. He knows exactly what he's doing. He tightens his grip around my throat slightly as he pushes his cock into me, and all the sensations together have me feeling delirious. He rocks hard and fast inside me. My hands go to his back, my nails scraping across his skin.

He continues a relentless pace as he fucks me hard and deep. I try to keep quiet as we are in the middle of a public campground. I'm building higher and higher. My hand goes to my mouth to soften my noises.

Josh leans down and whispers, "Be my good little slut and come on my cock so I can fill your pussy with my cum."

His words send me over the edge, and I clamp down around him and bite into my hand to quiet my screams as I come so violently my vision turns black. I slowly make my way back to the living and hear the tail end of Josh's release.

He stays above me as we work to catch our breath. We make eye contact and Josh brushes a few stray pieces of hair behind my ear.

"Are you okay?"

I see the hesitation in his eyes, like he's worried calling me his slut was too far. I wrap my arms around his neck, my fingers gripping his hair as I pull him down to me for a passionate kiss.

"Babe, I'm perfect. That was amazing. I think the name-calling worked for me because it was possessive. You didn't just call me a slut, you called me your slut, and I know you respect me. You would never call me that outside of sex. I'm perfect. Please trust me enough that I will tell you if a line is crossed."

He smiles down at me before placing a chaste kiss on my lips, pulling out of me, rolling to his side, and pulling me into his body. His hand trails lazily up and down my back as my fingers trace absently over his chest as we lie in silence. I look up at him and place my chin on top of my hand that rests on his chest.

"Thank you," I whisper.

His hand stops for a second as he looks down at me. His brows are drawn together, and his face is full of questions.

His hand continues to move along my back as he asks, "For?"

"Trying new things with me. For being patient. For being you." I smile up at him and his face relaxes.

"Babe, you don't have to thank me for any of that. I enjoy doing all of it with you and there is nothing to be patient with. We communicate with each other. That's how this works." I can't take the smile off my face.

No relationship I've ever had has felt this good. I would never have been able to tell any of my past partners that there were things I wanted to try in the bedroom. There was never this overwhelming sense of calm and safety in those relationships, but with Josh, I feel all of that. I know I can trust him, that he'll always listen, that he will always support me and have my back no matter what. He is my safe place. He is who I want in my corner every day. He is who I want to come home to after a long, hard day at work. He is who I want to do all these trips with, who I want to share all these memories with.

Josh is still looking at me, his hand still running up and down my back. "I love you," I whisper.

His hand stops and a smile breaks across his face. "You do?"

I nod, and he moves, rolling so I'm on my back as he hovers above me.

"I love you, Olivia Carter," he says before sealing our lips together in an intimate kiss that shows me just how much he loves me. I spread my legs as my hands move into his hair, gripping it and holding him to me. He positions himself between my legs and slowly makes love to me, holding my hand as he stares into my eyes. I can see and feel his love for me, and I hope he feels mine for him.

CHAPTER 24

Josh

I wake to the feeling of warmth on my face as sunbeams stream through the siding of the tent. Olivia is wrapped around me, her arm thrown over my stomach, her leg over mine, and her face on my chest. I smile, thinking about last night. The look on Olivia's face when she told me she loves me, the absolute bliss that went through me when she said those three beautiful words. I never thought hearing those three words would mean so much to me but hearing them from Olivia makes me feel like I can conquer anything.

She nuzzles into my chest, and her arms tighten around me. My hand moves lazily up and down her back. A while ago, I told Olivia she would stay in my bed every night, but she still hasn't moved her things from the spare room into mine. She spends every night in my bed, but all her things are still down the hall, keeping this gap between us. I know she was planning on finding a new place before the summer is over, but I can't stand the thought of her leaving. My stomach tightens in knots at the thought of her moving into her own place, of not being able to come home to her every night, not being able to curl up on the couch beside her while she reads her book and I work on my computer, not seeing the little things she does around the house like purchasing fresh flowers, or how she artfully throws the throw blankets on the back of the couch, and how every room smells like her.

"What are you thinking about so hard this early in the morning?" she asks.

I didn't realize she had woken up. I look down at her smiling and kiss the tip of her nose.

"Stay," I say.

"I'm right here, Josh." She smiles.

"I mean, don't move out at the end of the summer. I want you to stay. I want you to move in. I want all your clothes in my closet, your shampoo and conditioner in my shower, and your stuff on the nightstand beside my bed. I want to come home to you every day. I want to fall asleep and wake up beside you every day. Stay."

Her eyes dart between my eyes. She continues to stare at me for a few seconds and my stomach turns, wondering if I came on too strong. Then a smile pulls at her lips.

"Yes."

One word, that's all it takes for my stomach to settle, my heart to race, and a huge smile to spread across my face.

"Yes?" I ask to confirm.

She nods, still smiling her beautiful breath-taking smile. "Yes, Josh. I'll stay. I'll officially move in."

I roll us so she's below me and I kiss her deep and slow, breaking the kiss, our chests heaving, and I rest my forehead against hers. "I love you," I whisper while staring into her eyes.

"I love you too."

Her legs spread further, and I settle myself between them. I kiss her again as I position myself at her entrance. I take my time, slowly making love to her. I groan her name into her neck as she brings me with her over the edge.

I pull out and lie beside her. I turn and face her and she's smiling at me. My hand finds the back of her head as I pull her closer for a kiss. When we pull apart, I just rest my forehead against hers and look into her eyes. I see and feel the love in them. I know there are no other eyes I want to spend the rest of my life staring at like this. I wasted so much time by not making a move on Olivia. We've missed out on so much and I'm not going to let us do that anymore.

I'm going to grab the bull by the horns and take control. I want Olivia to be by my side for the rest of our lives.

I give her a quick kiss before unzipping the sleeping bag. "We should get a start on the day. Lots for us to do."

I quickly throw on some clothes before getting out of the tent and making us a quick breakfast. After eating, we pack up and head into the downtown area of Banff.

As we walk hand in hand down Banff Ave, Olivia sees the Christmas store and drags me inside. She wanders around slowly, looking at all the decorations and ornaments. I kiss her temple before telling her I need to make a quick call. She smiles and nods and continues to work her way around the store.

I don't really need to make a call, but there is something I want to grab without her knowing. I pop into the store I'm looking for and make the purchase before putting it in my pocket.

I come back to find Olivia at the register when I return. She wears a happy smile as the attendant wraps her purchase in tissue paper and hands her the bag. I grab it for her, and we walk outside.

It's a warm day. The street is full of people going in and out of stores, dining on patios, enjoying the summer weather. I pull Liv to the median in the street, dropping her hand before pulling my phone out, taking a few steps away from her, turning and positioning myself to take her picture with the beautiful mountains in the background.

After a few pictures, I join her, and she asks for a few selfies of us. I'm not usually one for selfies, but I would do anything for Olivia. I wrap my arm around her shoulder and pull her into my side as I lift the phone and take a few photos, then I kiss her temple and take a few more.

She grabs my phone and does something before handing it back to me. Locking it, I shove it back into my pocket before asking, "How about lunch?"

"Sounds good. What are you thinking?"

"There is supposed to be a really good pub just down the block. Why don't we try that?"

"Okay."

We cross the street back to the sidewalk and make our way to the pub. We manage to get a table right away and order a couple of drinks. We browse the menu and order. As we wait, Olivia shows me the Christmas ornaments she purchased. One is a pair of black bears sitting inside a wreath with Banff written underneath them, and she got three matching ornaments with three black bears with Matt, Olivia, and Gianna handwritten underneath the bears, one for her, Gi and Matt so they can have matching ornaments on their trees.

"Is Christmas your favourite holiday?" I ask as our food is delivered.

A wistful smile appears on her face. "Yeah, it's one holiday where we are guaranteed to spend it together as a family. We've all missed other holidays here and there even though we try not to, but we are always together for Christmas. I love it. We have our own little traditions, like Matt is always Santa, passing out the presents from under the tree. Ever since we were kids, Mom always had the hard-set rule, breakfast, then stockings, then presents, and it's the same today. She always gets us new Christmas pyjamas that we wear on Christmas Eve. We watch a Christmas movie after presents and then, usually after everyone naps, we play a few games before dinner. I love the family time and the traditions. It's something I want to carry on with my kids one day. I want them to love it the same way I do."

I can picture Olivia and I with kids of our own, a beautiful tree we decorated with all the ornaments Olivia has collected. Breakfast together, opening stockings, and the look on our kids' faces as they open their presents. A dog curled up on a dog bed nearby chewing on its newest toy, both of our parents there showering the grandkids in love and presents. The image sends a sense of contentment through me, a feeling of peace. That's what I want. I want a future with Olivia with all of it, the house, the pets, the kids, the family, the traditions.

Olivia nudges me. "You okay?"

I smile at her. "Yeah, perfect." I reach out and grab her hand, rubbing my thumb over the back as we continue to talk.

After we finish eating, we resume our wandering around downtown, stopping into stores and browsing. Around dinner time we decide to order a pizza from a little hole-in-the-wall spot and take it back to our campsite.

When we get back, I start a fire and we settle into our camping chairs, sharing a blanket spread over our laps. We sit and eat pizza while sipping on our drinks and watching the fire crackle. Later, when we settle into the tent, I pull Olivia into my side, kiss her temple, and whisper, "I love you" against her skin.

Her arms tighten around me and she places a kiss on my chest. "I love you, too. Good night, babe."

"Good night."

In the morning, I wake to Olivia peppering kisses across my chest and up my neck. She nibbles my ear, pulling it between her teeth, before kissing across my jaw. I open my eyes and roll Olivia onto her back, pinning her arms above her head.

"Good morning," I say with a huge grin.

"Good morning, my love," she says with a matching grin. I lean down and kiss her, rolling my hard cock into her centre. She bucks against me and I pull back, breaking the kiss. "As much as I would love to fuck you senseless right now, babe, we need to pack up. We've got something to do before we head out of town."

She gives me her sad face with the puppy dog eyes that usually gets me to fold and do whatever she wants, but I hold my resolve and give her a quick kiss before getting out of the sleeping bag.

"Babe, you know how much I want to, but we can't right now. I'll make it up to you tonight," I say.

Her face turns serious as she looks at me. "You better. I'll hold you to it," she says before getting out of the sleeping bag.

We pack everything in the car before we head into town and grab a quick breakfast. We then make our way to the hot springs. We head inside and get ready in the dressing rooms. I find a spot in the pool and wait for her.

Olivia comes out in a black swimsuit, showing off all her curves. Her bikini top shows off her ample chest and her bottoms come to her waist with sheer material on the sides. My mouth goes dry as I watch her make her way to me. As soon as she's within arm's reach, I pull her into me and kiss her, a kiss that lets everyone here know she's mine.

When we pull apart, she smiles up at me. "What was that for?"

I lean down so my lips are right beside her ear. "You look so damn sexy in that bathing suit I needed every man in here to know you're mine. That only my hands will be on this sexy body. Only my lips will be on yours, and tonight when we're alone it will be my name you cry out every single time I make you come."

I step back and see her chest rising and falling. A deep blush has spread across her cheeks, down her neck, and across the tops of her breasts.

She moves to my side, and we sit along the edge of the pool for an hour, enjoying the hot water and the beautiful view of the mountains before we head back to the dressing rooms to shower and change. When we meet outside, we load up and start the drive to Calgary; we listen to another one of Liv's books and I'm beginning to understand why she enjoys them. Not that I'm going to start reading them on my own, but I understand and appreciate her love of them. Getting lost in problems that aren't your own all while still being able to connect with the characters and their plights. I get it.

When we get to Calgary, we check into our hotel and head out to explore the city. For dinner we opt for room service and a movie before heading out. I haven't told Olivia who we are seeing yet, and when we round the corner to the arena, she sees the signs and stops in her tracks, pulling me with her.

"Excited?" I ask as she continues to stare in silence. Her mouth opens and closes a few times before she turns and meets my eyes, and nods. I managed to get us tickets to the Arctic Monkeys concert, which was not an easy task, but anything for Olivia.

"How... How did you get tickets? They've been sold out for every show for forever. I never thought this would be the concert we were going to." I can see her mind turning in that pretty little head of hers.

"They had been holding back a few and I happened to snag them right after they released them."

She stares at me for a few seconds before she wraps her arms around my neck, pulling me into her for a hug. I wrap my arms around, her taking in the feeling of her body pressed against mine and the feeling of her warm breath on the side of my face. She steps back, and I miss the feeling immediately. I take a deep breath and adjust myself in my pants before we make our way into the arena for the concert.

I wouldn't be surprised if Olivia has no voice tomorrow the way she screamed in there. We walk out with the sizeable crowd and Olivia is still pumped full of energy. Her cheeks are red, and she's trying so hard to keep her energy inside that she's almost shaking. She talks about all her favourite parts of the concert on our way back to the hotel. Inside the room, she gives me a quick kiss before grabbing her bag and heading into the bathroom, closing the door behind her.

I change into a pair of gym shorts and while I'm taking off my shirt, the bathroom door opens. Olivia is leaning against the door-jamb in a black negligee with two of my ties hanging from her outstretched fingers.

The fabric of the negligee accentuates all her curves, hugging her large breasts - I'm not sure how they're still inside the fabric - down her soft stomach and around her wide hips. She looks sexy as fuck, and she's all mine. I am the one who gets to see her like this. I am the one she chooses to share this part of herself with, and I couldn't be luckier.

A mischievous grin spreads across her face as she stares at me, standing there with my shirt halfway down my arms, and mouth agape. I close my mouth and clear my throat as I do another head-to-toe once-over of her body.

"Josh, if you're done eye-fucking me, I thought we might be able to get to some actual fucking," she says, amusement lacing her voice.

I finish removing my shirt and drop it to the floor. A light, breathy laugh leaves Olivia as she walks up to me. She goes onto her tiptoes and wraps her arms around my neck. My arms instinctively wrap around her middle, pulling her into me. She kisses up my jaw, painfully slowly. I want to take her to bed and worship her, but she obviously has an idea for tonight and I'm going to let her run with it.

When her lips find my ear, she whispers, "I thought we might check another item off that list tonight. You up for being at my mercy?"

I groan as I tip my head back and close my eyes. This woman is going to be the death of me. I will do anything she asks of me. Word-lessly, I grab her hand and walk over to the bed, where I climb on and lay on my back for her. A slow smile spreads across her face as the realization hits her. She grabs my left hand and wraps the tie around it, tying it securely. She then climbs onto the bed and does the same with my other wrist, she leans down and brushes her lips over mine, just enough that when I lick my lips, I can taste her, but she withdraws quick enough that I can't deepen the kiss. I groan, wanting more, needing more contact from her. She grabs the ties and brings them to the headboard, forcing my arms above my head, where she secures them.

Her tits hang over my face, and I lean up and scrape my teeth over one of her hardened nipples. She moans before she pulls away and scurries off the bed. She stands there with a grin taking me in, tied to the bed, completely at her mercy.

Olivia licks her lips as she brings a finger to my leg, just below the bottom hem of my shorts, and slowly runs it down my leg as she walks down the bed. Her finger jumps to my other leg as she does the same in reverse. When she reaches the bottom of my shorts, she doesn't stop. My cock is hard and wants relief and I want to have my hands in Olivia's hair, pulling her to me as I use my tongue to taste her.

Her finger moves over my shorts until she reaches the waistband. Her other hand joins as her fingers snake inside and pull them down. I lift my hips to help her.

She forces my legs open as she makes eye contact with me and crawls up the bed between my legs. Pre-cum leaks from the tip of my cock as I watch her. When she reaches my cock, she takes it in her hand and my hips buck at the contact, begging for release. She gives it a quick squeeze as she smiles at me with a devilish grin. She leans down and licks me from base to tip, slowly, like her tongue wants to memorize every centimetre of it. When she reaches the tip, she flicks her tongue across it, gathering the pre-cum on her tongue before she moans as she tastes it. This girl and her little noises drive me crazy. The way she is taking control and is so confident while she does, it just adds to my love for her.

She leans back down and wraps her lips around me and works her way down. When she hollows her cheeks, I buck into her mouth and she moans, sending vibrations through my cock and up my spine. One of her hands works the part of me her mouth can't while the other rolls my balls, she finds a pace and settles in.

I try to let her have all the control. Her hand that was working my balls releases them and I feel her finger work its way along my crease until she finds a spot and applies pressure, causing my hips to buck and my balls to feel heavy. She presses again as she tightens her grip around my cock and hollows her cheeks, sending me over the edge, releasing everything into her mouth. I can't breathe as she works every last drop from me, licking her lips when I've finished.

She climbs over me, startling me. I can feel her soaked pussy over my dick when she settles. She's not wearing any panties under that sexy thing. She leans down and kisses me. I lick at her lips, coaxing her to open for me. She does, and I taste myself as I explore her mouth with my tongue. I groan when her fingers grip my hair.

Breaking the kiss, she lifts her hips slightly as she reaches for my now hard cock and positions it at her entrance. She slowly sinks down, her head rolling back as she works to take every inch of me. When she's taken all of me, she rolls her hips and my hands pull at my bindings; I want to grab her hips and set the pace, to drive into her so forcefully she'll be feeling me for days.

She continues to roll slowly. "Olivia," I groan. She looks down at me with a smile on her face as she continues. "Take that off. As sexy as it is, I want to see your tits. Take it off, Olivia." She reaches for the hem as she continues to work herself on me and painfully slowly, takes off the negligee. Once it's off, she places her hands on my chest as she lifts until only the tip of my cock is inside her soaked pussy, and she slams down on me, eliciting a loud groan from both of us.

She continues this for a while. She leans down and whispers in my ear, "Josh, I need you to fuck me, and fuck me hard. I need to feel you in the morning." She then reaches up and unties my wrists. As soon as they're free, I'm gripping her hip and thrusting up into her, making her tits bounce. The sound of sweaty skin slapping and our moans fill the room.

I reach out and spank her ass. "Yes, Josh! Yes!" she moans.

I roll us, lifting her leg to her chest as I continue to fuck her hard.

"My naughty little slut wanted to tease me tonight, huh?"

She nods as she tightens around me and a low moan leaves her. My free hand reaches between us as I find her clit, pinching it. She calls my name, and her nails scrape into my back in response. I position us so my chest holds her leg in place, and I use my newly free hand to slap her ass again. She tightens around me and her back arches; I do it again and pinch her clit.

I fuck her faster, working out every last bit of her orgasm. I feel her building again. Leaning down, I latch onto a nipple, sucking it into my mouth and flicking my tongue over it. One more slap to her ass sends her over the edge and me with her.

I withdraw from her and lie beside her on my back as I pull her into me. I kiss the top of her head as we lay in silence. That was amazing. Her confidence in herself and what she wanted.

I've loved Olivia for a long time, but tonight made me fall for her even more. I don't know how I have gone so much of my life without having her by my side.

CHAPTER 25

Josh

Looking forward to dinner and TV with Olivia tonight, I walk into the living room, but I'm surprised to see she's not there. I make my way to her old room, knowing she was planning on moving her stuff this week. When I get inside, I don't see her, but I hear crying coming from her closet. Standing in the doorway, my heart is ripped from my chest at the sight before me. Olivia is in a ball in the corner, her arms are wrapped around her legs, her head resting on her knees as she cries.

I rush over and pull her into me. Kissing the top of her head and running my hand lovingly through her hair as I talk to her.

"Babe, what's wrong?"

Her hand fists in the front of my shirt, like she's scared I'm not real. She works to catch her breath through her sobs. I feel her take a deep breath before she lifts her head and looks me in the eye.

"I don't want to lose you," she whispers. If my heart was crushed before, now it's downright destroyed. Why does she think she's going to lose me? There is nothing she could do that would have me going anywhere other than right by her side.

"Babe, I'm not going anywhere. Why do you think you're going to lose me? What happened?"

She reaches beside her and hands me her phone. It's opened to a text conversation from an unknown number.

UNKNOWN

Do you really think anyone's going to stick around if you don't lose the weight? No man will when you look like that. It's fun at first, but then it's just downright sad.

Enjoy it while you can. You'll be crawling back to me in no time.

Link to www.weightlossnow.com

I know what you like. Just come back to me and we can be happy again. I'll help you lose the weight.

You know no man is ever going to truly love you when you look the way you do.

I want to punch something. Break something. Throw something. But I can't. I need Olivia to know the bullshit this ugly, heinous man is spewing is just that, bullshit. I put her phone down and pull her into me.

"Olivia, I'm not going to leave you. I love you. Every part of you. To me, your curves are sexy. I love the feeling of holding you against me, my hands on your hips, or holding your sexy tits. I love how easy it is to talk to you. You don't judge me, you listen and are compassionate. You are smart, kind, and courageous. You are great with my family and friends. I know you are an amazing teacher, and one day you will be an amazing mother. Block his number and ignore him. He is trying to manipulate you into getting back with him, but you are mine, and I'm not letting you go."

I settle myself up against the wall and move Olivia so she's straddling my lap.

She looks me in the eye, tears running down her cheeks. "I love you, Joshua Mitchell Lincoln." Her lips ghost over mine, but I'm not having that. My hand grips her hair and holds her close to me as I kiss her, pouring all my love and devotion into this one act. I roll us so she's on her back on the floor. I kiss down her neck, nipping as I go.

"Olivia, I want you to really pay attention, because right now I'm going to show you how much I love you. I want it to sink in that pretty, little head of yours. I love you. I love every part of you, and I have for a long time."

I push her shirt up over her tits. Leaning down, I latch my mouth over her black lace bra as I flick her nipple with my tongue. I move and do the same to her other before I kiss down her body. When I reach the waistband of her shorts, I flick the button open and pull them, along with her panties, down her legs.

Sitting up, I stare down at her. Her eyes are wide as she watches me. I lean over and kiss her soft stomach, placing kisses over her stretch marks. Looking back up at her, I see a tear slide down her cheek.

I use my hands to hold her thighs open as I position myself between her legs. I lick from her entrance to her clit, her taste hitting my tongue, and I groan. Her hand comes down and fists in my hair as she moans my name.

I continue to use my tongue to taste and tease her. When she bucks against my face looking for more, I use a finger and enter her slowly. I twist it inside her, teasing her, drawing out her pleasure, but not allowing her to come, yet. When she finally comes, it will be explosive. She will feel it in her entire body. I massage her g-spot with a couple of strokes before I pull my finger out and add another one.

Entering her with two fingers, slowly, I use my tongue to flick her clit. I slowly pick up the speed of my fingers and the strokes of my tongue. When I feel her begin to clench, I pull away.

I take my time kissing up her body. I kiss across every part of her soft stomach, her stretch marks, up to her breasts, across her chest, up her neck, until I make my way to her lips. I kiss her, forcing her to taste herself on my tongue. Reaching between us, I undo my belt and slacks, before shoving them and my boxer briefs down. I don't have the time or desire to fully undress myself, so with my shirt still on and my pants just below my ass, I grip my cock and tease her entrance before thrusting inside her.

Her hot pussy grips me tightly, and I groan into her neck. My hand goes to her hip and I grip her tightly. She'll likely have bruises tomorrow in the shape of my fingers, but good - she'll have a reminder of how gone I am for her. How desperate I am to have her. I work in and out of her at a slow pace, building her pleasure slowly.

Her fingers claw at my back as she moans, "More. Harder. Faster. Fuck me."

I kiss her and nip at her bottom lip before I lift her right leg to her chest. When I have the new angle, I fuck her harder, making sure I hit that sensitive spot inside her every time. She meets every one of my thrusts. She screams my name as she comes. If there was anyone else in the house, there's no way they wouldn't have heard her, and I honestly wouldn't be surprised if the neighbours heard her.

When she comes down, I pull out and have her get on all fours. I push her chest into the floor so her ass is up in the air. I rear back and spank her right ass cheek and she cries out before I massage the red mark.

I lean over her body. "That was for thinking I would ever leave you."

I do it again, this time on her left cheek. "That is for questioning my love for this beautiful, sexy body of yours."

Wack. Her right cheek again. "That was for letting that man make you question your self-worth. You are amazing, Olivia."

Wack. "That was so you never question my love and devotion to you ever again."

I grip her hips and position myself and thrust harshly until my balls bounce off her ass. My grip is tight as I fuck her fast and hard, drilling my point into her mind. It only takes a few thrusts before she's coming again. I don't stop or slow; I keep up my fast, relentless pace until she's coming for a third time, and this one takes me with her. She slumps below me, her hips moving back down to the carpet, and I lay beside her.

I brush her hair from her eyes and tuck it behind her ear before leaning in and kissing her. Slowly. Lovingly.

She smiles. "I got it." She half laughs.

I smile back. "I'm glad. I don't ever want you to question what I feel for you. I will spend the rest of my life making sure you know just how loved you are in this life."

I get up and help her to her feet. We make our way to our bedroom and into the washroom, where I start the shower. We step in and I take my time slowly washing every inch of her beautiful skin, peppering kisses across stomach, thighs, and stretch marks, showing all of her my love. I then slowly help her wash and condition her hair. When we get out, I wrap a towel around my hips and then use a fluffy towel to dry her off, before wrapping her in a bathrobe.

I change while she sits on the edge of the bed. I order us a pizza to share, and we settle onto the couch in the living room, with her cuddled into my side. My fingers running through her hair as we watch one of her comfort movies. When we go to bed, I hold her close and whisper, "I love you, Olivia Rose Carter," before we both drift off to sleep.

CHAPTER 26

Olivia

On Wednesday, while Josh is at work, I move my things into Josh's room. We make plans for our camping weekend. Josh booked two side-by-side campsites, so the girls and I are going to share a tent and the guys are taking two tents and they will pair up.

Josh has been extremely affectionate this week after finding me in the closet. He is constantly making sure I know he loves me. We've had sex all over the apartment, and I'm not sure who has initiated more, me or him. It doesn't really matter, as the sex has been mind-blowing. I'm surprised I can walk straight after last night's session.

We are taking the first ferry to Nanaimo, out of West Vancouver, we were lucky everyone was able to take this Friday off so we could leave a day early. Before leaving for the ferry terminal, I grab my forwarded mail and bring it with me into the car. When we arrive, I text our camping group chat.

OLIVIA

Josh and I just got here in lane 5.

ZOEY

Just pulling into the lane will probably be a few cars behind you.

GRAYSON

Caleb drives like a cop. 5 minutes away.

HAN

Maybe because he is…

LIZ

Down girl.

HAN

Not my fault he said something stupid.

MATTY

Geez, a little early for this, isn't it???

HAN

I've had a few years to adjust myself to dealing with Grayson in the morning, unfortunately.

CALEB

Okay, what the fuck did Grayson do??? It's got to be big to be eliciting this kind of snark.

HAN

Snark? Just pointing out the obvious over here.

OLIVIA

Can we keep this weekend civil, please?

HAN

For you, babe, anything!

ZO

I need coffee, join me inside girls?

OLIVIA

Be right there

"Do you want some coffee, babe?" I ask Josh while putting my phone away.

"Sure."

I lean over and kiss him before heading to the building that has a coffee shop and a few souvenir stores. I meet the girls and we make our way to the coffee shop. I place an order for a Venti mocha and Grande Americano and we wait for our coffees.

"Okay, Hannah. What happened with you and Grayson? We're all stuck together for an entire weekend. I would like for everything to go smoothly," I say.

Hannah rolls her teeth over her bottom lip, pondering what to tell us. She takes a big breath and lets out a sigh, as if she's decided.

"A little over a year ago, Grayson had made it seem like he was interested. We went out to dinner a couple times, and it seemed like things were progressing. We had plans to go out to dinner one night, then I walked into a supply closet and found him going at it with another nurse from my department. I was mortified. He never tried to explain anything. So, ever since I have tried to avoid him. Yet, everywhere I go, at work and in my personal life, there he is. He's always flirting with the nurses. I've heard from other people about his sexual escapades, and it's just kind of gross. I just wish he had some more respect and some common decency for other people."

I look around at my friends and nod, taking in all that Hannah just shared with us. Hannah's not an overly emotional or sensitive person, so this must've really done something to her if she is still wound up about it a year later.

We grab our coffees and make our way outside. The guys are sitting at a picnic table, chatting. The girls and I all look at each other when we spot Grayson and plaster smiles on our faces and walk up to them. I hand Josh his coffee with a smile and Matt looks at me with a big grin and asks, "Where's my coffee?"

I grin back and say, "Inside, you just gotta walk up to the barista and order it. She's pretty cute. Maybe she'll give you her number and you can have a new fuck buddy for a while." His grin drops a bit before it's back on his face.

"So, my best friend gets coffee from my sister, but not me?"

I place a hand on Josh's shoulder and squeeze. "Well, Josh is doing the driving for this trip, which means I can nap, and he's letting me play my music. So yes, I bought him coffee."

Grayson looks between the two of us and squints his eyes. "He's letting you play your music?"

"Yup," I say, popping the p.

He looks to Josh with mock offence as he clutches his chest. "Josh, man, I thought we were friends. You never let me play my music in your car."

"That would be because you have some shit taste in music," Josh retorts.

The guys all start laughing like Grayson's taste in music is some inside joke. Grayson's cheeks pinken a little as he rebukes, "It was one time, and it wasn't my fault." There has got to be a good story behind this.

Zoey scoots into the free space beside Matt and places her chin on her hand as she says, "Please, do tell."

Surprisingly, Caleb is the first to break. "At poker one night about a year ago, Grayson went to hook his phone up to Josh's speakers and One Direction started blaring through the system. He swears it was some chick and that it wasn't his." Hannah is covering her mouth, trying to hide her smile and the start of a laugh. "But when we scrolled through the playlist, it was riddled with boy bands and teeny-bopper songs."

Eliza, Zoey, and I let it loose and Hannah joins in. I have a feeling Hannah may have been behind the incident. The announcement asking everyone to return to their cars comes over the loudspeaker, and we head to our cars. When we get in, I ask Josh, "What are the chances that we can skip going upstairs for breakfast with everyone and stay here in the car?"

He reaches over and squeezes my thigh. "Babe, not a chance in hell. If Zoey and the girls don't come looking for you, it will be Matt. Might as well head up and avoid the hunt."

I know he's right. Upstairs, we order food and find a table big enough for the eight of us.

"Do you know how difficult it's going to be going a whole weekend not sleeping beside you, not being able to kiss you when I want, not being able to touch you?" Josh asks softly beside me.

"I know, but I was thinking, maybe after your game on Tuesday, we could go to dinner with Matt and tell him about us."

That has him grinning. He reaches for my hand, giving it a quick squeeze. "Yeah, I'd love that."

"You'd love what?" Zoey asks as she slides in beside me. I didn't even see them coming.

Josh and I let go and I turn to her, making sure the guys aren't nearby. "Josh and I are going to tell Matt on Tuesday after their game."

I get a variety of looks from the girls. Eliza looks shocked, Hannah looks excited, and Zoey looks happy. Zoey grabs my hand and squeezes. "It's going to be great."

The guys join us shortly after and we dig into our breakfast. Once we finish, I wrap my arms around Matt from behind. "I'm going to go walking around with the girls. I'll see you when we get to the campground."

I release Matt and look at Josh. "I'll meet you at the car when the announcement goes off."

He nods and I go to walk past him. He reaches out and grabs my hand before I can. "Keep your phone on you, Olivia." I nod and join the girls, pulling my phone out and shooting him a quick text.

LIV

Yes, sir.

MY MAN

Careful or I might need to find a secluded spot tonight to spank the snark right out of you.

LIV

What if I don't want to be careful?

MY MAN

Then maybe you'll have one very pink ass tonight.

LIV

😈

"You're texting Josh, aren't you?" Eliza asks as we make our way down the hallway toward the stairs to the upper deck.

"Yes," I grin.

The three of them shake their heads despite their large smiles. "Let's get upstairs so I can fill you in on how our trip went last weekend."

We find a spot and position ourselves so we can see if the guys make their way up here. I don't want them to hear any of this. I tell the girls about camping, the audiobook in the car, the new things Josh and I tried together, the scenery, me telling Josh I love him and him saying it back, and Josh asking me to stay, and finally about my breakdown in the closet on Monday.

The girls listen intently and when I finish, Zoey says wistfully, "He's your lobster." She just finished a romance novel where the female main character kept talking about finding her lobster and she has adopted the phrase.

I nod, and she pulls me into a hug that turns into a group hug. "I'm happy for you," Eliza says once we break apart. "I'm happy that you found someone who treats you the way you deserve. You've been so much happier since you moved into his place. He's good for you."

I tear up at her words. They are kind, but I'm not sure why they're causing this reaction. We continue talking until we make our way back downstairs, parting ways on the vehicle deck. Back at the car, I find Josh already in the driver's seat, scrolling on his phone.

Getting in, he looks at me before finishing and locking his phone. He leans over the centre console and gives me a quick kiss, which isn't enough for me right now. My hand moves to the back of his head and I grip his hair, holding him close as I lick the seam of his lips. He groans and opens, and I deepen the kiss immensely.

The sound of cars turning on has us breaking apart. He reaches down and adjusts himself in his jeans before turning the car on. We drive off the ferry and are on our way to the next. I fall asleep with Josh's hand on my thigh as I lean against the door. I stir when we make it to the next ferry and again when we make it to the one after that.

I can feel Josh brushing my hair back from my face, and I hear him whispering, "Babe, we're here. It's time to wake up." Just then, I start to fall out of my seat as someone pulls open the door, but I'm caught by several hands. The next thing I hear is a group of laughter and I look around and see that Zoey and Eliza are holding me as Hannah, Caleb, Matt, and Grayson stand behind them, laughing. I scramble back into my seat and undo the seatbelt before scrambling out of the car. I give Zoey and Liz light slaps for, one, scaring the shit out of me, and, two, causing a scene in front of everyone.

Zoey whispers in my ear, "You two are lucky the back windows are tinted. If we hadn't done that, the guys would have seen how sweet Josh was being with you. We saved your ass."

"You still scared the shit out of me," I whisper hiss before softening my tone. "But thank you."

They nod and we all get to work setting up our campsite. By the time we're done, it's lunchtime and the guys get to work on the barbecue. The girls and I set the table with everything we may need before settling down with some drinks. We tell each other about the books we've read recently. Eliza is partway through her update when

Caleb asks, "You guys actually read that stuff?" We all turn and look at him, waiting to gauge his reaction.

"It's all we read," Hannah says.

"Seriously?" Matt asks.

"Yup," I say.

"It's basically porn," Grayson says.

"It's not, but if you really want to know what your girl wants, read her books. Find out if she highlights or tabs them, then maybe you'll be able to satisfy and keep a woman," Zoey says with a saccharine smile.

"Oh, I have no problems pleasing a woman," Grayson says, grinning and taking a sip of his beer.

"It's the keeping them you struggle with," Eliza says, which isn't like her, but after what Hannah told us, I'm not entirely surprised. The girls and I all take a long sip of our drinks while the guys have mixed looks of amusement and curiosity on their faces.

"Have any of you ever read a romance novel?" I ask, diverting the conversation.

Grayson, Caleb, and Matt all say, "No," while Josh remains quiet, although the guys don't notice.

"Okay, how about this, pick a medium. E-book you can read on your phone, a physical book, or an audiobook, and then we will recommend a book for you guys to read. You can choose to all read the same book or we can select a book for each of you."

They look at each other and nod. "Okay, we will all read the same book," Caleb says.

"Why don't we do an audiobook so we can listen to it together and get it over with," Matt says.

The girls and I stand and walk away from the table. We opt to stay away from dark romance, and decide that since the guys play hockey, we should have them listen to a hockey romance. I scroll through my reading tracking app; I find a book and show it to the girls and a grin spreads across their faces and they nod and we join the guys again.

"Okay, we've taken some mercy on you guys. We didn't pick a dark romance, and we stayed away from reverse harem books and MM romance, so you'll be listening to *The Deal* by Elle Kennedy.

It's a little-to-medium spice book, so it shouldn't be too much for you guys," I say.

Matt pulls his phone out and downloads the book while the rest of them finish lunch. We sit and eat our barbecue together and when we are done, we clean up and the girls and I change into our swimsuits.

It's a nice summer day, the sky is cloudless, and a light breeze comes off the water. We slowly wade into the cold Pacific Ocean. I stand there and close my eyes, taking in the sounds of the water lapping at the shore, the birds overhead, and the people around us. I've always enjoyed spending time in nature. It's been so nice to do that again this summer.

After a few minutes, we see the guys making their way toward us. My eyes immediately find Josh and make their way down his body as he walks toward the water in his swim trunks. My mouth goes dry and my chest is rising and falling faster. I know what it's like to run my hands down his body, what he smells like as I nip at his ear and pull the lobe between my teeth. How his abs tense as I run my fingers over them. I squeeze my thighs together, feeling myself getting wet.

Hannah elbows me, letting me know that I'm staring. No matter how long we've been together, how many times I've had fun running my hands down Josh's body, kissed him, or slept with him, I am always going to stare at him because to be perfectly honest, the man is hot, but also because I am still in awe he chose me. He wants me. He loves... me.

Somewhere along the way, I convinced myself I had to settle. I think that's why I let my relationship with Drew get to where it was; I felt like I had to make concessions in the relationship because of my size, like I had to let him get away with things because he was with a big girl and I was lucky to have someone interested in me. Josh has shown me how wrong that mentality is. He has shown me what it is like to be cared for, cherished, and loved. He makes time for us, and not just by accomplishing my summer list, but also by being home in time for us to enjoy dinner together. We watch shows together; he answers my texts during the day and if he's going to the store on his way home, he checks if I need or want anything. It's the little things Josh does that I didn't realize I was missing in my last relationship.

I look toward the beach as the guys rush toward us. They each seem to have a target. Matt is running toward Zoey, Josh towards me, Caleb to Hannah, and Grayson to Eliza. The girls notice just after me and we try to make our way out to the sides, away from where they're aiming, but we aren't fast enough. The guys grab onto us and drag us under the water with them. The water is cold as it rushes up my nostrils as Josh pulls me into his chest and completely under the surface.

I wiggle against his body, trying to free myself and get to the surface, but Josh's grip tightens around me and I feel him hardening against my ass. I freeze for a second and then decide I am going to make this fun for myself. I reach behind me and grab the waistband of Josh's swim trunks and shove them down. He releases his grip on me and I surface and swim away as fast as I can, laughing.

Josh surfaces as I swim away. "Olivia, you are going to pay for that," he shouts after me. I swim faster, feeling the burn in my arms and legs, trying to gain distance from Josh. I hear him getting closer and closer.

"Faster, Liv," Zoey calls while laughing.

"You can beat him," Hannah calls. I try to move faster, kicking my legs harder behind me when I feel a hand wrap around my ankle. I scream as it's yanked back, dragging me with it.

The force of the pull brings my head underwater and I try to twist to force him to release his grasp, but he doesn't. I now have my hips twisted as I force my face to the surface of the water. When Josh has me pulled all the way to him, he reaches out for my shoulder to dunk me again, but I quickly manage to wrap my arms around his neck, pulling him in with me. He releases my ankle from his grip, and I wrap my legs around his hips, pulling me flush to him. His erection presses between my legs.

When we surface Josh is standing with the water landing around my waist and my legs wrapped around his hips, Josh's hands gripping my ass, and my arms around his neck as we throw our heads back, laughing.

As my laughing dies down, I hear a throat clear behind me. I look back at Josh with a smile and say, "Now, Josh, what have we learned about dunking me?"

He grins back and chuckles. "That you'll pants me and run."

"Yup, every time!"

"But, Olivia, remember that I'll always come after you," he says with a grin and squeezes my ass before I release my legs from around his hip and jump into the water. His tone is playful, but I see the seriousness of his words in his eyes.

"I'm sure you will, Josh."

I turn around and see everyone watching us. The girls are standing to my right with knowing grins on their faces and the guys all have questioning looks. Matt quirks his brow as he asks, "Did you really pants him?"

"Yeah," I shrug. "Figured cold Pacific Ocean straight to the balls with no barrier might force him to let me go. Bet it would work on you, too. Should we test the theory?" I say with a mischievous grin.

Matt throws his hands up and takes a few steps away from me. "I'm good, thanks though, Liv. Appreciate it."

I chuckle as I make my way over to the girls. "I'm going to dry off and read on the beach. Who's joining me?" I ask.

Zoey loops her arm through mine and Hannah and Liz do the same as we make our way slowly out of the water. We grab our blankets and books and lie down. A little while later, we hear the guys come up and move to the campsite. As I lay there, I hear them start the audiobook and I look at Zoey and Liz, who nudges Hannah, who is listening to her audiobook. She pulls out a headphone and looks at us and smiles when she hears it. I close my Kindle and listen.

After a few chapters, I wrap my towel around myself before making my way towards the fire the guys have started. Grayson and Caleb are sipping their beers watching the fire, Matt is scrolling on his phone, and Josh is sitting with his ass on the edge of the chair, his legs straight out with his ankles crossed and his head resting against the back of the chair.

Josh looks up as I approach like he knows it is me, and a soft smile appears on his face. I grab a chair, pull it between Matt and Josh and settle in, watching the fire as I listen with them.

I remember the first time I read this series; I powered through the physical books. I loved them and the characters. I've heard bits and pieces online of the audiobooks, but listening to it now, I'm falling in love with the book all over again.

The girls slowly join us. Zoey and Hannah grab a blanket and two chairs and settle between Caleb and Matt, while Liz passes me a blanket before settling between Grayson and Josh.

At one point, someone brings over the cooler and roasters, and we start roasting hotdogs as the sun sets and the only light left is the fire. As chapter twenty-three comes to an end and chapter twenty-four begins, the girls and I look at each other with grins and I get comfortable so I can watch the reactions of the guys. It takes a little bit before we get to the spice, but as it begins, I see the changes on the guys' faces. Grayson is grinning like a fool, Caleb looks cool as a cucumber, Matt is adjusting himself in his chair, and Josh is giving me side glances as to avoid staring at me. I think they are beginning to realize why we read these books. We don't read them just for the smut, but it is a nice addition to the romance story.

After a few more chapters Josh reaches over and pauses the book and clean up. I grab the plates to be washed and Josh grabs the dish soap and the two of us make our way towards the dishwashing station near the washrooms using the flashlights on our phones.

The fire provided a lot of light, but as soon as we leave our campsite, it's completely dark. Josh and I silently walk down the pathway. The only sounds are the light breeze in the trees and the crunch of sticks and leaves beneath our feet. When we get close to the washing station, Josh grabs my hand and pulls me into a cluster of trees off the path and turns his flashlight off, grabbing my phone and doing the same. He pushes me up against a tree and kisses me.

It's an urgent, hungry kiss, like he couldn't go another second without his lips on mine. I drop the plastic plates as I wrap my arms around his neck, pulling him close to me.

It's hard being this close to him and not being able to touch him when I want to. Not being able to give him a quick kiss when I walk past him.

He reaches up and cups my breast through my bathing suit. They are more sensitive than normal, but in a good way. When he rolls his thumb over my hardened nipple, I moan into his mouth and arch my back, shoving my breast further into his hands. He breaks the kiss and I reach for him again, needing him now.

He kisses along my jaw and up to my ear, nipping my earlobe

before he whispers, "Can you be my good girl and stay quiet, Olivia?"

I nod. I want to moan his name and show him how much his touch affects me, but I listen to him.

"Good girl," he whispers, and my pussy clenches.

I have soaked my bathing suit bottoms, and I couldn't care less right now. Wordlessly, Josh drops to his knees, and God, it's a sight to behold to see Joshua Lincoln on his knees for me. His hands skate up my legs slowly, reaching my knee, he grips my right leg and lifts it over his shoulder, holding me in place. His hands move up my inner thighs until he reaches my pussy. His finger hooks the fabric of my bathing suit bottoms and pulls it to the side, exposing me to him. I am so unbelievably turned on and all Josh would have to do is barely slide a finger between my folds and he would feel it.

He leans forward and trails kisses up my exposed inner thigh. When he gets to my pussy, he parts me and licks me from my entrance to my clit, circling it with his tongue. He pulls back and says, "My beautiful Olivia, always wet for me."

I nod, trying so hard to remain quiet. He leans forward and licks me again, before sucking my clit into his mouth. I buck my hips as one hand moves to his hair, gripping it tightly. The other moves to my mouth, stifling the moan that comes out as his teeth graze my clit. He inserts two fingers into me and says, "Good girl, Olivia, stay quiet. We don't want anyone to hear just how much my dirty girl likes to be eaten out in public." His words make me wetter, and he grins before flicking my clit with his tongue.

His fingers work in and out of me at a relenting pace. I grip his hair tighter and bite down on my hand. His teeth graze my clit again. That's all it takes before my vision blurs and I'm seeing stars as my orgasm takes over my entire body. Josh continues to work me, as he holds me up against the tree when my legs give out.

He pulls his fingers out and stands to his full height, keeping eye contact with me as he places his fingers in his mouth and sucks my cum off them. He leans down and kisses me tenderly, full of affection, and I kiss him back, showing him the same.

He fixes my bathing suit bottoms before he picks up the dishes I dropped. We make our way toward the washing station, and I have a huge smile on my face as we work together to wash and dry the dishes. Before we reach the campsite, I stop Josh and kiss him, and make sure there's nothing stuck to his knees.

After packing the plates, I say, "Thanks for the help, Josh."

I say goodnight to the guys before climbing into the tent with the girls. They're all changed into their pyjamas and in their sleeping bags. They stop talking when I enter. I put my finger to my lips and point outside, reminding them the guys can hear us.

I zip up the tent and climb over to my sleeping bag. I change into my pyjamas and we circle up.

"Why were you gone for so long?" Liz whispers.

"Josh sort of pulled me off the trail, dropped to his knees and gave me an earth-shattering orgasm," I whisper.

"You're so lucky to have someone like him. I miss orgasms. I really need a non-vibrator-induced one too," Zoey whispers.

We talk for a few more minutes before we get ready to sleep.

The next morning, I wake up to the sounds of people talking outside the tent and the smell of something cooking. The smell makes my stomach turn. I climb out of my sleeping bag, slip into my flip-flops, and unzip the tent. Josh, Caleb, Matt, Zoey, Hannah, and Eliza are all up and sitting around the picnic table as Josh cooks. I scrunch up my nose at the smell. Josh looks at me and smiles. "Good morning, sleeping beauty," he says. He must register the look on my face because a look of concern takes over his as he asks, "What's wrong?"

"Morning, umm... What are you cooking?" I ask.

"Eggs, you okay? You usually love eggs for breakfast."

"Um, I'm not sure. My stomach doesn't feel great."

I watch as he moves the eggs to prevent them from burning and my stomach flips. I run to the edge of the campsite and bend over puking. I feel someone's hands reach and pull my hair back out of my face and a hand rub circles on my back. After a minute, I turn and see it's Zoey. I give her a small smile as Liz hands me a bottle of water. I rinse my mouth out and spit before I slowly drink the bottle. I turn around and Matt and Josh both watch me with worried expressions.

"You okay?" Matt asks.

"Yeah, it's probably just heat exhaustion. Too much alcohol and sun yesterday and not enough water."

Matt walks over and pulls me into a hug and I have to ask him to loosen it as the tightness is hurting my breasts.

Hannah comes out of the tent with our toiletry bags and we head to the washroom to brush our teeth.

CHAPTER 27

Josh

Yesterday and this morning have been beyond difficult. Being so close to Olivia and not being able to touch her, hold her hand, kiss her when I walk by, hold her by the fire or in my tent last night. This morning was worse, though. Seeing Olivia sick and not being able to comfort her, to be the one that held her hair back and rubbed her back and then to hold her in my lap after and let her know that I'm here for her. I'm glad Zoey and the girls took care of her.

Matt looked worried, but once the girls had her, he relaxed a little. I decided that after breakfast I'm going to offer to take Olivia home so I can take care of her and she can relax in our bed.

While the girls are in the washroom, I finish the eggs and throw on some bread to make Liv toast. I'm not sure what caused her to be sick, but I'm worried about her. While the bread toasts, I check the cooler to make sure we have plenty of water and other things to help her today.

I grab the orange juice, pour a cup, and then butter the toast, putting it on a plate. When the girls come back, Caleb wakes Grayson.

Olivia is sitting as far away from the griddle and eggs as she can. I place the toast and orange juice in front of her and run a hand over her head. "You need anything else?"

She looks up and gives me a soft smile. "No, I think I'm good."

I give her a slight nod and sit beside Matt as everyone piles eggs, bacon, and toast onto their plates. Olivia reaches for some bacon and when she takes a bite, she releases a moan that has me instantly hard. I grab my water, clearing my throat before I take a sip.

After breakfast, Olivia goes to help, and I put my hand on her lower back and whisper. "Babe, just relax. I'll clean up. Everyone else is helping. I want you to take it easy. I don't want you getting sick again."

She nods and sits down again. She pulls out her phone and I hand her a bottle of water out of the cooler. She shakes her head. "For me, please," I plead. I'm going to make sure she keeps her fluids up and is hydrated.

Once everything from breakfast is cleaned up, everyone goes to change into swimsuits. "Olivia, do you want to head home and relax there?" I ask.

"No, I'm good, I'm feeling better. I'll let you know if I need to leave."

She reaches for my hand and squeezes it before she changes, too. I do the same and we all meet out by the water. Olivia lays a towel out and settles in with her Kindle. Eliza is beside her while Zoey and Hannah are in the water with Matt, Caleb, and Grayson. I lay my towel beside Liv's and take a seat, watching the water.

I take in the smell of the ocean, the faint smell of Olivia's sunscreen, the feeling of the slight breeze coming off the water, and the heat of the sun on my skin. As I sit here, a sense of contentment washes over me. Being here with Olivia and seeing her smile and laugh yesterday—there's nowhere else I'd rather be. It's like when I'm away from her, my entire body is on edge and the minute she's near me, my entire body relaxes, the air filling my lungs feels fresher, and all the stress from my day fades.

I look over to Olivia as she lies on her stomach, reading. She adjusts her legs, crossing them and uncrossing them. Her cheeks have a slight pink to them and she's biting her bottom lip. She's reading a spicy scene.

I lean towards her slightly, and goosebumps climb up her arms. "Watcha reading, my love? You look a little flushed. Are you reading a spicy scene?"

I whisper just loud enough for her to hear. She turns to me slightly and looks at me through her lashes, and subtly nods.

I run my fingers lightly over her arm and feel the shiver that runs through her body. "And what about it has got you so worked up?"

She looks around to see how far away the guys are, apparently not caring if Eliza hears. "The hand necklace, the possessiveness, and the dominance," she whispers.

"Are you wet Olivia?"

"Yes," she says breathlessly. Her chest is rising and falling at a quicker pace now. I think our conversation is turning her on more than the book.

"Do you want me to take you up there and make you come, Olivia?"

"God, yes," she quietly moans.

I lean into her until my mouth is right beside her ear. "Aren't you my needy little whore, ready to spread your legs for me, begging for me to make you come?" She bites her lip and nods. "Be a good girl then and walk to the bathroom and wait for me. I'll be there in a couple of minutes."

She quickly closes her Kindle and hands it to Liz before making her way up to the campsite.

I wait a few minutes before following her. She is leaning against the building, biting her lip when I approach. I grab her hand and pull her into a single stall. As soon as I have the door locked, I push her up against it and kiss her, one hand gripping her hair tightly, the other on her ass pulling her into me. She moans as I press my erection into her stomach. My lips leave hers and trail down her neck and along her collarbone before moving up to her ear, where I nibble on the lobe. "Is my needy little whore still wet for me?" I whisper. She nods and I tighten my grip on her hair to that precise point between pleasure and pain. "Be a good girl and use your words, Olivia."

"Yes, I'm wet for you, Josh."

I release my grip, moving my hand from her hair to her throat and my hand on her ass moves to the inside of her thighs. I make my way up her leg and grab her swimsuit bottoms and pull them to the side. I run my finger through her folds and groan. "You're not just wet for me, Olivia, you're soaked. Such a good girl."

I plunge two fingers inside her as my thumb finds her clit and work her slowly, building her release at my own pace. I remove my hand from her throat and pull her top down enough to reveal her pert pink nipples. I suck one into my mouth as my free hand pinches the other one. She groans and I press my hard cock into her thigh, showing her just what she does to me.

When I feel her begin to tighten around my fingers, I pull them out and say, "Today, you're going to come around my cock."

I push my shorts down, freeing my erection and grip the back of her thighs, lifting her as she jumps and wraps her legs around my hips. I line myself up with her entrance and with one thrust, I'm fully inside her. With her arms wrapped around my neck and my hands on her ass, I pump into her at a relentless pace. I feel her tighten around me and my grip on her ass tightens. I adjust the angle. Two more thrusts and she's falling over the edge, moaning my name like it's the only thing she can think or say.

I pull out of her, and she releases her grip on my hips. Once her feet are on the ground, I spin her and push a hand between her shoulder blades, and she bends just like I wanted her to. I line myself up again and get a grip on her hair before sliding back inside her. She arches her back as I pull on her hair, and one of her hands reaches back and goes on top of my hand in her hair.

I lean over and say, "You and this pussy are mine. Mine to use. Mine to love. Mine to take care of."

"Yes, yours." She moans and bucks her hips back, needing more.

I release my grip on her hair and slap her ass before grabbing onto her hip and fucking her hard and fast. The small bathroom fills with the sound of our moaning and skin slapping.

"Spank me, Josh. Spank me," she calls, and I do. One slap to each ass cheek leaving a slight pink mark on each, I grip her hair, pulling her up and use my other hand to slap her clit. It sends her over the edge, her pussy grips my cock tightly, taking me with her. I release everything I have in her, calling her name as I finish.

I pull out and wet some paper towels to clean her up. I adjust her bottoms back into place and when she turns around, I place my hand around her neck and kiss her deeply, knowing that I won't have another chance to do it again anytime soon. I give her a few pecks on the lips, and I lean my forehead against hers. "I love you, Olivia," I whisper and tap my thumb against her neck three times.

She smiles. "I love you, too."

I kiss her forehead before she leaves the bathroom, and I wait a few minutes before going out. I wish we could tell Matt today, but I respect Olivia's decision to wait until we do dinner after our game on Tuesday.

When I get back to the campsite, Olivia is sitting in a chair beside Liz and Hannah, talking. I look at Hannah and ask, "Where are the guys?"

"The water. They said something about coming in soon."

I grab the chair next to Olivia and sit. I know the girls know about us, so I lean over and kiss her and she smiles. I pull out my phone and respond to some work emails from Friday while the girls continue talking. Feeling a hand clamp down on my shoulder, I look over and see it's Grayson.

"Man, you chose to hang out up here with the girls rather than in the water with us. What's up with that?"

"Just thought I'd respond to some emails right now."

"We need to find you a girl to drag you away from your work, get you laid. How long has it been?"

I'm not about to tell him I just had amazing sex about thirty minutes ago in the bathroom with Olivia. "I'm good, Grayson."

"You're good with what?" Caleb calls, and I look to see him, Matt, and Zoey making their way towards us.

"I was just telling Josh here that we should find him a girl to drag him away from his work, at least get him laid. I haven't heard of any conquests, so I'm guessing it's been a while." Zoey starts some weird cough that she's using to cover a laugh and Matt pats her on the back.

"Not all men are man-whores," Liz calls with a little malice in her voice, and Grayson turns to look at her.

"Are you calling me a man whore, Eliza, because I don't know what I've done to give you that impression?" Grayson says.

"Just an observation, but just so you know, calling women a conquest doesn't help your argument," she retorts with a little bite.

"Okay. Well, Josh if you want, there is this cute girl I know that I could set you up with if you're interested," Caleb says, trying to diffuse the conversation.

"I'm good, no need for that," I say.

"So, you're having sex, then?" Grayson asks.

"Do we really need to be having this conversation right now?" Zoey asks.

"I just want to know if my friend is getting laid," Grayson says with a grin.

"Best sex of my life. Is that enough for you?" I ask, then look around the campsite and the girls are all trying to hide their bug-eyed expressions. I stretch my arms out over my head and then to my side, tapping a finger three times on Olivia's arm before returning them to the armrest of my chair.

Grayson sits next to me and places his arms on his legs as he leans forward. "Best sex of your life, okay? Now you gotta share. Who is giving you that?"

Everyone takes a seat like what I have to say is the most interesting thing in the world. I get up and grab a beer, popping it open and pass a water to Olivia, before taking a seat again. Everyone is still watching me, waiting for an answer. Olivia is playing with a string on her cover up and avoiding looking at me.

I take a sip of my beer and look at Grayson. "She's beautiful, kind, smart, funny, and loving." I don't want to say too much before we get a chance to tell Matt.

"When do we get to meet her?" Caleb asks with genuine interest.

"Soon."

"So, I'm starving. Who else is hungry?" Zoey asks, slapping the tops of her thighs, thankfully changing the conversation topic.

"Ohhh, you know what I could really go for? A burger," Olivia says before excitedly turning to me. "We brought the ingredients, right?" she asks hopefully.

I chuckle. "Yeah, we did. I'll make you a burger, just the way you like. Anyone else want one?"

Everyone raises their hand, and I begin to make burgers. I season the meat while Zoey grabs the pasta salad she made, and Liz grabs some fruit and veggies. Once the burgers are finished, we sit down and make our buns. Olivia bites into her burgers and lets out a deep, sexy moan.

"God, this is the best burger you've ever made," she says, taking another bite.

I take a bite of mine and it tastes the same as usual, but I'm glad she's enjoying it. Thankfully, Matt plays the book from yesterday, so

I don't have to worry about Grayson bringing up the topic of my sex life again. I'm surprised the guys agreed to listen to a book. I do it for Liv because I know how much she enjoys them, but they really aren't the guy's thing. I guess the girls just taunted them enough.

When Olivia finishes her plate, she asks me, "Do we have any pickles? I have a hankering for a good dill pickle."

I don't think we even have pickles at home. I don't think I've seen her eat one since we were kids.

"Are you on a pickle kick, like when we were kids?" Matt asks, raising an eyebrow.

"No, I just really want a pickle," she says.

"I don't think we have any, but we can run to the store if you want one," I say, and a huge smile breaks across her face.

"Really?" she asks. I nod and move to stand.

"I'll take her," Matt says, and I hand him my keys. Olivia goes to walk behind me toward her tent to grab her purse and I reach into my pocket and hand her my credit card; she tries to walk past me without taking it and I grab a hold of her wrist and put the card in her hand and pull her closer to me. "The code is 0515", I whisper, and I see the moment she understands the meaning of those numbers. Her birthday.

"Why don't you grab some of those popsicles you like and some iced tea too," I call as she and Matt make their way to the car.

CHAPTER 28

Olivia

Matt and I make our way to the grocery store. It's close by as the island is very small and doesn't have much. I watch the trees pass as we drive through the campground to the main road. I enjoy watching the nature and families enjoying the outdoors together, parents slathering their children in sunscreen, siblings chasing each other, the sound of the squeals and giggles. I want that one day, going camping with my family, my kids playing with each other, running around, and giggling while I sit with a book and watch them.

"We haven't had a lot of one-on-one time. I wanted to make sure you're doing okay. I know Drew showing up at Mom and Dad's a few weeks ago was a lot for you, but otherwise, are you doing okay?" Matt asks, breaking me from my people-watching and thoughts.

"Yeah, I think getting out of that relationship was best for me. Now that it's done, I noticed I had made changes in myself to accommodate him, and now I'm back to myself. I'm happy again, like truly happy," I say, not able to keep the smile off my face as I think about the last few months with Josh.

With Josh, I never have to think about changing the way I act. He loves and accepts me for me, and he doesn't suggest that I should hit the gym more or I should eat differently. He has tried to understand and enjoy my hobbies too. He doesn't pick on me for reading romance books.

"I'm glad. You'll let me know if you need anything, right?" he asks, glancing at me before looking back at the road.

I reach over and give his arm a reassuring squeeze. "Yeah Matt. I'll let you know. Do you have any plans after the game on Tuesday?"

"No, what's up?"

"Josh and I are going to grab dinner after the game and were hoping you'd join us."

"Sounds good. Just let me know where."

"I will. I don't think we have settled on a place, but I'll let you know."

We pull into the grocery store parking lot, and I hop out and head inside for my pickles, as well as Josh's requested items. I meet Matt at the cash register. He has an arm full of snacks and I shake my head. We are only here until tomorrow afternoon, so I'm not sure why all the snacks. I put my stuff on the belt, and Matt grabs a divider and puts his stuff up too. The cashier rings up all my items and I pay with Josh's credit card. I'm still stunned that his code is my birthday. As soon as we are in the car, I pop open the jar of pickles and grab the first one I can and take a big bite of it, moaning as the acid and dill flavours hit my tongue.

"You really wanted that pickle," Matt says with a chuckle.

"Yeah," I reply and finish my pickle as we make our way back to the campground.

When we get back, we hop out and I take the bag with the popsicles and iced tea to Josh and hand him back his credit card.

"She didn't even make it out of the parking lot before she had the pickles open. She's on like her third one already," Matt calls from behind me.

I turn and face him. "I really wanted pickles, and it could be worse," I say.

Josh gives my hip a quick squeeze, "You're alright, babe, don't worry about it. How are you feeling, though?" I barely realize his slipup of calling me babe, but I don't think anyone else caught it.

"I'm better, thanks." I give him a smile before settling into a camping chair and grabbing a bottle of water.

"That wasn't so bad, was it?" Zoey asks the guys when the book finishes.

"Top tier book boyfriend," Hannah says. All the guys, including Josh, look at her with questioning looks.

"Book boyfriend?" Caleb asks, using a napkin to wipe his face.

"Yeah, a guy in a book that all girls wish he were real because of how amazing he is. We all have book boyfriend lists, some guys are listed as book husbands, and that's a separate list," I say.

"You all have lists?" Matt asks and all four of us respond with a nod and, "Yeah."

"Who is on your list?" Grayson asks.

"We all have different lists, and it varies depending on our moods usually," Hannah says.

"Sometimes it's the more morally grey characters, other times it's the more golden retriever, although Liz, I think your list is usually more morally grey, not sure how that happened, I would have thought that would be more of a Liv thing," Zoey says with a chuckle.

"Morally grey?" Now it's Josh questioning us.

"Yeah, the mafia guys, the serial killers, the stalkers. They often have the 'touch her and die' vibe going on," Hannah says.

"And why do you think Olivia would be more into the morally grey book boyfriends?" Josh asks.

"Because there is a sense of security that comes with them, as well as a sense of devotion," Zoey says. "Liv, who is your top morally grey book boyfriend?"

"Zaddy Zade." The words are out of my mouth before I've even had a chance to think them through. All heads turn to me.

Matt and Josh have quirked eyebrows. "Zaddy Zade?" Matt asks.

"No comment," I say as I curl into myself. Why the fuck did I add the 'Zaddy' in there? Why couldn't I just say Zade? This is not a conversation I want to have with my brother, boyfriend, and their friends.

The girls are giggling. I grab an empty can and throw it in their general direction, and it hits Hannah in the arm. She puts her arms up in surrender and tries to rein in her laughter and nudges Zoey, who is sitting beside her.

"Who is this Zaddy Zade?" Josh asks with a hint of laughter.

I mimic zipping my lips and throwing the key away, and then the guys look to the girls, and Zoey is the one to crack. "Fine, Zaddy Zade is Zade Meadows from Haunting and Hunting Adeline, he stalks her in the first book and is determined to make Addie his. Zade would basically burn the world for her if she asked."

Everyone's eyes are on me now. "Hey, you all liked Zade too, not just me and I have more golden retriever energy ones on my list. Garrett Graham, Dean Di Laurentis, Nate Hawkins, all three of the Cane Brothers, although Huxley is more grump than a golden retriever, same with Brendan Taggart, Fox Thornton, the Eden brothers, Dylan Reed, the Rhodes Brothers, Dante Romano, Aiden Graves, Jack Hawthorne, Evan Zanders, Ryan Shay, top tier book husband for sure, Damien Martinez, Nathan Donelson, and that's only part of my non-morally grey list, which is significantly longer than the morally grey list," I say trying to take the attention off the fact that my first response was Zade.

"You just listed, like, eighteen guys there and some were brothers, so there are more and that's just part of your list of non-morally grey book boyfriends?" Grayson asks, his voice laced with confusion.

"Sounds about right," Hannah says before taking a sip of her drink.

"Yup," Zoey and Liz say too. "All our lists are very similar, but our top ten or so is what changes depending on our moods. I would one-hundred percent agree with the guys on Liv's list so far, although remind me of Nathan Donelson?" Zoey asks.

"*The Cheat Sheet*," I say, and the girls all make sounds of recognition.

"I'd say Damian is also a top-tier book husband, but that's me," Hannah adds.

"Oh, yeah, of the list Ryan, Damian, Knox, Nate, Jack, and Garrett are all book husband level," I agree.

Zoey and Liz nod their heads in agreement. "Sometimes I think I'd add Huxley too, depending on my mood," Liz adds.

The guys all look at us with confusion. "Would you take these book boyfriends over a real guy?" Caleb asks.

"No," I respond quickly. I see the smile playing on Josh's lips at my quick answer. Josh gives me everything I need. I couldn't even imagine trading him for anyone else.

"I'd take me a Damian Martinez right about now," Zoey says.

"That man eats pussy like it's his favourite pastime," Hannah says and I hear a couple of the guys choke on their drinks, and the girls and I break out laughing.

"Is that why he's a top-tier book husband?" Matt asks.

"No, it's the way he makes her feel about herself, how he helps her self-esteem after she finds out her boyfriend was cheating on her because she was 'too much' because of her love of pink and how her ex had said that what she does for work is pathetic, and commented on her size, then when Damian finds out the petty little revenge pranks she pulls on him because of all of that, he's proud of her, he builds her up while letting her be herself," Zoey says while looking at Josh.

I know what she's doing. She's comparing him with Damian, and she's right. They are alike in many ways.

"Plus, the man loves to eat pussy and always knows how to make his girl come, and usually more than once," Zoey adds, still looking at Josh.

"So, you idealize these male characters because they treat the female main characters how you would want your man to treat you," Caleb summarizes.

"Have you guys come across so many shit guys you now idealize these fictional ones?" Grayson asks skeptically, and the four of us girls all swing our heads in his direction with very serious expressions as we say, "Yes," at the same time.

"You realize that not all men are the same, right?" Grayson asks.

"Rich, coming from you," Hannah mumbles just loud enough that everyone could barely hear her.

"So, I think it's time for bed," Liz says, jumping up and taking Hannah's hand, pulling her up and out of her chair, and leading her toward the tent. Zoey and I get up to join them, saying a quick good-night before heading into the tent. We change into our pyjamas before climbing into our sleeping bags. I look for my forwarded mail as I haven't looked at it yet. When I find the stack, I notice it isn't as thick as it was before.

"Have you guys seen my mail?" I ask.

Liz and Hannah say, "No," but Zoey is suspiciously quiet. I turn and look at her, but she avoids my gaze. "Zo," I start. She lets out a sigh.

"I only took the letters from Drew. You didn't need to see them. The last thing you need to be reading is nasty notes from him," she says.

"Did you read them?" I ask.

"Babe, they aren't good. Just ignore them."

"What did they say?" I push.

She stares at me for what feels like an entire minute, but she must know I'm not going to let it go because she says, "He said he'd win you back. That he deserves you and you won't find someone who will put up with your size, so you're better off just going back to him. It's all the same shit he's been spewing. Not a word in those letters is true. You are in a healthy relationship now with someone who loves and cares about you, who doesn't want to change you."

I nod and settle into my sleeping bag, allowing her words to sink in. I think it was the final kick in the ass I needed to not let his words affect me as much as they have been. She's right. I'm in a healthy relationship for a change. I fall asleep allowing this revelation to sink in.

In the morning, we eat breakfast before we pack the campsite. I stay away from the eggs, the smell still making me queasy. We pull out of the campsite at exactly 10:45 a.m., fifteen minutes before check-out. We make our way to the ferry terminal; I hook my phone up to the stereo and put on my variety playlist, and Josh places his hand on my thigh as we drive with the windows down. When we pull onto the ferry, Taylor Swift's "Paper Rings" comes on, I turn it up and start jamming out to it. Singing along, counting with the song and just as the chorus hits, Josh's hand comes up to his face as he watches and tries to cover his smile. I continue to sing the song, having fun. When it finishes, I hear clapping and cheering from behind me and turn to see that Caleb has pulled his truck up to the spot beside us and Matt is filming me while the guys watch.

A rush of heat hits my face in embarrassment. I turn to Matt and point at him. "That gets deleted right now. That video will never see the light of day," I say.

Matt chuckles. "I don't know, this might be great to show your future kids how crazy their mom is." He grins.

"Matt, I'm your younger sister, the younger sister who spent most of her time growing up hanging out with you and Josh. Do you actually think that I don't have something that would be, in your words, 'great to show your future kids'?"

"Liv, you love me too much. You don't have anything on me," Matt says with confidence.

"Really? Might I remind you of your dry grad night, that wasn't so dry, and our backyard?"

Josh starts laughing and Matt's jaw drops. "You wouldn't?" Matt asks.

"Oh, I've got pictures from before Josh and I helped you inside."

Matt sends a look to Josh. "You let her take pictures?"

Josh tries to rein in his laughter but isn't entirely successful. "Man, I was pretty toast too, and I was laughing. I couldn't stop her; it was too funny."

"Fine, never seeing the light of day," Matt says.

"What happened after your dry grad?" Grayson asks with a shit-eating grin.

"Not talking about it," Matt says tersely.

Grayson and Caleb both look at me and I put my hands up. "Nope, that video stays gone, and I won't say anything."

The ferry docks, and we drive off and make our way to the next one. We don't see anyone this time and make our way down the island towards Nanaimo for our last ferry. As we get closer, a craving for a Timmie's bagel with cream cheese and an Ice Capp hits, so Josh takes us through a drive-through.

We board the ferry and I text the girls that we are making our way to the top observation deck. Josh and I get up there and we go to the front of the ferry. I lean against the railing and Josh stands behind me with an arm on each side of me. He kisses my neck and temple whispering, "I love you."

He removes his arms and moves to stand beside me, and I look at him with a smile and whisper back, "I love you, too."

We stand there for a bit, taking in the view. The wind whips through my hair, pieces being pulled out of my ponytail. I finish my drink as the girls join us. Zoey looks at my drink and a big grin spreads across her face. "Josh stopped at Timmies for you? He really is a good one."

I look over at Josh, and we grin at each other. "Yeah, I know."

When the guys join us, we find a group of seats inside. We talk for a bit and when I get tired Josh and I decide to head back down to the car. I give Matt and the girls hugs and say goodbye to Grayson and Caleb. The girls all hug Josh before he says his goodbyes to the guys. I fall asleep in the car and don't wake up until Josh wakes me when we get home.

When we get upstairs, I get all our clothes from the weekend together and put them in the washer while Josh unpacks the cooler.

"Babe, do we still have the jar of pickles?" I call as I make my way into the kitchen.

"Yeah, they're right here."

Opening the jar, I grab a pickle. "Was Matt right? You back into your pickle phase from when we were kids?"

I shrug. "Not sure. I just suddenly really wanted some pickles. I don't know what brought it on. Any thoughts on dinner? I was thinking Chinese?"

"Sure, babe, sounds good. I have to answer some emails before work tomorrow. Why don't you curl up on the couch and I'll order us some food shortly?"

"Okay, have fun."

I spend the evening reading on the couch before dinner and we eat together before I jump in the shower and climb into bed.

Tuesday is Josh's hockey game, so I spend the day around the house until Josh picks me up. We head to the rink and I give him a quick kiss before leaving the car and he goes into the dressing room. The girls join me again tonight and we find our seats on the bleachers. When Josh comes out, we do our pre-game routine before puck drop.

The puck drops, and the other team gains possession, passing behind to the defenceman. He passes it cross-ice to another player who crosses centre before drop-passing it and the next player manages to make it into our d-zone. A quick shove into the boards has us gaining possession and shooting it down the ice. Josh picks it up, before passing backwards to Grayson, who brings his stick back and shoots it, aiming for the top shelf, but their goalie gloves it and the whistle blows.

Josh wins this face-off and passes back to Matt, who connects with it. He sends it across to Luke, who wraps around the goal before passing to Josh, who manages to make it just over the pads of the goalie and scores.

The girls and I cheer. The rest of the period moves quickly, ending in a 1-0 score. They move to centre ice for the beginning of the second period. This period feels more intense than before, and more physical. Both teams have shots on goal, but none go in.

Between the second and third, I ask the guys, "What's up with this team? Seems like there's more to it than this game."

Grayson takes his mouth guard out before saying, "Last season, we kind of whipped their asses. Looks like they're trying to pay us back for it."

I nod and settle back on the bench. The third period starts, and I feel the tension. Ten minutes in, Josh gets possession of the puck and makes a wraparound goal. They meet at centre ice, and the puck drops. From the second it drops, it seems like the other team's #7 is targeting Josh. Josh sees the guy coming and passes the puck and five seconds later the guy cross-checks Josh so hard he's falling backward and his head bounces off the ice.

I scream and my entire body goes cold. My hands are in fists so tight my nails dig into my palms. When after thirty seconds I don't see Josh move, I'm off the bleachers and pushing past the guys on the bench, moving through the open door, and running onto the ice.

There's a group gathered around him, including the guy who hit him. I try my best to stay upright as I run toward him. I make my way between people and fall to my knees beside him. Tears are running down my cheeks. I place my hands on either side of his face and speak softly. "Josh, look at me. You're okay."

He doesn't move, and the tears continue. I brush his hair off his forehead. "Babe, look at me, you're okay, you've got to be okay."

He groans and opens his eyes, looking at me. "Olivia, what are you doing on the ice?" he asks.

"You scared the shit out of me when you didn't get up. You can't do that to me," I say through my tears.

Matt and Grayson help him get up and I stand and face #7, and without much thought, I pull my right arm back and punch the guy, hitting him straight in the jaw. He falters back and holds a gloved hand to his jaw. "That was a dirty check, and we all know it," I say. "Maybe next time you should pull your head out of your ass before you go playing dirty," I say, poking my finger into his chest, so hard my finger hurts, but anger is boiling in me. Arms wrap around my centre, pulling me back into a chest. "Olivia, babe, I'm fine. You can leave him be now."

I spin in Josh's arms, pulling myself out of them. "Don't 'babe, I'm fine' me. You didn't get up right away. I remember when you took hits in high school, you never stayed down. You scared the shit out of me."

I open my palms and show him the crescent shapes my nails dug in. "I clenched my fists so tight this happened." I let out a huge sigh when he grabs both my wrists and kisses each palm.

"I'm sorry I scared you. I'm okay. I'm not as young and spry as I was in high school."

I close my eyes and let out another sigh. "Okay," I say. "We have to get you checked for a concussion, though. Promise me."

"I promise."

"Your girl packs a mean right hook there," #7 says to Josh, who full-on belly laughs, and says, "I'm sure she does, haven't been on the receiving end of one." He looks down at me with a smile. "Babe, let's get you off the ice so the game can finish."

"Fine, but you're not playing anymore," I say before turning around and walking back to the bench, feeling the stares of Josh's team. The girls are watching me with shit-eating grins.

When Josh steps off the ice, I grab his hand and pull him towards Hannah. "Han, can you please do concussion protocol on my boyfriend here?" She smiles and nods, motioning for Josh to sit. She goes through everything and says he looks fine, but to monitor him and if he starts displaying symptoms to have him see a doctor.

There is still some time in the game when Josh heads into the dressing room. He assures me he's fine and will let me know if he starts to feel sick. The girls and I head upstairs as he showers and changes. Poor Josh is probably going to have to answer some questions from my brother.

CHAPTER 29

Josh

Opening my eyes and seeing Olivia on the ice was weird, and if that didn't out our relationship, me wrapping my arms around her, pulling her away from the guy who checked me and calling her babe definitely did.

I sit down in front of my changing station, take my jersey off, and lean down to unlace my skates. When the door opens, Luke is the first to walk in.

"Fucking your best friend's sister, dude, seriously?" he retorts as he makes his way to his change station. I shake my head because, of course, that's all he thinks it is—sex. Why could it be anything more?

When everyone is in the room, Nick asks, "Matt, you're okay with Josh dating your sister?"

Matt looks directly at Nick. "Yeah, why wouldn't I be?"

Nick doesn't say anything right away. "It's your best friend and your sister. You guys have known each other for years."

Matt sits next to me. "Yeah, Liv and Josh have known each other for just as long. I know he'll treat her right and protect her. I've seen him stand up for her firsthand. I've noticed a change in her since her stupid ex, too. She smiles more, has more fun, she's obviously happy. Why would I be upset by that? Plus, seeing as my sister tells Zoey everything, and Liz and Han probably know, and they like Josh enough to hug him goodbye this weekend, my guess is they approve, and if they didn't, well, I don't even want to know what they might do."

Grayson, being the shit disturber that he is, says, "Because, best sex of his life."

Luke and Nick's eyes go wide, and I shoot a glare at Grayson, who just grins back at me. I turn to see Matt's reaction. He looks me in the eye, and points at me. "That. I don't want to know anything about your sex life with my sister."

I nod because honestly, I don't want to share that with him. I get it. The last thing I want to know about is my sister's sex life.

"So, the night we all had dinner, and she said her sex life was satisfying, that was you?" Luke says and I throw a roll of tape at him. He catches it laughing.

"That was Olivia knowing how to get under Matt's skin," I say.

"Her book boyfriends and book husbands don't bother you?" Grayson asks.

Most of the guys in the room are staring at us in confusion. "No, I feel secure in my relationship with Olivia, and I've listened to a few books with her. She played them in the car when we went to Banff, Calgary, and the ice fields two weekends ago. That was hours of books." I look at Matt. "You're not going to want to hear this," I tell him and then turn back to Grayson. "And knowing what books your girl is into can be very helpful. If you really listened to that book this weekend, I'm sure you could learn something. All four of the girls said that Garrett was one of their favourites."

"Wait, you guys went to Banff and Calgary?" Matt asks.

"You remember the character's name?" Grayson asks.

I look at Grayson first. "Yeah, because it's important enough to Olivia that she remembers." Turning to Matt next, I say, "Yeah, last weekend was our third trip this summer, the weekend before we camped in Banff and then we went to a concert in Calgary on Saturday, drove up the ice fields, stayed in Jasper and drove home. A few weekends before we went to Whistler. After doucheface, she made a list of things she wanted to do this summer. I said I'd help make sure she does them all. We're going to Victoria and Seattle this weekend."

I grab a water bottle out of my bag and take a large sip. I was hoping this conversation wouldn't be taking place in the dressing room after a game, but here I am. "Why didn't she ask me to help her with her list?"

I choke on the water and cough. When I finally compose myself, I turn to Matt with a serious face. "Matt, you, under no circumstances, want to see that list."

"Now I want to see this list," Luke calls, and I give him the deadliest look I can. "No man, under any circumstances, will see it," I growl.

"Oh, there's a sex list, isn't there?" Nick says before laughing.

"Emily saw it, that's bad enough," I mutter, and Matt breaks out laughing. "Dude, your sister saw this list?"

"Yeah, and Zoey, Hannah, Liz, and probably Gi, so there's that." I guess I'm going to have to get used to all these women knowing details of my sex life.

"Three trips and she's still living with you. Must be serious," Caleb finally says, and that seems to quiet the room down a bit. I reach into my bag and grab the thing I hid in there last week and toss it to him.

"Serious enough for you?" He opens the ring box and the entire dressing room seems to go to a standstill.

My body tightens as I wait for a response. I know Olivia and I haven't been dating for a long, but I've waited, and I've wasted too much time. I'm not going to do that anymore. Caleb and I stand, and he hands it back to me before pulling me in, patting my back. "I'm happy for you, man, congrats."

"Thanks, I haven't asked her yet," I say with a chuckle.

"She'll say yes, based on how she fussed over you on the ice, the way she punched that guy who had several inches and pounds of muscle on her because of a dirty check, then had Hannah do concussion protocol."

I hope so. I'm not sure I could take her answer being no.

"Thanks, man."

I sit back down, passing the box to Matt. "I'm not asking permission because she would kill me if I did, but I do want you to know. That was why she asked you to dinner tonight. She was so worried about our relationship ruining yours and mine, but I love her. She will always come first to me and there is no one else I want to share my life with."

He passes it back to me and claps me on the back. "I guess now we will actually be brothers," he says with a huge grin.

"I need to hurry up. Knowing Olivia, she's probably upstairs freaking out, and likely wants a freaking bagel and cream cheese from Timmies, and I need to get more pickles before the store closes, too. You should hurry up too, so she knows you're not totally pissed at us."

Matt nods.

I grab my towel before heading toward the shower. "Josh," Grayson says, getting my attention. "You might want to grab a pregnancy test when you're at the store getting pickles," he says quietly.

My heart races. Could Olivia be pregnant? She said she was on birth control. We haven't really discussed a timeline for having kids, but I don't think she was planning on having them this soon.

"Why would you say that?" I ask.

"Well, this weekend she got sick because of the smell of eggs, which I'm guessing is a new thing, seeing as you said she usually likes them for breakfast. She is suddenly craving pickles for the first time since she was a kid and is now craving a very specific bagel and cream cheese combo. Are her breasts more sensitive? Are her emotions and moods changing? Has her sex drive increased?" he asks.

I remember her breasts being more sensitive when we were in the woods; she has been wanting more sex, and the cravings are new and weird. It all clicks, and a huge smile breaks across my face as the realization dawns on me: Olivia is probably pregnant. I kind of hope she is. I can't wait to start a family with her. I know she will make an amazing mother.

I move as quickly as humanly possible, showering and changing. I grab my bag and make sure the ring is in there. Matt joins me and we make our way upstairs to meet the girls.

We get into the bar and find the girls sitting at a table to our left. When Olivia sees me, she smiles, and tears begin to run down her cheeks. I make it to her and brush them away with my thumb. "Babe, why are you crying? I'm okay. You don't need to worry," I say.

"I don't know," she says with a laugh.

I see a drink in front of her. "What are you drinking?" I ask.

"Long Island. Needed to calm my nerves," she says.

I push the drink toward Zoey. "I think that those won't be your go-to for a while," I murmur, and Hannah's eyes widen like she realizes why I did it and I just smile at her. At least she seems to be the only one that heard me.

Olivia sees Matt over my shoulder, leaving me, she hugs him. "I wanted to tell you Matt, but I didn't want to be the reason anything comes between you and Josh." He holds her and tells her it's alright and he understands.

When they separate, I grab Olivia's hand. "Babe, we should get going. I have to stop at the store before dinner, and I'm guessing you also want a Timmie's bagel?"

She smiles. "I do. You're amazing, you know that?" I lean down and give her a quick kiss in response.

She looks over at Matt, who's smiling at us. "Where do you want to get dinner?" she asks him.

"Why don't we do something this week? You two go home and relax after the hit he took, seeing as your news is out."

"Wednesday, why don't you come over and we'll invite Emily and Gi too," she says.

"Sounds good. I love you, sis."

"Love you, too." She hugs him and the girls before we make our way to the car. I grab Olivia her bagel before heading to the grocery store and grabbing the few things I need. We pick up a pizza for dinner on our way home.

We get home and settle on the couch, eating while watching TV and once we're done, I pause the show and face her. My heart is racing as I look at her. She is everything I want, and I hope this goes how I want it to. I rub my hands down my thighs to get rid of the sweat. I take a deep breath.

"So, this isn't how I wanted to do this," I say, feeling my nerves increasing. "But I feel like you need to see item one before I show you item two."

Olivia adjusts her position and looks at me hesitantly. I reach into my pocket and pull out the ring box. "Olivia Rose Carter, I love you, you bring so much joy into my life. You make me laugh and smile and being with you is the happiest I have ever been in my life. I want to fall asleep and wake up next to you for the rest of my life." I get down on one knee and open the ring box. Her hands fly up to her face and her eyes turn glassy as tears pool in them. "Will you marry me?"

She nods and throws her arms around my neck. "Yes, yes, yes, yes, yes," she says into my neck.

My shoulders relax at how quickly she says yes and how happy she is.

When she pulls back, I take the ring out of the box, slip it onto her finger, and look at my fiancée's face. I brush the tears off her cheeks before leaning in and placing a kiss on her lips. The smile on my face is huge. I can't contain my happiness, but now there is the next item, and I just hope she's ready for it.

I sit beside her on the couch again. Reaching beside the couch, I grab a brown paper bag I got at the store. "So," I start. "I originally had a more romantic proposal in mind, but after the game, Grayson recommended I grab this for you. I wanted you to know that proposing to you had nothing to do with this. I've had the ring for a bit and wanted to find the right time." Olivia's face is full of questions after my long-winded ramble.

"Josh, now you're kind of scaring me. What's going on?" She grabs my hand and squeezes it.

I pass her the bag and she looks inside and her eyes immediately widen. She pulls the pregnancy test out of the bag and looks at me, and I can see the wheels turning in her head.

"Grayson noticed you'd been sick from the smell of the eggs this weekend and I was talking about your new cravings, and then he asked a few questions and recommended I grab you one of these."

She continues to stare at me, and my heart races. Is she going to be mad that I grabbed the test for her? That I took away being able to tell me? Will she be upset if the test is positive?

"Birth control," is all that slips past her lips.

I reach out and place my hands on either side of her face and kiss her. "Babe, we have always wanted kids. Our children will be loved, whether that's now or in the future. Olivia, I love you. I want the future with you and if that means in nine months, we get to welcome our new baby into our lives. I want that because it will be with you."

She closes her eyes and takes a deep breath. After a few seconds, she opens her eyes and looks at me. She reaches for me and pulls me into a kiss, and I kiss her back, showing her just how much I love her and can't wait for the future that we're building together.

I break the kiss and lean my forehead against hers. "The box says it's better to test first thing in the morning. Right now, I want to take my fiancée to bed and show her how much I love her," I say. Olivia nods and I help her off the couch.

When she's standing in front of me, I wrap my arms around her waist, pulling her flush against my body. She wraps her arms around my neck and goes onto her tiptoes, her lips brushing against mine as she whispers, "I love you, Josh. Forever and always."

I close the distance between our lips and lick at the seam of hers. She moans, giving me access, and I take full advantage. My tongue sweeps through her mouth, tangling with hers. She moans as I continue to taste her.

I reach down and remove Olivia's shirt, tossing it on the floor somewhere behind me. I run my fingers over the smooth skin of her back and over her hip. Staying connected, I walk us backwards toward our bedroom. Between the couch and our bedroom, we managed to remove all our clothes.

Leading Liv to the bed, she climbs on, resting her head on the pillows. I climb between her legs and begin placing soft, reverent kisses up the inside of her leg all the way until I reach the top, then I repeat the process with the other. Olivia moans and bucks her hips as I make my way further up her leg, and I smile against her skin.

When I reach her hip again, I use my hands to hold her legs open. I lean down and taste her before circling her clit with my tongue. I suck it into my mouth as I use a finger to circle her entrance. She moans and I slowly push my finger inside, crooking my finger and finding her g-spot, I massage it. Olivia's hand is in my hair. She grips tightly, holding my face close to her pussy.

I pull my finger out and add a second as my teeth scrape over her clit. Her hips buck and my hand moves faster. She tightens around me. She's close. I use my teeth to scrape her clit again, and she comes, moaning my name as her grip on my hair tightens. I help her ride out her orgasm before I kiss up her body. I show love to each part of her beautiful body, kissing reverently over her hips, her soft stomach, up her rib cage, and each of her breasts. When I reach her lips, I kiss her, allowing her to taste herself on my lips.

She wraps her legs around my hips, pulling my body closer. She breaks the kiss and we're both breathless.

"Make love to me, Josh," she says against my ear before she pulls the lobe into her mouth, her teeth scraping over the skin.

I line myself up with her entrance and slowly push my hips forward. I feel her stretch around me. I breathe deeply until I'm fully inside, resting my forehead against hers, looking into her eyes as her arms wrap around my back.

Looking into her eyes, I see everything. I see our childhood friendship, the crush I developed on her, us reuniting and falling in love, our future, our children. I kiss her deeply as I begin to move slowly in and out of her. My hand finds hers as I intertwine our fingers and hold our hands beside her head.

I kiss down her neck and along her collarbone. Her orgasm builds, and I move faster. I continue to place kisses along her skin, my teeth scraping her earlobe before I whisper in her ear, "You and me forever, Olivia. I love you." My whispered words send her over the edge. Her back arches as her pussy grips my cock and her hand squeezes mine. Her orgasm sends me over the edge. I call her name into her neck as I empty inside her.

We both work to catch our breath. I roll over beside her and pull her against me. Nothing could ruin this moment and how on top of the world I feel right now.

I run my hand over her soft skin until it rests on her stomach. I look her in the eyes and smile before I lean my head down and kiss her belly.

I know she hasn't taken a test yet, but I know our baby is in there right now. I give Olivia a quick kiss before I climb out of bed and head into the washroom, getting a washcloth wet with warm water before cleaning her up. When I'm done, she walks into the washroom and does her business before climbing back into bed with me. She lays her head on my chest as I run my hand lazily up and down her back and play with the ends of her hair.

She rests her chin on her hand and looks up at me. "You'd really be okay if I'm pregnant?" she asks in a soft, tentative voice.

My hand stops moving, and I look down at her, making sure I make eye contact with her before saying anything. I need to make sure she knows I'm completely okay with this. That I want this.

"Babe, I am positive about this. If that test comes back negative in the morning, I think I'm just going to start working on putting a baby in you anyway." She smiles as a tear runs down her cheek. I use my thumb to brush it away. "I want this. I want this future with you. I don't ever want you to doubt that you are what I want. I will always be here for you. My world begins and ends with you, and it will be the same with our children."

I kiss the tip of her nose, and she cuddles closer to me. I run my fingers through her hair, listening to her breathing. Her breathing evens out when she falls asleep. I continue to play with her hair. A smile spreads across my face as I think about our future and what that test could say in the morning.

CHAPTER 30

Olivia

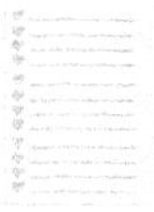

I eat stretch with my arms above my head before I rub my eyes and something scrapes across the skin above my left eyebrow. I stop for a minute and look down at my left hand.

My heart races as I look at a beautiful diamond ring. It's round with an elevated stone surrounded by more diamonds. The band is platinum and looks like an infinity sign surrounding the main stone. It's absolutely gorgeous and exactly what I would have selected for myself.

Memories of yesterday all come back. The nasty check against Josh at the game, running onto the ice to check on him, coming home and sitting on the couch with Josh while he said that 'this isn't how he planned to do this' effectively scaring the crap out of me before he got on one knee and proposed.

I'm still staring at the ring when I hear Josh come in. "You're not changing your mind, are you?" he asks.

I instinctively close my hand into a fist and pull it closer to my body. "No," I rush out. "Of course, I'm not. I guess it just hasn't completely sunk in yet."

A huge smile spreads across his face as he comes closer and leans over me, placing fists on each side of my head. I smile up at him as he leans down and gives me a kiss. When he pulls back, he tucks a piece of hair behind my ear while still smiling.

"Well good. I rather like calling you my fiancée." He kisses me and strokes my hair again before pulling back. I check the time. It's 9 a.m. and, by this time, he has usually been in the office for at least an hour, if not longer. I look back at him and sit up, and he takes a seat in front of me.

"Why aren't you at work?" I ask. "Not that I don't love the wake-up call, but you're not usually here at this time."

His hand runs up and down my leg in a soothing manner. He watches his hand for a few seconds before meeting my eyes again.

"I was hoping you might take that test with me here this morning."

The memory of Josh showing me the pregnancy test last night hits me. My hands fidget with the blanket as my mind begins to roll down the hill of what being pregnant could mean.

Are Josh and I ready for that? I would have to take maternity leave at school. Can I afford to take maternity leave? What will our families say? We haven't been together that long, and Matt only just learned that we're together. I'm ripped out of my spiral by Josh's fingers on my chin, forcing me to look him in the eyes.

"Babe, I don't want you to freak out. We will do this together. We love each other, we have each other no matter what."

I stare into his beautiful eyes and happiness and love stare back at me. The vice that had wrapped itself around my entire body loosens and an overwhelming sense of calm washes over me.

Josh and I can handle anything together.

I lean closer to him until I can feel his breath on my lips. "You're right," I whisper and kiss him.

"The tests are in the bathroom," he says, and I climb off the bed and head in there.

Josh joins me afterwards while I wash my hands. He wraps his arms around me from behind, placing his chin on my shoulder. I allow myself to lean into him as my hands join his on my stomach.

His thumb rubs softly up and down and he places a kiss on my neck before I feel him stiffen quickly. I look down at the tests and when I see both screens say 'Pregnant', I turn in his arms and he grips my face tightly before completely devouring my mouth. I meet his tongue with the same fervour. I wrap my arms around his neck and pull him as close as possible.

When we are both breathless, he leans his forehead against mine and smiles. "We're having a baby," he whispers, and I nod.

He drops to his knees in front of me. I'm still naked from last night, and he places kisses on my stomach.

"Hi baby. Daddy's here," he says between kisses.

I don't realize I'm crying until I taste the salt on my lips. I run my hands through his hair as he stays kneeling in front of me with his face pressed into my stomach. After a few minutes, Josh gets up and grabs my hand, pulling me toward the kitchen.

"We need to feed you, Mamma," he says, and encourages me to sit on one of the bar stools. I watch as he makes his way around the kitchen, making bacon, toast, and cutting fruit. He hasn't made eggs since we got back from the camping trip, and I'm not sure I really want to try that out right now.

He places the food in front of me before taking a spot beside me. His hand rests on my thigh as we eat in companionable silence. When we both finish, he turns to me, grabbing my hands and rubbing his thumbs over the backs of them. I feel the warmth that often surrounds me when I'm with him.

"So, I know we're supposed to go to Victoria and Seattle this weekend, but how do you feel about going the following weekend and having a barbecue in the park this weekend with our friends and family to announce the engagement? I don't think I can keep it a secret any longer than a few days."

I don't think I can either.

"That sounds perfect."

I look over at the clock in the kitchen and notice we've been up for nearly two hours now.

"As much as I love that you're here with me right now, you should get to work, and I should get to planning this barbecue."

I'm woken by the feeling of a hand stroking my hair. I nuzzle into my position and hear a deep chuckle from above me. I crack my eyes and see Josh smiling down at me. I smile and rub the sleep out of my eyes.

"Hey babe, have you eaten dinner yet?" he asks.

"No, what time is it?" I mumble.

"Just after seven."

I yawn. I somehow managed to sleep for three hours.

"I'm not hungry right now, but if you are, I can make you something," I say before sitting up, allowing Josh to sit in front of my crossed legs.

"It's okay. I'll wait to eat with you."

"How was work?"

He grins. "I spent much of my day distracted. Ended up spending some time looking at baby stuff. You know, I can't wait to go shopping with you and build the nursery."

A smile spreads across my face at his excitement. It makes me happy that he's not only happy about the baby but also excited about all the little things that go into preparing for a baby. This has me running my hand over my stomach.

"This afternoon, I made a doctor's appointment for tomorrow at noon if you want to come with me. I made it around your lunch time hoping that would be easier for you to fit in," I say hopefully.

"Yeah, I can make that. Just let me know the address and I'll be there."

I turn and cuddle into him as we sit on the couch in comfortable silence. Contentment consumes me. I listen to Josh's breathing as he runs his fingers through my hair that fell out of the ponytail.

Breaking the silence, I tell him about all the plans I came up with for the barbecue this weekend, asking if he would like me to include anything else. As we finish discussing the menu for the barbecue, Josh's stomach growls and I laugh.

"Guess we should get you fed," I say, tapping his stomach before heading into the kitchen. I don't see anything I want in the fridge, so I dig in the freezer and find a frozen lasagna I bought for lazy nights.

"You good with lasagna, babe?" I call out.

"Yeah."

As I'm preparing everything, my phone buzzes on the counter and I check it. I have several missed texts and a missed call from Mom.

I open the girls' chat, seeing my last text sent and all the new ones.

LIV

You guys able to join us for a BBQ in near my parents this Saturday? We'll meet at the park around noon.

ZO

For sure! Let me know what to bring!

HAN

Sounds fun! Count me in.

LIZ

I won't be able to get there until 1ish, I have an appointment in the morning.

LIV

I have everything planned. Just bring yourselves.

All good Liz!

I check my other texts. Everyone confirms, and people ask what they can bring. Mom never responded to my text, so I return her missed call.

"Hey sweetheart, how are you?" she says when she answers.

"I'm good. Sorry, I missed your call. I kinda passed out on the couch earlier."

"Oh, don't worry about it, sweetheart. I just wanted to check on you and see if you wanted me to bring anything to this barbecue you guys are doing?"

"No, I think we're good. I ordered everything online to be delivered tomorrow afternoon and I'll prep it all tomorrow and Friday so it's all ready."

"Okay, well, let me know if you need anything." Mom hesitates before she continues. "So we haven't talked in a while. How is everything going living with Josh?"

I realize I haven't told my mom about Josh and me yet, plus we just got engaged, and the pregnancy means I'm about to give my mom a bunch of surprises.

"Um... Things have been good," I say, not exactly sure how I should tell her.

Josh walks into the kitchen, sees me on the phone, and raises an eyebrow. *Mom*, I mouth and he nods as he opens the fridge, grabs a bottle of water, and offers it to me. I shake my head and he opens it, taking a sip.

"Just good?" Mom's always been able to tell when something's on my mind, and it hasn't changed as I've gotten older.

"Well, great actually. We're together now." I run my teeth over my bottom lip, waiting for her reaction. Josh watches me curiously from his position, leaning against the counter.

"Oh, sweetie, I'm so happy for you." My shoulders relax as I hear her genuine happiness. "You two have always been so close."

I grin. "Yeah, we have. It's been amazing. He makes me happy."

Josh smiles, listening to my side of the conversation.

"So, it's serious?" Mom questions.

"Yeah Mom, it's serious. I love him."

I walk over to Josh and grab his water, taking a quick sip.

"So you'll be giving me grandbabies soon?"

I cough. Josh pats my back lightly before rubbing it in circles, and I hand him back the water. I mean, I am pregnant, but she doesn't know that, and I literally just told her we're together and she's already pushing the grandbabies thing.

"I mean, we both know your brother won't be giving me some anytime soon," she says.

"Mom, I literally just told you about us and that's your first question? You didn't ask about grandbabies when I was with Drew," I say and both of Josh's eyebrows rise. I see all the questions flickering across his face. I put my phone on speaker and place it on the counter, turning to the oven and removing the film from the lasagna.

"Well, that's because I always hoped you'd see the truth and he wouldn't be sticking around for long." Mom sighs. "You always deserved someone like Joshua. I've seen the way the two of you have always looked at each other. You had a crush on him when you were kids. Don't think we didn't see it."

I feel the heat rising in my cheeks as Josh listens.

"And he might think that no one noticed when his crush grew, too. If you don't count that and the looks you two gave each other, then there's the fact that during the few weeks he was home from school in December every year, you guys watched every game together without fail." Trying to keep myself busy as mom talks, I grab some cutlery out of the drawer. "And when you passed out on the couch during a movie one night, I walked in on him placing a blanket over you and whispering 'Sleep well, Sunshine.' It was the sweetest thing. He looked so content looking at you."

I feel the colour drain from my face. *Sunshine.* Mom had heard him call me *Sunshine.* All the anonymous flowers I've received on my birthday used that nickname.

Josh sent them all.

I make eye contact with him and I can tell he knows I've made the connection as he worries his bottom lip between his teeth and pink spreads across his cheeks.

"Sunshine," is all that comes out and I'm surprised Mom hears it because it doesn't feel like it's more than a whisper.

"Yeah, I never told him I saw or heard him. I'm not sure why he didn't say anything to you during any of his trips that he had feelings for you, because he obviously did. Does Matt know?"

Her question pulls me out of my fog. "Yeah, he found out yesterday."

"How did that go?"

"It went well. Mom, I'm actually working on dinner. Can we talk at the barbecue on Saturday?" I ask, wanting to talk to Josh about all this new information.

"Yeah, of course, sweetie. I'm happy for you. Let me know if you need help with anything for Saturday. I love you."

"Love you, too."

I hang up and look at Josh. He looks hesitant, like he's not sure I'll react positively to all of this, but how could I not? The person I've had feelings for, for years, who has supported me emotionally and asked me to marry him, and is also the father of my child, has been doing little things out of love for me for years.

The birthday flowers have always made me smile and feel happy. I've always wanted to know where they were coming from, and now I do. The amazing man standing in front of me.

A smile breaks across my face as I stare at him. "Sunshine, huh?" I ask with a teasing tone and his shoulders visibly relax. I walk up to him and wrap my arms around his neck, and he wraps his around me, resting his hands just above my ass as he smiles down at me.

"Yeah, you have always brightened my days. No matter what my head space is, I get into a room with you and I see your smile or hear your laugh and it's like a weight has been taken off my shoulders. Everything seems brighter, like you've filled the room with sunshine. You're my sunshine."

No one has ever said something so nice and heartwarming about me. I mean, my siblings and I are close, and we're always there for each other, but to know I have such a profound impact on someone's life is insane.

"So, you've been sending me flowers on my birthday? Why haven't you said anything before?" I ask, genuinely curious.

I am beyond happy with where Josh and I are right now, but the what-ifs can't stop racing through my brain. What if we started dating sooner? Would I have not lost part of my feeling of self-worth like I did the last few years? Would we be married and settled and already have started our own little family? Nothing can change the past, but I want to know why he kept it a secret.

He takes a deep breath. "Well, at first, you were sixteen, and I was nineteen. You were still in high school, and I tried not to feel anything. I thought it was wrong. Then when you graduated high school I was worried about what your reaction would be, plus I was still on the other side of the continent, and when I was finally about to pull my head out my ass and tell you and see if you'd let me take you out I found out you were dating Drew. I wanted you to be happy and wasn't going to break something that made you happy."

I turn his words over in my mind, understanding his hesitation when I was sixteen and the distance that was between us, and his not wanting to end something he thought was making me happy. All of what he did was with the best intentions in mind, doing what he thought was best for me. I continue to look into his eyes as my fingers scrape at his scalp.

"For what it's worth, I had a crush on you when we were kids, like for as long as I can remember. I always viewed you as unattainable. If you had asked me out, I would have one hundred percent said yes." He leans down and places a soft kiss on my lips and leans his forehead against mine. "But I have to say I'm extremely happy with where we are now. So why don't we eat dinner and then head to bed where I can show you just how happy I am to be with you now?"

"That sounds great, Sunshine."

I grin at hearing him call me this secret nickname he's had for me for years.

I kiss him before pulling the lasagna out of the oven. We sit at the kitchen island and eat our dinner, enjoying each other's company.

CHAPTER 31

Josh

Olivia leads me into the bedroom. I had planned on telling her about the flowers eventually, although I wasn't sure just how she would react to the news. As Olivia's mom started revealing things to her and I saw her connecting the dots, it had me wound tight. I know she loves me, but I was worried it would change her view of me, and it did, but in a positive way.

The what-ifs have gone through my mind several times over the years. If I had opened up to Olivia earlier, would I have been living a happier life? Would we already have started a family? Would I have saved her from some of the heartache she's been through, or would she have gone through different heartache? At this point, there's nothing either of us can change, but I can spend the rest of my days showing this amazing woman how much I love her, raise our beautiful children, and love them as fiercely as I love their mom.

As soon as the bedroom door closes, Olivia is kissing me. One of my hands grips the hair at the base of her head, while the other goes to her hip, pulling her into me. I nip at her lip and a moan leaves her throat, sending heat through me. I walk her backwards towards the bed, gripping the bottom of her shirt and pulling it over her head, discarding it on the floor.

She takes advantage of the new space between us and reaches for mine, and I help her remove it. Her lips meet my chest as she kisses across it using her tongue to flick each of my nipples the same way I do hers. It still surprises me that it does something for me.

She continues to kiss her way down until she drops to her knees in front of me. I'm hard as steel in my slacks. She reaches for my belt, deftly undoing it, leaving it in the loops around my waist as she undoes the button, then the zipper before gripping the waistband and slowly pulling them down my legs. She looks up at me, licking her lips, and I groan.

"Christ, woman, you're driving me crazy."

There's a lustful glint in her eyes as she grips me through my boxer briefs before she leans forward and licks me from root to tip through the fabric. I feel the heat of her hot mouth through the fabric. My hand grips her hair tightly, pulling her back and tilting her head so she has to look at me.

"Olivia, stop fucking teasing me and take my cock out."

She visibly swallows, and I track the movement. Reaching forward, she pulls my boxer briefs down and I pop free. She grips me in her hand, stroking me twice before she licks the entire length of me, flicking her tongue over the head. My head drops back and a guttural groan leaves my throat as she wraps her lips around me.

She uses her hand to pump the base, while her other one rolls my balls. She continues to suck my cock until I feel my balls get heavy. I'm about to come. Before I can, I pull my hips back, put my hands under her arms, lift her to her feet, and kiss her.

Our mouths fight for control. I break the kiss, lean her down on the bed and remove her leggings and panties in one movement before climbing between her legs and hovering over her. My lips find the soft skin of her neck as I kiss and lick all her sensitive spots. She moans and bucks her hips when I find that particular spot behind her ear.

"Stop teasing me, Josh," she mewls.

I position my hard cock at her entrance and fully thrust myself inside her, consuming her loud moan with a kiss. I move slowly, drawing out the pleasure. She meets each of my thrusts as her hands roam over my back, her fingers scraping at my skin.

"God, you're perfect," I say as I pick up speed.

"Josh." Her fingers scrape harder. "You fill me so well, Josh."

I lean back, positioning myself on my knees, and lift her legs so

I'm holding them under her knees and relentlessly fuck her deep into the mattress. I watch as her tits bounce with each thrust.

"Look at you, Olivia, taking my cock like a good girl." She clenches around me, loving the praise. "I love watching those beautiful tits bounce as I fuck you."

Her fingers come and play with her nipples and she tightens around me. I release one of her legs and use my thumb to find her clit. Two quick swipes and she detonates around me, my name on her lips. After a few more pumps, I follow, collapsing on top of her. We both lie there, chests heaving. When the air comes back into my lungs more easily, I place a quick kiss on her lips before I withdraw from her and roll onto my side.

Olivia gets out of bed and when I hear the shower turn on, I join her. Stepping in behind her, I grab her soap and meticulously wash every inch of her body. On my knees, I place my hands on either side of her stomach, kiss it, and rest my forehead against it for a few moments. I grab the shampoo and wash her hair, using my fingers to scrub her scalp in the way I know she loves. After I condition it for her, she does the same for me and we climb out of the shower, drying off before climbing into bed.

I leave work early the next day and meet Olivia outside her doctor's office. We get her checked in and take a seat in the waiting room. I'm so full of nervous energy my knee won't stop bouncing. I'm excited to see how far along she is and hear the baby's heartbeat. She eventually leans over and places her hand on my knee and holds my leg still. I look over at her and give her a small smile.

"Sorry babe, just excited."

"I know." She laughs lightly. "But the knee shaking is driving me batty." I chuckle.

A nurse comes out and calls her name. Hearing them use her last name only makes me more excited to get married and hear her use my last name. Olivia Lincoln has a nice ring to it. I grin at the thought.

We walk to the end of the hallway where the nurse opens the last door on the right, and hands Olivia a gown and tells her to get changed and take a seat on the exam table.

As she changes, I move the spare chair right beside the table, grabbing her hand and placing a kiss on the top. Posters about the different stages of pregnancy and diagrams of baby positions fill the walls, filling me with an overwhelming sense of nervousness mixed with excitement. My stomach tightens as I read the warnings on the posters. Olivia sees where I'm looking and squeezes my hand reassuringly. The door opens, and the doctor walks in.

"Good Afternoon Miss. Carter, my name is Dr. Conway. How are we feeling today?" Dr. Conway is a petite woman in what looks like her forties, with smile lines around her eyes that come out as looks at Olivia and me.

"I'm feeling okay. Nothing too strong today."

"So, I take it you're experiencing symptoms then?"

"Yeah, I've had some morning sickness, though it hasn't been too bad. Food aversions and cravings too, but Josh here has been good at helping avoid the foods that make me sick and keeping me stocked on pickles." She laughs, and I squeeze her hand.

"Well, that's good. Sounds like you two are doing this together well. Today, we're going to do a vaginal ultrasound and try to get a look at your baby and listen to the heartbeat. We will measure the gestational period and generate a due date for you. I'll give you some prenatal prescriptions and set up a plan for the rest of your pregnancy."

Olivia lies back on the table and puts her legs into the stirrups as the doctor rolls her stool to the foot of the table along with what must be the ultrasound. She puts on her gloves and puts a wrapper over the ultrasound wand she grabs. She then puts some lube on it.

"You'll feel some pressure for a second, but that's it," she warns Olivia.

After a few seconds of her pressing some buttons, a sound fills the room. My heart stops for a second, and my hand tightens on Olivia's.

It's our child's heartbeat.

Dr. Conway reaches forward with her free hand and moves the screen to face us and points at a spot. "That right there is your baby." Tears fill my eyes. I'm not usually a crier, but sitting here, getting to see my baby and listen to their heartbeat for the first time is overwhelming. Sharing it with Olivia makes it so much better.

I kiss her, wiping away her matching tears. "Our baby," I whisper against her lips and she nods.

"Our baby, Josh." I brush her hair behind her ear, then place a kiss on each cheek over her tears, her nose, and forehead before looking back at the screen. Dr. Conway presses a few more buttons and smiles at us. The machine prints a few images, and she hands them to us.

"Here are some pictures of your baby. You're about eight weeks along now. I want to schedule appointments for every four weeks right now and once you're further along, they'll become more frequent." She hands Olivia a piece of paper. "Here is your prescription for prenatal vitamins. Do you have any questions for me?"

"Um," Olivia runs her hand in circles over her stomach. "I was drinking before I found out I was pregnant this week. Will that hurt the baby?"

"No dear, as long as you stop now and make sure you're eating and taking care of yourself, your baby should be perfectly fine. Many mothers drink until they confirm they're pregnant and have healthy babies." Olivia and I both nod.

"I'm going to let you get dressed now. Just stop at reception on your way out and schedule your follow-ups. Congratulations, Mom and Dad."

Olivia and I both say our thanks as she leaves and then Olivia gets dressed. We schedule her follow-up appointments and I ask the receptionist for scissors. I cut off one of the sonogram photos from the printout of four and hand the three remaining ones back to her. She has a questioning look on her face as she looks at them and then back at me. "I want to keep one in my office," I say.

Outside, I kiss her goodbye and say, "I love you. I should be home around 7 p.m. tonight." She climbs into the car and does her seatbelt before I close the door and watch her drive away. I order an Uber and head back to the office, positioning the sonogram photo on my desk beside a photo I have of Olivia so I can see them both as I work.

By the time Saturday rolls around, Olivia has everything for this barbecue completely planned and prepped. Loading up the car with everything, we make our way toward the park. I hold her hand on the centre console and play with her engagement ring. I love seeing it there, knowing she's agreeing to spend the rest of her life with me.

When we arrive, we set up until our parents show up and help us. As trickle in, we start the barbecue while people mill around and talk or play some games Olivia set up.

When everyone is here, I join Olivia and wrap my arm around her waist, whispering in her ear, "You ready, babe?" She looks at me over her shoulder and nods. Grabbing her hand, I pull her over to the side, raise my beer above my head and call for everyone's attention.

"Well, first Olivia and I would like to thank everyone for coming and joining us today. While we love spending time with all of you, there was a purpose behind today." Laughs sound out from everyone. "These last few months have provided a lot of change. Change that I'm extremely happy about. Olivia and I have been seeing each other." I lift her left hand as I hear murmurs from our friends and family. "And on Tuesday I asked her to marry me and she said yes!" I look down at her and she's beaming at me.

Congratulations are called by our friends and family, and people coming up and giving us hugs and people wanting to see her ring bombard us. She's eventually pulled away and I'm left standing with my parents and Emily. They each hug me.

"Congrats Josh, I'm happy for you. I'm glad the two of you finally got your heads out of your asses and realized you love each other," Emily says with a small laugh.

"Emily," Mom chides, but she's smiling. "Well, I'm happy for you too, Josh. I'm glad you two are happy."

"Thanks, guys." I look at Olivia over Emily's head and then back at my family. "We are. It all feels so natural. It's amazing how she can completely read me without me saying anything. And I know this may seem fast, but I don't want to miss out on anything more because I didn't take what I wanted, when I wanted it."

Mom lets out a small laugh. "Josh, you two have loved each other from afar for years now. We've all known. We just want you to do whatever makes you happy and we can see Olivia's that for you."

"Thanks, Mom."

"We're proud of you, son, and Olivia has always been family. You guys should come by for dinner soon," Dad says.

"Thanks, Dad, we will for sure. I'm going to go chat with the guys, but I'll let you know when we can make it."

I lean down and place a kiss on both Emily's and Mom's cheeks and clap Dad's shoulder before I head over to join Matt, Caleb, and Grayson.

"Well, if it isn't Mr. Domesticated," Grayson calls.

"Say whatever you want, fucker, but I'm happy," I say as I stand between Matt and Caleb.

"Congrats, man, happy for you," Caleb says as he claps me on the shoulder.

"Congrats, I trust you'll take care of her," Matt says, tipping his beer to me.

"I will spend the rest of my life making sure she's happy," I say honestly.

While we stand around talking, I see Olivia head towards the washrooms. I keep my eye out for her as she wanders off by herself.

CHAPTER 32

Olivia

After Josh's announcement, our friends and family surround us, offering their congratulations. Matt hugs me and kisses the top of my head. "I'm happy for you two," he says before stepping back and I'm pulled into Gi.

"Oh my god, Olivia, I'm so happy for you. You guys look so good together, too."

I feel the heat rising in my cheeks as I thank her. She grabs my hand and looks at my engagement ring, which is absolutely gorgeous. Mom walks up beside her and looks at it, too. They both have huge smiles. I'm so happy our friends and family are supportive and genuinely happy for us. Most people would question whether we're sure this is what we want to do. Do we want to rush into this? It's a serious step. We haven't been together that long. How can we be sure? I've loved Joshua Lincoln for years. It started out as friends, and then he became my first ever crush, and my love only grew actually being with him and being loved by him. I could not be more sure about this decision, and not a single person has questioned us so far.

When Mom and Gi drop my hand, Dad pulls me into a big hug, burying his face in my hair. "I'm so glad you're happy, baby girl. All I have ever wanted for you is to be happy and to be treated well, knowing you have that makes me happy." Tears gather behind my eyes and he pulls back and kisses my forehead. "You two can always count on us if you need anything."

I wipe my tears with the back of my hand. "Thanks, Daddy."

"So, you were engaged when we talked?" Mom nudges me.

I let out a little chuckle, "Yeah, but we wanted to tell everyone together," I reply, and she smiles.

"I know, sweetie, it's all good. I'm going to let you enjoy this. Let me know when you want to start the wedding planning, and I'll help with whatever I can."

"Thanks, Mom."

"Excuse me, Mr. and Mrs. Carter, but can I steal Liv for a little while?" Zoey asks from beside me. Mom and Dad smile at her. "Of course, Zo, we will see you soon Liv," Mom says before Zoey drags me towards Hannah and Eliza.

When we get to them, all three girls hold their hands out in front of them and I put my left one in front of me and they stare at the ring before Zoey is squealing and running in place, Eliza has her mouth open, and Hannah grins and says, "That man knows what he's doing."

They ask for the story of how he proposed, and I tell them, leaving out the details about the pregnancy. They have tears in their eyes as I tell them the sweet things Josh said. After I finish, I have an urgent need to pee, so I make my way to the washrooms on the edge of the park. It's not too far from our area, but it's a nice little walk and the weather today is perfect. It's twenty-five degrees and a subtle breeze blows through occasionally.

I'm on my way back when I hear my name called from behind me. I freeze as the hairs on the back of my neck rise. I know that voice. It's a voice I hoped I would never hear again.

Drew.

Turning around, I see him making his way toward me and before I can turn, make my way back to the group and ignore him, he's standing right in front of me.

"Olivia, baby, how are you?" he asks, and it takes everything in me to not slap him across the face. He makes a move as though he's going to pull me into a hug or kiss, and I immediately take a step backward.

"Don't touch me, Drew. First off, we're not together, so stop calling me baby. Secondly, what are you doing here?" He straightens, hearing the harshness in my voice, and shoves a hand through his hair. I clench my fists at my side, hoping to hold in my anger. Now that I'm in such a happy relationship, I wonder why I ever settled for the scraps that Drew gave me.

"You haven't been answering my texts, and I wasn't sure where you're living now. I thought I'd see if you were at your parents' house, and I saw you as I was driving past. We need to talk, baby. Please hear me out."

I take another step back. "Drew, you need to leave. You were not invited, and I have no desire to talk to you or see you ever again. Please leave me, my friends, and my family alone."

I go to leave and his hand wraps around my wrist, stopping my movement. I turn and glare at where his hand is, but he doesn't remove it.

"Olivia, you owe it to me. After two years together, you owe it to me to hear me out."

Anger rises inside me. How dare he say that I owe him anything, especially after I walked in on him cheating? I still have no idea how long that had been going on. Had he been cheating on me for the entirety of our relationship? Was he ever exclusive with me? Did he only say he loved me because he thought that would make me stay? As these questions continue to swirl in my mind, he continues to speak.

"I've tried to talk to you for months and you haven't responded. Hear me out. Let's leave and get some coffee. I deserve that, at least."

I rip my hand forcefully from his grasp, causing him to stumble forward before he stabilizes himself. "I owe you nothing," I hiss. "You were cheating on me. I walked in on you the day we were supposed to sign a lease to our new apartment, fucking some blonde chick in your bed. Don't you dare say that I owe you anything."

I turn and make it a few feet before he grabs my wrist again, spinning me, and yanking me against him. "I love you, Olivia, and I know you love me. Just give us another chance. It meant nothing and I deeply regret it. She means nothing to me. I love you."

"I highly recommend you get your fucking hands off my fiancée," Josh's deep voice comes from behind me and I hear the absolute rage in it.

"Fiancée?" Drew questions. It looks like there's pain in his eyes, but I don't feel sorry for him one bit. He lost me because of his own actions and I'm happier now.

"Yes, fiancée," I tell him.

His grip loosens just enough that I'm able to free myself and stand beside Josh as he wraps his arm around my waist. Drew's face grows red, staring at where Josh's hand is resting. My left hand goes to meet his and I see the second Drew sees my engagement ring.

"So, you won't listen to me after being together for two years, but you'll jump straight into this asshole's bed? Are you just willing to spread your legs for anyone, Olivia?"

Josh's already rigid body stiffens more, which I didn't think was possible with how tightly he was already wound. "Be careful how you speak about her," Josh warns, jaw clenched so tightly I worry he might break a tooth.

"I was with her for two years. I've fucked her more times than you could count. I'll talk about her how I want to." Drew's words make me feel dirty, remembering the ways he used to touch me, that I had sex with someone who could treat me so horribly.

Josh releases me, takes a step forward, and with two fingers jabs Drew in the chest as he says each word. "Watch. Your. Fucking. Mouth." Drew just snarls at him. I feel and hear more of our friends and family begin to surround us. Wanting to leave the situation, I grip Josh's forearm and try to drag him back.

"Babe, he's not worth it. Let's just go."

Josh looks over his shoulder at me. "But you are worth it, Olivia. I will always stand up for you, and I will always protect you."

He turns back and faces Drew. "It's time for you to leave. You need to stop contacting Olivia. You will never talk to her again. She has told you she has no desire to talk to or see you again, and you need to respect that." Anger spews off Drew as he stares Josh down.

"I deserve to be heard out. Olivia owes me that," Drew spits.

"Olivia owes you nothing after you cheated on her," Josh growls. "But I have to say it's lucky for me. I got the best thing that has ever happened to me because you were too stupid to appreciate what you had."

Drew looks at me pleadingly. "Olivia, I was going to propose. We were going to start a family together. Are you really prepared to throw that all out for this man?"

"Yes, Drew, because Josh is twice the man you ever were or will be."

"You don't mean that baby, I know you still love me. We can get married and start a family together. We can get past this. Please give me another chance."

"Drew, I've meant every word I've said. I'm marrying Josh. I love him. I'm starting a family with Josh." My hand instinctively goes to my stomach. Drew catches the movement immediately and his face pales completely.

"You're just marrying him because of the baby?" he grits out, and I stiffen, knowing everyone is witnessing this ordeal.

"No, Josh proposed before we found out," I whisper.

Drew begins laughing. "You really think this man is going to love you when you gain more weight? Do you really think he'll stick around? That he won't find some skinny chick to fuck on the side? You really are delusional." Drew's words are laced with anger and hatred, but they hit the exact points he was looking to. My arms wrap around myself tighter as I try to ignore him, but it isn't easy. These words are all my insecurities out in the world for everyone to hear, including Josh.

"You actually are an idiot. I would never do that to Olivia. Like I said, she is the best thing that's ever happened to me. I find it a privilege to share my life with her. And she is growing my child, that just makes her more beautiful in my eyes. I proposed before we knew about the baby, and the baby just makes it all the more special. Now, why don't you leave before you embarrass yourself anymore, you pathetic piece of shit."

Drew launches himself at Josh, but Matt and Caleb get to Drew before he can land a hit and pull him backwards.

"Okay, it's time for you to leave now before I arrest you. If you in any way contact Olivia, or her friends and family again, you will be arrested for harassment," Caleb says.

"What... You, you can't do that?" Drew sputters.

Caleb lifts the edge of his shirt covering the waistband of his shorts and shows him the badge clipped there. "Yeah, I can. I've witnessed this situation and have heard you be told to leave multiple times. It's time to go."

Drew doesn't say anything more, he stomps off in the direction of his car. My entire body relaxes and the tears begin to build. Josh turns to me and immediately pulls me into his chest. His hand runs soothingly over my hair as he whispers that everything will be okay, that he's here for me.

After a couple of minutes, I manage to pull myself together and pull back, wiping the lingering tears from my cheeks. Josh's hand stops running through my hair and grips the back of my head. I feel such a sense of safety and contentment in this position right now, and I smile up at him. He leans down and places a quick kiss on my lips. "I love you," he whispers against them.

"I love you, too."

"You know what he said isn't true, right, babe? I love all of you, and I'm excited to watch you grow with our baby."

I'm not sure I will ever truly be able to move past these insecurities that I have. They have all been so ingrained in me since childhood by the bullies and the magazine ads. Everywhere you go, you see ads about diets and weight loss, about how being skinny is the only way to be attractive. I need to push those thoughts away. Josh has spent the last few months showing how he loves every inch of my body. He has kissed my thick thighs, my soft stomach, my stretch marks, my breasts that aren't perky. Joshua Lincoln has kissed and shown every inch of my body love.

When I turn in his arms, his hands rest on my stomach and his thumb moves in slow strokes. The girls come up to us as soon as I turn around. They look at where his hands are resting and then look back at us. "You're pregnant?" Zoey whispers, and I nod. I know a lot of people heard the conversation, but it's nice to confirm it with my best friends.

Zoey and Hannah start to scream and jump, and Eliza is hugging me, then Zoey and Hannah join in. Josh is being a good sport about being in this group hug with my friends and I love him even more for it.

Matt walks up to us, and the girls break apart. "What are you girls screaming about?" he chuckles, used to our antics by now.

"I'm pregnant," I say, and a huge smile spreads across his face.

Matt pulls me into the biggest hug, whispering congratulations in my ear, and I'm over the moon. I know he's going to make an amazing uncle because he is the best big brother I could ask for. He breaks from our hug, moves over, and gives Josh a back-slapping hug. "Congrats man, I'm happy for you guys."

Josh chuckles. "Thanks man, I'm happy and excited. Just so you know, I proposed before we found out she's pregnant."

Matt just smiles and pats him on the shoulder. I turn and look up at Josh. "I guess we should tell everyone now that the cat's out of the bag," I say.

He leans down, kisses me, and says, "We better, before your friends let it slip." I kiss him back and we make our way over to the barbecue.

Mom stops me when we're close. "Are you okay, sweetie? I have no idea how he knew that we were here."

"Yeah, I'm okay, Mom. He was on his way to your place to see if I was there when he saw us, but he shouldn't be a problem again. I think Caleb scared him enough."

"Okay, well, I'm here if you need me for anything."

"Thanks, Mom, actually, before we tell everyone in a minute, we were going to wait, but the cat's kinda out of the bag." I squeeze Josh's hand, and the other comes to my stomach. "I'm pregnant, Mom."

Her jaw drops for a second, and then the first tear begins its trail down her cheek. I hug my mom fiercely, and she holds me tight. "I'm so happy for you two. You'll make amazing parents." Hearing that from my mom makes so many of my worries fade, not completely because this is such a tremendous change, but to know my mom believes in us means the world. Josh and I love each other, and we will face whatever comes our way.

I release my mom and hand in hand, Josh and I stand beside the barbecue while he gets everyone's attention.

I squeeze Josh's hand when everyone is gathered around and share, "After Josh proposed earlier this week, we got some news. News we are both incredibly happy about. In April, we will welcome baby Lincoln into our family, and we couldn't be more excited."

There are cheers around us and Josh leans down and kisses me in a deep, soul-searing kiss that shows me just how much he loves me.

He rests his forehead against mine. "I'm so excited about our family, Olivia. I will spend the rest of my life earning you and our children." He kisses my forehead before people surround us, giving us even more congratulations and well wishes.

We spend the next few hours with our friends and family, eating and playing games before we pack it all up and head home. I am so exhausted when we get home that he takes me straight to bed, where I fall right asleep in my fiancé's arms.

CHAPTER 33

Josh

Over the next few weeks, Olivia's morning sickness fades, but her food aversions and cravings are still here. We both agree we want to be surprised about the sex of the baby. Her stomach is becoming firmer as the pregnancy progresses and she looks absolutely beautiful. Hormones wreak havoc on her emotions, and I've learned she hates having it pointed out. In the madness, we managed our final getaway to Victoria and Seattle.

Getting home from work, I walk into the living room, finding Olivia watching *Criminal Minds* while cutting out laminated items for her classroom. I kiss her before sitting beside her. She pauses the show and looks at me, smiling. "How was your day?"

"It was good. Nothing blew up today, so I can't complain. How about you? Your students adjusting to being back in school?"

"Yeah, I like to ease them into it, so it's going well."

"That's good. I was thinking about ordering a pizza for dinner tonight, you good with that? Looks like you brought work home with you."

She laughs. "Yeah, pizza sounds great. As a teacher's husband, you're going to have to get used to having all my teaching supplies around. And pretty soon there will be baby stuff too. Your perfectly pristine place is going to be full of my mess." She laughs again.

I kiss the tip of her nose. "It's our place, babe, and I don't mind having your mess around because that means you're around."

A blush spreads across her cheeks as she smiles and returns to her project and show. I grab an extra pair of scissors and one of her laminated sheets and start cutting.

"You don't have to do that, babe," she says.

"I know, but I don't mind helping you."

I kick my feet up on the table and continue cutting while we watch TV. When the pizza arrives, we stop and eat. Once I finish my last piece, I turn and face her.

"So, I know we've spent a lot of time working on getting my office moved so that we can set the nursery up, but there is something else I want to talk about," I say.

Olivia puts her plate down and faces me, grabbing my hand and running her thumb over the top.

"Okay, what's up?"

"I want you to have the wedding you want, but I also want us to be married before our baby gets here. I want you to have my last name when they're born and honestly, I'm selfish and want to call you my wife sooner than later."

The smile that lights up her face is blinding. I reach forward and tuck a piece of free hair behind her ear.

"I want that too," she whispers. "What do you think about a backyard wedding, at one of our parents' places, just close friends and family, nothing big?"

"I want whatever you want. As long as at the end of the day I get to call you my wife, I'm happy."

Leaning forward, I kiss her. Her hands end up in my hair and she tugs it, causing me to groan. I lean her back and position myself between her legs, and she wraps them around my hips. She nips at my bottom lip and I roll my erection into her, feeling the warmth of her. Her pregnancy hormones have made her completely insatiable.

I break the kiss, brushing my lips down her neck and over her collarbone. I feel her getting impatient. She moans and bucks into me. "Josh, please," she whines.

"My impatient little slut wants me to fuck her?" I say into her ear and she moans. "You'll take what I give you, Olivia."

My hand glides down her front, squeezing her breast before I move my fingers delicately down her stomach to the top of her leggings, where I tease her. When she moans again, I allow my hand to slide under the waistband and inside her panties, where I tease her more. My finger runs up and down her slit, but not dipping inside. Her grip on my hair tightens and I kiss her, nipping her bottom lip until she relents and gives me access. My tongue tastes her, playing with hers.

My finger dips inside her, gathering her moisture and moving up to her clit where I circle it slowly and as soon as my finger makes contact, she is writhing beneath me, causing me to chuckle. I slowly enter her with two fingers while my thumb finds her clit, adding pressure while my fingers work her from the inside. I press my length into her thigh as she rides my hand, seeking the release she so desperately wants.

I pull my hand away and she whines before I add another finger and enter her again, working faster than before. I send her over the edge, calling my name. Once she's caught her breath she opens her eyes, staring at me. I lift my fingers to my mouth and suck on them, moaning around my fingers as I get every last drop. I place my lips right beside her ear as I whisper, "My favourite flavour." She shivers beneath me.

She reaches for the hem of my shirt, pulling it out of the waistband of my slacks, and I help her remove it before I reach for hers, dropping it beside the couch with mine. She's wearing a black lace bra that barely contains her gorgeous tits. I place my mouth over her nipple through the bra and my tongue laps at it. She arches her back, shoving her tit farther into my face. I reach behind her and unclasp her bra. Removing my mouth, I slip it down her arms before it, too, ends up on the floor.

I kiss across her chest, showing her other breast the same attention before I kiss my way down her body. When I reach the top of her leggings, I remove them and her panties. Once they are off, I lift one of her legs so that it rests on the back of the couch and settle between her legs. My hot breath ghosts over her centre and she arches her back and moans.

"Josh, I need you. Please don't tease me."

I lean forward and leisurely lick my way from her entrance to her clit, giving it a quick flick before repeating the movement. I go to pull back and her hand is in my hair with a death grip, holding my head in its position, and I chuckle.

"So needy, Olivia. You really are my needy little slut."

"Only for you, only yours." She moans, sending more heat to my cock. Hearing her call herself mine always makes me hard.

My mouth latches onto her clit while two fingers enter her. I work her to the edge of an orgasm before backing off, repeating the process three times before I allow her to come. I lap up her orgasm as she drenches my face, working every ounce of it out of her. When she's come down from the high, I stand and undo my pants before pushing them down with my boxer briefs.

I give myself a couple of pumps while standing over Olivia. "Aren't you just my pretty little slut, all laid out, waiting for me?"

She presses her thighs together, her vain attempt to get some relief. I spread her legs again, the same way I had them when I was fucking her with my tongue and fingers.

I grip my erection again, running it through her slit, gathering her wetness so I can slide in easily. I use the tip to tease her clit, causing her to grip the cushions on the back of the couch. Using my free hand, I pinch a nipple before moving over and doing the same to the other. She writhes beneath me and I finally give in, pushing inside her torturously slowly. Inch by inch until I'm fully sheathed inside her.

I grit my teeth as I stay still, taking in how tight and hot her wet pussy is. She moves her hips, trying to get me to move, and I grip her hip tightly and she stops immediately. Once I've grounded myself, I begin to move, building a slow rhythm as I nip her earlobe and kiss along her neck, finding her most sensitive spots that make her shiver. As I pick up speed, I kiss her, using my tongue to open her lips. She kisses me back just as urgently. Our chests are both heaving as we pull apart and I drop my face into the crook of her neck as her hands run up my back and she moves to grip my biceps.

"Josh, please, I need you to make me come," she moans as I thrust harder. "Yes, Josh, just like that. I need you."

Her words are my breaking point and I reach back, grabbing her legs and push them up toward her chest and fuck her relentlessly. Her eyes stay on mine as I watch her orgasm build. "Hold your leg," I grunt as she grabs hold of it so I can use my now free hand to circle her clit. Three swipes of my thumb and she's coming, calling my name as her pussy clenches like a vice around my cock. Her orgasm sends me over the edge and my hips jerk in uneven movements as I empty my release into her.

I collapse on top of her. Once I catch my breath, I lift myself off her and kiss her lazily. I pull out and she mewls at the loss. I grab her hand and we shower before we head back into the living room, resuming our earlier task.

Olivia and I agree on a simple wedding and she gets to work planning it. My parents offer for us to use their backyard and to help with whatever planning details we need help with. Our guest list is small, we want an intimate ceremony, so decorations are minimal. Her mom offers to bake our wedding cake and we meet with a caterer for the dinner and other desserts.

In between the wedding planning, we go shopping for the baby, we research car seats—which ones are the safest options, and we look at different strollers, cribs, change tables, and all the other things we are going to need for the baby. We put together a registry, per the instant nagging of our friends and family. Her mom and Gianna are working on throwing together a baby shower, and we've been sure to let everyone know we aren't going to find out the sex of the baby until they're born.

We pick an early-October date for the wedding, and before we know it, the date of our wedding arrives. I couldn't be happier. I don't have words to describe how ready I am to be married to Olivia. To call her my wife, and for us to share the same last name. She and our baby are my everything.

CHAPTER 34

Olivia

I stand in one of the spare rooms of Josh's parents' house and I run my hands down my wedding dress. It's a simple, white, and strapless with a sweetheart neckline, and empire waist with lace detailing down the skirt. I absolutely love it. I stare at my reflection, taking it all in, realizing that in an hour, I will be Mrs. Lincoln and married to my best friend. I run my hand over my belly.

"Mommy and Daddy love you, bug, and we can't wait to meet you."

I feel hands on my shoulders and meet Zoey's gaze in the mirror. She's my maid of honour, and Hannah, Eliza, and Gianna are my bridesmaids. I'm so happy to have them up there with me today. They have stood by me through all the ups and downs, and really are the best friends a girl could ask for.

"Josh asked me to give this to you," she says, handing me a square box. I open it, and gasp. Inside is a beautiful charm bracelet and necklace. The necklace has a rose charm hanging on it and my mind instantly goes to the bouquets he's been sending on my birthday. I look at the bracelet next and it has charms representing the items on my list, a charm from Whistler, Banff, Calgary, Victoria, Seattle, a camping charm, a hockey charm, a car, a two-piece charm with a flat circle with the engraving *to me, you are perfect* and an overlay of a heart, and two charms that look like they represent our birthstones. There is one loose charm in the box, and I pick it up. It's a *just married* charm and I see a folded piece of paper stuck in the lid.

> *Sunshine,*
>
> *We have made so many memories together and I look forward to the many more that will create as husband and wife. I wanted you to have something tangible of the memories we made and a place that you can add to them for years to come. This has been the best year I've had and I owe it all to you. Thank you for choosing me. I don't know how I came to deserve you, but I will spend the rest of my life proving that I deserve to have you as my wife, as my partner, and the mother of my children.*
>
> *There is another charm in here for you to add right after our 'I do's'. Can't wait to see you down there.*
>
> *I love you, forever and always.*
>
> *Josh*

I read it a second time as I wipe away the tears, fold it, and tuck it into the top of the box. I grab the necklace and bracelet out and have Zoey help put them on.

"You ready?" Zoey asks with a smile.

I smile and nod. We make our way out of the guest bedroom. The photographer is downstairs to capture a first-look moment with my dad. He looks up at me and I make my way down.

When I get to the bottom, I see the tears he's holding back. I don't think I've ever seen my dad cry in my entire life and here he is, seeing me in my wedding dress, starting to cry. His tears have me fanning my face to hold mine back, not wanting to ruin my makeup.

"You look absolutely gorgeous, sweetheart. I'm happy for you. I know the two of you will make each other happy."

I hug my dad and whisper, "Thank you," before we make our way to the doors leading to the backyard. The doors open and the girls begin their walk down the aisle. I take a deep breath, ready for the next chapter of my life.

The music starts and the guests stand as Dad and I make our way to the top of the aisle. When I get there, my eyes lock on Josh and I can tell the moment he sees me. His jaw drops slightly as he stares at me, and I feel the first tear fall. So much for protecting my make-up. When Dad and I make it to the end of the aisle, he kisses my cheek, passes my hand to Josh's, and shakes his hand. I know there's mutual respect between them and I'm so happy they have the relationship they do. Looking up, I meet Josh's eyes and see he's tearing up, too. Seeing the men in my life who don't usually cry, with tears in their eyes, is sending me overboard. I tilt my head back and take a couple of deep breaths, trying to centre myself.

Our justice of the peace begins, and before I know it, we're saying our vows. We decided to write our own. I'm going first because I would not be surprised if Josh's makes me cry. Zoey hands me the piece of paper I asked her to hold on to earlier today. I unfold it and begin reading.

"Josh, I have spent the last twenty years getting to know you. I was only four when you started coming around with Matt after school. As I got older, you and Matt let me tag along when you played and you went from Matt's friend to mine, too. As we got older, you became the cute older boy who still let me hang around, to the hot high school hockey player who let me come up with pre-game rituals with you." Some laughs come from the crowd.

"You then became the man who would watch hockey games with me when you were home on break and never made me feel bad for yelling so loudly at the TV screen." More laughs and I take a deep breath as I continue. "You then became the man that has been there for me unconditionally in every situation. You have become my very best friend, my confidant, my safe space. Being with you makes all the weight of the world fall away and my days brighter and happier. You make life fun and exciting.

Today I stand before our friends and family promising to be your best friend, your safe space in times of need, to be your vault of secrets, to spend the rest of my life making sure you know you are loved, cherished, and respected. You will make the most amazing father to our child, and I can't wait to watch you bond and grow. I know our relationship can stand the test of time because we have built on friendship, but I ask that you humour me for a second. It's brought you luck when you play hockey, so I figure we can only hope it brings us luck in our marriage."

I hold my hand out for the beginning of our pre-game ritual and Josh looks at it, smiling. We go through the motions, and then I reach down and grab the water bottle I stashed earlier and spray his hair. He grins before he gives his head a good shake, sending water droplets in every direction, and everyone laughs.

He runs a hand through his hair, reaches into the inside pocket of his tux jacket and grabs out a folded piece of paper.

"Olivia, when I was young, I referred to you as Matt's younger sister. Eventually, that changed to Olivia, my friend. You used to get upset when I called you Olivia because you insisted that everyone call you Liv, but I had thought why let such a beautiful name go to waste? I still think that to this day. In school, we had a school project about the meaning of our names. Joshua means 'deliverance from God', and I decided to see what yours means. It means "peace", and I could not have thought of a better meaning.

You bring peace to my life, no matter how crazy the outside world is. The moment I see you, it all fades away. With you, I know I can face and conquer anything. I can reach the unattainable, and I can be the best version of myself. I owe your parents a lot of thanks for bringing into this world my two soulmates." Laughter fills the air. "The man who is always down for whatever and was with me through all the craziness of high school and college, and the most amazing woman who has chosen to love me the way that I love her. Who will stand with me through anything, allows me to be vulnerable without judging me, has accepted my family as her own, and knows me so well she knows what I need, sometimes before even I do. Today I promise to support your dreams and aspirations, to be a place that you can dream, to be your safe place and protector, to always stand by you and our children, to love and respect you, and to make sure that every day you walk this earth, you know you are loved. It's always been you, Olivia."

The tears are running heavily down my cheeks by the time Josh finishes and it takes all my effort to not let the sob break free. I barely manage to whisper, "It's always been you, Josh."

The justice of the peace announces it's time for the rings and Matt leans forward and hands them to Josh.

I give Josh back my left hand and take his ring in my right. He smiles down at me and I smile back. Placing my hand flat for him, the officiant says, "Do you, Olivia Rose Carter, take Joshua Mitchell Lincoln to be your lawfully wedded husband?"

I say "I do" as Josh places the ring on my finger.

The officiant continues. "Do you, Joshua Mitchell Lincoln, take Olivia Rose Carter to be your lawfully wedded wife?"

Josh says, "I do," with total conviction, and I place his ring on his finger.

"By the power vested in me by the province of British Columbia, I now pronounce you husband and wife. You may kiss your bride."

The last words have barely left their mouth before Josh's lips are crashing onto mine. His kiss consumes me. I feel the heat of it from the tips of my toes to the top of my ears. My arms wrap around his neck and when we both need to breathe again, he rests his forehead against mine.

"Hi, Mrs. Lincoln," he whispers, and my smile gets even bigger.

"Hi, Mr. Lincoln," I whisper back.

Letting me go, he grabs my hand, and we walk down the aisle and into the house. He drags me up the stairs as quickly as I can go until we're in the room I used to get ready. As soon as we are inside, he presses me against the door and kisses me. He runs his tongue along my lips until I open to him. He explores my mouth like it's all new, and his hands grip my ass, pulling my body into his, and groans.

When he breaks the kiss, his fingers come up to the necklace sitting on my rapidly rising chest. "You wore it," he whispers.

"Of course, I did. It's from you."

I move out of his arms quickly and make my way to the dresser and grab the extra charm. I replace the one on my necklace and put the rose on my bracelet. Once it's secured, I look back up at him and a mischievous look fills his eyes as he smiles down at me.

"Think we can get away with another twenty minutes before heading back?" he asks.

"I think they'll live without us for that long," I say, and he immediately walks me back to the bed before spinning me around and pressing my upper body into the mattress. He flips the skirt of my dress until my backside is fully exposed, covered only in a lacy white thong. He groans as he drops to his knees behind me. I squirm in anticipation.

Leaning forward, he licks me over the fabric of my panties, and I groan at the delicious friction. He does this a few more times before hooking his finger into my panties and pulling them to the side. He licks and sucks at my dripping pussy like a man starved and I'm his first meal.

His finger comes up, and he circles my entrance before it slowly enters me. I moan his name while I try to squeeze my thighs together. He works faster and I grip the comforter under me in my fist and bite at it, trying to contain my moans so our entire wedding doesn't hear how well Josh is working me. He adds another finger, and I arch my back and push back against his face, looking for more. Needing more. It only encourages him. He goes faster and his teeth scrape against my clit, sending me soaring over the edge. I squeeze my eyes as tightly as I can as I ride out the throes of my orgasm. When I open them, it's like stars are floating in my vision.

Just as the stars fade, I'm shutting my eyes again as Josh thrusts his cock into me, filling me more than I think I can take some days. He grips my hips so tightly I'll probably have bruises tomorrow, but I don't care. He moves in long and fast thrusts. I almost wish I hadn't done my hair so meticulously this morning because all I want is for him to grab my hair and yank my head back as he continues to fuck me.

Like Josh can read my mind, knowing I need more, that I need to feel like he's completely in control. One of his hands comes around my throat and pulls me back towards him. When he has me positioned just how he wants me, he applies pressure on the outsides of my throat and the delirious feeling has me on the brink of an orgasm.

"Look at how well my wife takes my cock," he whispers in my ear. "Taking every inch of it like a greedy little slut." I tighten around him, and his free hand moves to my clit as he circles it. "Come for me, wife." His words send me over the edge, and I grip at his forearm as I try to hold myself steady as all of my energy is ripped from my body and the orgasm crashes through me. A few more thrusts and

Josh is following me. His grip around my neck loosens, he leans me back down on the bed gently and pulls out of me. I immediately miss the feeling of him. He returns with a wet washcloth and he cleans me up before helping adjust my dress and making sure I look presentable enough to go back out to our guests.

Before Josh opens the door, he gives me a quick kiss, grabs my hand, and we walk downstairs.

CHAPTER 35

Olivia

O ur friends and family are wandering around talking, laughing, and drinking when we get downstairs. Grayson is the first one to see us as soon as we walk out the back doors and he claps, everyone else joining in. I feel my face flame. I'm sure everyone here knows what we were doing. Josh pulls me close to him, smiling as he kisses me, sending more cheering among the group.

We make our rounds, thanking people for coming and catching up until dinner is ready to be served. As soon as most people are finished, we move into the speeches. Matt, being Josh's best man, is first.

"Good evening, everyone. For those of you who don't know, I'm Josh's other soulmate, and Olivia's older brother Matt." Laughs go around, and Matt continues, "In school, I always heard guys say their friends weren't to touch their sisters, that it was against bro code, but I never understood that. If your friends are good enough for you, if you trust them, why would it be the end of the world for them to date your sister? I've known for years that Josh and Olivia have been in love with each other." Josh and I shift in our seats and stare at Matt, and he grins at us. "You two were not exactly subtle about it. I think everyone knew, except the two of you." He laughs. "Even recently, people have asked if I'm okay with Josh and Liv being together. Well, who do you think put a little bug in Josh's ear that Liv needed a place to stay because her lease was up? Me. I love you both. Josh, you are my best friend and I trust you with my life, as well as with my sister's life, and heart. Liv, you have always been an amazing sister to both Gi and I, and we're lucky to have you. I know you will love my best friend the way he deserves."

He turns to the crowd and raises his glass. "To Josh and Olivia Lincoln, wishing them a lifetime of happiness and a beautiful family." The crowd responds with, "To Josh and Olivia," before they clink their glasses for us to kiss.

Zoey is up next, and I just cross my fingers that she says nothing to embarrass me.

"Good evening, I am Zoey, Olivia's best friend and maid of honour. I met Olivia back in school, and we bonded immediately. She was the sister I wished I had, especially since I grew up in a house of five brothers." People laugh. "The first boy I ever heard Liv talk about was the infamous Joshua Lincoln. I had never met him, but when I did, I understood the fuss that Olivia made. And it wasn't because I wanted Josh, it was because I saw the way he looked at her and the way he acted around her. He may not have come to terms with what he was feeling until after he left for college, but it was all there. He loved her, and she loved him. They had inside jokes, and their own little rituals, and they never seemed to tire of one another's company. I was so happy when you two found each other again and decided to take your relationship further. You two have a love that many aspire for and many fail to find. Protect it. Cherish it. I love you two and can't wait to watch your family grow and meet baby Lincoln."

Tears are running down my face. Both Matt and Zo's speeches were so sweet, and that mixed with my hormones means I really hope my mascara is as waterproof as advertized.

"And just a reminder that today is October 9, and I take payment in the form of cash and e-transfer." Zoey says. I stare at her slack-jawed, and see a proud glint in her eyes. "For those of you who don't know, including Liv and Josh, we kinda had a bet going, and I won, I bet Josh would be the first to make a move and that you would be married before Thanksgiving." She chuckles. "And you would announce a baby before Christmas, so I was three for three."

Josh and I stare at her, and I look around and see quite a few people reaching for their wallets or phones. I stand and make my way to her, grab the microphone from her hand and ask, "Who all was in on this?"

I watch as the hands go up: Matt, Caleb, Grayson, Zoey, Hannah, Eliza, Gianna, Emily, my parents, and Josh's parents. I'm speechless. All these people had bets about us. All of them suspected. Now, I need to know their guesses.

"Okay, now you need to fess up to your guesses," I say as Josh comes up behind me, wrapping his arm around me, and pulling me into his chest.

Zoey moves behind the table and grabs a giant poster board and sets in on an easel beside the dance floor. It shows all the guesses.

The guesses for who would make the first move are split down the middle, while Josh's dad had us getting married the earliest by the end of summer. Christmas was a popular guess from everyone for a baby.

Josh rubs his hand over my belly, and we sway a little as we stand here reading the bets our friends and family made about our relationship. I guess we can't be too upset because they were all betting on us, not against us.

I look at Josh over my shoulder. "Should I be worried that so many of them were positive we would announce a baby before the end of the year?" I ask.

"I guess they all know that when I decide something, I'm all in," he says before kissing me. He grabs my hand and brings me out to the dance floor as we start our first dance.

I rest my head on his chest as we sway, and I know that there is nowhere else I'd rather be.

CHAPTER 36

Caleb

I sit and watch Josh and Liv as they have their first dance, and I can't help but feel a pang of jealousy at what they have. After my tour overseas and all the baggage I came back with, I have resigned myself to never having what they have. I wouldn't ask a woman to deal with my random emotional changes and nightmares. It's too much to expect of anyone, so I work out, go to work; hang with my friends and spend time by myself with my black lab, Finn. I have the occasional hookup, but I never stay the night. The last thing I need is to scare the shit out of a woman because I've had a nightmare.

My mother doesn't understand why I don't date. She thinks it's high time I get serious about settling down and starting a family. My older brother has been married for 3 years and they are expecting their first baby. You'd think that would get my mom off my back, but it's only made it worse.

Grayson breaks me out of my thoughts when he slaps a hand on my shoulder. "You good, man?" Grayson knows the most out of the guys about my time overseas. We knew each other before I left, and he saw firsthand the change in me when I got back.

I take a sip of the beer I'm holding. "Yeah, man. You?"

"Just peachy, think I'm going to find a beautiful woman to dance with and maybe I'll get lucky and she'll bring me back to her place."

Grayson wasn't always this playboy, but after an incident in high school, he uses it as a way to protect himself.

"Careful man, you know Liv would kill you if you hurt one of her friends."

He pats me on the shoulder again before walking away and calling back at me, "I'll be good." I chuckle, knowing that we have different definitions of the word good.

The rest of the evening moves smoothly and before I know it, the bride and groom are on their way out, heading for their honeymoon. I make my way over to their guest book, write a note, and flip through reading the notes that others have left for them.

Seeing how everyone believes they are made for each other makes me wonder if it's possible there is someone out there who could deal with all my fucked-up shit and not crumble.

Epilogue

JOSH

Six Months Later

As I lay beside Olivia asleep in her hospital bed, I smile down at our beautiful baby girl in my arms. After her water broke at 6 a.m., we came straight to the hospital where she was a champ and went through twelve hours of labour before she delivered our beautiful Catherine May Lincoln. I haven't wanted to put her down since she came into this world.

Olivia stirs just as a knock comes at the door. Peeling my eyes away from Cate, I see Gianna poking her head inside. She smiles at me and the bundle of joy in my arms.

"I've got a small crew out here. You guys okay with visitors?"

I look over at Olivia, who has a sleepy smile as she nods. Gi makes her way into the room, followed by both of our families.

Anticipation fills the air as I stand, turning to show everyone her face.

"Everyone, meet Catherine May Lincoln," I say, telling them her sex and name for the first time.

Everyone smiles, and I turn to Olivia. She knows what I'm asking without me having to say it and she nods. Walking over to Matt, I stand in front of him. "Catherine, meet your godfather, your Uncle Matt."

I place her in his arms as he stares at me. Once she's settled, he looks down at her, sticking one of his fingers inside her hand and giving it a little shake as he sways.

"She's beautiful," he murmurs.

I run my finger over her cheek. "Just like her mamma."

"You guys really want me to be her godfather?" Matt asks, disbelief filling his voice.

"Matty, you're the best big brother a girl could ask for, and I know you'll be the best uncle, too. If anything were to happen to us, I trust that you and Zoey will take care of her," Olivia says with complete conviction. I agree with her. Matt will do anything for his family, and that includes our little girl.

Gi and Em have climbed into the bed with Liv. It's like an Olivia sandwich. I smile at the view.

"Grandma would like to meet the beautiful girl." My mom walks over to Matt, and he transfers her to her arms.

Cat is passed around to everyone before she starts to cry. I take her and pass her to Olivia so she can feed her. Everyone leaves after a while, giving us time to relax.

"You did amazing today," I whisper into Olivia's hair as I kiss the top of her head. She tips her head back, making eye contact with me, and smiles. "I couldn't have done it without you." I give her a quick kiss before moving to the couch and settling in for the night.

The next day as we walk out of the hospital with the car seat in one hand and Olivia's hand in my other, I wonder how I got so lucky. I have everything I could ever need with these two and I'm going to spend the rest of my life ensuring that they are happy.

OLIVIA

Six Months Later

Watching Josh with Cat leaves my entire body humming with happiness. You can't help but see the love shining in his eyes as he looks at our daughter. In the beginning, he got up with me every night when she cried. After we were able to build a supply of milk, we began alternating night shifts, but he took more than me. I think he really enjoys using the evening feeds to bond with her. There is no doubt in my mind she'll be a daddy's girl. When we're out and there are a lot of people, her favourite place to be is in her daddy's arms and she has him wrapped around her finger.

Watching them together makes me think about growing our family sooner than we thought. I always enjoyed being closer in age to both Matt and Gianna, and I don't want to wait too long before we have another, but I also want to enjoy this time with Catherine.

Watching Matt with Cat has been some of my favourite memories with him. She can do no wrong in his eyes. She has all the guys wrapped around her finger. It makes me laugh. When the guys come over for poker, she finds a way to end up in one of their laps instead of hanging out with me, and they all love it. None of them complain when she reaches for a card or chips and tries to put them in her mouth.

All our friends were over the first time she rolled over and it was such a sight to see a group of adults crowded around her cheering as she did it again.

The last year has been surreal, and today Josh and I are celebrating our one-year wedding anniversary. Gi and Emily are coming by tonight to chill on the couch and watch movies while Cat sleeps and we go out for dinner. Our friends and family have been amazing with helping us. We don't leave Cat with other people often, but it's nice to know that if we want to go out, there is a village surrounding us that will help.

I fix my hair in the mirror before slipping into my heels and making my way to the living room. I lean against the wall as I watch my gorgeous husband dressed in a suit dance with Cat in his arms. This isn't the first time I've walked in on him doing this, but I still pull my phone out and start recording. A smile tips my lips as I see he's singing to her.

"Before we know it, you'll be dancing with her at her wedding," I say, teasing him. He is constantly complaining that she's growing up too fast, and I agree, but I love to get a rise out of him.

He stops in his spot, faces me, and points. "There will be no talks of her wedding. She still has many decades before that will ever be a problem."

"Okay, Daddy." I walk up and wrap my arm around his waist on the opposite side that he has Cat positioned. I bop her nose. "Hey bug, your Auntie Em and Auntie Gi are coming over to spend the night with you."

There's a knock on the door, and I answer it. I quickly hug each of the girls and they make their way to grab Cat from Josh.

I give her a quick kiss on her cheek. "Be good for your aunties," I say, giving her a small finger wave before we make our way out of the apartment.

Josh made dinner reservations at Blue Spoon. Walking into the restaurant, I realize it's been a while since I've been here, since that birthday lunch I had with Matt and Josh. On my last birthday, with Cat being so young, Josh made me this amazing home-cooked meal that was to die for.

I smile at him as he pulls my chair out, and I take a seat. He kisses me before taking his seat and grabbing my left hand, running his thumb over my rings.

"Happy Anniversary, babe," he says, kissing my knuckles.

"Happy Anniversary."

We sit and eat our dinner, enjoying conversation and making plans for the upcoming holidays. When we finish, Josh pays the bill and we walk out hand in hand, but he doesn't lead me back towards the car. Instead, we head in the other direction.

"Where are we going?" I ask.

"I thought we'd enjoy more of our evening and take advantage of having our sisters watching Catherine."

I follow behind him until he pulls me into the lobby of a hotel, and I know what that means. I quicken my steps beside him and when we make it to the reception desk; he checks in under a reservation he apparently made beforehand.

The minute the doors close on the elevator, Josh's lips are on mine and his hands are fisting my hair. I moan into his mouth as he devours me. Even after all this time, I still feel how much he desires me. I was worried after having Catherine that it would be another reason for him to hate my body, but all he did was show me why he loved it. He kissed every new stretch mark and thanked them for helping grow our beautiful daughter. The first time he did it, I cried, and he continued to kiss each of them before he held me in his arms.

Every time I feel insecure about my body, Josh is right there telling me he loves it.

When the elevator doors open, Josh manoeuvres us toward our room, quickly sliding the key over the reader and opening the door. Before it's even closed, his hand reaches for the zipper behind my back, pulling it down and pushing the straps of my dress off my shoulders until the dress is in a pile at my ankles. As soon as it's off, he has me pushed against the door. His lips trail across my jaw and down my neck as he nips and licks along my skin.

When I moan, he presses his erection into my soft stomach, and I fumble with his belt before undoing his pants. Reaching my hand inside, I wrap it around his hard length. He jerks in my fist as I work up his cock, relishing in how he reacts to my touch. He pulls back and makes quick work of his shirt buttons, removing it and dropping it on the floor with my dress.

He drops to his knees in front of me and lifts one leg over his shoulder. Leaning forward, me licks me through the drenched fabric of my panties, applying just the right amount of pleasure that I bite my lip and let out a quiet moan.

He pulls his head back and looks up at me. "No hiding your moans from me tonight, Olivia. You don't have to be quiet. I want to hear every one of your sounds tonight."

He leans forward and roughly presses his tongue against my clit, and my back arches as a loud moan rips its way out of my chest. I grip his hair in my hand and hold him in place, begging for more. He pulls my panties to the side and slides his tongue against my exposed clit while pumping a finger inside of me.

I moan and call his name as he continues to work me. It's not long before I feel the telltale signs of an orgasm and I know he feels it, too. He adds another finger and presses his tongue against my clit. I detonate. My back arches, my legs shake, and my grip on his hair tightens. If it wasn't for him holding me up, I would have collapsed on the ground.

When my orgasm subsides, Josh stands to his full height and kisses me. I can taste myself on him. He brings me to the bed and strips off my panties and heels before following with his pants and boxer briefs. He climbs the bed between my legs and kisses me again, taking his time.

He positions himself at my entrance and slowly fills me with every inch of him. His kiss absorbs my moan as I feel the delectable stretch of him filling me. He starts slowly, lifting my leg over his hip, and builds up the pace until I'm panting and writhing beneath him, begging to come. His hand sneaks between us, his thumb finding my clit; a couple of swipes, and I'm soaring. Stars flash in the blackness of my vision as I clench around him. His orgasm follows right behind mine.

He pulls out and lies beside me, panting and holding my hand. I feel his release as it leaks out of me. I turn my face to look at him. When he looks at me, I say, "You forgot a condom."

He smiles and adjusts himself so he can tuck a piece of stray hair behind my ear.

"You ready for more kids?" he asks softly.

"If it happens, yes, but honestly, I wouldn't mind another six months with Cat before we get pregnant again."

"Okay, I'll try to remember to use condoms," he says, leaning in and kissing me. "But, so you know, I'm ready for more when you are." He kisses me again before getting up and dragging me with him into the bathroom and starting a bath for us. Two more rounds and four more orgasms later, we make our way home to our baby girl. Nine months later, our son, Oliver Liam Lincoln, joins our family.

THE END

Want more of Josh and Liv's? You can now in the bonus epilogue:
https://BookHip.com/VQARQQX
Want to read Caleb and Bailey's story? You can now in Saving You
http://mybook.to/dlsavingyou
Missed Caleb and Bailey's bonus epilogue? Check it out now!
https://BookHip.com/PJNKDBG
Can't wait for Grayson and Hannah's story? Pre-order Keeping You
now: https://mybook.to/dlkeepingyou

Book Boyfriends

If you would like to read about the girls' top tier book boyfriends and book husbands, check out:

Alex Volkov: Twisted Love - Ana Huang
Christian Harper: Twisted Lies - Ana Huang
Zade Meadows: Haunting and Hunting Adeline - H.D. Carlton
Garrett Graham: The Deal - Elle Kennedy
Dean Di Laurentis: The Score - Elle Kennedy
Nate Hawkins: Icebreaker - Hannah Grace
The Cane Brothers: A Not So Meet Cute, Not So Meant to Be, and
A Long Time Coming - Meghan Quinn
Brendan Taggart: It Happened One Summer - Tessa Bailey
Fox Thorton: Hook, Line, & Sinker - Tessa Bailey
The Eden Brothers: The Eden series - Devney Perry
The Rhodes Brothers: Queen's Cove series - Stephanie Archer
Dante Romano: Mastermind Duet - Morgan Elizabeth
Aiden Graves: The Wall of Winnipeg and Me - Mariana Zapata
Jack Hawthorne: Marriage for One - Ella Maise
Evan Zanders: Mile High - Liz Tomforde
Ryan Shay: The Right Move - Liz Tomforde
Damien Martinez: Tis the Season for Revenge - Morgan Elizabeth
Nathan Donelson: Cheat Sheet - Sarah Adams

Dicktionary

Acknowledgments

It was a long journey to get here. When I started writing Josh and Liv's story, I never thought I would publish it. My amazing beta readers told me how much they enjoyed reading about Josh and Liv, and it gave me the courage to share their story with the rest of the world.

My husband has been amazingly supportive through this entire journey, lifting me up even when I thought I couldn't do this. He has believed in my success even when I didn't.

Beth, you have been someone I could rely on through all of this. You beta read for me, were an extra set of eyes for editing, helped with content creation, and let me rant and vent to you. Thank you for your support and encouragement. I'm so glad I got to go on this journey with you.

Chelsey! This process has been crazy and you've been there for so much of it and I'm so happy that we've found each other and I get to call you one of my best friends. Thank you for your love and support.

To my friends who were so excited when I shared with them about this new step I was taking. Your excitement only grew mine and I am so grateful to have you.

Thank you to my editor Sophie who has put a great deal of work into this book. I'm so glad we got to work together on this project.

To my character artist Paige, thank you so much for bringing Josh and Liv to life. You were so fun to work with and I'm excited to watch you bring future characters to life.

Kim. My amazing cover artist. I don't have words to express how grateful I am for you and the work that you put into this cover. I'm eternally grateful for you and I'm so excited to work on the rest of this series with you and all the other books we get to do together.

Thank you to all the amazing indie authors out there who share your stories with the world. Your stories bring comfort and joy in times of need. To the authors of Liv and the girl's top tier book boyfriends, thank you for writing men we can all wish were real.

Most importantly, thank you to those of you who have picked up Always Been You. Thank you for reading Josh and Liv's love story. Without all of you, this wouldn't be possible and I can't wait to share more stories with you!

About the Author

Living in the Vancouver area of British Columbia with her husband, Alex enjoys spending her free time reading, watching Hockey (go Canucks), watching Disney movies and crime TV shows, and spending time outdoors. She started writing in 2023 when her first story just wouldn't leave her mind. From there, the ideas of a series formed and she's never looked back.

She enjoys talking to other authors and romance lovers. Her TBR is never-ending, but that doesn't stop her from adding at least one new book every day. Alex looks forward to experiencing more in the indie author community and can't wait to share her books with the world.

Connect With Me:

https://www.instagram.com/authoralextaylor/

https://www.threads.net/@authoralextaylor

https://www.tiktok.com/@authoralextaylor

alex@authoralextaylor.com

www.ingramcontent.com/pod-product-compliance
Lightning Source LLC
Chambersburg PA
CBHW051500030726
47592CB00006B/2016